A COMING STORM

BOOK ONE: The Beautiful Mrs Graham

Peter Craigie

Published in paperback by Lulu.com

Copyright © 2007 Peter Craigie. All rights reserved.

This novel is based on actual events that took place between 1776 and 1780.

My thanks to Naomi Tarrant for her advice on 18th century dress and manners, and to Stephen Wood, research consultant, for advice on military matters and for all his encouragement. Also to Gregan Crawford for his technical assistance in cover design.

Thomas Gainsborough's portrait of 'The Honourable Mrs Graham' appears by permission of the National Gallery of Scotland.

ISBN 978-1-84753-666-2

ONE

"My name is Charles George MacPherson, named for two kings as my fool of a father used to say. Though little good either one of them did for him. Here at Lynedoch House in the sovereign State of New York this twentieth day of August 1844 I set out to record the events of my life, so much of which has passed away in a kind of storm. But it is time at last to recall some of the people I have encountered and the great events seen." He glanced at his words. 'At last,' he thought with a smile. 'Well, it may come to that!'

The day was drawing to a stifling close and he pulled back the red velvet curtains to admit a little more light from the darkening sky. In that instant a flash of lightning illuminated the study and filled the room with vivid colour. The dull reds and greens of the book-lined walls leapt brilliantly into life, even the tired colours in the turkey carpet seemed briefly restored to youthful vigour and all around the room the glass and polished metal and mahogany of old scientific instruments blazed out in the vivid blue-white light. Then with barely a pause the thunder struck directly overhead, shaking the panelled walls of the room and rattling the small panes of the windows.

Charles was aware that his own end could not now be long delayed. 'So many of my friends have gone before me,' he reflected sadly. The awareness had come quite naturally to him, indeed almost comfortably, with the slowly developed acceptance of age. That was so very different from those other insights that had regularly blazed into his consciousness throughout a long life, often without logical explanation. He frowned, for he had never quite been able to understand these events and what Charles George MacPherson could not explain logically still made him uneasy.

Yet intuitions had flashed unbidden into his mind for as long as he could remember, certainly since childhood, and he had long accepted that they were a part of him. In time he had grown to trust them and more than once they had provided uncanny warnings that had saved him or his companions in the midst of apparent chaos. They had also proved an infallible predictor of how cards and dice would run at the gaming table and in days when money was still of some consequence they had regularly allowed him to anticipate the outcome of events before even his swift brain had calculated the odds and the rational probabilities.

As the thunder faded away in a long reluctant rumble, echoing around the hills, a succession of half forgotten memories flickered across his mind. He glanced down at the old electrical machines that littered the floor. "Benjamin Franklin with his lightning jar," he mused. "Luigi Galvani and the charming Alessandro Volta---- had not the dreadful Napoleon made him a Count for his scientific exploits? And had he not accepted the honour, the dog! The awful Edward Bancroft, clever but quite mad and treacherous too as it proved. Henry Cavendish and Augustin de Coulomb." All with their theories of how to control electricity, how to harness its terrible power. He sighed: for after all the efforts of these great minds, seventy years later no-one was much closer to understanding the true nature of electricity.

A hundred years ago the old Dutch settlers in these valleys had seen the lightning in the summer sky and heard the thunder rumbling around these same mountains. But they had known the answer, of course. It was Rip van Winkle up in the Alleghenies, playing skittles with the Giants! 'So much for Galvani and Volta and their clever electrical machines,' he thought with a smile.

'Wise old Alberto Massimo in Bologna,' he remembered suddenly. 'So modest and kind and a true gentleman.' An obscure figure, yet with as much right to be remembered as any of them. More indeed, for it was Massimo who had explained how the eye of the meridian worked and in the process revealed the mathematical secrets of the solar system. All these people might be gone. But in the Basilica of San Petronio the eye of the meridian would still be sweeping across the marble floor, year by year, endlessly tracking the movement of the heavens.

Another memory came suddenly and illogically into his mind. "Charlotte Pemberton," he murmured. "And the odious Reverend Snape." The amiable, rather pathetic Mrs Pemberton, whose name had not occurred to him in forty years or more. Yet all at once he recalled her plump good-natured, rather coarse face. She was dead now like so many of them. 'The snows of yesteryear,' he thought wistfully. Like his own little wife, and of course the wonderful Juliana Ritchie.

Dearest of all of course had been Mary Graham. 'The Beautiful Mrs Graham' people called her after Gainsborough painted her in that glorious dress beside that classical pillar. Dearest Mary! He smiled at the memory of how the artist had painted her again and again, each time in a more modest, simpler dress, as if desperate to reveal her true beauty the world

Mary Graham had become famous then and fashionable too after she was taken up by Georgiana. Ah yes! Georgiana, the flamboyant young Duchess of Devonshire. Of course gentle Mary Graham had never sought fame and the two women could not have been more different. Yet they had become firm friends. Mary, it went without saying, had been a world away from Charlotte Pemberton. A world away in every respect.

But like his dear own wife and Charlotte and Juliana and the little Duchess, Mary Graham was gone. 'Ou sont les neiges d'antan?' he thought sadly. Mary's charming and able brother William Cathcart was gone. Even Thomas Graham: seemingly indestructible and a devoted husband to Mary, even he had finally gone, though he had soldiered on longer than any of them. Of course cunning old Ben Franklin was long since dead. Yes, all were gone. Though Rip van Winkle might still be about, he thought with a thin croaking laugh.

With a sigh he tossed the quill down on the desk and turned to stare out across the darkening valley. Another blue flash lit the underside of the clouds and flickered mysteriously around the crests of the wooded hills above the Finger Lakes. Had people like Edward Bancroft, he wondered, truly imagined that something so elemental could be captured and contained, let alone used to cure the human condition? Mind, he thought wryly, handled carelessly it can certainly do just that! Especially if you are crazy enough to try to catch it in a jar, as Franklin did! But then who else would have attempted it? Only a madman or a genius like Benjamin Franklin.

How they had lionised him in Paris, he recalled inconsequentially, his mind drifting again. And how completely had homespun honest Ben bamboozled the French sophisticates. How he had played his role of the simple Puritan rustic! Even wearing a coonskin cap, the old fraud! But perhaps they had all been frauds in one way or another. Not Mary Graham of course. Not the beautiful Mrs Graham. The thunder, though still deafening, came just a fraction later. It was moving away, he decided as he shifted uncomfortably in his chair.

Where was he? Ah yes, Charlotte Pemberton. The first woman who had taken him to her bed. She had taught him to speak French and a great deal more besides in the late summer and fall of 1776. Though to his shame he had almost forgotten her, she had been a crucial factor in that eventful year, a factor that sent his life off on a path totally unplanned.

Of course it had all been his own doing, admittedly in the first heat of youth. But none the less--- . Had it really been so very long ago? He gave a silent grimace. How had it begun? He did not even remember, so much was vague and half forgotten now. He was ashamed to say that even a clear recollection of Mrs Pemberton escaped him, her image merging curiously into the memories of the other women he had known.

But all at once that final afternoon in Charlotte's bedroom in the Pemberton house leapt clearly into his mind. The house, it was scarcely more than a cabin in those days, stood not so very far from where he now sat and as today the heat and humidity in the valley had built up steadily until it seemed to be draped over them like a heavy damp blanket. Not a breath of air came through the open window as they lay naked and panting on Charlotte's ornate bed. There was only silence from the woods outside as the world lay dormant in the heat, everything living longing for the cool rain of late afternoon to break the deadlock.

Mrs Pemberton as usual had lost herself completely under his thrusting love-making and as usual, gazing down on her round flushed face, her full lips, her eyes firmly shut, he found himself wondering where she was at that precise moment. Into what secret recess of thought or feeling had she retreated? At the same time he was aware of the thunder as it rolled around the hills beyond the valley.

Rip van Winkle playing skittles he thought, casually timing her climax and his own to coincide with the next great crash of thunder, relishing the effect, though he knew it was almost certainly lost on her. The flash of lightning illuminated the rough walls of the small bedroom as he listened to her cries of pleasure. He studied her face with a certain detachment. She had still a kind of animal beauty, he observed clinically. But also a coarseness that he had not before noticed. Immediately he regretted the thought as unworthy. For there was about Charlotte Pemberton a kind of eager pathos and he knew that she was giving him all that she could give: all indeed that she had to give.

He should have felt more, he knew, and was vaguely ashamed of himself. Then the Pemberton's long-case clock struck sharply, sounding very close at hand through the distant ominously rumbling thunder. Five o'clock. "Oh Charlie," Charlotte murmured, her eyes still closed. "You must go now!"

Damn that clock, he thought. It was her true pride and joy of course. "The latest rococo!" she had trilled, after poor old Pemberton had shipped it back for her from Philadelphia, perched precariously on his rickety wagon. A journey that had done its fine action no good at all. "In the new French style from Thomas Affleck himself!" The old fool had spent weeks adjusting the thing to keep a semblance of time.

Charlie rolled away from her glistening plump body and glanced across at the clock in the corner. Even his untrained eye had to admit the finely carved oak case stood out from the rest of the house like an aristocrat in a work-house. Pemberton must dig deep to keep his young wife happy, he thought fleetingly. Though he could well afford to. For Pemberton owned the biggest general store in the area and made a nice profit, according to Charlie's father. "For no more than shipping hardware and tools up from New York and Philadelphia," James MacPherson had said bitterly. "Some make their money easy." It was on a trip to

Pennsylvania that Pemberton had met Charlotte, only daughter of a French Huguenot family.

But five o'clock it was now. Or as close as damn and Charlie slid easily off the bed, reached for his clothes and pulling on his breeches he adjusted the dirk on his belt. He stood tall and slim, looking down at her with youthful arrogance as he knotted the ties of his rough cotton shirt, dark hair still damp with perspiration and slicked back from his high forehead. Charlotte gazed at him with pleasure for a moment. Then she sat up and began to fuss with her hair, at the same time pulling a light shift around her. "You are very handsome, Charles George MacPherson," she said quietly in her still accented English. "Et quel nomme superbe!"

Charlie glanced down at her and felt a sudden surge of irritation. A frown spread across his tanned face and his usually good-natured brown eyes hardened. "Named for two kings, as my fool of a father says," he muttered half to himself. "Two kings that he has followed loyally, more fool him! Little good it did him last time. And when the British finally go, damn all good it will do him this time either. You'd think he would have learned his lesson back there in Scotland." His good humour had drained away completely.

But in spite of his words he knew that sentiment in the colonies was still mixed and the issue of independence was poised precariously, in spite of the events of the previous year at Lexington and Concord and the battle in Boston at Breed's Hill. Of course the Declaration had created a watershed of sorts and at the very least it had crystallised support for the patriots.

But British troops had died, the first to be killed deliberately by the colonists. Feelings were hardening on both sides and King George was showing little willingness to relinquish any part of his empire, though it was said that some politicians in Britain were sympathetic to the American cause. However it seemed that more soldiers were on their way. Many more, according to the rumours that spread through the colonies. The latest report to come up the Hudson was that a huge army under Lord Howe had landed on Staten Island and was threatening the city of New York. It was said that they had filled the harbour with ships and that a man could practically walk across the straits from vessel to vessel. Clearly nonsense, Charlie thought. But still--- .

He knew that many settlers were still loyal to the King, some fanatically so, especially here in New York. Many, even outstanding patriots like Franklin, had been slow to recognise the inevitability of the situation. Then there were the others like my father, Charlie thought irritably. James MacPherson had fought against the Hanoverian crown in 1745 and lost disastrously, when like so many highlanders he had been driven from Scotland in the dreadful aftermath of Culloden, all that he owned sacrificed to that futile cause. All to favour one king against another! Now Charlie knew that his father and many like him were simply not willing to fight against another British king, not willing to risk losing in another rebellion what they had so painfully created out of the wilderness.

Loyalist, that was what his father called himself, Charlie thought contemptuously. Under oath to resist the independence movement in the colonies. "Never fight against yer King," James MacPherson repeated endlessly and in his more reasonable moments Charlie understood his father's fears, though he did not share them. For James MacPherson had much to lose if the rebellion succeeded. After Culloden the highland clan chieftains had fled to France and been made welcome there, after a fashion. At least they had enjoyed a life of relative ease. The leaders like the great MacPherson of Clunie, a remote kinsman of his father, had done well enough. But for the ordinary clansmen there had been only loss and humiliation. The answer for many had been to flee as far away as possible, in particular to the Americas.

There in up-state New York James MacPherson had acquired a tract of land, cleared the forest and created a home of sorts on the banks of the Mohawk River. He and his neighbours had fought off the Iroquois Indians and then the French, made an uneasy peace, and as the years went by built up in a lucrative fur trade with the interior tribes. MacPherson was still a highlander at heart: quick tempered, trenchant and at times unpredictable. But like most of his kind he was a tough and resilient little man who knew how to survive in a hostile environment.

He had marched with the Rogers party that struggled relentlessly through hundreds of miles of trackless marsh and wilderness in 1754, all the way up to the Great Lakes on a reprisal raid against the Indian settlement at St Francis. Cold revenge had been his driving force then, for James MacPherson never forgot a slight, far less a betrayal. For him a debt of honour was a debt for life. He had been one of the few to make it back down the Connecticut River to safety.

Over the next few years James had built a profitable business in partnership with Sir William Johnson, a genial Irishman who had married well and settled in the valley west of Schenectady on land owned by his wife's family. There Johnson had created his own empire in the wilderness, thirty miles up the river, and in time was awarded a baronetcy from the King for loyal service against the French.

Sir William had also earned the respect of the local Mohawk for his fair dealing and, unusually for a European, he had learned to speak their language fluently, at times dressing in native clothing. Soon he had been accepted by them as a trusted mediator in their all-too-frequent disputes with the colonists and eventually he had even been adopted into the tribe. After the death of his European wife he had taken an Iroquois bride, Molly Brandt by name, a formidable woman and sister to Joseph Brandt the legendary war chief of the Mohawks, himself a loyal supporter of the British.

James MacPherson's land bordered Sir William's and in spite of very different backgrounds the two men had become friends as well as business partners, bonded by shared experiences and firmly held views on the British crown. In the early dangerous years Johnson had built a great stone stronghold, Fort Johnson, at the heart of his sprawling township and its patchwork of farms: this had served as a place of safety for the settlers of the area, including James MacPherson and his young son.

At the end of the French wars when peace seemed assured Johnson had turned the fort into a grand mansion extraordinarily fine by the standards of the Mohawk Valley and filled it with the best furniture and fittings that Europe could supply. There were paintings and marble fireplaces in the very latest vogue, all transported at enormous cost from London. The house was also well supplied with books of every nature. Sir William was no intellectual. But he knew that a gentleman's house needed books.

Charlie had never known his mother---- she had died in childbirth, after which James had seemed to lose interest in the boy and become a strange remote figure. Mostly he was away, far in the interior setting up trading agreements with the northern tribes on behalf of himself and Sir William and in consequence the boy had been left in large measure to fend for himself. But when Charlie discovered Sir William's library it was as if a curtain had been pulled aside to reveal a new and wholly different world and a rich source of pleasure.

As a result of his father's frequent absences Charlie had grown up as part of Sir William's large mixed family. He became a particular friend of Francis, one of Johnson's sons by Molly Brandt and it was from Francis and his Mohawks that Charlie had learned what he knew of woodcraft, riding, hunting and weapons. He and Francis also had shared political views and soon the two young men had concluded that their fathers were grossly mistaken in their loyalties and that the time would soon come when the colonies would free themselves from British control.

"Oh Charlie! What would your father think to hear you say such things, good loyalist that he is? You must not say these things! Not in this house! If my husband was to hear you, he'd have you arraigned as a rebel!" Charlotte still half naked had the grace to blush as the ridicule of her remark struck her. But she tossed her head and continued defiantly. "And you've learned nothing of the use of the subjunctive today!" she added plaintively.

Charlie was still laughing as he slipped out of the house and mounted his little mare, turning her head along a rough track that led through the trees towards the township. It was true that his French lessons had been neglected of late. But he knew he had a natural flair for the language, which indeed was what had first brought him to Mrs Pemberton's attention as a promising student. Even without the subjunctive he had no fears for the future. But the lovers had become careless of late as the hot summer wore on and though Pemberton was miles away in Albany on Loyalist business there were others in the community who knew that the afternoon meetings involved more than French lessons.

Another dull roll of thunder died away and Charlie's laughter floated back to the ears of a secret listener. A tall, pale, saturnine man dressed in the sombre clothing of a clergyman, with a wide brimmed hat, his curiously dark eyes dead and flat, stood hidden in the trees behind the house. He had been there for much of the afternoon, chaffing at the sound of their love-making. Now he moved bleakly towards the house.

But the Reverend Snape was a newcomer to the colonies and more at home in the city than the woods, so that he was quite unaware that for an hour or more another figure had lain nearby and that he in turn had been watched by steady hunter's eyes. Snape pushed open the door of the cabin and moved familiarly through into the bedroom where Charlotte Pemberton stood still only half dressed, splashing her face and neck with cool water from the large porcelain bowl on the dresser.

She turned at the sound of his footstep. "You?" Her eyes opened in surprise as he stepped closer. She smiled nervously. "Have--- have you just arrived?"

"Whore!" the minister said and struck her across the mouth with the back of his white hand. As she fell back onto the bed he strode across the room and pushed her to the floor. "French whore! You and that cursed MacPherson boy are both damned to Hell!"

He stared down at her in disgust. But in spite of his anger the sounds he had heard earlier had excited him. He knew he could take her here on the crumpled bed. The knowledge of what she had been doing inflamed his desire. But he could not quite bring himself to use her like that. Not after---. Slowly, almost unthinkingly, he loosened his clothing. Then abruptly he seized her hair and pulled her towards him. She looked up at him, pale as he forced her face closer to his body, ignoring the blood that dripped freely from the cut on her lip and stained the front of his dark breeches.

The hidden watcher in the woods, dark skinned and naked apart from long fringed leather leggings, a breech cloth and a round leather skull cap heard the sound of the blow and paused for a moment before slipping away over the rough hillside. Moving easily through the trees on moccasin-clad feet he cut swiftly across country, unimpeded by the long Pennsylvania rifle he carried in one hand, heading for a point where he knew that the track crossed a narrow stream at the edge of the township, where he would intercept the rider.

As Charlie rode slowly in the heat he watched the jagged lightning play with increased vehemence around the hilltops in the gathering gloom.

Unconsciously he was waiting for the inevitable downpour of cooling rain, Mrs Pemberton already lost from his thoughts. But the power of electrical discharge had fascinated him for as long as he could remember. Even as a young child he remembered watching the lightning flash and wondering at it. Then he had written a precocious letter to the great man about his experiment with the kite and the Leyden Jar. It was Franklin's first attempt to capture the power of lightning, an experiment that killed the next three men who attempted it.

To his surprise and delight Charlie had received a reply from Benjamin Franklin. For many days he had carried it with him, tucked carefully inside his shirt, and had stared at it again and again, wondering at the familiar words and the famous signature. Naively, Charlie had asked whether the sage had ever considered how the amount of the electrical fluid he had identified might be measured. In words that Charlie could forever quote from memory, Franklin had referred him to the latest research in the subject. Though he himself had moved on to 'other pursuits' as the great man said, there were clever men in the universities of Europe who were exploring this very question.

'Europe,' thought Charlie as he rode. 'Perhaps one day I shall go to Europe and learn the truth on this matter.' The little mare picked her way unbidden down the track towards the small settlement of Schenectady, a collection of log cabins with an inn and tavern and in the centre a communal meeting house that doubled as a blockhouse in the event of an Indian attack. Not that there had been much trouble in that regard in recent years, not since the French had been pushed out. Though the British might still try to use their loyal tribes when the fighting spread to the interior, as Charlie hoped, indeed was certain, that it would.

Fifty yards ahead of him a figure materialised from out of the woods, a tall figure standing motionless beside the track. Charlie strained forward, peering into the gathering darkness beneath the overhanging canopy of trees and loosened the dirk at his side, at the same time feeling in a saddle pocket for his pistol. The figure stood waiting impassively while the mare stepped daintily down the track towards him. As he drew closer Charlie made out the strong angular profile and the Mohawk dress and he relaxed slightly. His father had very good relations with the Mohawk, much of his trade being with them and Charlie of all people had little reason to fear them.

Still, in these times one could not be certain. Another jagged brilliant white flash lit up the gloom and for an instant the man was clearly illuminated. Charlie grinned and raised his hand in friendship. "Francis!" he cried out in delight. "I thought you were in New York with my father setting up shipping for next years trade."

Francis Johnson smiled back at him and in that moment his European blood suddenly seemed to prevail in spite of the darkness of his skin. A product of Sir William's second marriage, he and Charlie had been inseparable until Francis had been sent to school in Connecticut. He had returned better educated by far than Charlie, who had been left more or less to educate himself. Yet Charlie too had made good use of his time, every spare hour spent devouring indiscriminatingly but enthusiastically the books with which Sir William had filled his library in an effort to recreate a gentleman's mansion in the wilderness.

Sir William's choice of books had been haphazard in the extreme, gathered at random on visits to London or created ad hoc for him by his agents. As a result the library was an eclectic collection of literature, pornography, philosophy, science and mathematics. But Charlie had plundered it eagerly, exploring everything with equal voracity, though inevitably leaving great unknown gaps in his knowledge.

Science and mathematics had from the beginning fascinated him and he discovered, with no great surprise for he had no means of knowing how rare a gift it was, that he had a particular flair for numbers. Anything that could be expressed numerically seemed to hold no secrets from him, however abstruse the subject or complex the analysis. Rapidly he had learned the delights of prime numbers and surds, proportions and probability, trigonometry and logarithms. Even miracles such as compound interest, which he quickly realised could produce amazing results, were instantly obvious to him.

So for Charlie numbers came to seem the very essence of everything; a source of a delight such as other people, he understood, derived from music and the arts, which to Charlie meant nothing, for Sir William and his agents had neglected that aspect of his library.

What the library did contain however were the very latest works on probability theory, including the writings of Edmund Hoyle and in particular his analysis of card games. For his lonely entertainment, armed with sets of playing cards, the boy had spent hours verifying Hoyle's theories and throughout long dark cold winter evenings he had patiently and systematically played out innumerable hands of whist and piquet and endless deals of pharaoh, until he could read the mathematical probabilities of those games as clearly as the pages of any book.

Francis Johnson, given his more conventional education and good social connections might easily have adopted the life of a colonial settler, though the baronetcy would inevitably have passed to his older European half brother. Like Sir William, he found himself able to move effortlessly between the European and the Mohawk culture. But Francis found himself drawn more and more to his native roots and increasingly had opted to return to the ways of his mother's people. He seldom spoke about this decision to Charlie and certainly never explained it. His Indian name was Silent Owl.

But when Francis Johnson did decide to speak it was wise to heed his words. He spoke now, quietly, to his friend. "I bring you a message from your father. He is gravely injured and wants you to go to him in New York."

Charlie stared. "My father injured? But how injured?" His distant independent father had never asked for assistance from any man, least of all from him. He steadied the pony as a great peal of thunder crashed immediately over their heads and the rain came in a sudden solid wall of drenching warm water, driving great spurts of brown mud up from the track. Charlie leapt down and leading the pony behind him followed Francis deeper into the trees. They stood together under cover, waiting for the torrent to subside. "What has happened?" he asked again. "Why does my father want me?"

Francis stared at him silently for a moment. "Your father was wounded in a skirmish a few days ago and now the wound is turning bad. I am told that he is being well looked after," he smiled enigmatically, "by some new friends--- an English milord. I think he has plans for you, Charlie." He shrugged. "But he would not tell me, of course." Charlie's father knew only too well that Francis did not share his opinion about the rebellion, in spite of his family connections.

Francis went on inconsequentially. "In New York after the independence proclamation the people knocked the head off King George's statue and melted down the body to make musket balls."

Charlie laughed out aloud at the idea. Then he fell suddenly silent. "But where am I to find my father?"

"He is in the city now. At first he was moved to Staten Island. But the English milord is having him cared for in the city." He shrugged. "Most of the merchants seem to favour the British and expect their army to take New York soon. It seems that Washington and his men cannot stop them." Francis tilted his head in a gesture of silent acquiescence. "Let them have the city," he went on quietly. "But when they come into the woods----." He gestured to the wilderness around him.

Charlie nodded thoughtfully and started to mount the mare. The rain had ceased as quickly as it had arrived and the air was cooler now, smelling sweetly of the shrubs and plants. He must decide what to do next: either to join his father and confront their old disagreements or to stay in the Mohawk valley and allow events come to him, as they were bound eventually to do.

He swung up into his seat on the mare as Francis placed his hand on Charlie's knee and looked up into his face. "Charlie," he said, "You were seen with Mrs Pemberton today. Be careful of the man from the church. He means to harm you if he can."

Charlie frowned. "Snape? Old Snape, you mean?" he asked. "Not the Reverend Snape? But--- ." He knew that Snape was an Anglican and a declared loyalist. It was rumoured too that he was well connected in

England and had been sent to the colony to preach against the new and dangerous evangelic ideas that were infecting the churches there.

In truth these new ideas left Charlie cold, repelled him actually, for he cared little about religion. But since they seemed to challenge the establishment in London Charlie had little sympathy for Snape's point of view, especially as it was said that he had been sent to the colony by John Butler, a powerful and fanatically anti-American churchman. It was even rumoured that Snape's connections went higher still: that his mission was as much political as religious.

"Old Snape is after all a man," Francis said simply. "And Mrs Pemberton---- ," He let the sentence hang in the cool air. "So be careful, Charlie. We live in uncertain times. Watch your step."

"Old Snape and Charlotte? No, it cannot be!" His lip curled, unconsciously. But whether at Charlotte or at Snape or indeed even at himself, Francis could not tell. Charlie reached down and grasped his friend by the shoulder. "Thank you Francis. Be careful too. Not all your people share our views on the future." He cantered off in the gathering gloom towards the township, his hand raised in salute.

Francis stood in silence as he went. He knew Charlie well and was aware that in spite of his friend's contempt for his own people the blood was still strong. At heart he knew that Charlie had the same weaknesses as the highlanders he so disdained, including an arrogance and a quickness to take offence. And when he did take offence?

"Be not too casually, young Charlie," he muttered. "Please, not too casual. But since you will not take care, I must watch your step for you." As he stood watching Charlie disappear it was as if his own European persona gradually evaporated too. Finally Francis merged into the dark woods and vanishing in the growing shadows.

When Snape entered the White Hart Inn Thomas Pemberton was sitting staring uncertainly into his tankard of ale. A big burly man, powerfully built and somewhat overweight with a round ruddy face and bulging blue eyes, Pemberton was not a man usually much given to self-doubt. Certainly his business associates and drinking companions could never have imagined him in such a mood. Outside, the rain had relieved the oppressive heat and true darkness was now falling. It was past time to ride home.

Yet Pemberton lingered over his beer uneasily. He knew that he should never have stopped at the inn, should have ridden straight home to his young wife at their house on the edge of town. He had been, still was, genuinely proud of Charlotte. She was pretty and charming and he was equally proud of her other attainments--- education and social skills: all the things he lacked. Still Pemberton stared morosely into his ale. He was under no illusion as to why she had married him or the part his money had played in her willingness to move to the wilds of the Mohawk River from the relative comforts of Philadelphia. Money, marriage and security were not unusual attractions for a woman and to some extent he had accepted the differences between them, uneasy as they often made him feel.

But that was not the cause of his present unease. Not accustomed to introspection, Pemberton had slowly become aware that try as she might Charlotte did not, perhaps could not, truly care for him as he did for her and this awareness caused him pain. At first he had gone to any length and spared no effort to please her. But she had remained indifferent. Always polite and obedient it is true. But still indifferent. Now this truth lay between them like a thick pall.

It was worse now than it had been in the beginning when all had been new and exciting between them. Now Pemberton, a straightforward physical man, was unable to express his fears even to himself and least of all to Charlotte. He felt shame and a growing sense of anger at what was happening. Why was he unable to enjoy her physically now? Why could he not be the man with Charlotte that he knew he could be, indeed frequently was, with other women whom he encountered on his travels?

It was with a sense of irritation then that he saw the Reverend Snape peering through the smoky darkness of the interior in his direction and making his way across the rough wooden floor towards him. Pemberton watched him with some surprise, for it was strange to see the cleric here, especially someone so austere as Snape.

"Mr Pemberton, I have to speak to you on a matter of some delicacy." Snape whispered in his soft ingratiating tones, his head bobbing and an apologetic half smile on his sallow features.

Pemberton pushed his tankard aside and half rose with a respectful nod. "Pray sit down, my dear sir." He knew of Snape's reputation and had every sympathy with the political views he held. "The damned rebels aren't causing more trouble, I hope? I've been away for a few days, so I'm out of touch. But I can tell you Albany is awash with them. I don't know where it will end."

Snape's smile turned instantly to a quick involuntary sneer. "Have no fear, Mr Pemberton. Lord Howe and his troops have landed and will soon be here. There is also a strong force coming down from Canada. Washington's rabble will soon be scattered." His voice rose shrilly before he recovered himself, paused and rearranged his features into a more pious and concerned exterior.

He leaned forward solicitously, his long pale hands folded before him on the rough deal table. "No, Pemberton, my concern is of a more personal nature. I must speak to you of something that concerns your wife--- a matter I am reluctant to take up officially out of consideration for her feelings and reputation." Pemberton's eyes widened and Snape added rapidly, "And of course your own." He eyed the other man's alarm for a moment with a secret satisfaction and then went on. "My dear sir, I think you should go straight home and tend to her."

Pemberton stared at him in alarm and Snape raised his hand. "Oh, she is well enough, sir," he added with a reassuring smile, "in spite of her shocking experience," he went on smoothly . "But I felt it right to warn you---- ,"

"What the devil---," Pemberton began.

"Yes," said Snape severely. "The devil indeed! You know the young MacPherson boy, do you not?"

"Yes, I do," Pemberton said slowly. "His father is James MacPherson, a good loyalist and Tory. My wife Charlotte has been helping the boy with his French."

Snape sniffed. "The father may be sound enough in truth. But the boy is contaminated with serious rebel tendencies, I fear. Still, that is not the issue," he went on quickly. "I have to tell you that today the boy quite forgot himself with your wife. He---, well, he tried to force himself on her. But all is well." Snape held up a pale hand again as Pemberton started up from his seat.

"She, fine woman, fought him off. But in his wicked lust I'm sorry to say that he did strike her a blow. I fear you will find that she is slightly injured," Snape said solicitously. "Nothing serious, I hasten to reassure you. But she was still in some distress when I called at your home, quite by chance this afternoon and I felt that I should explain the circumstances to you. For she, dear soul, may wish to defend the boy, perhaps from some misplaced sense of charity," Snape added, his black eyes fixed on Pemberton's face. "But I thought you should be forewarned," he ended with a faint consoling smile.

Pemberton's normally florid face was pale with anger. "The young swine! How dare he! I'll have the skin off his back!" He rose abruptly and headed for the door.

But moving with surprising speed Snape caught him by the sleeve of his coat. "Please do not act hasty, my dear Mr Pemberton. Remember the perilous times we live in." He smiled comfortingly. "But see to your wife. Assess the situation and confirm my account. You will find a suitable punishment for him then, I am certain."

Back at the cabin, though Charlotte did her best to conceal the bruise, Pemberton had taken only a moment to see the livid mark on her face and scarcely more to confront her. "The truth, my dear," he had demanded. "For I know what happened here today with the MacPherson boy. Do not attempt to deny it." Charlotte stared in horror, petrified at what she thought was to come. "He was here, was he not?" Before she could speak Pemberton raged on. "And he attacked you, the vile animal! Thank God you were able to fight him off. The Reverend Snape has told me everything."

Charlotte made a rapid and simple choice. Lowering her eyes she confirmed Pemberton's version of events. "Please do not seek to punish the boy!" she cried out virtuously. "He is young and perhaps I was unwise to see him here alone. Perhaps, unwittingly, oh yes, as God knows, quite unwittingly, I may have given him cause to think--- ." She blushed quite convincingly. "Forgive me, Thomas! And please, please do nothing in haste!"

TWO

Charlie had risen early and was standing outside the MacPherson cabin sluicing himself down from a wooden water trough, clad only in a pair of buckskin trousers and relishing the warm sun on his shoulders.

Overnight he had decided to go to his father in New York, though why he had been summoned Charlie could still not imagine. But his father needed him and so he must go. Absorbed in his thoughts he was unaware that Pemberton and two of his men had emerged from the woods behind the cabin.

Charlie did not see them until they were almost upon him and when he did Pemberton was only a few yards away and riding down on him like a maniac. With a sickening blow his powerful mount struck Charlie with its shoulder, knocking him sprawling half-stunned to the grass.

"Hold him!" he heard Pemberton call and before he could recover his wits the men had seized his wrists and dragged him bodily across the low water trough. As Pemberton dismounted they held his wrists painfully against the rough uprights. Twisting his head around, Charlie could just see the bulky figure that stood over him, silhouetted against the early morning sun. "This will teach you a lesson, young MacPherson. Never go near to my wife again!"

The first blow from the riding crop lashed down on Charlie's naked back and he shouted out involuntarily with shock and pain. But as blow after blow fell he bit his lip and took his punishment in silence. Though the pain was acute he was aware in a curiously detached way of the strange mixture of emotions that swept through him. Pemberton in his rage continued to thrash down at his bruised back. But it seemed almost as if Charlie's mind was functioning in a different body. His guilt was beyond doubt, he reasoned. He had cuckolded this man and his first thought was a kind of relief that the truth was out and the affair finally over.

But as Pemberton continued to flog at his naked back and as the blows and the pain mounted his mood changed. A new emotion filled him:

a cold slow hatred and a desire for revenge, however long it took. With total clarity he knew that he could never forgive this man for the pain and the humiliation, especially the humiliation. Regardless of the cause and the offence was undeniable, sooner or later he would have to settle with this man.

A kind of madness had grasped Pemberton and he flogged viciously at Charlie, bringing blood to the weals across his wounded back, cursing as he lashed down at the boy. All pretence of self-righteousness was gone and now even the men holding Charlie began to murmur their concern. One of them released his wrist and Charlie slumped limply onto the trough, half in the icy water, gasping desperately for breath. Pemberton stood over him, trembling and panting, his rage slowly subsiding. "There!" he spat out. "Take that as a lesson." In spite of his bitter justification an awareness of his own secret fears struck suddenly at him. As his big heavy gelding pranced about nervously, unsettled by the smell of blood, Pemberton jerked its head angrily down.

While the men remounted Charlie rolled painfully over and pulled himself unsteadily to his feet. Clinging to the wooden fence for support he stared up at Pemberton. "I pity you, Thomas Pemberton." he said slowly. "But if you ever cross my path again I shall kill you."

Pemberton gazed down at him in astonishment. There was a look in Charlie's young eyes that he had never before seen in any man's. For an instant he was taken aback, all moral certainty gone. Then recovering he shook his riding crop at Charlie angrily. "Learn your lesson, boy, before it is too late." He wheeled his horse and urged it away.

Charlie watched them go. "It is too late, Thomas Pemberton," he muttered coldly. "You will pay for this. I don't know how. But you will certainly pay."

He stumbled painfully towards the cabin but before he had reached the sanctuary of the open door a Mohawk woman, one of Francis's many half-sisters, appeared carrying a pot of herbal salve. She motioned for him to stretch out on the bunk and then applied the ointment gently and silently to the ugly wounds on his back. Charlie winced at first but as the pain eased he thanked her. "Tell my friend Francis that I go to meet my father," he told her in her own tongue.

The woman smiled and nodded. "Francis will know," was all she said.

Hours later, with the sun dipping behind the circling mountains and the woods darkening, Charlie reined in his little mare at a familiar fork in the track south of Schenectady. All that day he had lain in the cabin, resting while the Mohawk ointment worked its magic, his young body shaking off the physical effect of the beating.

Finally he had dragged himself off the bunk, still moving stiffly, still cold with rage at the indignity of what had been done, and gathered up his few possessions including the prized letter from Benjamin Franklin. Arming himself for what might prove an uncertain journey to meet his father in New York he had mounted the mare and headed south away from the valley.

But now he hesitated. Which way, he thought, as the mare shook its bridle as if to ask the same question. Straight on to Albany? Or the well-known turn that would lead him towards the Pemberton house? As he considered, he heard the faintest rustle in the undergrowth beside the track. Unconsciously he reached down to loosen his pistol, at the same time scouring the dark woods for a sign of movement. He would not be taken by surprise a second time in one day. But there was only silence in the woods.

He delayed only a moment longer. For honour's sake, come what may, he should see Charlotte again. If only to make certain she was not in harm's way. He owed her that at least. Though in truth his foremost feeling was a sense of distaste for the whole episode and a desire to leave it all far behind.

He wheeled the mare down the path towards the Pemberton house and trotted on, mentally rehearsing how he would take his farewells from Charlotte. As to what he would do if Pemberton was at the farmhouse Charlie had given no thought at all. If past experience was a guide it was unlikely that he would find Pemberton at home at this time of day. He would be in town, almost certainly drinking at the tavern and bragging about the beating he had given the young MacPherson boy. Charlie rode on with a cold hatred growing in his heart, almost hoping to find Pemberton waiting at the house, certainly no longer caring if he did. 'Let us see how he fares without his helpers,' he though grimly.

But suddenly events spiralled out of his control. Rounding a bend in the track he saw Pemberton galloping towards him. The two recognised each other at almost the same instant and the older man uttered an outraged bellow of anger, spurring his horse on. Charlie barely had time to see that Pemberton was flourishing a weapon of some kind over his head as they closed rapidly on each other. The next few seconds passed in a flash. But in spite of the speed, at one level it seemed to Charlie as if what happened followed a slow, carefully rehearsed, almost preordained sequence.

Ducking under Pemberton's blow and instinctively drawing the dirk from his waist, Charlie felt the familiar hilt in his grasp and found himself striking upwards into the man's chest with calm deliberation. The momentum of Pemberton's rush carried him hard onto the blade, driving it deep and tearing the knife from Charlie's hand as the two mounts recoiled from the collision.

Charlie spun the little mare quickly around in time to see Pemberton still upright in his saddle, his eyes staring and mouth gaping open, the dirk projecting darkly from his chest. As Charlie watched, the man slumped forward over his horse's neck. Then very slowly he toppled sideways and slid to the ground with a heavy crash. The woods settled back into a deep silence, broken only by the snorting and stamping of Pemberton's anxious gelding as it circled its master's body.

'Hell's teeth and damnation,' Charlie thought in dismay. 'What now?' For he had little doubt that the man was dead. He knew equally well that his own action had been deliberate, possibly even premeditated. Yet in truth he felt no sense of guilt. He thrust that awkward thought out of his mind to be examined at a later date and started to dismount.

In that instant the heavy foliage by the track parted and a silent figure stepped onto the track, stooped over the still body of Pemberton, tugged the knife from dead man's chest and calmly drew it across the defenceless throat.

Charlie stared in shock as Francis Johnson straightened and looked up at him solemnly. "Go, Charlie!" he said. "Go to your father in New York! This is no place for you. These woods are full of treacherous Indians!" There was not a flicker of humour on his face as he spoke. Francis wiped the knife clean in the soft earth and handed it back to Charlie. "Go to New York. Leave this to me."

Charlie stared at him in silence as slow comprehension penetrating his astonishment. He nodded. "I shall never forget this, Francis," he said quietly, leaning down and grasping his friend's hand. Wheeling the mare he disappeared back down the track towards Albany, his arm raised in a gesture of farewell.

Francis watched him until he was out of sight. Then drawing his own knife he swiftly cut around the top of Pemberton's head and expertly tugged back the hair, smoothly slitting away the scalp. He tucked the grisly trophy in a pouch at his waist and looked around cautiously before dragged the body deeper into the woods. There would be a search when Pemberton failed to appear. But it would take time before the body was found and by then Charlie would be a long way off. With any luck a killing like this, with a scalp taken, would not be linked to a settler. Though the Reverend Snape would continue to be a problem until he was dealt with finally, Francis thought grimly.

At each stopping place down the Hudson valley the news of the war changed. Amongst Albany's high gabled Dutch houses, where he left the mare with one of the Johnson men and took to the river, there was a growing excitement in the streets. Astonishing rumours circulated of a British fleet so enormous that it had filled New York harbour and its approaches. There were accounts moreover of masses of troops and equipment of every description being landed on Staten Island, including it was said vast numbers of brutal Hessian German mercenaries, a rumour that particularly outraged American opinion on both sides of the argument.

On the other hand, it was being said that the American army was well established in their Battery at the foot of Manhattan and in strong positions on Long Island. In addition General Washington held key forts in commanding positions on the natural ramparts that bordered the Hudson River and these were considered invulnerable to attack. In any case, so the generally held opinion went, soon the British would see sense and negotiate a settlement rather than fight against their kith and kin, particularly with foreign troops like Hessians.

But in case they were stupid enough to attack the colonists, General Philip Schuyler, an aloof and admittedly unpopular gentleman who owned extensive estates in the area, had been asked to organise the local American troops. Schuyler was an odd sort of revolutionary, thought Charlie, but nevertheless dedicated to the cause. He had been charged by Washington with stopping the British from moving up the Hudson Valley to Canada and thus splitting the colonies into two parts unable to communicate effectively with each other.

That evening Charlie joined the throng milling around outside Schuyler's elegant white mansion, drinking in the rebellious mood and revelling in the excitement. In spite of his father's summons he was greatly tempted to join the fight there and then. But though events seemed to be moving fast it was unlikely that the British would reach Albany for weeks or months, if indeed they ever came so far. Charlie kicked the ground angrily. His father's summons was most unusual and to judge from Francis very urgent. In any case, he thought with a mental shrug, further down the river towards the city he would be closer to the action. Next morning he begged passage down the Hudson on one of the big flat-bottomed cargo scows that plied to and from New York.

By the time the old stone houses of Poughkeepsie came in sight the news had become worse, worryingly so. General Howe, it was said, had moved against Washington with an army of disciplined Hessians and the American troops had been put ignominiously to flight even from strong positions on Long Island. Patriotic spirits were low. But Colonel Knox and three thousand men with artillery still held the Battery in New York, surely impregnable, people muttered. Moreover Washington was even now fortifying new strong points on Haarlem Heights to the north of the city and awaiting the next British attack.

As the clumsy scow rolled on down the slow moving majestic Hudson, Charlie lay in the bluff bows gazing up at the towering cliffs on each side of the steadily widening river, listening to the distant thunder rumbling around the horizon. That the season was moving on from summer was clear and from time to time the entire river would vanish from sight as a white curtain of rain and mist rolled towards the boat, swallowing up everything in its path and wiping out every navigational aid, driving Charlie down into the shelter of the hold.

Francis had said that nature is our best defence, he thought as he stared out at the cliffs. And the high palisades and the heavy chains and blockades that General Washington was stringing across the river must make it totally impassable to the British ships. There was surely no way in which they could force a passage up this great river. Sooner or later they must realise the futility of trying to hold this wilderness against a determined opposition. Sooner or later the British would have to go away.

The scow moored at sunset just beyond Jeffrey's Point, safe under the guns of the twin forts, Lee and Washington, that stood like Scylla and Charybdis on each side of the river. Charlie scrambled up the steep slope to Fort Washington and stared in amazement at the hundreds of green-clad patriotic defenders who milled about in the complex of trenches that protected the landward approaches of the fort.

Some of the men crouched around camp-fires that flared red and yellow against the night sky, preparing evening meals. Others lay stretched out, resting or speaking quietly to their neighbours. Some, even at that late hour, staggered into the camp carrying timber and rocks from the surrounding farm lands and woods to reinforce the already stout earthworks and redoubts. No, Charlie thought, forts like these could never be taken by any human force. And with guardians such as these the upper Hudson was surely impregnable.

The determined mood in the American garrison transmitted itself to the crew of the scow and all were cheerful when the scow set off next morning, heading south on a brisk ebb tide down the ever-widening river estuary towards the harbour of New York.

As they drew near however Charlie noticed a thick black cloud that was drifting ominously to meet them on a light breeze. He frowned, his doubts growing by the minute as they approached the old landing stages on the west side of the city. The Battery at the south end of the island was now almost completely shrouded in smoke.

Suddenly a random gust of wind parted the smoke for a moment and Charlie saw fluttering fitfully in the half gloom a British flag. Staring in disbelief at its garish colours, erratically appearing and disappearing as the light wind rose and fell, Charlie realised that the unthinkable had happened. New York was ablaze and in British hands! The boat slowly approached a jetty and now he could clearly see scarlet uniforms on the ramparts.

Making his way through the smouldering streets Charlie noted resentfully that amid the shambles of the old harbour area were throngs of smiling happy Tory loyalists, many known to him personally as friends of his father. Women too, he thought contemptuously, were welcoming the redcoats and their blue-coated Hessians mercenaries with open arms, literally in some cases. A few shops and stalls had survived the fire and were open for trade with the mostly drunken British soldiers, many of whom had giggling young local women hanging on their arms.

He walked north up Broadway, gazing in dismay on the devastation about him. Smoke and ash drifted cheerlessly on the swirling wind and what had once been a splendid avenue of fine houses was now row upon row of burned-out ruins, smoking grey ghosts of what they had been. The whole west side seemed to have vanished and the east side was a waste land almost to the river. Already a shanty town of rough huts had been hastily thrown together using charred discarded timber and beams and covered over with sailcloth, replacing some of the finest buildings of the city. Already these had been occupied. But not by the merchants and traders of a few days earlier. Now the lowest riffraff of the city had taken over, prostitutes and their protectors, eager for English gold and openly engaged in their trade with drunken soldiers.

A few runaway slaves and the occasional Indian from up-state lounged around, watching impassively or raking through the remains of deserted mansion houses for loot. New York was little more than a dark shell, the smell of smoke and the all pervasive stench of charred animal carcasses adding to the overwhelming sense of destruction.

Charlie headed towards the Trinity Church, stepping carefully to avoid the worst of the debris. Then he stopped abruptly and stared in disbelief. The lovely old church was gone! Its great steeple, once visible for miles out to sea, lay in smoking rubble where it had crashed to earth, half blocking the broad road.

'Why?' Charlie thought in dismay. 'Why ruin a city that might have been a comfortable winter headquarters for them, that would have given them shelter, full as it is of Tory sympathizers?' He was gazing around in bewilderment when he noticed that some of the buildings had been crudely daubed in red paint with a large letter 'R'. He caught at the coat of a man hurrying by. "Tell me friend," he asked, "what signifies the letter 'R' in these parts?"

The man paused and stared at him in astonishment for a moment. "Why lad," he said, almost contemptuously, "That means Rebel! These are the houses of damned rebels. At least they were!" he added with a laugh. "Some of the leaders, God curse them. We marked them to let the British see where their enemies lived."

Charlie, checking his anger, held back a hot response. "Rebels, eh!" he said, groping for words. "Well, since you seem to know these parts so well, can you tell me where the Tontine Coffeehouse might be?"

The man pointed further up the broad avenue. He thought it might still be intact. "Most of the west side has gone," he said, "right up to St Paul's Church. But I hear the Tontine has survived."

As they parted Charlie called after him, "Tell me, why did the British do this?" He indicated the devastation around them.

The man stared at him again. Clearly he was dealing with an idiot. "Why bless you lad, it weren't the British as done this! It was the damned rebels! They set the fires as they ran away, hell mend them! They tell me it was started last night in a grog shop near Whitehall. But the wind spread it too fast to check. The damn fools had melted down the church bells to make guns and there was no way to sound the alarm and no fire crews to help!" The man spat his disgust.

"Rebel swine were running around all night helping to spread the flames with matches and fire-balls. Even cut the handles off the water buckets! Paid the price for that too, some of them. Saw one myself knocked on the head by an English grenadier and thrown into the fire for his pains!" He laughed bitterly. "Another one caught with matches was hung on the spot. Good riddance too!" Appalled, Charlie walked away wordlessly through the chaos that had been New York.

As he went north the devastation seemed to lessen until eventually he came to a small group of buildings that appeared to have escaped the fire entirely. There was the Tontine tavern and coffee house, miraculously intact. Charlie entered and as his eyes adjusted to the internal gloom he saw a small group of British and Hessian officers in splendid scarlet and blue uniforms lounging back on the rough wooden benches, drinking and talking quietly in a desultory way, black cocked hats and beribboned helmets scattered about them. After a cursory glance at Charlie they pointedly ignored him. He hesitated for a moment, looking about until he caught sight of the local man who ran the tavern. "I'm looking for my father," he said. "James MacPherson of the Mohawk Valley. I believe he was here. Have you seen him at all?"

Before the man could reply one of the British officers leapt to his feet and came eagerly towards him. Not much more than Charlie's age, he was a good looking young man of medium height and build, immaculately turned out in the red silver-buttoned coat, white buckskin breeches and black top boots of a Dragoon officer. His fair straight hair was pulled back from a high forehead, his complexion fresh and his manner friendly and open.

He approached Charlie and inclined his head politely in his direction. "My dear sir, do I understand that you are the son of James MacPherson? If so I am very much at your service, sir." he said with a smile, reaching out his hand. Charlie thought that he detected a Scots accent under the cultured tones. The young officer went on quickly. "But I have sad tidings for you, I fear. Your father is very ill--- badly injured, I'm afraid. My physician is fearful for his survival."

Charlie stared in amazement at the good-natured young man. So this was the hated enemy! The young officer seized his hand, shook it enthusiastically. "I am William Cathcart, sir, Cornet in the 16th Light Dragoons. I am deeply indebted to your family, sir, and to your father in particular." Seeing Charlie's puzzlement he brushed aside the unspoken question. "But now you want to see your father. Of course. Please, come with me. The doctor is with him now," he added over his shoulder, picking up his helmet and with a smile indicating to Charlie that he should follow him up a steep flight of rough wooden stairs. Charlie noted resentfully that the brass helmet, gaily swathed with a scarlet turban around its base, bore an ominous death head insignia. Underneath was inscribed the motto, "Or Glory!"

The young officer bounded up the steps to a bare wooden door at the rear of the building. Then he paused and said in reassuring tones, "Believe me, Edward Bancroft is a very fine physician. A distinguished scientist too, I understand. Member of the Royal Society of London. Friends in high places, in government and so on. It is very fortunate that he was here in New York when we needed him. He has a great reputation and if anyone----."

He leaned against the door and grimaced at Charlie, sympathy in his large brown eyes. "But of course you don't know what happened? What a fool I am! Do forgive me for the clumsy way I have broken this news to you." He gestured and led the way to a small window that provided what light there was on the landing. "You see your father has been wounded--- very badly wounded. At Kipp's Bay on the 15th, when we drove off the rebels from their redoubts. Lord how they ran!" he said, with an unaffected laugh. "And that gave us New York, you see. For now they have been forced to withdraw up the island to the heights at Harlem."

Misunderstanding the mute disapproval on Charlie's face, Cathcart broke abruptly off. "But more of that later." he said half to himself. "You want to see your father, of course and here I am rattling on--- ." He gazed at Charlie, suddenly seriously again. "It is enough to say that he saved my life that morning, without a doubt. It was an act of such,--- " he shook his head and choked back his emotions. Then he smiled amiably at Charlie. "There I go again! Plenty time to tell you about it later." He knocked gently at the door and stood aside to allow Charlie to enter.

The walls were of plain unadorned wood and the rough flooring creaked beneath Charlie's feet. But the room was light and airy, lit from one large window that looked south over what was left of Broadway. By the window was a night-stand with a bowl and water jug. Apart from that a small Dutch dresser and a couple of simple wooden chairs were all that furnished the room, save for the bed in which his father lay. Charlie advanced cautiously towards him and groped his way slowly into one of the seats, his eyes fixed on his father's face, only half aware of a tall figure standing by the window.

His father, the indestructible James MacPherson, lay propped up against a pillow, gaunt and drawn, his face filled with a deathly pallor that had wiped away the natural colour from his weather-beaten features. His arms were stretched out by his sides and Charlie was shocked to see that even his hands seemed suddenly frail. His eyes, set deep in dark hollows, were closed and his breathing rapid and shallow.

The man by the window spoke. "Mr MacPherson," a strong cultured voice said firmly, "your son Charles has arrived." James open his eyes and his head moved slowly, searching the room and finally fixing on Charlie's face.

"Charlie, it's you," he whispered. "You have come just in time, I am thinking."

Charlie reached out and took his father's hand in his own, wondering at how thin and weak it was and trying to remember when he had last held his father's hand, if indeed ever he had. "I am here now father," he said simply.

A half smile flickered across his father's pale face. "I fear that I'm done for, Charlie," he said hoarsely. Charlie looked sharply across at the tall figure by the window, who simply shrugged philosophically. "This wound is the end of me," James MacPherson went on slowly and painfully, grasping his son's hand with something like his old strength.

"Where---," Charlie started to ask.

"A belly wound," James said hoarsely. "Not good." He shook his head weakly. "No matter," he went on, closing his dark brown eyes. "But I must tell you what I have arranged and not leave you to read it in my will."

Charlie started to speak. But his father shook aside his half formed words. "No lad, it's all right. Just don't interrupt me. I have little enough strength or time." The impatient gesture seemed to exhaust him and he sank back on the pillow with his eyes closed.

After a moment his eyes reopened and he gazed up at Charlie. "You have always gone your own way, son," he whispered weakly. "But for once I want you to do as I ask. Promise me that, boy? God knows, I've asked very little of you! But now swear to follow my wishes, Charlie. It is all written down, legally and binding. And it is all for your own good, believe me."

He indicated with a faint movement of his head towards the tall figure by the window. "Dr Bancroft will explain. But listen to Sir William--- you must trust Sir William Johnson for he is to be your legal guardian now. Follow his advice as you would a father." He smiled feebly. "In truth he has been that to you these several years, I think. More so than myself, I fear." He brushed aside Charlie's faltering denial. "No, I'm no fool, Charlie. I know---." He paused again to summon his strength. "But that is of no consequence now. Above all Charlie," with an effort he raised his head from the pillow to emphasise his words, "I want you to accept the help of young William Cathcart."

He sank back exhausted. "The Honourable William Cathcart," he murmured half under his voice, so that Charlie had to strain to hear him. "Eldest son of Lord Cathcart. A noble Scottish family." He seemed to lose the thread of his thought for a moment and lay back muttering vaguely. "On the wrong side in '45. Though many fine gentlemen were, God knows. If only--- ."

Recovering some strength James went on. "The gentleman in question feels a debt of honour to our family and has promised to help you. He will be the Lord Cathcart one day, Charlie, and I want you to accept his help. Promise to respect my wishes in this, Charlie."

Then summoning up all his failing energy he raided his head and stared at Charlie, speaking with something like his old vehemence. "I know your political views, Charlie. But I want you to follow me in this matter. Promise me you will leave the colonies, at least for a time. I dread what is coming and I do not want you to suffer on the wrong side. Swear it now, lad, for I have little time to argue with you." He sank back exhausted for a moment. When his dark eyes opened Charlie could see empty death in them. "Swear it!"

Charlie took his hand, feeling the chill that was spreading through his father's bones. "Leave America?" he said in despair. "I certainly want to do as you wish, father." He squeezed his father's hand lightly. "But there will be time to talk about this later."

He glanced across again at Edward Bancroft, who simply shook his head silently.

THREE

Three months later and Charlie stood in the waist of the brig 'Mercury' as she battled her way into a wintry English Channel, an easterly gale having abruptly turned what was set to be a near record crossing from New York into a bitter struggle to reach France. But at least now he had quite gained his sea legs, his first days on the ocean having reduced him to a sadly weakened creature quite unconvinced by the assurances of Edward Bancroft and the officers of the packet that they were enjoying a wonderfully smooth and speedy crossing to Nantes. How he had longed for a steady horse under him and the green hills of the Mohawk Valley as he lay retching, clinging desperately to the sides of his cot in the dark damp cabin that he had discovered he was to share with Bancroft.

Balancing easily against the pitching of the ship and with a confident grasp on the mizzen stays, he breathed deeply of the cold clean winter air and watched the tall regular grey waves sweep towards him and crash white against the side of the small vessel, throwing salt spray high in the air. Even now he could scarcely believe the course of events that had changed his life so fundamentally and with such speed.

His father had died almost within the hour of Charlie's arrival, even as he had been taking a simple meal of bread, cheese and ale in the tavern below and listening to William Cathcart's account of the British landing at Kipp's Bay a few days earlier.

"It was just before dawn on the15th--- that was when your father saved my life, as he most certainly did. I am temporarily attached to General Clinton's staff--- you see we don't have many horses here as yet and I did so want to be involved--- and when we crossed the East River I was sent to scout out the land with a few loyalists who knew the area well. Including your father," he added with a sympathetic smile.

"Lord, the noise! Some of our frigates were in the river and how they bombarded the rebel breastworks! It was like the end of the world, as it proved to be for a lot of them, of course. Their positions were blown to pieces almost at once. Quite blown to pieces! Lord, it was the most tremendous peal I ever heard! Shouldn't have liked to be on the receiving end. Though I have to say that our fellows did not seem all that happy with the water business, crammed together in boats in the half dark. Quite defenceless too as they were shot at on the way over the river." The young Cathcart laughed uproariously at the memory. Charlie paused with a piece of bread half way to his mouth, frowning at him in wonderment. Soldiers clearly took a different view of life, he thought, and of death too, for that matter.

"The Hessians and their Jagers hated it, I can tell you. They were stuck bolt upright in the boats, unable to move and terrified of being spilt into the water! Then would you believe it, they started to sing hymns! As they were crossing the river! I don't know who was more surprised, the rebels or our Highlanders who shared the boats with them! Though the Scots were pretty noisy as well. But it weren't hymns they were shouting out, I can tell you!" William Cathcart's honest laughter was irresistible and in spite of himself Charlie found himself grinning at the thought.

"Well, the defenders scattered quickly and their support troops broke almost as fast, disappearing into the ravines that abound in that area. That was when it happened." The young man's tone changed suddenly. "I was running quickly up the slope with your father alongside me and a handful of other local fellows who knew the lay of the land. We were badly outnumbered, you see, and had no artillery at that stage. We knew they had a few cannon on a hill nearby--- they'd been firing on us quite heavily. So we raced up towards the Inchenburg, I think it is called. To clear them out and secure the landing." He shrugged casually as he described the scene.

Charlie tried to imagine the chaos of landing from the crowded boats onto a strange terrain in the dim light of dawn, cannon balls and musket fire whizzing around them as they scrambled up the steep slopes. Cathcart went on more solemnly. "That was when your father saved my life," he said simply. "The Inchenburg is the commanding height but we took them completely by surprise, moving as fast as we did. They had a new brass howitzer and quite a store of ammunition. All of French manufacture, if I'm not mistaken. Also they had more men than we had bargained for," he admitted ruefully.

"I had just disposed of one rebel with my sabre when another came at me out of the darkness with a bayonet." All his relish at the memory of the fight ebbed away from the young man's voice. "I saw the thrust coming out of the corner of my eye. But there was not a thing I could have done about it, such was my position. It all seemed to happen damned slowly. Curiously slow. Or so it seemed in the moment." Cathcart grimaced at Charlie.

"Then out of nowhere your father flung himself at the man and took the bayonet thrust in his own body. A thrust that was meant for me and would have done for me for sure." Cathcart bit his lip and shook his head. "At the same time he killed the rebel with one blow of his sword, while I was crouched there, every second expecting the rebel's blade! Your father saved my life, Charles--- you don't mind me calling you that, do you? It is my younger brother's name and it comes easy to me. He's a clever devil, my brother," he added inconsequentially. "Much smarter than me, of course."

No one had ever called him Charles before. He had always been Charlie to his father, and his mother of course was an unknown figure to him. But sensing the genuine friendship behind his new companion's words he nodded his head in silent acquiescence, curiously moved at hearing of his father's role in Cathcart's escape from death. The Hon. William Cathcart took his hand again. "You see Charles, I am most blessed in this life, that I well realise. A good name, a good family, wonderful brothers and sisters." He hesitated and flushed in embarrassment. Then he went on awkwardly, "and a noble title." He made a vague self-deprecating gesture. "But all of that, all my future life, everything I owe to your father. Charles, I want you to know that now and forever if ever I can help, if ever you need assistance, you may call on me and on my family. I give you my word that you shall have it," he said simply.

In the weeks that followed Charlie had been caught up in a bewildering whirl of activity as time sped past rapidly. The war was going badly for the Americans and every day seemed to bring news of some fresh reverse, with General Washington constantly being outflanked and repeatedly forced to retreat north and west.

Sir William Johnson had arrived in New York to join the conquering British army and took the opportunity to sit down with him to explain the details of James MacPherson's will. "You father's wishes are quite clear, Charles," Sir William said firmly, inexplicably adopting for the first time in their long relationship Cathcart's formal version of his name. Charlie stared at him, experiencing the curious sensation that in some way he was being recreated. "As your guardian and executor of your father's will, I am instructed to sell the MacPherson land at market rates and also to pay you a fair price for your father's share of our trading activities. I am in addition charged to ensure that you leave New York as soon as practicable."

Sir William went quickly. "Your father's wish is for you to continue your education in France where in your father's own words, 'you are to learn to conduct yourself as a European gentleman'. There is not a huge sum available. But in government funds it will provide you with a modest and secure income until you decide on a career and set yourself up properly in life." Sir William was to lodge the proceeds in a sound London bank and to ensure that the income was paid to the young man on a regular basis, 'providing always that he was following his father's wishes'.

Charles's first instinct had been to refuse. This war had scarcely begun and although events were not encouraging, his impulse was to stay and fight. Each day the city was filling with the red coats of more British troops and even worse the green and buff of local loyalists, the 'Royal Greens', particularly hateful to all patriotic Americans. It seemed at times that the entire colony was rejecting independence and was happy to aid the invaders provided there was money to be made from it.

There had been, he heard, a major battle at White Plains where in spite of inflicting heavy casualties on the British, once again Washington had retreated. Now only the twin guardians of the river, Fort Washington and Fort Lee, remained in American hands. Charles George MacPherson, since his father's death he had begun curiously to relish the sound of that name, found himself torn between patriotic loyalty and his recent promise, uneasily made for sure, but inescapably a promise and a death-bed promise at that.

The turning point arrived abruptly one morning in late October, with fall well underway and his thoughts turning longingly to the familiar beauties of the woods and hills around the Mohawk Valley. Charles was enmeshed in yet another stubborn debate on his future with his new guardian when Sir William's manner changed abruptly. Almost in mid-sentence his good-natured demeanour vanished . From the outset he had been well aware of the young man's reason for resisting the terms of the will and aware too of his own son's influence on Charles. The older man stared at Charles with uncharacteristic severity. Then apparently a propos to nothing, he said casually but with quiet emphasis, "You knew Thomas Pemberton, did you not?"

Charles stared back, a cold lump forming in the pit of his stomach, his mind racing. 'How much did Sir William know? What had Francis told his father? Nothing, if he knew his friend'.

"Pemberton is dead, you know." Sir William went on. "Died in rather odd circumstances. You knew him, did you not? Though I suppose you knew Mrs Pemberton rather better?" he added casually.

Charles stammered something trivial.

Sir William seemed oblivious to his confusion. "It looked like a stray Indian killing at first," he went blithely on. "There has been a bit of that sort of thing recently in the back country. As you know, the tribes have divided loyalties and a lot of old scores are being settled, one way and another." He gave Charles an innocent smile. "But," he said heavily, "there were some features of this killing that made it quite out of the ordinary. Tracks of a shod horse in the vicinity and so on. There was some talk that it was a political killing." He paused. "Or even personal," he went on, looking beyond Charles at something outside the window that had caught his attention.

Then he frowned. "But I have to tell you that the Reverend Henry Snape is putting it about that there was trouble between the two of you---you and Pemberton, that is. Pemberton was a staunch Loyalist as you will know, being a friend of the family so to say." He smiled again. "He was well known in the valley and in a way popular. Especially in the present climate of opinion. As for old Snape?" He paused and wrinkled his nose. "Well, no one much cares for him, of course. But still, he is a churchman and influential in his own way."

Charles rapidly considered what Sir William was telling him. The message was clear and the earlier warning Francis had given him rang in his ears. Why was Snape so much set against him, he wondered?

But then as quickly as his mood had changed, Sir William seemed to relax and with a snort he slapped the table. "You know young fellow, in your boots I'd grab at a spell in France! You'd be well out of things here for a time, if you ask me. In a year or two from now--- well, who knows?"

He beamed at Charles. "Be delighted to smooth your way in London. No shortage of friends there. And young William Cathcart is damn well connected everywhere. They tell me his sister is now Lady Stormont. Married to David Murray, a coming man, who is British Ambassador in Paris as well as being nephew to Lord Mansfield."

"Cathcart's older sister is Mary Graham, the one they call the 'Beautiful Mrs Graham'. So young William could be a good friend to you and he'll certainly provide letters of introduction that will open doors for you all across Europe. What more do you want, lad? My word, you can cut a swathe through those Parisian ladies!"

When it comes to the ladies, Charles thought uncharitably, Sir William presumably knew what he was talking about. For since the death of his first wife his mistresses had been legion and most of them had provided him with children. Before Francis's Mohawk mother took him in hand he had married several of these women in rapid succession, including a devout Dutchwoman whom he had agreed to wed on her death bed to enable her to meet her God in good order, as she hoped.

"I hear the old fox Benjamin Franklin is on his way to Paris to join the rebel delegation to the French court. The rebels here don't think Deane and Lee are making much progress with the damned French." Sir William smiled encouragingly at him. "You can be sure of some very interesting times there, I can tell you."

Charles's eyes lit up suddenly. Not at the thought of the famously loose French women but at the idea that he might share a city with his idol Ben Franklin. Perhaps there might even be a chance to meet the great man himself. After all, Paris could not be such a big place. The case for leaving New York had suddenly become more alluring.

For the first few hours after the swift-sailing packet had set sail from New York Charles had been carried away by the excitement of the situation, especially the near silent efficiency of the crew as they heaved up the anchor and swarmed up and down the bewildering network of ropes that he presumed held the whole vessel together in some devilishly clever way that he couldn't yet unravel.

At first the motion of the little brig had been smooth and he had enjoyed his very first contact with the ocean, staring eagerly ahead from a vantage point near the bows as if France might at any moment appear. A day out however and the packet had developed a most unsettling twisting motion, a motion that was neither a roll nor a pitch but was decidedly, yes, most decidedly unsettling. After vomiting once or twice over the side Charles hoped that his head would clear and the dull leaden lump in his stomach dissolve.

But the curious motion of the vessel only seemed to increase as the winds strengthened and for days he had lain green and wretched in his cabin. By that point he was quite careless as to whether the ship went to France or to the bottom of the grey sea. At times the ocean's depth was a clear favourite in his anguished mind.

During this period Edward Bancroft had been greatly in attendance, offering him a succession of foul-tasting draughts that he assured Charles would cure his sea sickness--- they did not--- and persuading him to swallow the odd mouthful of beef broth which probably did some good. It was during this period of overpowering illness that, having weakly confessed to an interest in electricity during a dramatic lightning storm that struck the vessel in mid-Atlantic, he had lain close to despair while Bancroft recounted in enormous detail his experiments in Guiana and Surinam with Torpedo Fish. These fish, according to Edward Bancroft, exhibited the most fascinating characteristics and could induce torpor in their victims by their electrical discharges. To Charles, sunk in a private torpor of his own, it seemed that Bancroft's enthusiastic account of his work had occupied many hours of his recovery and may even have delayed it.

But it was during this period of incapacity that Bancroft must have come across the highly treasured letter from Benjamin Franklin, which Charles presumed he had allowed to fall unnoticed to the cabin floor from a carelessly abandoned coat. It was not until very much later that it occurred to Charles there might be a less honourable explanation. For with hindsight he realised that it was from this point that Edward Bancroft's manner towards him had changed.

The sombre physician's saturnine features seemed to compose themselves in a more friendly fashion and the cool detachment and brisk professional attitude seemed to thaw. His dark eyes still studied Charles closely. But now they seemed to display a warmer interest and as Charles recovered the two men found themselves increasingly exchanging views on Ben Franklin, particularly his famous experiment to seize lightning from the heavens.

Then as the journey wore on and as Charles regained his usual good spirits, Bancroft had turned their conversations away from their shared interest in science and, at first subtly, towards Franklin's political activities and later to the independence issue in general. Finally, on deck one wild day with the wind whipping their words safely away to the south-east and without fear of being overheard, Edward Bancroft revealed to Charles his secret commitment to the cause of American independence.

"I have lived for many years in London and count many in that city as my friends. I did of course study medicine there, as you may know," he shouted, his mouth close to Charles's ear. "Member of the Royal College Surgeons; the Royal Society and so on. Regarded as a true Englishman, though actually I was born in Massachusetts. Did you know that?" He paused to look cautiously around and then gestured for Charles to follow him into the lee of the cabin. There he stared into Charles's face for a moment, his brown eyes suddenly vulnerable and troubled, as if at a loss for his next words.

"In truth I am a patriot at heart," he blurted out. "In fact I am on my way to be private secretary to Mr Franklin and Silas Deane at the American delegation in Paris, though that is not as yet generally known. On the recommendation of Mr Franklin himself, who is at this moment also on his way to France on an armed vessel, the 'Reprisal' from Philadelphia!" Charles's immediate thought was that Edward Bancroft would be an excellent means of meeting the great man in Paris.

Bancroft went on confidently, "I have a feeling, sir, that you share my sentiments in the matter of America's future status." He exposed his large yellowing teeth in a grin and held up a large hand. "There is no need to say anything at present. My position will become apparent soon enough. There will be a few folk in London somewhat taken aback, as I believe our nautical friends call it. Not that there is any lack of men in that city who are of our persuasion." He inclined his long-jawed face confidentially nearer to Charles. "I trust you will respect my confidence, even if you do not, though I feel that you do, share my sentiments."

He hesitated, as if assessing Charles's reaction before he went on. "There will be no need to point out to you the advantage of having a friend of America actually within the British Embassy in Paris," he continued. "You could be most helpful to Mr Franklin and to the cause."

He saw the frown cross Charles's face and seized his arm reassuringly. "Not, of course, that I would expect you to do anything dishonourable," he added quickly. "Or to betray personal confidences. Oh no! Of course not! We are all gentlemen after all."

Charles looked down at Bancroft's hand on his sleeve. Unnaturally large and powerful. The hands of a skilled surgeon. Or a strangler's hands? He shivered, in spite of himself, hoping that it would seem merely a response to the chill wind that whistled through the rigging.

"But as you can imagine," Bancroft went on smoothly, "Mr Franklin is eager to discover all he can about attitudes in England, especially the private views of influential men. Those could be most revealing and might help him greatly in deciding policies and strategies. Public opinion in England is very mixed, you understand, regarding this war. Have no doubt that we do have friends in England who seek an honourable settlement with us. Friends in some of the most surprising places," he added with a disconcerting smile, baring his big teeth again in what he took to be a winning smile. "So the most innocent of information, a snippet heard over dinner, a casual comment, here or there? An opinion expressed by a particular person, taken with other facts already known to Mr Franklin, could do for our cause what a regiment of infantry might fail to do."

There was undoubtedly something about Bancroft that Charles found disagreeable and the sudden outbreak of personal confidences, this newfound familiar manner which had replaced the physician's earlier cold detachment he found unconvincing and unsettling. "I do not like thee, Dr Bancroft. The reason why I cannot tell." Charles concluded. The rhyme might be wrong. But the sentiment was just right.

It was therefore somewhat stiffly that he agreed to maintain contact with Bancroft in France and to treat his revelation as a confidence until the true nature of Bancroft's mission became public knowledge. Though it seemed to Charles there was little point in making such a promise. For the news must inevitably become public almost as soon as they arrived in Paris, if indeed it was not already known.

However given the adverse winds, Paris was likely to be many days away and after landing it appeared that there would be a long and uncomfortable journey across country from Nantes, during which time he and Bancroft would inevitably be thrown much together.

Charles had concluded quite rapidly that he did not like the man. Yet in spite of his unfounded reservations he could not avoid feeling slightly flattered by his confidences and excited too at the prospect of possibly meeting his famous hero. With mixed feelings therefore he agreed to consider Bancroft's proposal. A world of intrigue seemed to await him in Paris. There would be famous men to meet, not least the great Benjamin Franklin: which prospect excited him rather more than Sir William Johnson's promise of sophisticated ladies.

Besides, perhaps it might be possible for him at last to make a contribution to the patriotic cause; the cause that however unwillingly he seemed to have abandoned.

FOUR

In fact there followed ten miserable days as the 'Mercury' beat back and forth against a savage north-easterly gale outside the mouth of the Loire estuary. According to Bancroft, well informed as ever, the splendid port of Nantes that lay nearby had built its wealth on trade in slaves and sugar and now boasted a host of splendid buildings, quite outstripping old New York in its fine architecture.

But for all that could be seen, Charles mused, clinging to the weather shrouds and staring hopefully into the low grey clouds that came endlessly racing towards them filled with flying spume and spray, the ship might well still be in mid-Atlantic. Land, if indeed it was there, was quite invisible and with the sky completely overcast it was obvious even to a novice such as Charles that for several days the captain had been unable to take any sightings of the sun to calculate the vessel's position accurately.

But then the mood on the brig changed. The wind moderated and backed sharply round to the west and the captain announced cheerfully that he intended to put the vessel into the nearest safe port. As they were now well inside the great curving headland of Quiberon, instead of Nantes they were bound for a small fishing harbour near the town of Auray. The 'Mercury' ran smoothly on and as the fresh wind swept the sky clear of cloud Charles caught his first sight of Europe.

He gazed fascinated at the strange land that was to be his new home; green damp hills beyond threatening black sea-cliffs that soared above them as they raced towards the shore. Then abruptly the land opened out into a sheltered pleasant bay and there was a tall church steeple dark against the green farm land and the first sign of the new civilisation that awaited him. In only minutes it seemed, they were tied safely to a low stone jetty, watched curiously by a handful of stolid long haired peasants.

Charles leapt ashore, staggering slightly as his legs adapted to the unusually steady land beneath his feet, the calm silence of the harbour sounding loudly in his ears after so many weeks in the roar of the sea. He stared curiously around him at the small harbour with its low slate-roofed houses. A group of locals stood in the background, broad-brimmed black hats pulled well down over their hair, short dark jackets of some unknown material, baggy breeches and tight gaiters, watching the packet complete its berthing with an air of stolid indifference.

Walking briskly towards them, Charles greeted them cheerily in what he assumed to be fluent French. But much to his chagrin they showed no sign of comprehension, merely staring blankly at him. He was suddenly overwhelmed by a terrible thought. Was his accent so impenetrable as to baffle them completely? The prospect of his new and brilliant social life in Paris seemed to be collapsing at the first contact and for one awful moment he wondered what language Charlotte Pemberton, a Huguenot when all was said, had actually taught him!

It was Bancroft, clambering ashore closely behind him, who gave a whispered explanation. "They speak neither French nor English in these parts but an ancient language of their own, older by far than either of those languages. They are Bretons," he said. At that moment a black-clad priest appeared and Bancroft addressed him confidently in a strange tongue that did have some vague familiarity for Charles.

"Breton?" he asked Bancroft in awe, but secretly greatly relieved. "You actually speak that language?"

"No, no, my boy!" the physician replied to him loftily, with a gesture in the direction of the smiling priest. "We are conversing in Latin! It is quite the only way to communicate in these parts, at least for an educated man and a scientist. This gentleman is from that great church we saw from the sea--- the Church of St. Pierre-Quiberon. I have just arranged for transport to take us on to Nantes."

Within half an hour the transport arrived, a rough wooden farm cart that carried them and their baggage on a jolting journey through ten miles of wild woods and thickets to the small town of Auray. Quite exhausted, they spent the night there in an inn which was as dirty and uncomfortable as any Charles had seen in the wildernesses of New York.

Next morning Charles was relieved to discover that his French was actually superior to that of Bancroft. Charlotte had indeed taught him well and so he had taken charge of the negotiations with a sullen peasant to purchase a small gig and a horse to take them in more comfort to Nantes, seventy miles and a three day journey away to the east. Though Charles was able and indeed anxious to pay his way from the funds he had been given by Sir William, his offer was firmly set aside by the physician.

For Bancroft did not seem to lack for gold, at the sight of which the peasant suddenly began to comprehend Charles a great deal better. "No, my boy!" Bancroft said grandly. "The pleasure of your company and conversation on the long journey ahead will be reward enough. It is rare that I meet anyone these days with a genuine interest in the science of electricity--- particularly one of your relative youth, if I may say so. For mark my words, electricity is the thing of the future! I am convinced that its mysteries will soon be revealed to the great benefit of mankind. By the way, have I ever told you of the fascinating study I made of the extraordinary Torpedo Fish of Guiana?"

Charles felt his heart sink. "Yes, I can well understand your astonishment," Bancroft went on smugly. "For would you believe it? The electricity generated by that strange fish proved not to be purely mechanical, you know. One researcher could touch the fish with an iron bar and another person whose hands were in the water would feel the shock! Also, if one person put his hand in the water and joined hands with another person who in turn touched the fish, both parties would feel the electric shock! Amazing, is it not? Just as van Musschenbroek discovered with the Leyden Jar---."

Charles gave a silent groan. It was going to be a long journey to Nantes and even longer to Paris, whatever excitements that great city held for him. "So I am convinced," Bancroft went on obliviously, "that medically the energy from those electric fish will soon prove wonderfully therapeutic for patients with gout, paralysis, headaches and fevers and the like. Dr Mesmer is quite famous for his treatments of that kind." Bancroft paused. "Though in truth," he admitted regretfully, "much of the benefits still remain to be demonstrated."

At Nantes they sold the gig and took to a coach which began the journey across France, roughly following the course of the River Loire to the bourgeois city of Tours and then northwards to Orleans, a lovely town set on a great bend in the river and dedicated, or so it seemed to Charles, largely to the memory of Joan of Arc. She had apparently once delivered the city and almost her country from the English invaders, Charles noted with interest. Then the road lay north again through the fertile farmlands of the Ile-de-France. The last night of the journey they spent at Villejuif, setting off next day for Paris itself.

Despite all his expectations, his first view of Paris came as a shock. As they crested a low hill a great mass of houses came suddenly into his view, stretching it seemed to the horizon in every direction: more houses than he had ever seen in his life, more houses than he thought might possibly exist in one place and all overhung by an enormous dense pall of smoke that poured from ten thousand chimneys, poisoning the air for miles around. In the distance, straight ahead, he could see a broad river winding its way through the city, glinting silver in the low sun.

But it was only as they descended towards the banks of the Seine that the full glory of the city became clear. The carriage rattled towards the centre through seemingly endless rows of superb buildings, magnificent edifices towering six stories high, rich elaborate shops, and stylish private hotels and palaces set in lovely formal gardens. 'Here is a place like nowhere else on earth,' thought Charles and in spite of his determination to remain sophisticated in the eyes of his companion, he was aware to his chagrin that he was actually gaping in wonder.

Behind the grandeur however it became apparent there lay another different Paris. For as the coach sped along Charles caught fleeting glimpses of squalid crowded alleys, cheek by jowl with the beauty and elegance and surprisingly, dangerously, close to it. In spite of all the magnificence it seemed that much of the city was still a labyrinth of narrow muddy streets and huddled ugly medieval slums, crammed together in total disorder and swarming with poorly dressed beggars and street sellers.

Bancroft tapped him on the shoulder to draw his attention away from the window of the coach. "Our ways must part soon, my dear young sir." His long lugubrious face displayed the fleeting smile that Charles had come to recognise and mistrust. "But not for long, I am certain," he went on. "I shall be in contact. But meanwhile I will take leave of you at my lodgings in the Rue de L'Université, while this carriage takes you on to Lord Stormont's home. I envy you my dear boy. Truly I do!" He gave his graveyard smile again. "But for reasons you will understand it would not do for me to be seen at the British Ambassador's residence." He gave a strange laugh. "No, not at all!"

The carriage drew up outside a house in a long street of tall formal buildings near the Quay d'Orsay, where Bancroft took his leave. At last Charles was left to his own devices in his new land and he breathed a sigh of relief, looking eagerly from side to side, delighted and fascinated by the extraordinary scenes as the carriage rumbled on across a crowded bridge spanning the broad river.

More than anything he was struck by the chaos; the incoherent mix of elegance and filth that lay on every hand and by the noise that assailed his ears as he leaned out of the carriage window. Crowds of peddlers and hawkers, male and female, were loudly selling their wares.

Everything from handkerchiefs to hats, perfumes and glasses of tisane, and perhaps more seemed to be on offer here.

He sat back and pulled out his letter of introduction, glancing anxiously at William Cathcart's bold hand to verify, as he had done a hundred times before, that he was indeed bearing a letter addressed to Mr William Fullerton, Secretary to Lord Stormont, Ambassador of Great Britain to France. The audacity of the venture on which he was embarking struck him afresh. 'What am I doing here?' he groaned inwardly. Why was he meeting these great ones who surrounded the Cathcart family? Suddenly the green valleys of the Hudson had never been so appealing.

But before he had time to grow truly apprehensive the carriage had rolled to a stop in front of the dignified façade of Lord Stormont's private residence. Carefully it negotiated its way through the narrow porte cochère and emerged into the hidden stylish courtyard within where it came to a creaking swaying halt.

Charles climbed stiffly down from the coach as a cloud of servants descended on him and spirited away his meagre baggage. He gazed about in some confusion. Then he noticed one especially distinguished-looking gentleman who was watching this process with apparent approval. From the man's magnificent dress and manner Charles wondered fleetingly if this was the Ambassador himself and was about to make a bow to this figure. But happily, before he committed a truly terrible faux pas, some instinct told him that the man was no more than a grand kind of senior house steward.

Suddenly conscious of his travel worn and rustic outfit, he made a mental note that he must quickly learn to tell the servants from the family. Perhaps he should spend some of Sir William's gold on a more suitable outfit. 'I dare say they sell decent clothes in Paris,' he thought vaguely. 'Someone will advise me, I'm sure, if I throw myself on their mercy and beg for advice.'

With great courtesy the superb figure of the steward conducted him into a long reception hall, finely colonnaded and brightly illuminated from a succession of tall windows that seemed to disappear into the far distance, with an elegant golden-framed mirror and a gleaming mahogany side-table set between each. The opposite wall was lined with small straight-backed seats and on one of these Charles was politely invited to wait while his letter of introduction to Fullerton was borne away. He gave a sigh of relief and relaxed slightly. Though still overcome by the grandeur of his surroundings, he was relieved that at least someone seemed to expect him in the home of Lord Stormont.

He scarcely had time to record his new surroundings before he heard firm confident footsteps sounding loudly on the marble floor and an assured voice addressed him clearly in English. "Mr Charles George MacPherson, you are most welcome to Lord Stormont's home." There was in the voice just the hint of an underlying Scots accent and Charles looked around to see a sparely-built man of middle height and dark hair, wigless, with lean tanned features, a raw-boned jaw and glittering intelligent eyes. He was dressed in sober grey coat and breeches, relieved only by a simple white shirt and cravat. "I am William Fullerton, his Lordship's secretary. You are expected of course and, as I say, very much welcome."

Fullerton smiled at Charles, who knew instantly that the shrewd grey eyes had missed nothing in their initial appraisal of him. He took the offered hand and felt the firm handshake, coming to conclusion that as his father might have said, this was a man you could do business with.

Lord Stormont's secretary led him out of the reception hall and up a great flight of stone and marble stairs. Outside a pair of tall mahogany doors he paused for a moment. "These are your rooms," Fullerton said unceremoniously, ushering him into a suite that seemed to run in every direction through a myriad of doors.

'I shall lose myself here, for sure,' thought Charles as he stared around in amazement.

"The Ambassador is away at present," Fullerton went on. "But needless to say Lady Stormont is quite beside herself with eagerness to meet you." Then he gave a discreet dry little laugh. "You can have no idea how much your visit has been anticipated in these parts, Mr MacPherson! Her Ladyship is desperate to learn from you how her brother was when last you saw him." He smiled at Charles. "Mrs Graham is of course equally eager to hear."

In response to Charles's look of puzzlement he added, "Mrs Graham is the eldest sister of the Hon. William Cathcart. She and her husband, Mr Thomas Graham, are staying here at present and you will be sure to meet them soon. As you can imagine, both ladies are eager to hear how their brother does. As indeed is Mr Graham, for he is a special friend of the Hon. William Cathcart. If it is suitable to you I shall have your baggage sent up and when you are ready, please go down to the green drawing room. Any of the servants will direct you," he added casually. "And do not fail to tell me of anything I can do to assist you here in Paris."

FIVE

The suite was magnificent, eclipsing totally anything that he had ever seen before. Sir William Johnson's mansion in the Mohawk Valley, which had hitherto been the last word of splendour for him, now seemed rural and primitive by comparison. In one corner of his new bedroom a long mirror stood above a splendid classical commode and in front of this Charles hastily attempted to tidy himself, gazing in despair at his homespun and travel worn image.

Then with emotions that ranged between excitement and expectation on the one hand and straight forward apprehension on the other, Charles took one deep breath and made his way down to the green drawing room, delayed only by the fact that, having misremembered which of the doors Fullerton had used, he wandered in several wrong directions before finding the great staircase again. "At least," he said ruefully to himself as he descended, "It should not be difficult to recognise the green drawing room. When all is said and done, it is presumably green."

And it was green, as well as being sumptuous beyond even his newly raised expectations. Charles stood for a moment in the middle of the elegant room, his senses reeling and scarcely able to credit how his life was changing by the minute. "I must not act like a country bumpkin in front of these people," he repeated desperately. "I must not act like a country bumpkin. I must not----." But before he could quite collect his wits he heard a clatter of neat feet in a corridor and one of the large mahogany doors flew open.

Charles gasped as a small dark haired bundle of perfumed taffeta and silk flew at him, seized him round the neck and hugged him furiously.

"Dear Mr MacPherson. Dear, dear Mr MacPherson, I am so glad to see you! How pleased we all are! May I call you Charles? That is the name of our other dear brother, you know! But how was William when you left him? He writes of course but never frequently enough and one can never be sure how he is being treated by those awful Americans. But oh dear, of course you may regard yourself as an American! Do not say that I have offended you already," she giggled. "Usually I have to know someone quite a time before I cause serious offence!"

Lady Stormont stood smiling delightedly up at him. Then releasing him, she led him by the hand to a huge and comfortable couch while Charles took rapid stock of this extraordinary young woman. For she seemed young, indeed very young. Scarcely more than his own age she was pleasantly plump and rounded with features that were pretty but which to Charles's eye fell just short of real beauty. However she more than compensated for this by the way she radiated enthusiasm with a special warmth and charm. Yet even in this moment of genuine delight he noted the strong jaw line and large emotional eyes and sensed the possibility of a turbulent storm from time to time. 'Quite a handful,' he mused. 'In more ways than one. I wonder how Lord Stormont copes with her?'

"Tell me, was my dear brother William in good health? That is the real matter. Did he look well fed and happy? He and Charles were so precipitate to be gone to this war in the colonies. I confess I do not know why." She took his hand in hers and Charles sensed a shadow of real concern flit for a moment behind the luminous brown eyes.

He smiled at her. "Your brother was in excellent health and spirits when last I saw him. He seemed to be enjoying himself immensely and my impression, for what it is worth, is that he is made for a military life." As he spoke he was aware that behind him a door had opened and that someone had entered the room. Louisa's gaze shifted and her pretty rounded face immediately broke into an affectionate smile.

She waved a pale hand in a gesture of welcome. "Mary, ma cherie, come and meet Mr Charles George MacPherson! We have already agreed he shall henceforth be known as Charles to us."

Charles rose to his feet and turned to meet the newcomer. A slim young woman stood before him, tall and erect, her head carried with an unconscious grace and poise. She smiled at him and Charles was instantly lost. His head swam and the blood pounded so loudly in his ears that he could scarcely hear Louisa's voice. It was as if every other person in the room had vanished. But through his confusion he gathered that Louisa was introducing him to her elder sister Mary, the Honourable Mrs Thomas Graham.

Speechless and entranced, he stared at her in silence. For Mary Graham was simply the most beautiful woman he had ever seen. Even in that remarkable room she was like a star, the gentle beauty of her pale oval face, the almond-shaped blue-grey eyes and the fine delicately formed features completely outshining the robust attractions of her young sister. And this in spite of the simplicity of her dress, which was a sort of polonaise of light brown linen, with only a narrow piece of pleated gauze at her slender neck as a tippet. Her direct gaze held his eyes frankly and openly without a trace of feminine wile. It was as if she had no concept of her own beauty.

Charles found he was having difficulty breathing, let alone speaking coherently. Completely bewitched, he gazed at her for what seemed an eternity. How he wished afterwards that he might have had the wit to turn some suitably charming phrase, something by which she would remember him for ever. Instead he stared in silence at her, listening to his heart pounding in a most indiscreet way. It was a bolt from the blue that shattered him like one of Mr Franklin's lightning strokes. Taking her slim hand he bowed as gracefully as he knew how, murmuring something inconsequential that afterwards even he could not recall.

Mary drew him willingly away to sit beside her on a nearby sofa. Then she turned towards him and gave a him smile of such kindness and warmth that Charles knew he had found a friend and perhaps even more. But there was also about her a haunting fragility that even then tore mystifyingly at his heart. It was an instinct of impending loss such as he had never known before, quite inexplicable to him in that moment.

"Do tell us how our dear brother William was when you saw him last," she said in a sweet low voice and Charles knew instantly that he would love her for ever.

"Your brother was well," Charles found himself stumbling over his mundane words. "He was very well. And enjoying his life in the army. That much was clear when last I saw him."

Then glancing up he realised that a dark haired man in his late twenties, very tall and athletic in build, had approached them. The newcomer placed one large brown hand tenderly on Mary's shoulder with a smile of pleasure on his lean open face and greeted Charles in the most unaffected way possible. "I am Thomas Graham, sir and most pleased indeed to meet you." He bowed his long raw-boned frame graciously towards Charles, who hated him instantly merely for being the husband of Mary. "You are more than usually welcome in this house. For we have all heard how courageously your late father behaved and of the great debt we owe to your family."

As Charles watched gloomily Graham said gently to Mary. "Come my dear, you must rest. Mr MacPherson will excuse us, I know." Then with great care he helped her to stretch out on a nearby chaise longue, gesturing to one of the footmen for a warm cover. As he spread it carefully over her slender legs and perched his heavy frame beside her, Mary gave Thomas a look of affection that pierced Charles through and through.

She looked sadly up at her husband and shook her head. "Why my brothers were both so desperate to dash away to the Americas to fight in this war I confess I shall never know." She sighed and took her husband's large brown hand in her slender fingers, frowning slightly. "I know that Mr Charles James Fox thinks the whole enterprise is extremely foolish and unnecessary. You have often said as much yourself, have you not, Thomas?"

Thomas Graham looked uncomfortable and cleared his throat, moving awkwardly on his seat. "War is usually a sad way to settle any dispute, my dear," he said vaguely. "This one seems especially unfortunate, with kith against kin and brother against brother in many cases." He coughed again and added quietly, "But as we are in Lord Stormont's house I think perhaps politics is a little out of the way." Charles stared at him. So Graham might be one of the people Bancroft had meant, who were by no means committed to the war in America.

"Besides," Thomas went on, "William and Charles are young men. They naturally want to make their way in the world, free of family, eager for excitement. That is quite understandable." He laughed in a slightly self-deprecating way and smiled across at Charles. "Not everyone finds cattle and crops as interesting as the laird of Balgowan, you know, Mary. Planning new roads and laying out rows of cottage, improving livestock is not such a great pleasure to every man. Let alone enough to satisfy their ambitions." he added half wistfully.

Mary squeezed his strong hand. "But you are so clever with all of that, Thomas," she said gently. "And the estates in Scotland do need improvement! You say so yourself frequently. Besides, you know your dear mother relies upon you so greatly."

Graham nodded. "Yes, there is much to be done. It does take time to improve the barbaric Highland customs of cattle raising and planting, which are scarcely out of the middle ages in some respects."

Charles felt a surge of completely illogical anger. He knew that he was being foolishly and unnecessarily argumentative and even as the words rose to his lips he bitterly regretted them. But still he went on with them, however unfair and insincere he knew them to be. "I regret, Mr Graham," he said piously, "that you find the Highland people so barbaric. Perhaps there is some good in them that you have overlooked."

Thomas looked aghast. "Oh my dear sir, do forgive me! I had not meant to speak so thoughtlessly. Of course there is much to admire in our Highland people and their culture! A great deal indeed! I spoke only with modern agricultural theory in mind, of the lack of technical development in the field of farming."

Charles, who knew nothing of Highland farming methods and cared even less, was nonetheless perfectly aware of the true source of his irritation and was just about to take further exception to Graham's remarks when Louisa intervened to save the situation. "Oh dear Thomas! I fear you are in danger of digging an even deeper hole in your theoretical farm!" Turning to Charles she said laughingly. "Do forgive him! What you must remember is that Thomas is quite a bore about modern farming methods. Positively lives for agricultural improvements and claims to be the first man to introduce Devon cattle to Scotland! What could be less interesting than that, I ask you?"

Mary had also sensed the underlying tension and detected its cause perhaps more accurately than her sister. A shadow of a frown flitted across her face and she looked reproachfully at her husband. "But surely Thomas, you would not wish to have gone to this dreadful war! Oh Thomas, I would not have you regret anything--- nothing at all!"

Before he could reply, Louisa burst in again, "What nonsense Mary! Of course Thomas has no desire to be thousands of miles away, fine soldier though he would make I am sure. Do you remember the way he dealt with those footpads in London? Such dash! Such courage!" Over Graham's protests and in spite of his obvious embarrassment Louisa carried on with the story she obviously loved to tell and just as obviously had done so on many an occasion.

"Sisters Jane and Mary," she said breathlessly, "just before their joint wedding in London--- Sister Jane is married to the Duke of Atholl--- were travelling by carriage with Thomas on their way to a ball and all dressed in their finery when a group of ruffians sprang out from a dark lane and seized the horses, stopping the carriage to demand money! They were armed with knives and a pistol too!"

Thomas Graham groaned in embarrassment. "Oh please, Louisa! No! Mr MacPherson does not want to hear this old history. They were merely unfortunate wretches, unemployed and underfed, desperate fellows and poor devils."

But Louisa was undaunted. "Thomas, completely unarmed of course, for he was after all on his way to a ball, sprang down from the carriage and grappled with them. He knocked one to the ground, covering himself with mud in the process, which strangely no one remarked upon later at the ball! Isn't that odd? Anyway, three of the men ran off leaving the one who was holding the horses. So Thomas took him in charge and handed him over to the officers who turned up just in time. Wasn't that an adventure! And such courage!" Charles tried to look impressed, loathing Graham all the more.

"What nonsense you talk, Louisa," Thomas Graham said gently. "There was not a whit of danger. The one who held the horses was an unemployed groom with a sick wife." He looked appealingly at Charles. "It was nothing to speak of, truly."

"Yes," concluded Louisa triumphantly. "And next day you begged him off the charges and actually gave him a reference for another position as a groom! Wasn't that splendid?" she asked Charles, who could only smile weakly and agree that Graham was indeed a paragon of kindness and bravery.

"But regarding this American war, you have often made it clear that you have little sympathy with it, Thomas. And to say the truth," Louisa added, "even Lord Stormont in private doubts its wisdom. In spite of the fact that his uncle is mad to pursue it as vigorously as possible." Louisa turned back to Charles and explained. "My husband's uncle is the Earl of Mansfield, who is Lord Chief Justice and a member of the administration. So of course he is bound to support the war! Though I must say," Louisa admitted, "David is quite strong on the legal obligations the colonies owe to the Crown and seems in no doubt about the need to force the war to a conclusion."

Then she gave a ladylike yawn and waved her white hands disparagingly in the air. "But what nonsense, " she cried. "Why are we wasting breath on such a boring matter?" With a demure look at Charles she appraised him diplomatically, taking in his home-spun outfit at a glance.

"Is there anything, I wonder that we can do to help you settle into Paris?" she asked sweetly.

With some relief Charles seized the opening. "Well, Lady Stormont, I believe that I may need some advice regarding what it is suitable for a gentleman to wear here----,"

But before he could say more she had burst into giggles and covered her face. "Well indeed, my dear Charles! I did not dare to mentioned it, thinking that perhaps you wished to rival your compatriot Mr Franklin in rustic simplicity! Do you know Mr Franklin, by the way? If not, I dare say you will bump into him somewhere in Paris, as you go about. He seems to be everywhere! Though as you can imagine we cannot have him here because of this silly war. That would be just too much for David!"

She studied his clothes again with a frown and a grimace. "But now you have raised the matter, I think that my sister and I can take you to one or two of the better tailors in this fair city and have you outfitted as befits a man of property. We shall have a wonderful time turning you into a young man of fashion, will we not Mary?"

Mary smiled at Charles sympathetically as her sister raced on. "What a delight! Mary, you will come with us tomorrow, if you are feeling well enough? No need to ask you, Thomas. I know your views on buying clothes."

Thomas Graham rolled his eyes in relief. "Have a quiet word with Fullerton," he advised Charles sotto voce while Louisa and Mary enthused about the latest cut of coat and style of gentlemen's cravats. "He knows what's what. A splendid fellow in every way. He will prevent you from ending up like a popinjay or some macaroni. Above all, do not fall into the hands of the ladies in this matter. That is my advice!"

SIX

"My dear Lord Cathcart," Charles hesitated, pen in hand, frowning at the paper. This letter was proving to be one of the most difficult he had ever composed, although in truth he had little experience of writing other than the occasional rough note to an up-state storekeeper. Certainly he had never needed to commit his personal thoughts to paper in this way.

The two young men, so very different in most respects, had yet come to understand each other during the period they had spent together in New York. They had also come to like each other surprisingly well. Surprising that is to the young American who had been prepared from the beginning to dislike Cathcart for purely political reasons. But apparently not surprising to the amiable young Scottish aristocrat, who was seemingly oblivious to his new acquaintance's barely concealed hostility towards the British occupation. Soon they had moved easily to first name terms. But now for some reason Charles found it difficult to formalise that relationship by using the other's first name in writing. He struck out his words and wrote firmly "My dear William," feeling instinctively that in the past few weeks, even days, he had crossed an invisible boundary that was changing his life.

Charles had adapted to life in the Stormont's home to a degree that surprised him, so easily and generously had the family, essentially strangers to him when all was said, welcomed him into their lives. He had been immediately absorbed into their energetic social programme and at once treated as if he had ever been a part of the household. Soon he sensed that he was regarded as a kind of surrogate for the absent brother.

Moreover this household was one of such general kindness as

Charles had never before experienced. Here in Paris, among strangers, he had discovered a warmth which made his life in the home of Sir William Johnson seem cold and almost barbaric by comparison. That early life he could now see dispassionately had, with all its interest and activity, been essentially a lonely one.

On his second morning in Paris he had been summoned by Fullerton to Lord Stormont's study and had followed the secretary not without trepidation through the echoing corridors. Aware perhaps of Charles apprehension Fullerton had maintained a steady flow of apparently casual conversation as they walked. How had his journey gone? Was the company on the voyage interesting? And on the long haul from Nantes to Paris, had he encountered anyone of note?"

Charles, half distracted with his mind racing ahead towards his meeting with the Ambassador thought little of the questions, which seemed natural enough. "Yes," he replied vaguely. "A rather long-winded physician and natural philosopher called Bancroft. Very learned on the subject of the medical applications of the new electricity. A little obsessive perhaps. But helpful to me when I was at my worst with sea-sickness."

Fullerton glanced at him as they approached the Ambassador's private study. "Edward Bancroft?" he asked curiously.

"Yes, the same," replied Charles. "Do you know him? I dare say he's quite famous in his own line."

Fullerton stood aside to allow Charles to proceed him into the study. "Edward Bancroft." he repeated casually. "Yes, I think I have heard something about him. Is he not attached to the American delegation here?" He smiled. "If so, I expect you will meet him again. Fashionable Paris is quite a small place, for all the sprawl of the place and people still meet socially, on neutral ground as it were." He opened the door into the study. "Neutral ground, at least for the moment," he added dryly.

Charles found the Ambassador to be more corpulent than he had imagined and disgracefully elderly to be married to the animated young Louisa. Still, even to his critical eye Stormont appeared a man of distinction, handsome even in a mature way and he proved to have an easy charm that soon won Charles over. The seventeen year old Louisa was Stormont's second wife, the Ambassador having lived alone for a number of years as a widower. But it seemed that this potentially awkward relationship of May and December was a happy, if at times turbulent, union.

Stormont welcomed him warmly. But he had one piece of news that shocked Charles. "I am sorry to inform you that your guardian, Sir William Johnson, has died suddenly in New York." Seeing his look of consternation Lord Stormont hastened to reassured him. "You need have no fear as to your own future however. You have lost a wise advisor, of course. But I understand that your funds are safely deposited in one of London's great private banks, Thomas Coutts & Co in the Strand. You will be able to draw on them either directly or by letters of credit, just as you require." Stormont smiled at him sympathetically.

"You may nonetheless wish to proceed to London at some point to formalise the position. If you need help of any kind please rely on my services--- Fullerton is at your disposal in this regard." He waved generally in the direction of the door of his study, behind which Charles presumed the secretary unobtrusively lurked. "Meanwhile, until you decide on your future plans I hope you will consider this your home. You are very welcome here."

The offer was of such sincerity that Charles could not help but respond favourably to him. It was flattering that this great man of state was taking such concern over his welfare. "I thank you, my lord. My own life seems in such a flux at present that I am deeply grateful for your support. And for the time to muster my thoughts." Lord Stormont smiled at him again and rose silently to his feet. It was clear that the interview was at an end.

As Charles approached the door it opened as if by magic and Fullerton materialised. Turning back to Stormont Charles blurted out, "Tell me sir, what news do you have of the war in America?"

"Nothing but success for our troops!" the Ambassador said cheerfully. "The mood in government is one of confidence. The war is all but won, it seems. Two principal fortresses on the river Hudson have now fallen----,"

"Washington and Lee? Surely not! There must be some mistake!" Charles could not restrain himself. "Their defences were impregnable. They cannot have been taken!"

His shock was obvious and Stormont shot a shrewd glance at him. "I can see," he said dryly, "that your sympathies may not be entirely with our soldiers!" Charles swallowed hard, judging it better to stay silent. "Well, that is not so unusual these days," Stormont went on with a laugh. "Half of London seems to share your sentiments. Eh Fullerton? Mr Fox certainly makes no secret of it and with less justification than our young friend here. Far less indeed." Fullerton lowered his eyes and silently showed Charles out of the Ambassador's study.

Since he had arrived in Paris Charles had given little thought to his own situation, swept along as he had been by changing events, new experiences and new people. Suddenly the realisation that he was genuinely a free agent struck home. Now he was at liberty to do much as he pleased and to go where he chose, with even the loose rein of Sir William's control removed. Another thought came to him, guiltily as something of an afterthought. What would be the effect of Sir William's death on his friend Francis? For in spite of political differences, Francis and his father had been close, his mother being very much a favourite of Sir William.

There had of course been no possibility of Francis inheriting the baronetcy, there being an older half brother by Sir William's first European wife who would automatically become the next baronet. But Charles hoped that his friend would not be left too isolated by this turn of events, for he was aware that the new baronet was a staunch British Loyalist. Indeed he was actively involved in prosecuting the war against the patriots and commanded the hated Queen's Own American Regiment or Johnson's Greens as they were known.

If what Lord Stormont told him was even half true, it sounded as if that war was not going well from the American point of view. So it would not be impossible, Charles thought sadly, for the two brothers to find themselves in direct opposition in the fighting, if Francis followed his instincts. Thomas Graham's words about 'brother against brother' rang in his ears. Life for Francis would not be easy now, for his strongly held views would set him against even his Mohawk uncle Joseph Brandt.

But in Paris the spring days passed pleasurably enough and Charles found himself completely taken up with the social life of the embassy. Indeed, given the entrée that came as a result of being part of Stormont's household, he might have spent all his time at soirées and every evening at balls, plays, concerts and the like, visiting the grand houses that lay on both sides of the great river.

Like the rest of polite society he would travel on such occasions by coach or on horseback, the filth of the Paris streets making it impossible to arrive in good order by any other means. Frequently he would cover the relatively short distances involved in the company of Mary and Thomas Graham. But soon he realised that in spite of a willingness to join in these entertainments, Mary and for that matter Thomas, did not have the same taste for society as the younger and more energetic Louisa. In particular, Mary tired quickly, her slight frame able to cope with only a limited amount of socialising. The effort of keeping up with Louisa seemed to wear her out and though she would make a gallant attempt to enjoy these evenings, Charles noticed that the couple frequently left long before the entertainment drew to a formal end.

Paris was not all high society however and from time to time Charles would find an excuse to escape from the civilised atmosphere of Lord Stormont's home. Then he would abandon his newly fashionable breeches and coats and plunge on foot into the seething mass of humanity that cluttered the streets of Paris, roaming the fetid narrow lanes with raw sewage flowing in open drains or with equal facility strolling along great tree-lined boulevards where the fashionable inhabitants went to observe and to be seen.

Gradually he came to understand this city. Dressed in his old homespun, his familiar dirk tucked discreetly into his belt, insulated from fear by youthful confidence, he would wander into the darkest corners, quite immune from the surrounding vice and sense of menace that hung like a miasma over the back streets. His strangely accented French, he noticed, passed almost unnoticed in a population made up of provincials drawn into Paris from every corner of the land.

Every habitable space in every courtyard in every alley, however squalid, seemed to have been divided and divided again into wretched accommodations or for small scale commercial use, rising two or three storeys above the infected streets with even the parapets of the bridges over the river pressed into service. Listening to the cries of the street vendors and the entreaties of the miserable prostitutes Charles came to realise that there was nothing, however bizarre or degrading, that could not be found in Paris.

Yet the city captivated him. Captivated but also greatly irritated him. Paris was undoubtedly an extraordinary place, with the most magnificent public spaces and monuments. But somehow it was as if these wonders had been scattered at random throughout the city, frequently swamped by adjacent collections of hovels and dank medieval streets.

The Place des Victoires with its splendid statue of King Louis was a delightful arena in which the indolent rich could stroll, meet and drink. The stunning vista of the Place Louis-Grand, though admittedly a sea of mud for most of the winter, nevertheless swept down magnificently to the river and discovered the commanding veterans' hospital on the left bank. Then there was the gracious Place Royale, an elegant strictly geometric arrangement of noble houses dating, Charles was astonished to learn, from a time when New York had been a collection of huts on an untamed island. The gardens of the Tuileries, the stylish Place Dauphine on the Ile de la Cité, with the river gliding smoothly past on each side and the astonishingly fragile beauty of the St Chapelle were all simply beyond comparisons.

Yet all this beauty was set amid a hideous morass of narrow dirty and dangerous alleys through which there was almost no way for a respectable man to pass and no way at all for a woman to move safely across the city. "Tell me," he burst out in frustration to Thomas Graham one evening as they sat sipping a glass of port after supper. "Why do they not simply drive some decent roads through that mess of slums? Let some light and air into the place! Open up a view of those wonderful public spaces?" Charles had found himself relenting in his antipathy to Thomas Graham, reluctantly coming to admit to himself that it was simple jealousy, if indeed there was such a thing as simple jealousy, which was the root of his initial feelings.

Thomas smiled at him. "You are not the first to have that thought, Charles," he said mildly. "A lot of clever devils have thought much the same. Men like Rousseau, Montesquieu, even Voltaire, have all had their say and all pretty much along the lines you suggest. Some would have gone further and fairly demolished the place." He laughed and shook his head. "But you see, old man, that would cost money. A lot of it! And if there is one thing the French are simply not keen on, it is paying more taxes! Certainly not to beautify Paris. For the truth is your provincial Frenchman does not love Paris. Not at all!"

He savoured his wine. "And the government here is such a tangle of bureaucracy and interest groups that nothing much is ever achieved speedily. Though I must say the present King is a decent enough fellow and means well." He shook his head sadly. "But Paris seems doomed to fall between several stools. There's the Parlement as they call it on one side of the river, trying its strength against the King who has only just allowed them to meet again after they have been suspended for several years. Then there is the city administration on the right bank, to say nothing of the royal Court at Versailles and all those ministers with their plotting and scheming and jealousies."

"All of them are trapped in an elaborate ritual dance," Thomas went on, "and don't overlook the fact that the King really does not care for Paris either. No more did his grandfather, the old King Louis. Dirty and hazardous! That is their view of Paris and who can argue with it? The French kings have had to deal with a succession of popular risings that always seem to begin in Paris. So who can blame them for distrusting the place?"

"But surely," Charles intervened, "that's just the point! It is dirty and dangerous and it needs change!"

Thomas shrugged. "But in the end it comes down to money, Charles. Money is what it is all about, at bottom. And money is just not there. Remember that the French have to pay their bankers rather more in interest than the British are required to pay." He laughed. "On account of the tendency the Bourbons have of defaulting on loans! Bankers don't really approve of that!" He shook his head again. "No. If there are any more taxes raised they will not be spent on cleaning up Paris. They will be for another war. Most probably against us, I wager."

He shot a glance at Charles. "Speaking of bankers, will you not go soon to London to meet your chap? Coutts, isn't it?" He smiled approvingly. "Well, you couldn't do better. Well respected and most extremely well connected. Sound fellow too--- very sound. Scottish, of course. Been a Scottish banking house there since 1692. You'll like Coutts."

Charles made a mental note that he must do as Thomas suggested. But lingering over Lord Stormont's port, he tried to tease out from Thomas a little more about the Cathcart family and even a little more about Graham himself, though that was like drawing teeth. Still torn by occasional and quite unreasonable pangs of jealous Charles gradually found his prejudices wane when faced with the man's obvious common sense and modesty.

Under questioning Thomas reluctantly admitted that the Grahams could indeed trace their descent from Robert the Bruce in Norman times, though he made little of the ancient lineage. "Oh, most of our old Scottish families can trace their origins back to the Normans, you know," he said airily. "If only they care to. That's nothing to the antiquity of the Highland clans of course," he added quickly. "Time immemorial there! Quite a different thing," he said with a shake of his head. "By the bye," he went on, eager to change the subject, "when I was a boy I had an excellent tutor by the name of MacPherson. James MacPherson was his name. He was a nephew of the famous MacPherson of Clunie who guarded Charles Edward Stewart after Culloden. A kinsman of yours perhaps?"

Charles frowned. "I think I have heard my father claim some connection with the great Clunie."

"No matter. You have heard of him in any event. Desperately clever fellow, James MacPherson. Though he failed completely to turn me into a scholar!" Thomas laughed merrily. "Apparently he discovered some ancient poems written in Gaelic by a fellow called Ossian. All Greek to me! He translated them into English and caused a bit of a fuss in literary circles. I believe the great Dr Johnson declared them all to be frauds, as I recall."

Charles remembered Dr Johnson from his long hours spent pouring through Sir William's books. "Might that be the same Dr Johnson who suggested that Americans were a race of convicts?" he asked with a smile.

"Indeed!" Thomas gave a roar of laughter. "The very same. And opined that they should be thankful for anything we allow them, short of hanging! So you can judge how much weight to put on that man's views!" A smile crossed his lean features. "I still recall the great pleasure of riding over the hills beyond Perthshire with James MacPherson when he was collecting material for the poems. Sleeping rough, shooting our dinner and cooking it over an open fire, talking to the old folk in the villages who remembered the stories." He sighed. "Happy times indeed."

Slowly Charles had come to admire Graham's straightforward approach to life, his royal associations not withstanding. Almost in spite of himself he found he was coming to like this man.

Though Thomas would have died under torture rather than say so, Charles discovered that he was equally well connected on his mother's side, from whom he would one day inherit great wealth. Lady Christian Graham still lived on the family estates at Balgowan in Perthshire and by all accounts ran that household with a tight grasp on every penny and with a grim puritanical zeal. This seemed especially incongruous, given that she was a daughter of the Earl of the Hopetoun, a family of enormous wealth and patronage, and that in addition she had a claim to the even wealthier estates of the Countess of Annandale.

Then of course there was Mary. She too came from a distinguished family, the Cathcarts, who had for six hundred years served their kings politically and militarily. Of course, they had benefited substantially from this tradition; a tradition that was now being continued by William and his younger brother in America, Charles reflected. He was uncomfortably aware that his feelings were inevitably still very mixed in respect of his new friends. He was also aware that though William Cathcart had been typically unassuming in New York, his young friend was actually the 10th Lord Cathcart, having succeeded to the title on the death of his father earlier that year.

The old Lord had been known affectionately within the family as 'Patch' on account of the black dressing he wore to cover the scar of a war wound on his face. He had served as aide-de-camp to the Duke of Cumberland and then had spent three years as British Ambassador to the Russian court at St Petersburg, an illustrious appointment by any standards. There Mary and the other Cathcart children along with their mother Jean had lived amid elaborate pomp and circumstance: yet for all that splendour they seemed to have emerged quite unspoiled and Charles found it touching to see how much simple pleasure they took in each others company.

For in spite of their grand associations, he reflected with an ignoble pang, they obviously enjoyed a happy family life--- one that contrasted starkly with his own strange childhood. Perhaps, it occurred to him, it was a life that contrasted equally starkly with Thomas Graham's austere upbringing at Balgowan.

But happy though the Cathcarts were, there was still no defence against tragedy. First their mother Jean and then the much-loved 'Patch' had died, both from the dreaded consumption that seemed to haunt the family. In a flash of insight Charles suddenly understood the unspoken fear that haunted Thomas Graham: that behind his facade of sturdy geniality Thomas was constantly prey to the gnawing dread that Mary's delicate nature would give way and that one day he would lose her to the same scourge. Of course, it dawned on Charles! That is why they travel so constantly, ever seeking a gentler climate or the latest medical treatment for the beloved Mary.

'Yes, the beloved Mary,' Charles thought painfully. For many a sleepless hour he had spent contemplating his true feelings for Mary. At first he had regularly awakened in a muck sweat from some amazingly realistic erotic dream. Now, gradually, he was coming to believe that there was no lust in his feelings for her. Of that he was certain. Well, almost certain. For who could honestly say what might happen between a man and a beautiful woman in the right circumstances?

Not that there was anything of Charlotte Pemberton in his feelings for Mary Graham, he thought quickly. No, that feeling had been very different. Indeed it was difficult to think of an emotion more different, he insisted to himself. That had been in the heat of youth, with curiosity and excitement, pride and ego and self-satisfaction at the conquest of an experienced woman by a young boy. But his feelings for Mary were of a different nature. Or so Charles persuaded himself. There was love certainly, though he was honest enough to admit that love was a word that rather begged the question.

What then were his feelings for Mary? Affection, admiration, and concern? Yes, all of that. Desire? A desire to cherish? Yes, undoubtedly. Perhaps, he thought rather wistfully, especially that. But was there also a physical desire, hidden from even his own gaze? Well, that was of no matter, he decided firmly. For it would never be put to the test, Charles had concluded, reluctant though he had been at first to accept the thought.

For now he knew beyond doubt that Thomas and Mary were a love-match that could not be shaken. According to Louisa it had always been so, since that day many years before when the young Thomas had ridden up to the Cathcart home at Schaw Park on estate business and seen Mary, seventeen years old and no longer the child he remembered but a beautiful woman. The couple still showed every sign of mutual devotion, as Charles could see plainly. So it was with no expectation of reward other than friendship that Charles silently dedicated himself to protecting the beautiful Mrs Graham and assisting Thomas in his life's task, quietly and undeclared.

But Charles was a young man and it had been many weeks since, somewhat shamefaced, he had availed himself of the services of New York prostitutes. Now his thoughts turned more and more to the sordid streets of Paris. Where, he wondered with a silent laugh, were Sir William's famously loose women?

The answer came from an unexpected source. Caught up as he had been in the hectic life of the Stormont house and in his own secret explorations of the Paris streets, Charles had almost forgotten Edward Bancroft. It was a surprise therefore when a few weeks after his first meeting with Lord Stormont he received a letter from Bancroft, written as if to an old friend.

Bancroft began by confirming that he was greatly enjoying his duties with the American mission which had now moved from Rue de L'Université to more luxurious accommodation at Passy, just outside the city walls. Would Charles care to ride out there to meet Dr Franklin, to whom Bancroft had spoken of Charles's great interest in the electrical sciences? First however, perhaps Charles would care to join him for dinner and an entertainment at the home of a good friend of his in Paris? The friend was a theatrical gentleman who lived on the Rue du Temple, where Charles would be assured of meeting some interesting people. It might also, Bancroft went on, be an opportunity to continue their discussions from the packet ship.

This last statement caused Charles to stir uneasily. Even on board the 'Mercury' he had instinctively felt Bancroft's proposition to be distasteful. Now that he was on terms of growing confidence with Thomas and Mary Graham and so far as he could judge was liked and respected by them in turn, it was impossible to imagine spying on his trusting hosts.

For spying it would be, however genteelly it might be put by Bancroft. At heart Charles knew that he had not changed his views on the political future of his country. Indeed he had never sought to hide his opinion on that matter from Thomas or even from Lord Stormont himself.

But what Edward Bancroft was suggesting was a very different matter.

SEVEN

Nevertheless on the evening in question Charles did ride over to the Rue du Temple in time for dinner, set in the French fashion for about seven in the evening. From his rambles around Paris he knew that the Temple was in the north-east of the city, an area that had seen better times, though a few fashionable private houses were still dotted about. But for the most part the district had been taken over by artisans moving in as the elite retreated west towards the grand boulevards.

Nearby, particularly around the bleak old prison, was even more louche. There he knew lay some of the most dangerous neighbourhoods in the entire city. There poverty and despair could drive the over-crowded streets to violence at any moment and after dark you were as likely to have your throat cut or your pocket picked with equal ease. Charles therefore, fashionably dressed though he was, carried a primed and loaded pistol in his saddle-bag as he clattered in through an imposing gateway and handed his horse over to the waiting groom.

He was shown into a large reception hall lined with the usual array of straight backed chairs and long rows of spluttering candles that reflected intermittently in the succession of tall mirrors. As he strolled past he could not resist a glance in one of the mirrors and saw to his surprise a tall dark-haired young man, now quite fashionable thanks to the efforts of Louisa and Mary and an altogether presentable figure--- very different indeed from the home-spun individual who had so recently left New York.

Footmen stood about with trays of champagne and Charles took a glass from one of them. In form this reception was very similar to those he had attended with Thomas and Mary and he moved through the crowds with confidence, looking about for a familiar face. But there was something different here. He frowned, trying to identify the source of his concern. For one thing the standard of cleanliness of the footmen's linen was not quite the thing, he decide. But there must be more to it than that.

Through a thick of people he saw Edward Bancroft. But once again he knew there was something different about the man. Previously a rather austere man of science, except when animated by the electric fish of Guiana, here he was flushed and over-heated. On his arm hung a plump lady of uncertain age, vivacious in manner, with a mass of red hennaed hair and to Charles's critical eye a large maternal bosom. Bancroft greeted him in English like a long lost friend. "My dear young man! I am so glad you are able to be here. Allow me to present you to my companion, Madame Briote." Charles bowed to the lady and murmured in French how enchanted he was to make her acquaintance, while she fluttered and cooed in response.

Turning back to Bancroft he asked politely about Passy. "Oh it is splendid. Quite splendid!" cried Bancroft, snatching another two glasses of champagne from a passing footman and thrusting one into the simpering grasp of Madame Briote. It was clear to Charles that the pair had already dealt with several such glasses. "So much more suitable. Quite grand! Do you know Passy? Very pleasant. Just outside the old walls of Paris and delightful now that spring is bringing everything to life again. A commodious house belonging to M. Leray de Chaumont, who is a zealous friend to the American cause," Bancroft leaned forward confidentially, "and very well connected in Paris! You will ride out tomorrow and visit us, will you not? Mr Franklin has expressed an interest in speaking with you. He is quite intrigued by your electrical interests. But come, let us find some food. I declare that I am quite destroyed with hunger."

He led the way into a grand salon, smoke-filled and crowded, in which a throng of well-dressed men and stylish very attractive young women were drinking and eating at a series of small tables scattered about the room. Beneath another row of spluttering candelabras a long buffet table was laid out with great platters of meat, fish and fruits. Charles caught at Bancroft's arm as he darted towards the food. "But tell me sir, who is our host this evening? For I have not yet paid my respects to him as I should."

Bancroft and Madame Briote descended on the buffet and waved away his question. "Oh do not stand on ceremony, Charles! Our host is not yet here. But you will meet him, do not fear! I imagine he is held at the theatre on business."

Charles followed them to a table with a plate of food, frowning. What kind of business would keep a man at the theatre of all places? A bank he could understand. Or a law court, yes, he could understand that also. But detained at a theatre? Gazing around he observed a very high percentage of attractive young women, indeed very attractive he noted approvingly. All were dressed a touch more boldly than he had seen before and were more animated, more casual in their behaviour towards the men in their company. Attractive, but not exactly of the style which he had been accustomed to seeing in Paris.

Bancroft's behaviour was not what Charles had expected either--- indeed far from it. The man was covering his food with vast quantities of cayenne pepper, leaning closer to Madame Briote to explain confidentially but in a voice loud enough to be heard by Charles above the general din of the room, the medical benefits of pepper in regard to male performance. "Particularly," he said with a leer towards the shrieking Madame Briote, "when washed down with copious, I say copious, draughts of burgundy!" So saying he emptied his glass and refilled it unsteadily from a large flask that stood on the table.

Charles watched him in silent astonishment. Was this the man of science he had met in New York? Was this his link to Dr Franklin? Of more concern, could this really be a reliable agent for the American cause? Shaking his head he excused himself and drifted out of the salon and into the first of a series of side rooms. There groups of guests, early diners or those with little appetite for food, crowded around small tables earnestly playing cards.

This, decided Charles, was more interesting. For though he had studied the theories of chance and the rules of card games in the solitude of Sir William's mansion he had never actually wagered real money. Indeed, gaming was an aspect of life in Paris he had not yet encountered. He strolled quietly about observing the choices that were available. Several tables had games of whist in progress involving stakes that Charles could not at first evaluate, though judging by the solemn demeanour of the players he decided the ivory discs that changed hands must be of serious value.

He watched in silence for long enough to note that the players were certainly serious and for the most part playing with sound scientific judgment. Here and there a number of silent pairs played piquet with equal care and every sign of rational good sense and here too the ivory tokens were changing hands regularly. But Charles soon calculated that this was happening in an even handed way, ebbing and flowing from player to player, much as he would have expected given the normal probabilities of chance and a reasonably even degree of skill.

Slightly bored, he pushed his way through a further set of double doors that led him into a smaller room at the rear of the building. Here immediately he was in a different world. In one corner was a large round table at which an animated group of guests were throwing dice. Charles quickly realise that they were playing a form of hazard, a game at which he knew large sums could be won, given a quick reaction to the fall of the dice and the ability to calculate the odds almost instantaneously. He observed the process for a time, silently noting the importance of the supervisor of the table, the so-called 'groom-master'. Interesting, he reflected to himself. 'That is a game I may try on another night, when I have money to risk.'

Then with a sudden flash of excitement he recognised at the rear of the room the layout of a pharaoh table and behind it the unmistakable appearance of a professional dealer, rapidly spinning cards out before an excited crowd of mostly half-drunken players. 'Pharaoh is illegal in France,' Charles recalled with interest. 'In spite of being invented here, like most of the pleasant vices.' He moved closer to the table, eager to observe the pattern of play.

The deals were being played out rapidly, two or three a minute he calculated, and such was the level of alcohol being consumed that it was soon apparent that most of the players were virtually throwing their money away. Some were wildly betting on cards that had no chance whatever of appearing, all four of that denomination having been dealt out previously, as shown by the table with which the dealer or his assistant should indicate the cards already out. But the dealer, Charles noted, always seemed a shade slow in keeping the record straight.

Charles frowned and studied the game more closely. Oddly, the way the cards were shuffled seemed to be producing unusual sequences of play and patterns that always seemed to fall to the advantage of the dealer. But caught up in the rapid pace of play the excited players rattled their tokens out on the table, seemingly careless to their losses.

Just opposite Charles stood a young blonde woman, somewhat too Junoesque for his new refined tastes but curiously reminiscent of Charlotte Pemberton. She was though more vivacious and altogether more attractive, he decided. Her round face was flushed with excitement and wine and she was clearly carried away by the thrill of the game; wagering wildly, as fast as the dealer could turn out the cards. She was also losing at every deal and Charles saw that she was frequently one of those betting on cards that were already dead.

Moving round the table he stood beside her and watched in silence until the deck had been almost fully dealt out and the winning options had become very limited indeed. She was reaching out to toss her wager on yet another dead card when Charles leaned quietly towards her. "That denomination has of course entirely gone," he said in her ear. She stared at him in confusion, her wide blue eyes revealing first surprise, then comprehension and finally a sudden flicker of interest. "All four have been dealt out," he said with a smile. "So that it is a pointless wager unless it is your wish to donate your money to this gentleman," he added, indicating the dealer who was by now staring at him with ill-concealed irritation.

By this time the play had finished and seeing that her choice was indeed a loss the young woman suddenly understood the point of the advice. "Why, thank you kind sir!" she said in a charming voice. "How very clever of you! I am most grateful. How can I thank you?" she added ingenuously, her smile a signal he could not mistake. But before Charles could shape a suitable reply, an older man, well-dressed and affluent in appearance, stepped between them. Not quite old enough to be her father, Charles thought to himself. But it was a close run thing.

"Come, my little one," the older man said and taking her arm he led her away. "Let us take some supper." As they left he turned back towards Charles. "And you, my dear sir," he added suavely. "If you set yourself up to be an advisor in such matters, I suggest you limit yourself to those who seek your advice." He bowed stiffly and then half pushing and half pulling he steered the blonde girl away. As she went she glanced back with a helpless shrug of her shoulders before vanishing into the crowd.

'Now I know why this game is illegal,' Charles thought dryly as he made his way back to the main salon. 'But there is certainly money to be made if one only stays sober.' As he re-entered the room Bancroft appeared and seized him by the arm. "Ah, there you are my boy. Come and meet our host."

He ushered Charles across the room to where a tall distinguished man stood surrounded by an audience of admirers. Wearing a well-powdered short wig, he was dressed in what, thanks to Louisa and Mary, Charles knew to be the height of fashion; a splendid coat of scarlet trimmed with silver lace, a pale buff waistcoat and dark breeches with about his neck an elaborate jabot. The badge of some impressive order was pinned to the coat and on his arm was a striking young woman in a green silk dress, a woman so striking that Charles could not resist staring at her.

Almost as tall as the man, her flaming red hair was coiled loosely about her head and tumbled unrestrained onto her half-naked shoulders. It was apparent even to Charles that unlike Madame Briote the hair owed everything to nature, its rich sheen glinting under the candle light. As her direct stare matched his Charles became disturbingly aware of her extraordinary green eyes. Quickly he switched his gaze back to her companion.

Bancroft was introducing Charles in his atrocious French. "Monsieur de Beaumarchais, may I present Mr Charles George MacPherson, a young friend from America." Then turning to Charles,

"Charles, this is Monsieur Pierre Augustin Caron de Beaumarchais, the world-famous diplomat, author and playwright, great man of ideas and a friend and benefactor to our American cause."

Beaumarchais was a good-looking man, upright and athletically built although probably already in his early forties, Charles decided. He bowed gracefully and welcomed Charles to his home with a genuine smile on his open friendly face, obviously relishing Bancroft's words. "I am always delighted to meet a citizen of your great country," Beaumarchais said to Charles in French, placing one hand on his heart beside the order he wore.

Charles studied the shining badge as best he could under the fluttering candle light but could make nothing of it. "Your country, I say!" Beaumarchais went on dramatically. "For whose struggle against English tyranny I have long had the utmost sympathy. And if I may say so," he added as an aside, with a modest smile, "to which I have made my own small contribution from time to time, eh, Bancroft?"

Edward Bancroft, who appeared to have followed only part of his speech, muttered something incoherent and grinned uneasily at everyone in the little group. Then turning back to Bancroft with a conspiratorial smile Beaumarchais added, "I assume of course that Mr MacPherson is of our persuasion in this matter?"

Charles assessed him rapidly. A man of grace and charm with an easy confident manner. Which will take you a long way as Charles had already discovered. But in ballast perhaps rather lacking and a touch too theatrical in manner for his own taste. As Bancroft tried to splutter out some kind of reply Charles intervened simply. "I am a patriot, sir." he stated. He looked Beaumarchais directly in the eyes. "I have no doubt that the destiny of my country is independence."

Beaumarchais beamed at him. "Bravo!" he cried. "Well spoken. I make no secret of my sentiments on this, as on other matters. Though it has been at some cost to myself," he added slightly ruefully. "Still, we will speak of this again, in more suitable circumstances. There are projects in which I can use the assistance of a young man such as yourself. Perhaps we might co-operate, if you will." Then recollecting himself, he smiled amiably at Charles. "But I presume too much. Go too quickly, perhaps. It is a fault of mine, I think. Though there is so much to be done."

He shot a curious glance at Charles. "But you speak our language well--- not a characteristic that I find too common in the people of your admirable land. Do you also speak Spanish? For if you do have that tongue--- ." He stopped himself in mid sentence. "No! I do presume too much! Suffice to say that as an American patriot you will not lack for friends here in France."

As Beaumarchais turned to the tall young red-haired woman beside him, Bancroft excused himself and set off in search of Madame Briote. "My comment on the language ability of your compatriots," Beaumarchais went on, "does not apply to my beautiful companion, who speaks our language as well as you do yourself." The woman gave a faint smile, her eyes fixed appraisingly on Charles. Then Beaumarchais bowed very low. "Allow me, sir, to introduce you to Mrs Juliana Ritchie of the city of Philadelphia."

Juliana Ritchie inclined her head towards Charles. "I am indeed from Philadelphia," she said. "Though I have lived for too many years in Europe now. So I am very pleased to meet a fellow American," she said. "Exactly from where do you hail, sir?"

Charles explained his early years in the Mohawk Valley. "Ah, a backwoodsman!" she declared. "And a patriot too! Perfection indeed! So many from that area are what they like to call Loyalists, are they not?" Before he had time to bridle at her remark, she went on easily. "And a friend of Mr Edward Bancroft?" Her green eyes never left his face.

"I would scarcely say a friend. We travelled together from New York where he happened to tend my father in his last illness. But I hope to be presented by him to Mr Franklin, whom I have long admired."

She gave a non-committal nod. "There might be other ways to achieve the same end," she said with a quiet smile. "Mr Franklin is quite ubiquitous here in Paris. It is indeed hard to avoid him at times. Tell me, where do you lodge in Paris, may I enquire?"

"I am staying for the present in the home of Lord Stormont."

Her eyes darkened a shade or two. "You are lodged with the British Ambassador?" She frowned. "A patriot in the lion's den, indeed! What kind of American patriot are you, sir?"

Charles could control himself no longer. "I am my own kind of patriot," he said coldly in English now, not wanting to embarrass his host. "At some pains to myself--- and needing no lessons in patriotism from any long-term expatriate." Instantly he regretted his words. Her retort had been fair, if overly direct to be acceptable in polite society. Yet she had unerringly touched on the very issue which was increasingly troubling him.

Mrs Ritchie's response was simply a delighted laugh. "Well said, fellow patriot! I see you can strike back!" she remarked, also in English and only half mocking in tone. "Tell me, do you by any chance know my own city of Philadelphia, our capital?"

At this point Beaumarchais excused himself to attend to new guests and vanished into the mêlée, leaving the two of them alone together. Charles was awkwardly aware that he was finding this woman more disconcerting than anyone he had ever encountered. Studying her from behind his wine-glass he noticed that her complexion was unfashionably brown, very different from the pale flesh, white or whitened by powder and creams, that was displayed by almost every other lady he had seen in Paris.

Indeed, with her high cheek bones and strong handsome features she looked almost as much a native Indian as his friend Francis Johnson. Almost but not quite, he thought, glancing at her low cut dress which revealed her shoulders and hinted at breasts that were indisputably white by nature. Charles decided she must be accustomed to riding or walking in the open under the American sun, an unfashionable thing for any Philadelphian lady of fashion to do. So had she too been raised in the backwoods? In which case perhaps her remark was a tease and not the snub he had feared.

"I'm afraid I have never visited your city," he said stiffly. "Though I did once have a friend from Philadelphia." He hesitated. "A language tutor, as it were." He paused uncomfortably, conscious that Juliana Ritchie was hanging conspicuously on his words, a small smile playing on her lips. Charles realised that she had been well aware of his close examination and for some reason had found it amusing. In spite of himself he flushed. He was not used to being made jest off and he found himself beginning to resent this cool lady. But gamely he ploughed on. "At least she was originally from Philadelphia--- ," he began.

"Ah," she cried mockingly, the green eyes widening in apparent astonishment. "It was a she! A lady from Philadelphia! Now who could she have been? Tell me her name! I dare say I will know her."

Charles realised with dismay that he had no idea what Charlotte Pemberton's name had been before her marriage. In any case he had thought better of the whole gambit, which was leading him onto decidedly unsafe ground. "I'm afraid," he confessed, " I do not have the lady's name to hand." To his relief Juliana Ritchie did not burst into immediate peals of laughter.

She simply inclined her head gracefully. "Not very flattering for the poor lady," she murmured. "Still, shall we take a stroll about the place?" Taking his arm she guided him through the salon, nodding to little groups of people whom she recognised. Judging by the number of people she appeared to know, Charles reflected, Mrs Ritchie must have met half of Paris.

But what half, he wondered? Certainly not the half that was known by the Stormonts and the Grahams. As they walked she turned towards him and such was her height she looked him almost eye to eye. "I hope you will not forget my name so easily," she said to him reproachfully. "You do remember it?"

Charles felt himself set at a loss again by this strange young woman. "Tell me about Monsieur Beaumarchais," he asked hastily.

She fixed him with her gaze; and turned a curious look on him. "Pierre Augustin Caron de Beaumarchais?" she said half mockingly. "Have you not gone to the theatre in Paris at all?" Charles shook his head. He did not care to admit that he had never set foot in a theatre in his life.

"Why Mr MacPherson! Beaumarchais is the talk of the town at the moment. He has just staged his new play at the Comédie-Française and in spite of 'Le Berbier de Seville' being rather severe on the French ruling classes it is a great success."

She paused and smiled charmingly. "Or perhaps it is just because they do not understand it. The plot is clearly a tilt at the situation here and not everyone in government is pleased by it. Still, the aristocrats seem to be willing to laugh at themselves." Then she added, more seriously. "At least for the moment it pleases them to pretend that it is an irrelevant comedy, the play being set in Spain. That is a country Beaumarchais knows very well," she added, giving Charles a curious look.

Ah, the theatre, Charles thought. Of course, at last he realised why there were so many vivacious young women at the party. "So," he said carefully, vaguely sensing he was moving onto dangerous ground again, "many of the younger ladies here tonight are his colleagues in the theatre?"

"Delicately phrased," Juliana said solemnly. "Delicately put indeed! Beaumarchais could not have chosen his words better!"

At that moment the crowd thinned around one dinner table and Charles caught sight of the young blonde women he had tried to help at the pharaoh table. "The one over there," he asked. "That young lady, the pretty blonde one, is she an actress?"

Juliana Ritchie followed his gaze just in time to catch the young woman with the poor gambling technique smiling across the room towards Charles. "Indeed she is," she said shortly. Her eyes had once again curiously darkened. At least three shades darker than before, Charles realised in wonder.

"That is exactly what she is. Since you seem so interested, Mr MacPherson," she added coldly, "I can tell you that she is a salaried member of the Théâtre Française. That gentleman with her, and you should note this well for it might save you some difficulty, is M. de Lapouyade. He is a sociétaire, very well-connected and a wealthy shareholder in the enterprise. He takes a special interest in that young lady's---, prospects." Not even Charles could miss the heavy emphasis.

Juliana Ritchie let go his arm and pulled away from his side. "Now damn you to hell, Mr MacPherson!" she said politely. "If you have not sense enough to enquire about one lady from another in these circumstances." Charles stood frowning, stunned and almost open-mouthed. But before he could react she had stalked away across the room to where Beaumarchais stood with a group of guests. Charles watched her smile graciously at the playwright and take his arm, the two of them vanishing into the crowd.

"Hellfire and damnation!" Charles muttered under his voice. "How is a fellow ever to understand these women?" He wandered about the room for a time, observing the card players in a desultory way and noting that the pharaoh table was being run as sharply as ever, though the players still seemed oblivious to what was going on. Judging by the amount of alcohol being consumed, he thought sourly, many of them will be oblivious to everything quite soon.

Charles decided abruptly that he had seen enough of the demi-monde for one evening. And a thoroughly unsettling evening it had been he reflected, as he made his way towards the entrance hall where Beaumarchais was taking leave of some of the guests. Charles noted that of Juliana Ritchie there was no sign.

Beaumarchais very much regretted his early departure. Would he not care to speak further with him, on the matters to which he had referred earlier? If so he would expect Charles to call on him at the Théâtre near the Tuileries; some time soon he hoped? He was to be found there most mornings and would look forward to meeting him again. Perhaps he would enjoy watching a rehearsal?

Charles had only the haziest notion what Beaumarchais had in mind. But out of simple curiosity he did agree to meet him there. Then turning to leave, he saw the young blonde actress nearby with her wealthy protector in close attendance. "Tell me, M. de Beaumarchais," he said. "The very pretty young lady over there. I understand she is an actress. Do you happen to know her name?"

Beaumarchais glanced across and smiled knowingly. "Indeed I do! She is an understudy for the role of Rosina in my latest play; Charlotte Barrault by name--- a promising young actress. You might well encounter her at the Théâtre when you call on me. Another reason for you to come, eh! But you face severe competition there, I must warn you!"

'Another Charlotte,' Charles thought wryly making his way towards the entrance hall. He had just called for his mount to be brought round and was strolling up and down impatiently near the great doorway when out of the half darkness he was suddenly confronted by Juliana Richie.

She wore a dark green velvet cloak thrown over her shoulders and under the fluttering torches he was acutely aware that she looked very beautiful. "Well, Charles George MacPherson," she declared firmly, fixing him with her green eyes. "I am going home now and I want you to escort me. You are not so ungallant I suppose as to allow a lady to travel alone at this time of night? My carriage is outside."

With that she swept away leaving Charles confounded yet again. Meekly following, he found that the full moon had lit up the ornate courtyard as bright as day and that a groom was holding Charles's horse. Juliana stood beside a splendid coach, its door held open by another servant. Charles was about to swing up onto the bay when she held up her hand. "Tie the animal up behind. On such a dark night, I need your protection--- close at hand."

Several hours later Charles rolled away from Juliana's naked body. There was in fact no sudden transition from brown to white, that much he had discovered in the course of the night. Rather there was a gradual shading to a smooth olive tone that made her firm limbs seem like a beautiful sculpture carved from pale amber. She looked at him, her green eyes half-dimmed by fatigue.

"You may know nothing very much about women, Charles George MacPherson," she murmured. "But what you do know is by no means bad." She began to giggle and he kissed her yet again to quieten her.

At some point in the night, after the initial rush of passion was spent, they had exchanged life stories. Or at least as much as each thought wise to reveal so early in the relationship. Tentatively, Charles had ventured. "Mrs Juliana Ritchie? Is there a Mr Ritchie?"

"There was once," Juliana said simply. "But he died in Philadelphia of the fever in the summer as our marriage. Philadelphia is a poor place for the fever, what with the river and the mud flats." She smiled at Charles. "In truth I hardly knew him. However he left me financially well provided. A widow certainly, but a rich one. Rich enough to indulge her whims as to travel, for I had no parents to advise me to the contrary."

Charles frowned at her enquiringly and Juliana went on in a

matter-of-fact way. "They were both killed in an Indian raid during the French wars when I was still a child. Though brought up on the frontier I had been sent away to town for safety. And so I survived," she said. Charles wondered if he detected just a hint of regret in her voice.

"Ah, yes!" he said triumphantly. "I guessed you were from the backwoods!" Juliana smiled as she recognised the allusion. They fell silent for a time, lying in the pre-dawn darkness of her bedroom. Eventually Charles whispered, half dreading the answer. "What about, Beaumarchais?" he asked hesitantly. "I suppose---. I mean, I thought---,"

"You thought I was his mistress," Juliana said sharply. "I am no man's mistress, only my own. Don't ever forget that, Charles George MacPherson!" Then suddenly she relented and smiled at him. "What a ridiculous name! I shall call you Charlie from now on," she said firmly and reaching up she brushed back the dark hair from his damp forehead.

Then she frowned at him. "This will no doubt come as a surprise to you, Charlie. But there are some men who are so much in love with themselves that they would prefer the world to think they enjoy a woman's favours when they do not, rather than actually to enjoy her in secret." She laughed. "No, I can see you do not understand that! But take my word for it," she said with a dismissive shrug.

"Besides, Beaumarchais is a buffoon." She went on. "A well-meaning buffoon and quite a charming one, it is true. But a buffoon, none the less." She looked at him seriously. "I believe that he is genuinely helping the American cause. I must give him credit for that, though I do wonder at his true motives. You know of course that he is shipping arms to America? Half of Paris seems to know about that--- paid for by the French government of course. But shipped via a Spanish company."

As Charles blinked in astonishment she went rapidly on. "So his heart seems to be in the right place." She laughed again. "To say the truth, it's Beaumarchais' head I worry about! For he is no judge of character and his choice of associates is worrying to say the least. Take my advice Charlie and do not become involved in his schemes, especially while you are staying with your friend Lord Stormont. You do know that Stormont has spies and agents everywhere in Paris?" She stared at him, her eyes clear and shining. "Charlie, I believe you when you tell me you are a patriot," she said. "But living in the home of the British Ambassador--- ?"

"Well, it is a very long story," Charles said. "Perhaps when I know you better!"

With a shriek she threw herself at him and it was another hour before they began to talk again quietly. Then he told her about his life in the Mohawk Valley and his political differences with his father and his friendship with Francis Johnson. He told her exactly how his father had died and of William Cathcart's kindness. "The British are not all bad, you see," he said wisely. "I've met some whom I now count as friends. But I am still a true patriot, believe me." He added a little about Charlotte Pemberton. But not too much, remembering how she had reacted to the other Charlotte earlier in the night.

Juliana seemed to understand most of the story and guessed at the rest. "Your tutor? Or your mistress? In any case she taught you well," Juliana whispered. "Though you had a natural talent anyway, I suppose," she added grudgingly. She sat up in bed and stared at him fiercely. "Now will you help me, Charlie?" she asked. "Help another patriot? And incidentally help your country."

Charles hesitated only briefly. "Help you? Of course. Provided it is honourable--- ." He stopped and considered his words. "By which I mean provided it does not involve betraying another friendship, any other trust."

Juliana gazed at him doubtfully for a moment. Then, "Ah well, Charles George MacPherson," she said quietly. "The time is coming soon when you may have to chose sides. Perhaps even compromise your fine principals." Charles flushed at her words. "But what I have in mind I do not think will be a conflict for you," she added. "Unless you are a dear friend of Edward Bancroft, as well as your British hosts?"

"Bancroft? No, certainly not! He's no friend of mine. But he is working with Benjamin Franklin as his secretary? Surely he is a loyal American patriot?"

Juliana Ritchie smiled delightedly at him. "That, Charlie, is exactly what we must discover. Now let me tell you just what we are going to do!"

EIGHT

Next morning, scarcely able to keep his eyelids apart, Charles was nevertheless in a happy and contented mood as he rode towards Passy. The village, as Bancroft had said, lay just outside the old city walls of Paris and was surrounded by ancient cottages half hidden in lanes of tall chestnut trees already clad in light green. Charles began to relish being back in a rural landscape, with late spring softening the air. It was as if he could already smell summer.

Winter had been eventful enough, he thought with a smile. What would summer bring? Everything here was so very different from his childhood in the Mohawk Valley, to which he found his thoughts turning frequently these days. Of course these woods of Paris were softer and prettier by far than the forests of his childhood; for this was altogether a more ancient human habitation. But trees and open green fields were a welcome escape from the stench and the heaving masses of Paris.

He gazed about with satisfaction. Franklin and the American mission must be enjoying this change of scene. Quite apart from the calm and quiet of the place it was infinitely more suitable for the sort of secret negotiations that he understood were underway with the French administration. Secret, that is to say, though half of Paris seemed to be aware of what was afoot! And where Edward Bancroft was involved, Charles was now convinced that the other half would soon know.

It was generally acknowledged that Louis would naturally be unenthusiastic about assisting the American colonists to remove a king. This was more than understandable as it would undoubtedly be an awkward and dangerous precedent to set. But gradually he was being persuaded by Vergennes, his Foreign Minister, to the idea of supporting the Americans if for no other reason than 'my enemy's enemy is my friend'. Or at least my temporary ally, Charles laughed cynically. For the French would undoubtedly have their own plans for North America and these in the longer term were unlikely to be agreeable to Congress. Nevertheless Bancroft had told him in discreet whispers that the French were very close to entering the war. Though having now seen Bancroft at play Charles realised that one should not use the words 'discreet' and 'Bancroft' in the same sentence!

The problem for both Vergennes and Ben Franklin was that the royal resolve was swayed by every piece of conflicting news that drifted across the Atlantic. That the news was usually tardy and confused, often deliberately so as both sides played the game of manipulating the information, merely complicated the issue. An American setback such as the loss of New York alarmed the King hugely and delayed French intervention. Contrariwise, an American victory made it more likely that the French would rush to share in the success.

For the very last thing the French wanted, Charles realised, was a strong young independent nation in North America, especially one not beholden to them. The true interests of France lay in retaining control of the land around the Mississippi River, ultimately perhaps in recovering their old territories in Canada. Meanwhile Franklin's mission was to put the best possible light on the news coming from America and to bring the French openly into the war as soon as possible.

Much earlier that morning Charles had slipped back into his own bedroom as the first of the servants were astir and had just time to bathe and take some breakfast, tired but elated by his night of revelations. Then he had gone in search of William Fullerton and taken his advice on travelling to London to meet his banker, Thomas Coutts.

As they parted, he to ride out to Passy and Fullerton to pay his first visit of the day to Lord Stormont in his study, he asked Fullerton what he knew about Beaumarchais. Fullerton smiled. "Pierre Augustin Caron de Beaumarchais?" he murmured quietly. "There is much to say about that gentleman! He is, how shall we say, a colourful character? Well known to us here." Charles frowned at him enquiringly and Fullerton went quickly on. "Let us say that he is no friend of England. Or of Scotland either for that matter," he added, with a glance that Charles could not miss. "Well, that is by the bye. You know of course that he has just staged a very successful play in the Comédie-Française? A clever writer I am told." He smiled briefly. "Too clever for his own good perhaps. He has a knack of making enemies, as well as strange friends."

"His history is certainly unusual. Began his life as a watchmaker, like his father before him. When still quite young he invented some ingenious kind of watch mechanism for the accurate control of time and was taken up by the royal court on the strength of it. He made a watch for Madame de Pompadour and King Louis--- the old King, that is--- asked him to make another for himself. So his reputation was instantly made! Oh, and he taught the royal princesses to play music. He is charming, presentable, talented and obviously has a way with the ladies. He married the widow of a senior court official and thus had enough money to buy a title. Which is when he took the name of Beaumarchais. That is how they do things here," Fullerton shrugged.

"His first wife, unfortunate lady, died within a year." Fullerton said. He raised his eyebrows fleetingly. "Then he married a lady by the name of Lévesque, who came with a good dowry. She also died within a year or so." Fullerton smiled thinly at Charles. "As you might imagine, there was some speculation about just how his wives came to leave the stage so quickly and so conveniently. Poison was mentioned, I seem to recall," he added with a shrug. "Since then he has been involved in a succession of, well, let us call them adventures! He has a flair for embarking on ill-judged legal disputes over money and also seems to enjoy foreign intrigues and high risk business ventures. Money always seems to plays a part with him--- usually other people's money." He sighed and shook his head. "Other than that, I'm afraid I do not know much about him."

Charles stared. "You seem to know a great deal about him," he said bluntly.

Fullerton glanced away. "We try to keep an eye on people like him," he said dryly.

So what Juliana said was correct: Lord Stormont did have his own secret agents and Fullerton probably knew most of what was going on in Paris. Not excluding, Charles thought uncomfortably, how he had himself spent the previous evening.

"The bold Beaumarchais has carried out a few assignments of a confidential nature for both the present King and his grandfather. But he is not by nature reliable and so he has come to our attention now and then. His chief characteristic is that he seems never far from scandal. In sum, a plausible rogue and a clever one, I should say." Fullerton gave Charles a quick look from under his brows. "But a rogue certainly. Take a long spoon when you deal with a man like that. He is also very close to your friend Bancroft," he added, as if in afterthought.

Charles rode past the ruined stone walls of old abandoned cottages towards the gates of a great house, reflecting that it was about time he distanced himself from both Bancroft and Beaumarchais. Given the personal distaste he felt for Bancroft, that at least would be no great loss. And since it was clear that Lord Stormont knew almost everything about Beaumarchais, including his pro-American activities, he was almost certain to know as much, if not more, about the good doctor.

It was an uneasy thought but Charles realised now that his own activities were probably equally well known in the Embassy. But did Thomas Graham and Mary know about his associations in Paris, innocent as they were? Or innocent as they had been until last night, he thought with a flush of embarrassment. 'No,' he decided firmly. Once he had established contact with Franklin, an ambition that he could not bring himself to renounce, he would find a way to drop Bancroft regardless of the outcome of Juliana's scheme.

He turned in between tall gate posts and saw before him a splendid baroque house with a very fine decorated façade and a long sweeping driveway, comfortably wide enough for the elegant carriage that stood before a double flight of stone steps leading up to the impressive front door. Whoever M. Leray de Chaumont was, and whatever his motives, he was certainly doing the American mission proud.

Immediately before the grand façade stood a twittering group of fashionable women, elaborately dressed with extravagantly plumed hats. They were being slowly and reluctantly ushered into the coach, while on the steps above them, bowing and cheerfully waving them off, stood a figure whom Charles recognised instantly. A large man, heavily built and elderly, unmistakeable in the plain brown home-spun coat that had made him famous in Paris, his greying hair falling straight from a thinning dome and framing plump rounded features. Clumsy spectacles perched perilously on the end of a rather bulbous nose and he was propping himself up with his cane as he waved an enthusiastic goodbye to the ladies. As the carriage drove away Charles dismounted, his heart pounding. He was about to meet his hero.

Franklin turned towards him. His large amiable brown eyes surveyed Charles calmly, taking in at a glance his French clothes. "Bon jour, monsieur," he said politely in excruciatingly accented French. Then he bowed very low to the astonished young man. Charles was to discover that Franklin made a point of bowing to everyone he met, including the servants whom he encountered in the great Parisian houses to which he was invited. This all contributed to his image as a quaint and simple man of the people.

Charles introduced himself in English. "I understand that Edward Bancroft may have---."

"Ah, yes!" cried Franklin happily. "Why, you must be Mr Charles George MacPherson, the young man from New York. You wrote to me about the need to measure electricity! A very telling point for one so young, if I may be so presumptuous."

Charles was too astonished to reply. Could the great man possibly recall a naive letter from a mere boy written years before? No, it was simply not possible! Benjamin Franklin, a man with great matters of state on his mind: not least agreeing to sign the Declaration of Independence, could not possibly remember him! He began to stammer something to that effect but then saw the broad grin on Franklin's round face. The older man roared with laughter and seized Charles by the hand.

His eyes sparkling behind the bi-focal lenses of his spectacles. "Oh you must not allow me to practise upon you! I must confess that I did not actually recall your letter. Though doubtless I should have done so," he said disarmingly, "for it was a shrewd point to make. But I receive so many letters. Do forgive me, my dear young man." He smiled charmingly at Charles. "No, it was your good friend Edward Bancroft who reminded me about your early interest." He beamed at Charles again. "Still, come with me." Charles followed him into the house. Yet again, he thought! Edward Bancroft had somehow become his friend in everyone's eyes. And if what Juliana suspected of Bancroft proved to be true, what then?

"For indeed, of course," Franklin was saying, "your question was extremely apposite. And in fact it still is apposite. From some points of view, a philosophical one of course but nonetheless valid, what cannot be measured may be of doubtful benefit." He sat down on a long chaise and nodded musingly, gesturing to a nearby seat. Charles sat down on the edge staring at the great man, concentrating on his every word. "Now we know that electricity is a single fluid of some sort that flows from one body to another it makes eminent sense to find a reliable way of measuring it." He looked at Charles approvingly. "It was extraordinarily shrewd of you, so young as I say, to see the thing."

Charles flushed. To have Benjamin Franklin talking to him as to an equal was so wildly beyond anything he could ever have imagined that he thought he might be dreaming! Franklin sighed, pondering the problem. "I wonder if something might not be done using Leyden jars of sufficient size?" He frowned. "Oh how I wish I had time at my disposal to look into the matter. But this damned war, so unnecessary and wasteful, consumes much of my life it seems."

He smiled sadly at Charles. "There never was a good war nor a bad peace, whatever the zealots say," he said ruefully. "Never forget that, Mr MacPherson. So many good men die in war, too many by far, on both sides." Then, pulling himself up with a start, he went on, "However this will never do. We men of science must not allow politics to intervene. First tell me about yourself."

Charles had scarcely begun before Franklin interrupted. "Ah, from the Mohawk Valley! Tell me, Mr MacPherson, is it still a hotbed of loyalist support?"

"I'm afraid, sir, that it is in large measure. Though sentiment is by no means uniform." Charles hesitated. "My own father was a loyalist---, though I am a patriot."

Franklin nodded sadly. "I am well aware of how families have been split by this unnecessary dispute. My own son---." He stopped short and waved the unwelcome thought away. "The world I think knows that depressing story only too well." He fell silent for a moment, no doubt thinking about his estranged son, now the loyalist Governor of New Jersey.

Then Franklin brightened again. "But what of your plans, Mr MacPherson? I suppose that you are not related to Mr James MacPherson who collected the works of the great Ossian? No, I dare say not. But now you are in Europe I expect you will be travelling to meet some of the savants who are engaged in the most advanced work in the field of electricity? It is a rare opportunity for someone like yourself. How I envy you having youth and time at your command."

His mind raced on. "Now, you must certainly call on Luigi Galvani," he said. "We hear of his work through the Royal Society--- I am still a member there, though I think King George does not entirely approve of me!" He guffawed delightedly and slapped a plump thigh. "Galvani writes to me regularly from the University of Bologna where he is Professor of Anatomy, as I expect you know. Have you followed his experiments on the muscles and nerves of frogs? The contractions of a leg touched with charged metal? Now he has apparently devised an arc of two dissimilar metals with which the same contractions could be induced. Intriguing, is it not?" He smiled happily at Charles.

"The current is created by the metals, it seems. So it is not, as was thought at first, a vital fluid within the animal itself. Yes, yes, Galvani! You must visit him! I'll write a letter of introduction for you and you must certainly let me know how you do." He beamed at the young man. "What fun you will have! If only my business here were over----. Ah well!" Franklin's face clouded briefly.

"Then of course there is Alessandro Volta, at Pavia," he went on enthusiastically. "Now he, I know, has become very keenly interested in measurement and becoming quite famous for his work on the subject. And of course there is my good friend Joseph Priestley in England, who has discovered that electricity follows the inverse-square law of gravity." He fell silent and shook his head in wonder.

Deciding he must set the matter straight, Charles tried to explain that he was very much a beginner in the field of electricity. "I have to say, sir, that I am a tyro in these matters, Mr Franklin. A complete amateur in many ways---," he began firmly.

"Of course, my boy! Are not we all, all of us, simply feeling our way? I remember that time I took my silk handkerchief on two cross-sticks and my key into the fields with a thunderstorm approaching--- I almost blush to think of it now! The rain falling and the sky darkening! Why, everyone thought I was a madman and greeted me with the ridicule which commonly attends early attempts in science!"

"Please tell me about that incident," said Charles eagerly. "I have read of it, of course. But I should love to hear from yourself how it was."

Franklin nodded. "I was attended by no-one but my son that day." A cloud of regret briefly darkening the large brown eyes again and he smiled thoughtfully at Charles. "He was scarcely older than yourself," he said sadly, "and not so unlike you either. It was he who assisted me in raising the kite with the metal key for weight. I remember one very promising cloud passed over without any effect and I was beginning to despair of the contrivance. Experiments rarely work at the first attempt, you should always remember that, my young friend. Then another cloud drifted above and suddenly I observed some loose threads of the hempen string standing erect, as if to avoid one another! It was just as if they had been suspended on a common electrical conductor."

"Electrical static," Charles murmured.

"Exactly! Then, wonder of wonders, when I presented my knuckle to the key I perceived a very evident electric spark and later when the rain had wet the string I was able to collect the electric fire very copiously, very copiously indeed. Ah, a great moment, Mr MacPherson. May I call you Charles?"

Charles knew from his study in Sir William Johnson's library that before Franklin it had been thought that electricity consisted of two opposing forces. Franklin had shown that electricity in fact was an single element which he called 'electric fire'. Everyone, at least everyone who was at all interested, now knew that this element could pass from one body to another, sometimes with great vigour, provided the bodies were electrified positively and negatively and that it could also be captured and stored.

But not yet measured, Charles reminded himself thoughtfully. Franklin had created a whole dictionary of words for this new science, terms such battery, electrical charge, condenser and conductor, a language still largely incomprehensible to most people. Charles was all too aware that he comprehended some of it only roughly himself and he was beginning to feel guilty about how the great man perceived him, wondering how he might correct the impression at this late stage. Then he recalled one of Franklin's own aphorisms. 'Silence may not always be a sign of wisdom. But babbling is always a sign of folly.' With an introduction from Franklin a whole new world would be open to him! His heart rose within him at the prospect and he decided to leave any misapprehensions alone for the time being.

"My friend Priestley lives in the north of England, where he is a member of an important Lunar Society." Charles could only imagine that this society studied the moon but decided on a policy of further silence. "But of course he is in London from time to time. Will you be going there, at all?" he heard Franklin ask.

Charles was just explaining that shortly he intended to visit that city when a small sharp-featured man, round-headed and plump, but with none of the comfortable good-nature of Franklin, burst into the room. "Franklin, it is time to depart for our meeting in Paris!" His narrow-set eyes took in the young man at a glance and dismissed him as rapidly. "First these damned women and now--- ."

Charles had risen to his feet politely and catching himself in time the little man nodded stiffly towards him. Franklin beamed at the newcomer. "Charles, allow me to introduce you to my fellow commissioner Mr Silas Deane. Silas, this is the friend of Edward Bancroft we were to expect. You may recall Edward spoke to us about Mr MacPherson. He is a good patriot from New York. A rare species these days, eh?"

Charles silently groaned. Yet another association with Bancroft and one hard to refute this time. Suppose Juliana were correct! But after the merest hesitation Deane ignored the young man completely. "It is time to go," he repeated to the older man. "Really, Benjamin!"

Franklin continued unabashed. "Mr MacPherson was telling me about his imminent visit to London." Turning back to Charles, "Given your interests you must call on my good friends Edward and Charles Dilly, the publishers. They have just arranged the printing of the Complete Treatise on Electricity by Tiberius Cavello, though he is a gentleman I have to admit I do not know. Still, I dare say you have read the book." He gazed approvingly at Charles, who marvelled at how simply he had been transformed into a scientist and with so little effort on his part.

"Now I must give you an introduction to my friend Priestley," Franklin had continued. "And to Joseph Banks too," he added as an after thought. "He has no special interest in your subject, being primarily a botanist of course. But he is extremely well connected in London and a leading figure in the Royal Society. Although too loyal a subject to speak out publicly, I know he is deeply unhappy about this unfortunate war." He sighed and took the young man's hand. "Now I must go it seems. I do enjoy a discussion like this and I thank you so much for coming. I shall not forget to send you those letters of introduction. Fear not! Edward knows how to find you, I dare say?"

Charles found himself being ushered briskly away by Deane. But to his surprise the little man's asperity of manner softened "You travel to London soon I understand," he said. His close-set eyes were studying Charles carefully.

"Within a few days. My friends are looking into travel for me." Charles replied shortly. Why was this man so much less sympathetic to him than his much greater colleague?

Deane stopped in his stride and drew Charles aside into an ante room, taking a small package of papers out of his coat. He contemplated them thoughtfully for a moment. Then he glanced up at Charles and smiled a smile that did not quite reach his eyes. Charles thought instantly of Edward Bancroft. "Edward assures me you are a loyal patriot." Charles only inclined his head graciously.

"As you can imagine, Mr MacPherson," Deane went on, "these days we must frequently pass documents of a confidential nature to our friends in London. So many of our usual routes are cut off or otherwise compromised and the normal post is invariably intercepted by British government agents in spite of every precaution we may take. As often as not it seems they know more about our business than we do ourselves." He shook his head sadly at the thought.

"It would be a great service therefore if you would carry these papers with you." He stared at Charles again. "Yes," he repeated thoughtfully. "It would be a great service if you would carry these with you to London. Deliver them pray to the person named on this separate cover." He held up single sheet of paper. "But remember well! The documents themselves have no address within or without. So it is vital that this address and these papers are kept apart." He glared at Charles severely . "Is that understood? It is a matter of the gravest importance for our country!"

Charles glancing down saw that the cover note was addressed to Stephan Sayre, Esq. It was a name that meant nothing to him. What harm could there be in delivering some papers to London? He had done little enough to aid the cause so far, he thought guiltily. Though Juliana's ploy might yet prove a valuable, if disruptive one.

"For reasons of state," Deane continued. Then he paused and nodded almost to himself. "Yes, for reasons of state. Exactly so! It is important that these documents are not under any circumstances associated with myself--- and certainly not with Mr Franklin," he added abruptly, shooting another severe glance at Charles.

"In fact," he said, "should their contents ever unfortunately become public, Mr Franklin must be able to deny any knowledge of them." He nodded once more. "Just so! Mr Franklin must not be explicitly aware of this transaction. Do I make myself clear, Mr MacPherson? Do not, therefore, even allude to it in his presence. How well do you know London?" he added, inconsequentially.

"This will be my first visit."

"No matter," said Deane briskly. "Stephan Sayre can be found at Jonathan's Coffee House in Exchange Alley. Or possibly at Lloyd's in Lombard Street. Sayre is a man of business," Deane said by way of explanation. Charles nodded solemnly and said nothing. "Failing those places," said Deane broodingly, "he may be difficult to find, for his movements are somewhat--- irregular."

Deane studied Charles doubtfully for a moment longer. "In which event, you must go to a man named John Almon. He is a journalist and the proprietor of the 'London Evening Post', one of the city's news sheets. He publishes a regular review of writings concerning our case for independence and is well connected with the opposition party in London."

He paused and stared fixedly at Charles again. "John Almon is sympathetic to our cause and incidentally a good friend of John Wilkes. He will know the whereabouts of Sayre, if anyone does. If you need to, but only if necessary you understand, you might ask cautiously for Sayre at the St James Coffee House near Pall Mall. The Whigs commonly meet there. But cautiously remember! For the British have spies everywhere."

NINE

The light of the full moon seemed to have leached all the colour from the gardens of the Tuileries, which lay pallid about Juliana Ritchie's coach, the trees reduced to unreal grey ghosts of themselves. She had dismissed her driver for a few hours and presuming his eccentric mistress was bent on some secret assignation, he had wandered off to find his own entertainment in one of the nearby taverns.

Now she sat alone with Charles, studying the moonlit spectacle. "This is the day, or rather the night, that Edward Bancroft invariably comes," she said quietly. "Each week at the same time and always to leave strange messages hidden in that same box tree on the south terrace. The one with the hollow bole." Juliana shook her head in the shadowy interior of the coach. "I extracted one of his earlier message but could make no sense of it. It seemed to be a simple letter of gallantry, addressed to some lady unknown. Yet it was signed ' B. Edwards'. Do you not think that significant, Charlie?"

Charles had read a copy of the message; a copy that Juliana swore was exact in every respect. It had been left by Bancroft a week before and was no more than a half-dozen lines of banality referring to a romantic tryst. To Charles the triteness of phrase seemed quite in keeping with the nature of the man, the only oddity being that the lines of script seemed to be written strangely far apart. A half-formed idea lurked obscurely in his mind.

"However," she went on, "I have not yet identified the man who collects the messages. Always it is the same man. But one I have never seen elsewhere in Paris. I hope you can solve that question for me tonight." Juliana gave Charles an affectionate kiss. "Simply follow the man to his lair, wherever it may be and so discover the identity of Bancroft's secret correspondent."

'Ah,' thought Charles, 'that is all'. Simply follow the man through half empty Paris streets unnoticed in the light of a near full moon. It was a task that Francis Johnson with all his woodcraft could scarcely achieve. Suddenly Juliana seized his arm urgently. "There," she whispered, peering past the velvet curtain that draped the rear window of her coach. "He comes!"

Twisting around Charles saw the tall figure of Bancroft, huddled in a long dark coat, his saturnine face half hidden behind its high collar but his patrician nose unmistakable even at this distance. He seemed to have come on foot from somewhere deeper in the gardens. Now he hesitated close to the tree that Juliana had identified, looking about to check his bearings. He peered in the direction of the coach as if to assess its significance. In the moonlight Charles saw a frown flit across his face. Obviously he was careful and suspicious. Praying that he would not risk approaching the coach, Charles held his breath and waited.

A lop-sided sardonic grin appeared on the dark lantern jaw and Bancroft visibly relaxed. He had probably decided that the coach was being used for an illicit assignation, far from uncommon in that area of the city. If so, the occupants would presumably be far too preoccupied with their own activities to notice his. As Juliana had predicted, Bancroft made his way to the tree with the hollow bole and Charles watched engrossed as he drew something from his long coat; something that glinted white in the moonlight. This he placed securely into the shadowy tree trunk and again he glanced around. Then he scurried away with an unmistakable loping gait into the darkness of the gardens.

"There!" Juliana whispered triumphantly. "Did I not tell you?" Charles started to climb down from the coach but she caught his sleeve. "No," she said urgently. "We must leave the message for the courier to collect. If a letter were to go astray they would know for certain they are being watched. That would spoil everything. No, the key is to follow the man who picks up the message and identify him. We must wait!"

"For how long?"

She peered at her fob watch. "Bancroft was exactly on time. It is just midnight, as usual. That means the courier will come in one hour precisely. It is an unfailing pattern. We have an hour to wait."

"Well, well." Charles murmured. "What can we do to pass an hour?"

Juliana giggled. "No! We must be vigilant!" she protested. "It would be a sin if we were to---," The precise nature of the sin she meant to avoid never became clear. But to any observer the sounds that came from coach would have confirmed Bancroft's earlier suppositions. As the hour approached however the two of them were restored to good order, if a shade out of breath and overheated.

They resumed their careful watch. But in spite of their vigilance they almost missed the fast moving figure that appeared from the trees, moving with such speed and plucking the message from its hiding place with such practised skill that Charles scarcely had time to slip from the coach in pursuit before the unknown courier was again lost in the darkness. "Will you be all right?" he whispered as he descended.

Juliana brandished a loaded horse pistol she had taken from a compartment in the coach. "Go!" she hissed.

Following at a cautious distance and using every patch of shadow and moving with a silence he had learned from many hunting trips with Francis, Charles stalked the man, cautiously at first as he would a wary deer. But gradually he relaxed. From the way the man moved through the streets without a backward glance it was evident that he had carried out this exercise before, probably many times before, and that he had no fear of being followed. It was also evident that he had a clear destination in mind, moving fast and obviously familiar with every twist and turn of the way.

But always, Charles realised, heading in a general direction towards the Rue St Honoré. A growing and extraordinary conviction came into his mind as the two of them wound their silent way through the darkened streets, deserted except for the occasional drunken groups straggling out of taverns or the importuning of the occasional late and underemployed whore. Soon he knew beyond any doubt the destination of the man.

The Stormont mansion, dark and firmly secured for the night, finally loomed up as Charles stopped and took shelter in a dark archway across the street. As he watched the man slipped down the side of the building and tapped softly at a small wooden door, used normally for tradesmen making deliveries to the embassy. The door opened promptly in spite of the late hour and the light of a lantern from within fell briefly on the man's face.

"Sewell!" Charles hissed jubilantly. The short dark hair and the lean tanned features were unmistakable. For the man who had collected Bancroft's message was John Sewell, a familiar enough figure in the embassy, though one whose precise function Charles had not so far been able to discover. But that Sewell was one of Fullerton's close associates he knew, having seen the two men speaking together more than once.

Charles stood in the darkness, his mind a whirl of speculation. Edward Bancroft, secretary to Franklin and confidant of Silas Deane, was in secret communication with Lord Stormont's private secretary! The full impact dawned on him. Bancroft must be privy to all the discussions with the French government and probably much more besides, thought Charles grimly. This man, who for reasons best known to himself had tried to enlist him to spy on his hosts, was in fact regularly sending messages covertly to the British from inside the American mission!

It was treachery and treachery of a most dangerous and confusing nature. What was more, it struck him more sharply, Beaumarchais was now very risky indeed to know! Charles had to assume that Fullerton and Stormont knew about Beaumarchais' activities in smuggling French arms to the Americans: yet here they were exchanging secret messages with one of Beaumarchais' close associates, Edward Bancroft!

Juliana had been correct. Now Franklin must be warned. But the mystery remained as to what information the secret messages contained. What lay behind the innocent words? For without evidence Franklin was unlikely to be convinced that he had a British agent within his inner circle.

A code was being used, that much was clear. But what kind of code? He must examine the copy of that earlier message more carefully. After all, a code devised by man could be broken by man, if only the principles were understood. He remembered from his readings in Sir William's library that in any message there would be patterns of words or letters or symbols; patterns that repeated themselves with mathematical precision, though different for different languages.

Still, Charles knew that if mathematics were involved he would find the solution, given time. He made his way thoughtfully back to Juliana's coach. The chief problem was how to make Benjamin Franklin listen to a woman and a young man like himself. For that he must have proof of Bancroft's treachery.

Much later that same morning Mary Graham glanced over her breakfast cup at her husband. Thomas seemed strangely ill at ease today she observed, his strong face unusually dark with some unexpressed concern. That he was preoccupied was clear. But with what? She knew Thomas generally did his best to spare her his worries. But he was certainly not his usual relaxed self. Some problem with the estates at Balgowan, she wondered? Or bad news concerning one of his beloved hunters? He did love fox hunting, she knew. He had come willingly enough to France when he realised that her separation from sister Louisa cut her so sharply. But Mary was aware how much he missed his regular ride to the hounds, to say nothing of the simple satisfaction of solving the daily down-to-earth practical problems of his tenants--- those men he knew so well and whose company he enjoyed so much.

She sighed and immediately Thomas glanced across at her, renewed concern in his dark eyes. Throughout their married life it had become a habit, almost regardless of other distractions, for them to take their morning chocolate together. It was a habit Mary valued greatly and in these quiet moments she might write some of her personal letters--- she wrote almost daily to one or other of her family or friends. Or she might simply organise her diary while Thomas would look through business letters or study the latest estate papers from Balgowan. It was a time of calm repose that she hoped would set the pattern for the day.

This morning however she knew Thomas was troubled and that disturbed her. Meeting his gaze, "My dear," she said gently, laying down her cup. "Is it something you want to share with me?"

For a instant Thomas looked surprised. Then his look changed to one of comfortable resignation and he gave a sigh of secret relief. There was little he could conceal from Mary, at least for very long. In truth there was usually little he ever wanted or indeed needed to conceal from Mary. Though like most married couples he imagined there were areas into which their ordinarily discussions never strayed. In his case these were areas to do with feelings: feelings that he could never or at least did not choose, did not dare, to reveal to her. Feelings and fears about her own health and well-being. He smiled at her a shade guiltily. "Lord, Mary. How well you can read me. It's as well that I have nothing much to hide."

She took up her cup again. "Perhaps," she smiled calmly. "Yet there is something that concerns you this morning?"

Thomas Graham frowned and grimaced uncomfortably. "The thing is, I don't see what I can do about it. For it concerns young Charles," he said brusquely. Then seeing her sudden look of alarm, "Oh, not our Charles," he said hastily. "That is to say, not your Charles." He laid an affectionate hand on her arm. "What a clumsy fellow I am, my dear. No, it's young Charles MacPherson. You see, our brother-in-law is becoming concerned about the sort of friends Charles is making in Paris, outside the embassy."

"What exactly did David say?" Mary asked, a rare frown crossing her gentle face.

Thomas groaned and lay back in his chair. "That's just the point. David Murray never says anything 'exactly'! He's the perfect diplomat! That is why I'd be no good at that sort of thing. But I can read between the lines as well as the next man." He paused. "Well, almost as well." Mary smiled quietly and sipped the thick sweet dark chocolate.

"No, the thing is, he made a special point of asking me about Charles. Who was he seeing in Paris these days, that sort of thing. Nothing specific. But you know how David Murray is--- what all the Murrays are like, bless them. They aren't given to idle chat and I'm certain he means it as a warning of some kind. There is something behind it that he does not like."

"Do you know anything about his new friends, my dear?"

Thomas shook his head. "Not a deal," he said. He looked uncomfortable and cleared his throat "There is a lady that he has been seen with recently." Looking more ill at ease by the minute, he went on awkwardly. "I understand that she is American and possibly not quite the thing," he said flushing. " But beyond that I know very little."

Mary lowered her eyes tactfully.

"But I'll wager David knows all about it," Thomas went on. "There isn't much Lord Stormont doesn't know about what goes on in Paris." He glowered at Mary. "Charles has taken to staying away nights, apparently. But what he is up to I cannot guess." He paused and reddened slightly. "Well, I can guess, of course," he said awkwardly. "But why David should be so concerned puzzles me. Besides what does he expect me to do about it?" he added almost petulantly.

Mary gave a knowing smile. "Ah, this explains the little hints Louisa has been dropping to me. David obviously hoped I might have some influence with the boy."

Thomas groaned aloud and clattered his cup into its saucer. "Oh Lord! It's as serious as that! And now since nothing has come from the distaff side, he decided to try me." He shook his head and stared moodily at his empty cup. "But what can he expect, Mary? A young fellow on the loose in Paris for the first time. Besides," he went on hurriedly, realising he had encroached on dangerous ground, "what can we do? It's not as if he is our son." Oh Lord, he thought instantly, such dangerous and painful ground!

"Any roads," he said quickly, "I assured David that young Charles is off to London soon to see his bankers. That should keep him out of mischief for a while. Old Coutts will keep him on the straight and narrow if anyone can. Though perhaps we should make sure he meets the right type of people in London. Also when he comes back I thought we might perhaps plan a trip together. Get him away from Paris, if you follow me. It might suit you too, my dear, now that the hot weather is coming to the city.

For it can be a foul place in summer."

Mary did follow him and her heart sank just a little, for she did not truly enjoy travelling. It tired her so and she would miss the company of her dear sister Louisa. Yet she knew Thomas was always eager to explore and to see new places.

"I had in mind to try the waters at Spa," he said. "They are quite the thing now, they tell me. Everyone is going there. It's just like Bath, they say, except you don't have to walk everywhere. It's foreign of course--- but quite nice for all that. And they say that the hot mineral springs are very strengthening and invigorating. You might enjoy it. Anyway, I thought we might invite Charles to accompany us." Then he gave a grunt. "Not that he needs much invigorating, by all accounts." Mary looked blankly at her chocolate cup again as Thomas coughed awkwardly.

"Still," he went on hurriedly, "he might enjoy the new English casino that has been built at Waux-Hall as they have christened it, after the London pleasure gardens you understand. Don't know if Charles is a gambling man but there's something called the English Club at Spa. Your father's old patron the Duke of Cumberland was its first President."

Thomas grunted awkwardly again. "Mind, perhaps we had best not mention that to young Charles. He seems deuced touchy about his highland connections, especially for a fellow who was born in the colonies. Still, a great many of our friends will be at Spa and you will enjoy meeting them, I'm sure. The woods and hills around the area are very like Perthshire. We can ride out when you feel strong enough or take a comfortable chaise and picnic under the trees. The scenery is lovely."

Mary nodded serenely. "Yes, Thomas. That sounds very pleasant indeed."

"Regarding young Charles, do you think we should say anything to him about David's concerns? It is difficult, I know."

She hesitated for a moment. "Is he about the place this morning, do you know?"

"He came in very late last night, I understand. Or more correctly early this morning if your brother-in-law is well-informed, as he customarily is. Fullerton will discuss his travel arrangements for London with him today. There are some embassy mails to go on the Dover packet which sails from Calais in few days time, weather permitting. I think the plan is for Sewell, Fullerton's man, to carry the letters to London. Charles can travel with him and stay in London for a few days."

Mary nodded. "Then I shall speak to him, if only to wish him a bon voyage. Or failing that I shall certainly see him on his return."

Thomas breathed a sigh of relief.

TEN

Charles stood at a first floor window of Thomas Coutts & Co at 59 the Strand gazing down in amazement at the crush of people and carriages below.

In spite of its impressive width the Strand was jammed with every sort of conveyance: horses, carriages and chaises, all jostling for a foot of space and a yard of progress, while on each side the impressive foot pavements were a bustling mass of people. The street was lined with coffee houses, taverns, shops and enterprises of every kind, some with enormous glass windows the like of which he had never before seen. Every trade and profession it seemed and almost every nationality in the world was here to do business in London.

The previous night a private chaise had carried Sewell and himself in relative comfort from Dover. As it made its way through the south of the city and across a great stone bridge into the Liberties of the Savoy, Charles had already seen enough to realise that Paris, with all its turmoil, scarcely began to match this city in either scale or organisation. His heart sank when he compared this spectacle of power with the provincial New York he recalled.

'Even supposing it had not been half burned to the ground,' he thought glumly. The unburned Philadelphia, to judge from Juliana's description, must equally seem parochial by comparison with this great city and for the first time he began seriously to doubt whether America could ever realistically challenge the great British realm.

That morning, having spent a comfortable night at an inn near the

Adelphi Wharfs chosen for him by Thomas Graham, he had walked through the crowded streets to the bank in the Strand where he handed over his two letters of introduction, Lord Stormont having bolstered his credentials by adding his voice to that of Sir William Johnson. A suspicious and initially unhelpful clerk in the front office had shown him into a private room and there he had waited with growing impatience for an audience with the great Thomas Coutts, the man who apparently had his money.

As he waited, observing the bustle of the London streets with one part of his mind, his thoughts turned back to Paris two night earlier, just before Fullerton had organised his hasty departure. With Juliana stretched out sleepily on her bed Charles had spent the last of the night and the early dawn hours trying to decipher the letter she had copied from Bancroft's hiding place. It consisted of a few widely spaced lines, at face value no more than a simple billet doux, a letter of gallantry and a clumsy one at that. Just the sort of thing that Bancroft might construct to a lady of no great taste Charles thought to himself.

But a billet doux signed with a false name and delivered secretly each week at the same time, to be collected in the night by one of Lord Stormont's staff? And moreover by a cautious and trusted member of the embassy, as Charles now realised.

Sewell, although polite and deferential, had made a point of avoiding him on the packet boat, pleading sickness and an unlikely aversion to sea travel. On the coach journey to Calais and later on the chaise from Dover to London Charles had tried to engage his travelling companion in conversation. What were Sewell's duties in the Embassy? Did he find his working hours congenial? Did they allow him to enjoy the pleasures of Paris, the night life and so on? How long had he worked for Lord Stormont? How good was his French? And for where was he now bound, exactly?

Sewell had talked freely enough, though it was difficult to place his manner. He had a roughness about him and his teeth were bad. No, Sewell was not exactly a gentleman. Charles had already learned to make that distinction, at least with English speakers. But neither was Sewell a typical domestic servant; his eyes were too forthright and questioning for that. Also, in spite of his apparent openness he had told Charles exactly nothing, though in a pleasant enough manner.

Oh, he had general duties: just fetching and carrying, that sort of thing, don't you know. Not very long in Lord Stormont's service. And he was bound for some offices in London. Government offices, he confided to Charles ingenuously, patting the belt of documents he carried around his waist. Diplomatic papers from Lord Stormont, the mails being so unreliable, he said with a knowing smile. Yes, it was obvious that Sewell was well regarded; a member of the Stormont's staff trusted sufficiently to handle Bancroft's secret letters. And perhaps with much more besides.

In Juliana's bedroom Charles had studied at the document. That there was a hidden message of some kind he did not doubt and he fancied that he remembered enough about codes and other secret writing to solve the puzzle, given time. But how much time, he thought, scratching his head as his candle finally spluttered out and he realised with a start that the dawn light was seeping through the curtains of Juliana's bedroom. She lay sound asleep, though still dressed, and he gently pulled a cover over her against the cool air. He was tired and his mind, he realised, had stopped working effectively some time ago. He blinked as spots flickered before his eyes, which felt as though they were on fire in his head.

Charles had tried every trick of encoding he had ever heard of; experimenting with every possible combination of substitution or displacement of letters. He had then looked for some numerical basis, such as hidden groupings of letters, formed by apparently natural breaks in the hand writing, for example, and then converted back into letters by a variety of techniques. But nothing had worked. In general, the most common alphabetic characters used in English seemed to appear more or less in the frequencies one would expect, though because of the shortness of the letter the statistical information was probably not very helpful. In desperation he had even translated it into French and examined it in that language for some hidden meaning, an unlikely ploy given Bancroft's low level of competence in the language. But it was just possible that he had assistance in his treachery. For it was clear now that Bancroft was a traitor in British pay. Why else would he be in secret communication with the Embassy?

Somehow, Charles thought drowsily as he stretched out on the bed beside the sleeping Juliana, he must find a way to solve the mystery. And to tell Franklin, of course. Yes, Franklin must be warned that he was being betrayed; that there was a spy at the very heart of the American mission in Paris. Charles tried to sleep. But his mind refused to release him and a half-understood phrase returned to his thoughts again and again. It simply would not go away. 'There must be a way to read this message,' he thought hazily as he descended into a half sleep; 'there must be a way to read between the lines. There simply must be a way.'

His eyes shot open. Between the lines! Of course! The lines of the note had been widely spaced; curiously widely spaced! He had noticed that almost at once but had taken it for one of Bancroft's eccentricities. There must be other writing on the paper, invisible to him all the while he had wrestled with the innocent text.

Yes, of course. There was some kind of chemical writing hidden there! Something that would require an appropriate liquid, some solvent that would react with the writing to reveal the truth; a liquid that Lord Stormont had simply to apply to bring up Bancroft's secret message. He lay back as sleep finally overcame him. Of course, he remembered drowsily, Bancroft was chemist as well as a physician. He would certainly have a knowledge of chemical writing.

Did he not recall in Bancroft's endless lectures, delivered as Charles lay supine on the voyage across the Atlantic, that the man had dabbled in the chemistry of dyes during his time in Guiana? Of course! It all began to make sense. He would tell Juliana when she awoke, he thought. But without a knowledge of the precise substance used and access to the correct chemical treatment their chances of reading the messages were negligible.

Charles still stood staring down at the hectic street below, thinking of Juliana, when he heard the door open behind him and a brisk voice with a clear Lowland Scots accent addressed him. "Ah, Mr MacPherson I presume. Forgive me for keeping you waiting. I had some business to contract on behalf of a noble personage. Correspondence to be approved and sent off urgently post haste."

Charles turned to see a tall, spare man, plainly but fashionably dressed in a dark grey coat with black velvet collar and impeccable white linen shirt front and cravat. He had a long face, intelligent, formal and even sombre in appearance, with dark curly hair close fitted about a high domed head. He looked not unlike Charles's idea of a Presbyterian minister.

Coutts strode forward and seized Charles confidently by the hand, a broad and welcoming smile splitting his long face. At the same time Charles was conscious of being scrutinised by a pair of amiable but shrewd eyes. "Mr MacPherson," Coutts repeated with pleasure. "That is a grand Scottish name. Yet if I do not err, you were born in the American colonies?"

"My father settled there after 1745," Charles said.

"Ah, 1745!" Coutts said with an understanding nod. "A sad time. Still, best not to dwell on that, eh?" he added. He shot a discreet glance at Charles from under his dark eyebrows, registering the French cut of his outfit.

Charles had been well briefed by his friend Graham and knew that Thomas Coutts and his family had their roots in Edinburgh where his father had first established himself as a banker. He had in fact been Chief Magistrate during the 1745 Rising, which meant that the Coutts family had been sound Hanoverian Whigs with little sympathy for men like Charles's father and had probably hanged a few of them. Later, on the strength of their loyalty to the British government, Coutts and his brother James had expanded their business into the lucrative London banking market, taking over an old established Scottish-owned bank, Middleton and Campbell in the Strand, which handled much of the Scottish money flowing into London in support of the developing trade and commerce.

The bank took the Coutts name after the two brothers became partners and only last year on the death of James Coutts the bank had finally become Thomas Coutts & Co. It had already acquired a large and growing list of prestigious clients, including much of the nobility and even some royalty. The Prince of Wales, heir to the throne, was a client with, it was supposed, a virtually unlimited line of credit. As Thomas Graham dryly commented, "this is something of a benefit for the Prince, given his lavish lifestyle and massive gambling debts."

Coutts aspired to the accomplishments and manners of a gentleman. But he was above all a man of business and punctilious to the last penny in dealing with debts, either owed to him or by him. Except, that is to say, where the gentry were concerned. These he treated, not with laxity, for their debts were never exactly overlooked. But he did treat them with extreme indulgence, managing each account personally against the day when the individual would marry well or come into their expected inheritance. Or where some other advantage, commercial or more likely social, would fall due to Thomas Coutts.

As a result of his acumen he had become extremely wealthy. But notwithstanding his careful approach to business matters he had also acquired a reputation for great public generosity. He was well known for giving freely to the poor and for dispensing hospitality liberally to his friends, paradoxically even to those he continued to hold to the last penny of their indebtedness to the bank. An interesting man, Charles decided instantly, who would make a better friend than an enemy.

"Now sir," he said to Charles, indicating a chair beside a small Chippendale desk. "You will want an account of the monies that your guardian, Sir William Johnson, lodged with us here." He frowned, his long face taking on an air of sudden melancholy. "A great loss, his death and a matter of grief for you, I am sure. Especially so soon after the loss of your own father. Still," he continued briskly, "life must go on and I expect a young man like you will have many plans, many plans indeed." He paused. "For travel," he went on. "And for a choice of career." He looked at Charles with a quiet smile.

"Let me first show you the accounts," he went on briskly. "And for a young man like yourself they make comforting reading, I dare say. For Sir William obviously gave your father's estate a very fair price for the land that was involved. Especially considering the uncertainties of tenure in the colony at present." He gave Charles a gloomy look. "For who can predict the outcome of this unhappy conflict. Sad indeed. And whatever the outcome it will not be good for business at all." After a moment's glum reflection he seemed to brighten up as he returned to the account book.

"In addition we have a payment representing your father's interest in the joint trading company in which he and Sir William shared equally. A substantial sum, I am glad to say, and again a very fair valuation." He beamed at Charles. If the money had been his own, Coutts could hardly have been more pleased. "There is also a small legacy, left to you by Sir William. I do not know if you were aware of his intentions?"

Charles expressed his surprise, indeed amazement at this fact. Nothing had been further from his thoughts. A total surprise. "Well, it is only a small amount," Coutts said. "Five hundred pounds. But it speaks volumes of the regard in which Sir William held you, I am sure. It was handsome, very handsome." Charles sat patiently as Coutts considered the account book reverently, nodding to himself.

"So the total capital you have at your disposal at this stage, Mr MacPherson, taking everything into account is something in excess of six thousand pounds." As Charles gasped Coutts went on unconcernedly. "Not a vast sum, of course, though it is attracting interest in the account. But adequate, more than adequate for a young man starting out in life. Invested in funds at say three and a half percent. Or even five percent if you are willing to accept rather more risk, which I personally would not recommend. But even at the more prudent level it will provide an annual income of ------,"

"Two hundred and ten pounds," murmured Charles.

Coutts gazed at him with approval. "Very good, Mr MacPherson. We could make a banker out of you, that is clear. I wish some of my other clients had as quick a grasp of the realities of life."

It seemed to Charles that something in excess of two hundred pounds was a substantial sum. "Just what does such an income represent in this country, Mr Coutts. I have little experience of such things."

"Well, it might not run to a carriage and servants in London. But many a professional gentleman lives well enough on two hundred pounds, especially in the provinces. Aye, and even raises a family. So you need have little concern as to the immediate future." He paused. "Of course you may wish to travel for a while. Before you settle down to a sensible profession. With a good marriage and family responsibilities and so on."

He beamed at Charles, whose stony face showed no obvious pleasure at this prospect. "But that is a long way off, I dare say," Coutts added quickly, seeing Charles's reaction. "A long way. Yes, I dare say. Still," he went on judicially, "it is never too early to plan for the future. Do you have any notion of a career for yourself, may I ask? The law for example, if you had no inclination to finance and other commercial matters. The law is a good basis for a gentleman and with the patronage of men such as Lord Stormont it could lead for example into parliament, if such is your desire."

Charles could only admit that he had given no thought to the matter and that perhaps he should. "I suppose that the subject of greatest interest to me, Mr Coutts is that of natural philosophy, the sciences, in particular the new study of electrical science."

Coutts frowned. "Natural philosophy? Electricity, is it? Well, I am sure it is all a very fascinating subject. But of what practical use, I wonder? Perhaps a suitable study for a gentleman at his leisure. But as a basis for a career, Mr MacPherson? I wonder at you. Truly I do." He considered Charles silently for a moment, with just a hint of disapproval. "Perhaps a period of travel about Europe to open up your perspectives. Or a term or two at one of our great universities. Edinburgh of course has several men of distinction teaching chemistry, geology and the like. Even Glasgow---- ," His voice tailed away as he sought something encouraging to say about that city.

Charles considered the events of the past several months in silence for a moment; Pemberton; his father's death and his abandonment of what had seemed a settled if potentially turbulent path in revolutionary New York. It was almost as if he was being swept along in some kind of storm. Of course Coutts was quite right, regardless of his dismissive and reactionary view of the sciences. He must think about his future more carefully. As his mind returned to the immediate matter, Coutts was explaining how he could draw on the account for cash or with letters of credit.

"Now sir," Coutts said finally. "Is there any other way in which I or my staff can be of assistance to you while you are in London."

"I'd like to thank you sir, for your kindness. And also for your well-meant and I am sure very sound advice to a young man."

Coutts flushed with pleasure at his words. "Genteel of you, sir. Very genteel."

As Charles was preparing to leave he asked casually. "Since you have been so helpful, do you happen to know where I might possibly find a man by the name of Stephen Sayre? I understand he is a banker in this city."

Coutts stared at him and any pretence of reserve vanished. "Sayre? Well, if he is out of gaol I would not know where to find him. And I need to correct you, Mr MacPherson. Sayre is by no means a banker. He is a bankrupt! Which is hardly the same thing, and certainly not a sound basis for a financial career." He gave a creaking laugh. "Lord, I must recall that turn of phrase. I do not often come out with such a good remark."

Charles felt himself bridle. But Coutts went on regardless. "Dare I enquire, sir, what the nature of your business with a man like Sayre might be? Nothing of a personal financial nature I trust. For he is by no means sound. By no means!"

"Not financial by any means," Charles said coldly. "I have merely undertaken to deliver a message to him. On behalf of an acquaintance in Paris, the post being so erratic." His voice tailed weakly away as he recalled Deane's repeated admonitions about the need for discretion in London.

"You are most likely to find Sayre in a tavern." Thomas Coutts said shortly. "Or a coffee house at best. He is out of the Tower now, where he was placed for seditious activities, and I understand he still dabbles on the most disreputable fringes of the insurance markets, where men place wagers against possible events. War or peace at fixed odds! Disgraceful! It is no better than gambling, sir. With little to distinguish it from the card table, which is a source of so much distress even amid the best of society." Coutts looked at Charles with open disapproval for a moment. Then gathering himself he went on coldly.

"But if he is sober you might find Mr Sayre at Jonathon's Coffee House in Exchange Alley. Jonathon's is not the place that it once was, of course. Not in the least the same. Since the stock-jobbers moved out to the Royal Exchange it has gone down greatly in the world." He smiled bleakly and inclined his head. "As has Mr Sayre, I fear. Now good-day to you, sir. Please let me know if I can be of further service. I shall be able to contact you at Lord Stormont's meanwhile, I presume? Now if you will give my clerk a sample of your hand, I must press on with other matters."

Within minutes Charles was back on the Strand, pushing his way through the crowded street, his mind whirring in confused speculation. What in the world did Deane want with a man of such reputation? For Sayre was clearly well-known in London and just as clearly there was something about him that Thomas Coutts knew, did not like and was not prepared to reveal.

Of course Coutts might simply be prejudiced. Sayre's political views would certainly not be to the taste of the cautious banker, that was perfectly understandable. Still, Charles thought firmly, he would judge Stephen Sayre for himself when once he had seen the man and assessed him. Assuming of course that he was out of gaol.

ELEVEN

Thomas Graham had outlined to Charles the geography of the city. "In spite of all its bustling affluence, you know, the centre of London is quite a compact area. One may walk briskly from one side to the other in an hour or two, from the Tower to Westminster Abbey. Though," he had added in a cautionary tone, " there are areas into which one had better not go after dark." The Strand and the river seemed to function as the two great thoroughfares of the city, running roughly parallel with each other east and west: the newly fashionable Strand with its rows of elegant townhouses only recently transformed from a long sweep of riverside wharfs, warehouses, docks, waterside steps and taverns and even stretches of shingle beach.

From his temporary lodgings in the Savoy Charles had already observed that the river seemed almost as busy as the Strand itself, packed as it was with every shape and size of vessel, from great North Sea barges to small skiffs that could be hailed from a multitude of landing stages and which for a modest fare would take passengers up and down, or to and fro across the great river.

To the west lay the smart political coffee houses and the ministry buildings of Westminster and Whitehall, Parliament and the Court, the royal parks and the fashionable new squares where lived the rich and the great men of England. To the east, towards which he was now bound, was the commercial heart of the city; the centres of banking, shipping, insurance and broking of all kinds, as well as industries like printing and publishing.

Further east still, as Thomas had explained, lay the dark

manufacturing areas where tinsmiths, brewers and distillers, textile workers and glass makers plied their dirty trades. Around them and beyond them, running down east were dank and dangerous slums where only the poorest lived in wretched conditions, generally dulling their senses with what drink or drugs they could afford.

Charles made his way steadily along the Strand and into Fleet street, crossing the bridge over the turgid Fleet Ditch and up Ludgate Hill towards St Paul's. Cutting through the great church precinct he found himself in Cheapside and Poultry, gazing with interest at the assortment of publishing houses and taverns as he went. Near the Exchange he enquired of a passer-by and was promptly directed to Jonathon's Coffee House in the nearby Change Alley.

Jonathon's may have come down in the world as Coutts had said. But clearly it was still well known, Charles decided. He pushed open the heavy wooden door and stepped into the dark interior, to be immediately assailed by a powerful smell of coffee and tobacco. As his eyes adjusted to the dim interior he saw a large low-ceilinged room, panelled in some cheap wood stained and darkened by years of smoke. A small fire burned in a grate halfway down one side and down the middle of the room ran a long wooden table littered with clay pipes, empty coffee cups and a scattering of newssheets and gazettes including the London Evening Post and the Morning Chronicle, providing the news of the day for a small charge. On one wall was a bookcase containing a few books, including, Charles noted, a bible, as well as an assortment of curious objects that at first glance Charles could not identify, some cups, bottles and dishes.

On the wall hung a mass of official-looking notices and rules describing what the customers might under no circumstances do. Charles noted that these included swearing, quarrelling with other customers, discussing things spiritual, maligning the political authorities and, at this he gave a short laugh, depressing the place by being maudlin in love. Games of chance and cards were also prohibited.

Making a mental note to avoid all of these things, he surveyed the room, which was empty apart from one small untidy figure slumped on a stool near the hearth and a large plump lady in a cap who stood staring at Charles with some interest. He made his way towards her and smiled. "Good day Madam. May I enquire if you know a gentleman by the name of Sayre?" he asked her pleasantly.

Just as she opened her mouth to reply the small figure by the fire stirred himself. "Who wants to know?" he grunted sourly, not even looking up.

Charles turned, still pleasantly but instantly smarting at the little fellow's rudeness. "Why, I want to know, my dear sir. That of course is the point of my enquiry."

"And who the devil are you, sir? I suppose you have a name that you are not ashamed to give."

"My name is Charles George Macpherson," said Charles stiffly. "And I am by no means ashamed of that name, which is esteemed both in Scotland and in New York." As he heard himself speak Charles was uncomfortably aware that he sounded like his father.

He was in the act of turned back to the woman by the fire when the man spoke again. "New York eh," the small man said. "So you are from the benighted colonies! Well, well!"

Charles studied him for a moment coldly, trying not to show the irritation he felt rising within him. The man was quite small and slightly built with a pale thin unhealthy face and large watery angry-looking eyes. Fair hair straggled down from a high forehead and there was a wispy beard and moustache around a weak mouth. He was dressed in an old fashioned but good quality black silk court-dress that had seen better days. Charles saw that his shoes were badly worn, in places actually split. Some poor crank, he thought and he knew he should ignore the fellow. But before he had time to collect himself he heard himself reply. "Colonies they are for the moment, perhaps. But at least that is where I call home."

The little man rose with shabby dignity. "And what may I ask does Mr Charles George MacPherson want with Mr Stephen Sayre?"

This was too much and Charles was about to answer the little man roughly when the use of the Christian name dawned on him. "Ah! You know Mr Sayre?"

"None better." The man turned towards the woman. "Maria, please tell our young friend who I am."

The woman cackled. "Why, I recall that last time the watch came looking for you they called you Mr Stephen Sayre! So I reckon that's your name! Now young sir, will you take some of our fine coffee?"

The man bowed to Charles in mock respect. "I am Stephen Sayre. At your service, of course. Now, may I ask again, what is your business with me?"

Charles stared at him, still smarting at the man's rudeness but vaguely aware too that others had entered the coffee house. "I have come from Paris lately." he said in a low voice, remembering Deane's warnings. There was a slight change in Sayre's watery eyes. "And I bring you a message from a mutual friend." Unconsciously he reached up to touch the letter hidden in his coat.

"Not here!" Sayre whispered violently, fairly spitting out the words. Then with an unconvincing smile he added in a more natural tone, "If you will give Maria here two pennies I will take a dish of coffee with you and give you such directions as you need."

In a lower voice he added. "Young sir, do not turn immediately. But pray take a cautious look at the man who has just come into the room. Dressed all in brown; black hair and he stands by the door reading the notices. Take a good look and tell me if you have seen him before. Perhaps in the street? But be sure to remember him, for you will almost certainly see him again." He gave a savage half-choked little laugh.

Charles paid for the coffee and followed Sayre to the far end of the long table, glancing casually towards the door as he did so. He sat down and shook his head. "I have never seen that man before. Who might he be?"

Sayre grunted. "One of Wentworth's fellows." Then seeing Charles's blank look, "one of Paul Wentworth's men," he said slowly and clearly, speaking as if addressing someone of weak mind. Charles sipped his coffee and shook his head, staring at Sayre silently. The man's words meant nothing to him and he was beginning to wonder if Sayre was drunk. Or possibly mad. Certainly Thomas Coutts had warned him to expect something odd from this meeting. Now it was Sayre's turn to stare. He pursed his thin lips. "Your message is from Silas Deane, I assume?" Charles nodded assent. "Why in God's name does he do it," Sayre muttered savagely to himself. "And where does he find such messengers?" He sat back and gazed disgustedly at Charles. Then with a sigh he leaned forward and spoke in a low voice.

"Wentworth is one of Eden's best agents, a loyalist from New Hampshire. One of our turncoats stationed in England and responsible for the surveillance of Americans in Europe. You know that I am from Philadelphia originally?" He gave a sneering smile. "Yes, an American, like yourself. Why else was I in the tower? Does that not make you think, young MacPherson?"

A cold chill struck the pit of his stomach as Charles considered the full implications of what he was hearing. He had no reason to doubt Sayre's words. Yet most of what he had to say was meaningless to him. "Eden?" he asked. "Just who is he?"

Sayre simply pursed his lips again. "William Eden? He is an English aristocrat, Eton and Oxford and all that sort of thing. A member of parliament who has run several important government offices in his time. Earlier this year Eden was appointed to the Board of Trade and

Plantations, which means that one of his prime tasks is the surveillance of Americans in Europe." Sayre glanced at him sardonically. "I dare say even you will know that we are seeking alliances to combat the British. Well, Eden has a network of agents who keep an eye on American activity in every major capital in Europe and send him reports on anything interesting. Do you think he knows about you, Master MacPherson? For he certainly knows about me!" Sayre broke into a loud cackle and punched Charles lightly on the chest.

Charles flushed. Quite soon this Eden fellow will know about me too, he thought grimly. Which means that Lord Stormont will also know, supposing that he was not already aware of my activities in Paris. Will he tell Thomas Graham? Indirectly probably; that's his way. Which in turn means that Mary too, will know-----.

His heart sank as he sat in silence sipping his coffee. He felt the sudden heat of embarrassment, his mind racing. Beaumarchais of course was already well known to Stormont. In which case----. Oh God! Juliana Ritchie! He groaned inwardly at the thought of facing his new friends with this new knowledge. For it seemed, almost imperceptibly, that the good opinion of the Grahams had become important to him.

"Do you know the bookshop of Edward and Charles Dilly in the Poultry?"

Charles shook his head. "No. But I'll find it." Sayre did not look too sanguine about that possibility. But Charles was too preoccupied with his thoughts to notice. Edward Dilly? Yes, he recalled that Franklin had mentioned that name. "Dilly the publisher?"

Sayre nodded briefly. "Who else? At 22, The Poultry, right by the Rose and Crown. The house will probably be under surveillance--- it usually is. But only friends are admitted there and as you already appear to be a marked man no harm will be done." Charles cringed inwardly at Sayre's words. "Meet me there at half past seven o'clock tonight and bring Deane's message with you. It can be handed over more confidentially there than in a public coffee house." He shook his head. "Really, I wonder at you, MacPherson."

Before Charles could respond, Sayre continued. "Now I shall leave and you shall remain for a half hour or so. That will give our friend by the door an interesting choice. But my guess is he will follow you rather than myself. The government knows all there is to know of me, I fancy, since my little sojourn in the Tower! Look out for him as you go. He or one of his fellows will not be far away!"

With that he rose and stalked from the coffee house, pausing only to collect a rather shabby court sword with a tasselled hilt from the rack by the door. There he turned and bowed graciously towards Charles.

That evening Charles presented himself at the home of Charles and Edward Dilly and gave his name to a large competent looking doorkeeper, sadly aware that all his well-intentioned plans to distance himself from Bancroft and Beaumarchais were dissolving. It seemed that events he could no longer control had taking over his life and he did not enjoy the feeling. For as Sayre had anticipated, the man in brown had followed Charles to his lodgings and was barely half a street behind him as he was admitted to the house at 22,The Poultry.

However there was no time for him to consider how to deal with the situation that would await him in Paris before he found himself ushered into the large comfortable drawing room of the famous publisher brothers. It was brightly lit, crowded with strangers and filled with a buzz of conversation. Charles was greeted at once by the tall and graceful Edward Dilly, well-dressed and bewigged, obviously well-to-do and wearing what Charles had learned was the standard blue coat and buff waistcoat of a pro-American English Whig. "My dear young man, you are most welcome to our gathering!"

Charles had been apprehensive about this meeting. But in the event he need not have worried, being required to do no more than smile and nod as Dilly, chattering non-stop, ushered him around the room making a bewildering succession of introductions to small groups of men and the few women, all of whom were deep in their own conversations and scarcely noticed Charles. Only one lady, a tall rather plain woman with dark hair and a long nose and face that reminded Charles rather ungallantly of a horse, took any note of him. She was dressed all in black and had been recently widowed by the death of a rich husband.

"Ah," she said in response to Edward Dilly's introduction. "I am always delighted to meet an American patriot. Why anyone should want to serve under a king anywhere is beyond me. But to do so in a land so remote, so very different and with such great potential would be very odd indeed."

As Dilly steered him around the room he whispered, "Catherine Macaulay. She of the 'History of England'. I think she is on the fourth volume at present, if I am not mistaken. Are you familiar with her work? Her defence of Oliver Cromwell has endeared her to many of the republican view and even to a surprising number of moderate Whigs. Though Edmund Burke calls her a 'republican Virago', ha, ha ha!"

From somewhere in the depth of his memory Charles dredged up something vaguely relevant. "I'm afraid the only one of your publications that I am familiar with is Cavallo's 'Treatise of Electricity'. By the way," he added casually. "Mr Benjamin Franklin asked me to give you his regards."

Dilly spared him a closer look. "Ah! You are a friend of Franklin and a man of science! Excellent, excellent! Now there is our friend Stephen. So I shall leave you to his care. But do circulate and meet the others when it suits you."

Sayre was sitting on a window seat, clutching a glass of steaming punch. "You have come," he said shortly and held out his hand. "I'll take our friend's instruction now." As he tucked Deane's letter inside his old court coat he nodded around the room. "All the great names of radical England," he said sardonically. "Some of them have even been in gaol for their opinions. Though most of them have done quite well out of it, unlike myself!"

Charles, relieved to have rid himself of Deane's communication, looked at Sayre questioningly. "You see the gentleman by the fireplace? The fashionable one with the very ugly face? The one all in lace? That is the famous John Wilkes. It is a trouble to know who enjoys hearing himself talk the more, Wilkes or Edward Dilly. Charles Dilly, his brother, is a different kettle of fish. He is here somewhere about. A man of moderate opinions politically. So he will do well." Sayre said dryly, draining his glass and looking about anxiously for a refill.

"You will know that Wilkes has been in trouble with the Parliament," he added casually, "over the publication of their proceedings. Though now he is a member of the House himself I dare say we will see a different side of him." He scowled across the room at Wilkes. "I do not care for him. He is a poseur. He makes a lot of noise and the mob loves him. But for me he lacks true convictions. Other than for publishing obscene poetry!" He sniggered at his own witticism. "No, I fear Wilkes does not have the stature to lead a radical political movement in this or any other country. At the moment he's more interested in becoming City Chamberlain and repairing his own fortunes than in support for liberty and freedom. Very wise too," he added sarcastically.

"What of the lady in black?"

"Ah, very different," Sayre said grudgingly. "Her heart is in the right place. If she has a heart, that is to say," he said with a sneer. "But she is a true friend of America and an enemy of the monarchy. It is a wonder that they do not conspire to send her to the Tower! But she is too clever for them and has influential friends. As well as money," he added morosely.

"You were in the Tower yourself, I understand."

"For five days only," Sayre said shortly. "A trumped up charge that my lawyer John Reynolds was easily able to overturn. That is him in conversation with Wilkes now. They are very close." Charles noted the elegant man, dressed in grey with a plain white cravat, who stood listening to Wilkes in deep concentration, nodding in apparent agreement as Wilkes expounded on something or other.

"So Wilkes helped you indirectly," asked Charles. "Is not that rather in his favour?"

"I suppose it is. As far as it goes." Sayre said shortly and fell into silence.

Charles ploughed gamely on. "Though I want nothing more than to remove the King from around our necks at home, I must admit that I have been impressed by what I have seen of London. It seems so much better ordered than what I found in Paris. Is there not something to be said for a system that produces such wealth and comfort for people?"

Sayre glanced at the young man beside him. There was the hint of a smile on his pale face. "After supper, when once we have eaten, let us take a walk, you and I. There are things in this fair city that I think you should see if you hope to understand the way this country is governed."

As darkness fell the two of them took their leave and Sayre led Charles out towards St Paul's, turning north into the maze of mean back streets that lay towards Smithfield, Clarkenwell and the Covent Garden market. "I dare say you've noticed the black people in this city; servants and coachmen, the waiters?" They had barely registered with Charles, accustomed as he was to seeing black slaves throughout New York.

Sayre stopped abruptly in the street and faced him. "Why man, do you not see! They are one of the awful results of the great English empire!" he cried out. "Of exploitation and slavery! People cruelly wrenched from their homelands and sold like chattels! How can any society tolerate such degradation without being dragged down to degradation itself? I tell you, this country contains within it the seeds of its own destruction. The trade with the East Indies is almost as vile! Making war on primitive defenceless nations and subjugating them for the sake of luxuries like silks and spices that only the rich and powerful can afford to buy."

Charles, stunned by his vehemence, murmured something about supposing these offences to be in the process of change and did not the religious establishment seek to improve the lot of these people? "You mean the church?" Sayre said scornfully. "I share the opinion of Tom Paine on that matter. Churches are no more than inventions to terrify mankind and monopolise power for the upper classes. In any case," he went on, "just look about you."

As Sayre had been lecturing him they had wandered into the dark sordid alleys around the Fleet Prison and across the fetid Fleet Ditch. Looking about in the darkness Charles could now see a very different London. The broad glass-fronted streets that he had admired earlier in the day, only a short way south towards the river, seemed to be in another world.

On every side amid the rubbish that littered the narrow lanes lay groups of poor drunken wretches, men and women, shabbily dressed and sprawled half-conscious in the filthy gutters, many still clutching half empty flasks of gin. Some of the women, almost all fat and grimy, had small children or infants clinging desperately to them, whimpering miserably and Charles was horrified to see from time to time some of the children being pacified with gin from their mother's bottle.

Looking about, Sayre pointed to where a small group of younger prostitutes lounged drunkenly outside one of the late night coffee houses. The women promptly broke out into shrill cries of ribald welcome to the two men. "There they wait," Sayre said sourly, "for customers willing to join them in their misery and infection. Are they and those other unfortunates not as much victims of this great empire as the blacks slaves? If only their male customers could see the filthy night-cellars the poor wretches return to when their work is done! Diseased, infested with rats and crowded with the sick and insane dregs of this society. Have you even seen a penny-a-night public lodging house, which at least has beds, albeit stinking heaps. But better by far than the dark basement cellars where the poor people of this wonderful city bed down each night, men and women together on heaps of straw and old sacking."

"I have not sir," Charles said rather primly. "And I have no desire to do so. However I take the point of your argument. As you know, I am no lover of a monarchy."

But still Sayre was not satisfied. "And let me assure you that even these pits of iniquity are better than the bulks." Charles look enquiringly at him, beginning to regret embarking on this walk with Sayre. "I dare say you have no idea about the bulks!" Sayre cried angrily. "They are the wooden shelves outside the market stalls in Covent Garden or Billingsgate or Smithfield, used for fish or meat or vegetables by day. Even there, in summer at least, amidst the rotting food you will find the poor devils who gain nothing and lose everything in this cruel city. In winter they wander further east and find a glass works and sleep, or try to sleep, on the warm ashes from the furnaces, rising from the ashes in the morning, if they rise at all, like grey ghosts." Sayre paused and flushed, perhaps realising that he had ridden his hobbyhorse too far.

"Does parliament not interest itself in what is happening here, almost in their faces?"

Sayre smiled bitterly. He drew his sword and made an aimless cut in the darkness. "Parliament sleeps soundly enough when it comes to such matters. You will find that they are more interested in maintaining their own privileges. Though when it comes to anything touching on them personally, why then you can be sure they are wide awake!"

By now their wanderings had taken them far to the west, almost to Charing Cross. Sayre looked about him, still with his sword unsheathed in his hand. "I need a glass of brandy. Come, there is a late night place over there. It calls itself a coffee house but after midnight only the houses of ill-fame are open. Still, they serve good liquor and if we mind our step all will be well."

He strode off across the dark street and was about to push open the door ahead of Charles when three men appeared swiftly from a nearby alley. Charles realised in a flash that they were going to attack Sayre and sprang forward with a shout just as one of the men swung a heavy club at his companion's head.

With a blow of his shoulder he sent the first man sprawling into the street and in an instant he and Sayre were standing back to back, he with his dirk in his hand and Sayre with the long blade of his sword. The other two men leapt at them and Charles saw the dim light of the doorway glinting on blades. Sayre, a much smaller man, parried one thrust from his attacker and then struck, the point of his court sword catching the man high up on his shoulder. At the same time, as one of the men raised a knife to slash at him Charles seized him by the wrist. For an instant he looked into the man's eyes and saw fear there.

Then deliberately turning his hand he smashed the hilt of his dirk against the man's throat. As his unknown enemy staggered back gasping for breath Charles kicked him in the groin. Swiftly turning to face the first attacker while Sayre watched, panting for breath, Charles clubbed the man heavily behind the ear as he tried to rise. The man flopped forward and lay still. The other two reeled away into the darkness and Charles gasped out, "My God! Robbers in the very heart of the city!"

Sayre heaved the prostrate body over and in the faint light Charles saw the face of the man from Jonathon's Coffee House. "No," said Sayre. "Wentworth's men. No doubt anxious to see what message you brought with you from Paris." He looked around furtively. "Let us get away from here," he said nervously. "Come, I'll walk with you to your lodgings. I dare say they will give us a glass of brandy, even at this hour." He gave a slightly forced laugh. "I must tell you that I need one all the more! But didn't I handle that fellow well?"

By the time they reached the inn Sayre had regained his swaggering stride and seemed to have quite recovered himself when they were seated by the brightly blazing fire in the deserted snug. "By Jove," he said as he downed his first brandy. "That was well done. But you too handled yourself well, my dear young sir! It was a treat to see the way you dealt with those scoundrels. I am truly glad you were with me tonight. Though when the news gets about it will not do your reputation any good in certain quarters" He eyed Charles thoughtfully. "They were obviously after the message you brought me from Deane. But how did they know you would be the messenger? It is usually Edward Bancroft who carries these notes. He comes to London frequently on his own or Deane's business. Between them they make a fair bit of money from time to time."

Charles stared at him. "Edward Bancroft the physician? Franklin's secretary?"

"Oh yes," said Sayre casually. "They are old associates. Deane was his teacher at one stage I believe and Bancroft was appointed to the mission on Deane's recommendation. Not that I would trust Master Bancroft with anything political. Nor anything to do with money, either," he added. "For I happen to know that Bancroft used to work as a surgeon for Paul Wentworth on his plantation in Surinam. Of course that was before Wentworth became a British agent. But even so it does not bode well. No, Bancroft is one to watch." He hesitated for a moment. "But he and Silas Deane have an excellent financial scheme that I should love to share in. You know that Deane takes a commission on all the supplies he purchases for the Congress. Not bad, eh?"

Charles shook his head in wonder. "Oh, that part is all legitimate enough," went on Sayre. "That much was agreed by Congress. But Deane has also a personal trade--- again it is quite legal. Except of course that he ships his cargoes without declaring them to be a private venture and not official business. Then, if they get through safely to Philadelphia or New York he sells them on his own account. But if they are taken by the British blockading fleet, why they are suddenly official! The cost is borne by the American people! Brilliantly simple, is it not?"

Sayre smiled half to himself and shook his head as he stared into his brandy. Then he looked slowly up at Charles. "You know, young sir, you did so well tonight that I am tempted to offer you a share in the wager. Would that suit you at all?"

Charles gazed at him. "Wager? What wager is that?"

A frown passed over Sayre's white face. Then a look of understanding came into his eyes. "Ah, I see Deane has not confided in you entirely. Of course he wouldn't!" He gave a snort. "A mean little fellow like Deane would share nothing, not even with a friend. If he had one, that is to say!" he guffawed.

He leaned over and patted his companion's the thigh, much to Charles's unease. "The wager--- the insurance--- is that England and France will be at war within six months." Charles gazed at him in astonishment. "I have odds of five to one against that event. Deane, who knows exactly how the negotiations stand," he gave a low snigger, "Deane is wagering £1,000 on the result. So he stands to gain £5,000 of course." He sat back with a thin smile. "I take a meagre percentage for my trouble." Sayre leaned closer. "A young man of means like yourself could earn a pretty sum if I were to act for you in an similar manner. What do you say?"

The full implication of what he was being told and the transparent truth of the matter struck Charles suddenly. He stared at Sayre in horror and immediately his new companion, misunderstanding his look, went on hastily, "But for you, of course, in view of our comradeship in arms and tonight's little affair, I would only take, say three percent. What do you say to that?"

Charles felt his head spin and his grasp on reality begin to slip. Could it be that Silas Deane, a man at the heart of the American mission to France and a representative of the Congress in Philadelphia, one of Franklin's closest associates, was no more than a despicable speculator? A man seeking to make personal gain from a privileged position while others, honest soldiers like Francis Johnson, lived in hardship and peril. And what of Edward Bancroft! Almost certainly a traitor and also a close associate of Franklin! It seemed there was treason and corruption on every side.

Anger and disgust rose up within him. He glared angrily at Sayre This was the man who had spoken so vehemently about the social degradation of England! Charles shook his head. "No," he said tersely. "I want no part of any such scheme."

TWELVE

This eventful year is wearing on rapidly, Charles mused as he rattled from Calais through the dark warm night. In truth all he wanted now was get back to Paris and set some things to right. Not that it would be simple, he thought uneasily. But above all he must ensure that Franklin was warned of the treason that surrounded him. Juliana Ritchie was key to that, of course.

Staring out into the blackness he considered his own future. Apprehension struck him as he realised that he must soon face Thomas and Mary and indeed all his new friends with the knowledge of his activities. For their good opinion seemed suddenly to assume great importance to him.

At heart he knew he was still an American patriot and always would be. Of that there was no doubt. But already he had seen great good indeed and kindness in those whom he had once considered enemies: first William Cathcart, then Thomas Graham and of course Mary and her sister too. Now he was aware that some of his fellow patriots were deeply flawed, just as flawed as any foe! How to balance these conflicting loyalties? It was a question that vexed him.

But before he could confront that issue it was essential for Benjamin Franklin to be warned about the treachery that surrounded him. Juliana was known to Franklin and more likely to be trusted than he himself. Had it not been her suspicions about Bancroft which had sparked the entire matter? Yes, Juliana was undoubtedly the best person to break the news to Franklin. After that? Well, after that he would have to see.

Charles did not hesitate on his arrival in Paris but went straight to the home of Juliana Ritchie, late though it was. The carriage rattled to a stop and he hurried into the small courtyard, half aware that another carriage stood silently in the shadows. He hammered on the door and waited impatiently. It was only just half past ten and he was sure that he would find Juliana still awake. The prospect of her warmth began to creep pleasurably into his mind. But quickly he focussed on the main reason for his visit. When the heavy door opened he saw Juliana's maid, an older woman who knew him well. She looked startled to see him.

Charles pushed past her before she could speak. "I must see your mistress," he said abruptly. "It is most urgent. Please tell her I am here."

The woman stood uncertainly in the hallway. "Madam has retired for the night," she said hesitantly.

"Go to her then and tell her I need to see her urgently."

The maid's confusion was obvious. "I---, I am afraid sir, that I cannot disturb her."

"Not disturb her?"

"No sir. Madam Ritchie gave specific instructions that she is not to be disturbed."

Charles stared at her in blank incomprehension. "But it is barely eleven o'clock!" he cried. "She is not unwell?"

The woman half smiled and shook her head. "No," she said simply. "Madam is not unwell. She is simply----," she paused and shrugged. "unable to be disturbed. Can Monsieur not understand?"

The truth dawned slowly and Charles felt himself flush with embarrassment. How could he have been so stupid, so presumptuous! Juliana was not alone in her bedroom. Of course, the strange carriage in the courtyard. A host of emotions rushed through him; initially a sense of shame at his own callowness. But also anger. How dare she do this to him!

He collected his wits and scribbled a note, handing it to Juliana's maid, who stood clutching her robe anxiously about her shoulders. "Here," he said curtly. "Make sure she receives this as soon as---- as soon as," he stumbled out, "as soon as she awakes in the morning. It is imperative that I see her."

As he mounted his own carriage he stared across at the other vehicle. There was a monogram on the door bearing the interlaced letters

'PACdeB'. Beaumarchais, he thought in bewilderment! But how could that be? Had she not told him quite clearly that Beaumarchais was not her lover?

His mind was spinning in a wild turmoil as the carriage bore him back across Paris towards the embassy. Was there no one in the world that he could trust? How could she have taken that buffoon to her bed! What right had she to betray him like this? Yet even in his turmoil he found a crumb of reason. What did Juliana owe to him? He had no special claim on her. She had told him clearly enough that she was no man's mistress.

Only his own egotism, he realised, had made him misunderstand that message; probably wilfully misunderstand it, he admitted. She was her own mistress, she had said that plainly enough. What she did with her body was her--- and only her--- concern. The initial sense of outrage had almost died away by the time he reached his own room. But still, as he fell into bed, a new sadness weighed heavily on him. Was nothing what it seemed? How he missed the old certainties of his earlier life!

Next morning early he rode back to Juliana Ritchie's house, dreading what he might find but knowing that he must see her. There was no sign of the strange carriage and Juliana received him promptly, still in a dressing robe, her red hair unconfined and falling about her face.

She was seated in her private sitting room with a tray of hot chocolate beside her. Ignoring his initial awkwardness she rose to give him an amiable kiss. "Charlie, my dear!" she said softly. "I am truly sorry about--- last night. But what is so urgent? Did something happen in London?" It was clear from her studied calm that she intended to ignore the events of the previous evening.

But Charles knew that he could not ignore it, the pain was too much to allow him to rest in peace. He drew himself together mentally. "First," he said shortly, "you must go to Benjamin Franklin and warn him about Bancroft. The man is without doubt a traitor and Franklin's whole mission is riddled with spies and corruption. He needs to be told and you can do it better than anyone."

Juliana listened in silence as he told her what he had learned in London, including Bancroft's long term relationship with Paul Wentworth. "I see," she said simply. "But why must I go to Franklin?"

"You are well known to him and he respects you as a declared patriot. He will believe you rather than myself, a newcomer living in Lord Stormont's home and relatively unknown to him."

Suddenly Charles found himself unable to continue with this logical train of thought. He slumped into a chair and buried his head in his hands. He had to confront her with his agony. He looked up at her. "Juliana," he began. He hesitated, hardly daring to put what he knew into words. "Last night--- ? Was Beaumarchais here?"

She looked at him levelly, her green eyes steady. "Yes," she said simply.

His heart dived again. "But, but----. Why?"

She gazed at him not unkindly. "Why do you ask?" she said calmly.

His head spinning, Charles blurted out, "Why do I ask? Because I thought--- ." He stopped, searching for the words that would set right this awful wound he felt. "I thought----,"

"You thought that because we had a couple of tumbles in bed that I belonged to you, is that it Charlie?"

He waved away the thought. "No, no! Of course, not that. But Beaumarchais?" He shook his head in dismay. "You said he was a buffoon! That he was nothing to you!"

Juliana smiled sadly at him. "He is a buffoon and he is less than nothing to me. Last night was nothing." She laid a hand on his shoulder. "It was quite unlike--- us." She said gently. "It was all over in a few minutes. Hardly worth thinking about."

"But why?" he said again, almost desperately.

"I wanted to know for certain where he stands vis-à-vis our cause," Juliana said, looking at him unflinchingly. "I knew he has been arranging to ship weapons to America--- he has made no secret of that. I dare say your friend Stormont knows all about that as well." Charles winced silently. "But I did not entirely trust him," she smiled. "To say the truth, I wondered if he could be such a fool as he seems to be. Or if he was playing some deeper game." She walked across the room and stood by the window, empty cup clutched in her hand.

Charles noticed absently how the late spring sunshine lightened her hair. "And?" he said dully, hardly caring now what she had to say.

"He is truly a fool." Juliana said with a wry grimace. "But after all an honest fool and a friend of our cause. Men tend to tell the truth on a pillow, I have noticed."

"I dare say," Charles said bitterly. Then he leapt to his feet suddenly. "And me? I suppose it was the same with me. A test of my loyalty? My God! I thought you loved me," Charles heard himself say hoarsely.

"No, it was not at all like that with you." Juliana shook her head. "It is difficult for you to believe me now, I know. Now or perhaps ever," she added sadly. "But in time you may come to understand that all you felt with me, all we felt together was real and true. And I can honestly tell you Charlie, that---," She hesitated, half turning to him, not quite daring to say all that was on her lips, not even daring to move a step towards him. "--- I felt the same as you."

She paused and Charles, staring at the carpet, shook his head. "I know you think now that you cannot not trust me," Juliana went boldly on. But she looked miserable and Charles glancing up realised with a sudden pang that he had never seen her like this. What do I really know about this woman, he thought desperately as he searched for words to reconnect with her. But the words were not there and he remained silently staring into her pale face.

"No," she said sadly. "You may never trust me again, Charlie," she went on, "and for that I will be truly sorry. More sorry than you can possibly imagine today." She turned away to stare out of the window. "Now I think you should go. I will speak to Mr Franklin. But please go now."

THIRTEEN

Two letters awaited him at Lord Stormont's house. He broke open the first and realised instantly that it was from Beaumarchais. With a curse he crumpled it into a ball and hurled it unread into the fireplace. With hands still shaking with rage he opened the other. To his astonishment it was from Francis Johnson!

"My dear Charlie," he read eagerly.

"I hardly know where to begin, so much has happened. First, let me hope all goes well with you in Paris. It must be exciting to be there now, with our delegation conducting discussions of such great consequence. Do you ever come across our people? In any case, I do hope that you are well and happy. I need hardly say that you are greatly missed here, not least by myself.

Life has been such a storm of activity here that I can scarcely believe the first winter of war has passed and summer upon us again, with all that means in terms of the military campaigns. Do not believe all that you may hear, Charlie. There have been some setbacks but true patriots are in good heart and do not doubt our eventual victory.

I grieve to tell you however that my people are very much divided between country and King, though perhaps no more than is the population in general, and as you might expect my uncle Joseph Brandt is hugely influential within the tribe. There is also a small group that seems to have gathered around myself to some extent and we have been helping our troops in the north east. In particular I have attached myself to General Benedict Arnold, who is a great leader, if somewhat unpredictable.

So we have much to do in the coming months. We hear that there is a strong British force coming down from Canada under Burgoyne to attack New York, while our old enemies the Huron have been making frequent raids into the upper Mohawk Valley. We believe a second British column will come down from Oswego to link with Burgoyne and this of course we will prevent at all cost.

I write particularly to tell you of an incident of which you should be aware, especially if you have any plans to return soon to New York, which incidentally I would not advise at present. It concerns your old friend the Reverend Snape, who true to form has been acting more and more against the patriotic interest. The Hurons have been coming sometimes in small raiding parties and sometimes with detachments of British and Loyalist troops, when they behave in a slightly more disciplined manner. Though I have to say not greatly so, for there have been some atrocious incidents against outlying farmsteads. Which is not surprising, as Burgoyne is paying them a bounty for scalps.

As you might imagine, with a cash bounty at stake the Huron make no attempt to distinguish between patriot and loyalist, killing, burning and raping randomly, which is greatly enraging feelings against all the tribes. I encountered one such incident near Fort Stanwix, where I was scouting for the besieged patriots in the fort. I stumbled on a Huron war party pillaging a loyalist smallholding, quite indifferent to the fact that these people are in theory their allies.

I was some way from the farmhouse and on the far side of a stream when I saw a group of five or six Huron. There was no sign of men folk from the farm and I saw that the raiding party were very drunk and arguing amongst themselves over possession of a young woman captive whom they were dragging away. You may know her, Jane McRae by name, a Presbyterian clergyman's daughter engaged to a loyalist lieutenant in General Burgoyne's army and hoping soon to be reunited with him, though this sadly is not to be. There was also another older woman whom at first I did not recognise, my attention being on young Jane McRae who was in such a bad state.

Before I could act, the disagreement flared into violence and the Huron first began to beat each other with their muskets, then several shots were fired and two of them fell dead. No loss, I thought, as that left me with only three to deal with. But tragically the young woman fell shot in the breast, whether by accident or design I could not tell as the incident escalated so rapidly. Before I could close with them one of the chiefs had taken her scalp and it grieved me to see that Huron toss the long and flowing blonde locks triumphantly into the air. I shot him at once and charged across the stream towards the others, when the two survivors ran off into the woods.

Miss McRae was already quite dead and I looked hurriedly at the other woman who lay in a swoon on the grass. To my surprise I saw at once that she was your old friend Charlotte Pemberton and at that moment I noticed a man hidden in a woodpile near the house and called to him, waiting only to see him emerge from his cowardly hiding-place before I went after the Huron. They were moving very fast and it was the best part of a day and a night before I caught up with them and killed them. They still had Miss McRae's scalp, which I burned, not wanting to be found with it on my person, as you will of course understand.

The important thing is that the man who hid himself in that cowardly way, abandoning the women to the Huron, was your old bête noir, the Reverend Snape, with whom incidentally Mrs Pemberton now lives, as his housekeeper some say. By the time I was able to return after dealing with the Huron, Snape, creature that he is, had aroused the local loyalists who were naturally incensed by Jane McRae's murder. Having persuaded them that the crime had been carried out by what he called renegade Mohawks, a group of locals then attacked one of our settlements further down the valley, where they killed members of my family including two of my sisters. This in spite of the fact that they were if anything inclined to support my uncle Joseph.

Snape had also villainously identified me as part of the war party who murdered Miss McRae, so that I had to flee for my life, the loyalists not being inclined to listen to my account. Snape and Mrs Pemberton have now vanished--- possibly fled to Philadelphia, which sadly is now in the hands of the British. I am determined, as you can imagine, to find Snape and deal with him for his crimes and treachery.

So for the moment all is in turmoil here. You can see how desperately we are divided amongst ourselves and Snape must wait for his comeuppance. But if you hear of him in England, where I believe he will sooner or later appear, please inform me of his whereabouts. You may guess now that Snape was responsible for some of your troubles and also that Charlotte Pemberton was a factor, in more ways than you imagined. In any event I write to warn you that he is still a danger and that he will almost certainly return to England eventually as that is where his influential friends are based. I am convinced that in spite of the present reverses there will soon be no place for him and his like here. So you would oblige me greatly by watching out for him and informing me if you have any news.

But be very careful, Charlie, for Snape has powerful connections in England. I am told that he has been acting for an English churchman called John Butler, who is a bishop of the church. Snape seems to be his agent here and my information is that Butler is fiercely anti-American and will stop at nothing to damage our cause.

Now I must say adieu Charlie, until we meet again. How I wish you were with us when such great events are at hand. But we both know why it was necessary for you to go. So very best wishes,

   From your good friend, Francis Johnson.

  Charles stared at the letter and for a moment or two he was carried back to the Mohawk Valley by his friend's words. Then the significance of what Francis was saying struck him hard. Charlotte Pemberton and Snape! The idea seemed at first so absurd that he almost laughed aloud. Then he was overwhelmed by disgust and then by a feeling closer to dismay and shame. Snape a sexual rival? How could she have come to that? And was Francis really telling him that Snape had been a rival all along? Perhaps even a rival lover! Charles curled his lip in silent revulsion. What could you think of a woman like that? And now Juliana and Beaumarchais!

  His sense of dismay quickly turned to a cold anger as he thought of the events of the previous night. The letter from Beaumarchais still lay near the fire. He recovered it now and spread it out on a side table, casting his eye over the elegantly formed words. A friendly letter, he thought with a scowl, reaffirming how much Beaumarchais had enjoyed their encounter, reminding Charles of their discussions and hoping to meet him soon to consider matters of mutual interest.

  It appeared that he had no idea that Charles and Juliana had become lovers. Why should he, Charles thought bitterly. And why would he care? With another curse Charles crushed the paper and hurled it back into the fireplace. This morning he could not bear to face his friends and without waiting to take breakfast he slipped silently and disconsolately out of the embassy.

  Wandering aimlessly into the city, his head still buzzing with rage and confusion, he was quite oblivious to the direction he took until he found himself in the garden of the Tuileries. There he rested for a moment on a small seat under a bower and looked about him bleakly. It was near here that he and Juliana---. His heart gave a lurch at the recollection and rising to his feet he silently swore to erase all the memories that so plagued him.

  He had turned and begun to walk away when directly in front of him he saw a small group of fashionable young women standing in active conversation beneath their parasols. Just beyond them he was vaguely aware that two men also stood talking, leaning casually on their canes. As he passed the women one of them turned towards him with a smile. It was Charlotte Barrault, the pretty blonde actress with the foolish gambling instincts.

Of course! He remembered her from the Beaumarchais house that first night he thought, with a pang as the memory of Juliana slid unbidden into his mind. "Why, it is my kind advisor!" Charlotte Barrault said, laying her hand on his sleeve. "How is it I have not seen you at the Comédie-Française? Are you not fond of a little drama? Or even a comedy!" The other young women, mostly actresses from the theatre, giggled as Charles, still lost for words, gazed speechlessly at the girl. She was very pretty, he thought. Not as beautiful as Juliana. But fresh and appealing. Her large emotional eyes, he decided, were the blue of cornflowers.

Bowing graciously Charles took her hand and kissed it. "I am no great hand at theatre. But I do hope I may be able to advise you again before long." As he spoke he was aware that Charlotte's eyes had widened in alarm and that she was staring at something just beyond his shoulder.

Suddenly he felt a blow on his shoulder that caused him almost to stumbled. Pivoting rapidly he saw the angry middle-aged man he also recalled from the Beaumarchais party. Juliana's words of warning came into his mind as the elegantly dressed man took Charlotte Barrault by the arm, turning his back on Charles as he did so. "Come my dear," he said. "This is no place for you."

As Charles realised later, when he had taken time to analyse his feels rationally, the savage emotion that rose within him did not stem from this stupid man's actions. But in the moment he forgot himself. Stepping forward he tapped Charlotte's protector firmly on his shoulder. "Forgive me sir," he said coldly. "I was speaking to your charming daughter and did not expect to be so rudely interrupted."

An exclamation of mixed gasps and ill-concealed giggles came from the small group of Charlotte's friends. The man stared back at Charles in astonishment, his face reddening. "How dare you---- ." he started to say.

But Charles continued relentlessly. "Of course, perhaps she is not your daughter. In which case you I hope you will forgive me. The all-too obvious disparity in your ages led me to that assumption. Meanwhile, I was in the midst of a conversation with the young lady when you intervened so rudely." Charles inclined his head to the man and half turned towards Charlotte, keeping the man in view. He was well aware of the deliberate offence he was causing. But at that moment he was beyond caring.

Charlotte Barrault's protector, red with fury, raised his cane and struck out at Charles, who half avoided and half blocked the blow with one arm. But as the man went to strike again, suddenly all the deep seated resentment and anger that Charles had been nursing flared into action. A kaleidoscope of feelings and memories flashed before him: Pemberton with a whip, the odious Snape and the foolish Beaumarchais all merged for an instant into a pure image of hate.

His fist crashed into his antagonist's hateful red face, sending him sprawling onto the path, only half conscious. He noted in a detached way that Charlotte Barrault had rushed to the man's side and that his male companion was helping him to his feet, dazed and shaken. He watched calmly as the two of them tended to the man, finally leading him away to a nearby carriage.

Then the man's companion returned. "Sir," he said stiffly to Charles. "I imagine that M. de Lapouyade will want satisfaction from you in due course. May I enquire where I shall be able to contact your representative to make arrangements?" Only half grasping the man's intention, Charles stared at him. "My name is Charles George MacPherson and I can be found at the home of Lord Stormont, the British Ambassador."

"Ah! An Englishman!" the man said smugly, as if that explained the bizarre nature of the incident.

Charles gazed at him icily. "No, sir. An American---- and as for my representative," he hesitated for just a moment. Whom could he rely upon in these strangely confusing days?

He heard himself speak the words that told him more about his feelings than he had been willing to admit even to himself. "My friend, Mr Thomas Graham will be happy to meet you and to make whatever arrangements you think appropriate."

FOURTEEN

Thomas Graham stepped back, looking grave as for the third time in five minutes Charles stooped to recover his sword from the floor. Then Thomas examined the blade of his own weapon in silence. But even before he or John Sewell, who stood morosely watching their exercise, could speak Charles knew his chances of surviving this kind of duel with de Lapouyade were slight, if not actually non-existent. Thomas gazed with a frown at the floor between his feet. "Well Charles," he said with an awkward cough. "You are obviously not a fighting man."

Suddenly conscious of Charles's outraged glare, he went on hastily. "I mean in the duelling sense, of course." He paused. "No more am I, for that matter. I have never been out on a matter of honour, as they call it." He smiled at Charles apologetically. "Never seen the need to. Never had the cause, I mean. Somehow it just hasn't arisen."

He gazed agonizingly at the young man, his big open face showing his concern. "If I had three months to work with you, I dare say you would put up a creditable show. You are strong and agile and given time----." He glanced over to where Sewell stood leaning against an end wall of the secluded basement room. Charles now knew that John Sewell was one of Stormont's personal guards and as an expert on weapons Thomas had consulted him confidentially. Sewell silently shook his head, his angular jaw set.

"But time is what we do not have." Charles said disgustedly. "I meet this wretched man Lapouyade the day after tomorrow, at some ungodly hour of the morning." He replaced the sword on a rack. "Now if I could just take a dirk to him---," he said quietly. The others looked suitably shocked at the notion. "No," said Charles firmly. "Pistols it must be. I know you say pistols are more likely to bring a lethal end to the affair," he said, turning to Sewell. "But as you can see, I am a complete novice at this other business. At least I know how to shoot straight."

Thomas Graham looked at them gravely. He had done everything that honourably could be done to avoid this outcome and though he had confided in Sewell he still hoped to keep the affair from the ears of his brother-in-law. Just as importantly, he wanted desperately to keep it from Mary. If Charles should kill this Frenchman it would become a diplomatic issue. But if Charles were to be seriously injured-----.

His heart sank at the thought of having to explain a disaster like that to Mary and Louisa, for the young man had become quite a favourite. Almost a substitute for their brother Charles, he thought as he eyed his new protégé. "In an affair of honour like this," he said slowly, "it is often enough for one party or the other to take a minor flesh wound. The merest scratch sometimes suffices."

He sighed. "Sewell here tells me that de Lapouyade has a reputation and has fought several times it seems. His life style apparently brings him into this situation surprisingly often," he added dryly. "In any event, he is an accomplished swordsman by all accounts. Perhaps a quick bout and a slight flesh wound----," His voice tailed away as he saw the look on Charles's face. Then, undaunted, he soldiered on. "Even at this stage an apology would be acceptable, I believe," he added hopefully.

"Not to me," Charles said calmly. "He attacked me with his damned stick! It was only then that I knocked him down." He gave a small grimace and a wave of his hand, glancing at the bruised knuckles. "Though I dare say I did my best to provoke him." He fell silent for a moment. Then he turned fiercely back to Thomas and Sewell. "But only after he had intruded on my private conversation with the young lady. No, damn him! Why should I apologise?"

He gazed out of the small window set high in the wall and saw a glimpse of blue sky, remembering the Mohawk Valley in summer. He shrugged his shoulders casually. "What does it matter in any case? I dare say both of us acted stupidly. But it is done now and it is only a case of paying the piper."

"Right," said Thomas Graham in a businesslike voice. "I have a pair of excellent duelling pistols which I shall prepare for you. Let us all three ride out to a quiet spot and see what you can do with them. I need not inform your opponent's second of our choice of weapons until this evening."

An hour later Sewell, Thomas Graham and Charles stood together in a small wood on the banks of the Seine near the secluded corner of the Champ-de-Mars that had been selected for the duel. Thomas pinned a playing card to a stout tree and paced out the twenty yards that would separate the adversaries the following morning. "You'll be firing north and south so as not to be blinded, either of you, by an early glint of sunlight. That is only fair."

He handed the first pistol to Charles who studied it admiringly. He had never seen such a lovely weapon, beautifully balanced and finely decorated. As he hefted it in his hand, judging the weight and gazing across the grass at the white card, he noted with a wry smile that by accident or design Thomas had selected the ace of hearts.

"You know how to shoot, do you Charles? I mean, do you need any advice?"

Charles smiled and took up the firing position that Sewell had explained to him, sideways to the opponent to reduce the size of target presented. He raised the pistol, which seemed as light as a feather in his hand, left arm by his side, took quick aim and fired.

Thomas gasped and John Sewell walked forward with a little smile on his face to study the card more closely. Then he turned back to them. "You have shot the heart out of him!" he called out delightedly. "Can you do that again?"

Charles took the other pistol from Thomas Graham, took an easy aim and fired again. Splinters flew from the tree as the card shattered and spun fluttering to the grass. Sewell picked it up and examined it. He shook his head happily. "I've never seen such a thing. Both shots in virtually the same place!" He stared at Charles in amazement. "Can---- can you do that or something like it every time you fire?"

Charles stood looking at the shattered ace of hearts. "Pretty much every shot," he said calmly. "The second pistol throws slightly to the right. But I dare say you knew that," he added in an aside to Thomas.

John Sewell guffawed and Thomas Graham laughed delightedly too, but more in relief than real amusement. He had not been looking forward to explaining to Mary and Louisa that their young favourite had been cut down in a hopeless duel on a damp field. He put his arm around his young friend's shoulders. "Pistols it will be," he said firmly.

"But when I see de Lapouyade's man I shall warn him what he is up against. He should be given an opportunity to withdraw his challenge. I only pray that you do not kill the gentleman, Charles."

Next morning Charles looked curiously around, trying to impress the scene on his mind. He did not intend to repeat this experience and he wanted to be certain that he would recall every detail of it. The sun was very low in the sky at this hour and still hidden behind one of the city's great basilicas far to the east. M. de Lapouyade's carriage stood a little way off in the half darkness that shrouded a small cluster of trees. A second carriage bearing a surgeon was discreetly positioned nearby. Thomas Graham and John Sewell had ridden over with him from the Stormont house in the last darkness of what had been for Charles a restless night.

To judge by his pale concerned face the night had been equally difficult for Thomas Graham. He was at that moment in serious discussion with his opposite number as to the details of the encounter. "I should warn you sir, that Mr MacPherson is deadly with a pistol," Thomas said unhappily in a low voice. "It is my hope that this matter could even now be settled by an mutual apology."

Lapouyade's official second, a florid faced military-looking man, shook his head vigorously. "My man feels that he has no reason to apologise, my dear sir. He was simply defending the honour of his friend Mademoiselle Barrault, who was being importuned by M. MacPherson, who then attacked him savagely and in full public gaze." He smiled thinly and shook his head condescendingly. "Of course, if your man wishes to apologise for the incident----?"

Thomas Graham bowed and turned away. "I regret this event greatly, sir. But if it must be----." He paused. "Let us pray that no one loses their life over it."

The seconds then paced out the twenty yards and Charles and Lapouyade took up their firing positions. Sewell stood midway between them and raised his hand bearing a white cloth. "Gentlemen, when I call fire and release the cloth, you may fire."

Charles stared down the barrel of the pistol at his opponent. He could see the white cloth in the corner of his eye. He took one deep breathe to steady himself. Then, "Fire!" and he saw the cloth flutter to the ground in the half light. The muzzle flash of Lapouyade's pistol came instantly, bright in the gloom and suspiciously early.

Charles had not yet fired and he felt a tug at his shirt front and then a sensation like a red hot poker being drawn across his chest. Glancing down he was shocked to see blood staining his white shirt. Suddenly the pain struck and only then did he flinch, half lowering his pistol. In the same moment he was vaguely aware of a flock of strange dark birds that soared and spiralled up with raucous cries of alarm from a nearby stand of trees, into the brightening sky.

For an instant his imagination told him they were lost souls from the nearby graveyard. Then he shook his head and gritted his teeth. The pain was sharp and intense. But he knew that he at least was not dead. A savage feeling of triumph rose in him and he raised the pistol again, feeling its lovely balance and sighted along the slim barrel. The pain of his wound seemed to melt away and his hand was steady as he took aim.

But now in his mind it was Beaumarchais who stood in front of him and he lined up his weapon on the top button of the man's waistcoat. At that instant a shaft of sunlight broke from behind the distant domes and illuminated his opponent in a curious theatrical way so that he saw Lapouyade clearly, staring at him, eyes wide open, his face white.

Charles knew that he could kill this man--- and in the same instant he knew that he could not do so. He raised his pistol until it was pointed into the sky and pulled the trigger, wincing as he felt the recoil wrench against his damaged chest. Then he bowed awkwardly towards his opponent. "I offer you my apologies for my part in this distasteful affair, M. de Lapouyade. Perhaps we can regard the matter between us as settled."

He turned away and staggered slightly as the pain began to bite again. Thomas gripped him by the hand. "Well done, Charles," he said quietly. "Damned well done! Now let us see to that wound."

FIFTEEN

The next few weeks were perhaps the happiest in the young life of Charles George Macpherson as he travelled leisurely across France towards Spa in the company of Thomas and Mary Graham, for long periods having the delight of sharing their coach solely with Mary. To his initial disgust, as it seemed to him deeply shaming, especially since it was untrue, Thomas had explained the young man's damaged shoulder as being the result of a fall from an awkward horse. At this Charles had weakly protested, suspecting correctly that Graham was simply eager to conceal the story of the duel from Mary and in particular his own part in the affair, which would inevitably then have come out.

Still, as day after delightful day passed and he luxuriated in Mary's undivided attention, Charles quickly forgave the subterfuge and sat back, glancing smugly from time to time at Thomas as he rode steadily along beside the carriage, while Mary fussed over him, propping cushions under his injured shoulder and regularly begged Thomas to urge the coachman to go more slowly. For the very first time Charles found himself alone with Mary Graham and for him every moment was like a dream realised. If he had loved Mary before the journey to Spa, her gentle charm and endless care now bound him to her for ever.

But progress was slow, seldom more than ten miles each day, and delightful as the journey was for Charles he could see at first hand the toll these rough country roads were taking on Mary's fragile constitution, how desperately weak she was and how quickly she would become quite exhausted. Repeatedly therefore, Charles, seeing her pale and worn out by the incessant jolting and bumping of the coach, would plead his own painful shoulder as an excuse for Thomas to find an early bed for the party in some comfortable inn. Though this was a stratagem that he knew did not in the least deceive his friend.

In this way, day by day as they travelled steadily north and east, Charles began gradually to discover a more about his companion. Quite soon for example he realised that Thomas Graham spoke French every bit as well as he did himself. Moreover, it was clear that his companion was familiar with the country through which they were travelling.

During long evenings in country inns after Mary had retired for the night he tried with limited success to tease out from his friend details of his earlier life. Finally, in the vicinity of Brussels where they were enjoying the comfortable hospitality of friends while Mary recovered her strength, Charles decided to be more direct. The two men were out one morning riding side by side in the Bois.

"Tell me, Thomas, how do you come to be on familiar terms with so many grand people in these parts? They seem to offer us such a generous welcome wherever we go!"

"Ah," said his friend awkwardly. "Well, as to that, after I left Christ Church my guardians sent me off on the Grand Tour." He gave a little laugh. "I fancy they thought I was destined for a brilliant career in diplomacy or government." He shrugged. "I suspect I have been a disappointment to them, for I was no great hand at studying. Most of my time at Oxford was spent hunting or playing cricket, as I recall." He laughed and then glanced sideways at Charles. "My father died when I was not much older than yourself and my dear mother's family is quite well connected, so they made certain that I met all the right people, so to say."

"Tell me about your family." said Charles.

"My mother, Lady Christian, is a Hope by birth--- daughter of Lord Hopetoun and a niece of the Countess of Annandale." Thomas said diffidently. "So I did not lack for friends and family around Europe. First I spent the best part of a year in Paris learning the language." Charles nodded silently. 'Ah,' he thought, 'that explained his companion's command of French and an accent that was irritatingly better than his own.'

"Then I travelled around a bit. Mostly in Italy--- Rome, Ravenna, Florence and Naples; that sort of thing. Lots of art and architecture. Very improving, I am sure," Thomas said with a laugh. "Met one of Mary's favourite uncles there, Sir William Hamilton, our ambassador in Naples." He hesitated momentarily. "A great collector of the arts. Interesting man. Keen on volcanoes." He coughed awkwardly and rode on in silence for a bit before continuing. "Anyway, in France especially I was introduced to quite a few influential people. Though to tell you the truth Charles," he glanced sideways at his friend again. "To tell you the truth, I do fear for some of them now--- those who will not bend to events. For there is a storm coming, I believe."

Charles looked enquiringly at him as he continued. "Many of them seem to have no notion of how perilously they are poised on the edge of a political volcano. For their excesses strike me as simply unsustainable. And though this French king means well, there is such a dead hand of inertia in the society that I do not see his reforms being successful. Or indeed possible."

Charles glanced at his friend in surprise, for he had never imagined Thomas Graham to be a radical. Or heard him express his thoughts so openly. "A revolution? Is that what you expect?" he asked.

Thomas rode on silently for several minutes. "I fear it may come to that. Or some new kind of tyranny." He smiled grimly. "Or perhaps both, for once civil society breaks down, who can tell what will arise in the chaos? Certainly I see no benign outcome here." He nodded across at Charles as they rode. "Not such as the one your countrymen are undoubtedly capable of establishing, once this foolish war in America is ended."

Charles looked sharply at his companion. It was the first time he had heard Thomas express such Whiggish pro-American sentiments, though on the previous day as it happened he had sensed his friend's silent disapproval as Mary read them a long letter from her brother William, describing some of the bizarre events that had taken place recently in Philadelphia.

It seemed there had been an extravagant farewell party to mark the departure of Sir William Howe as commander in chief of the British forces in the colonies. This 'Mischianza', as it was called, had been on a truly heroic scale, the centrepiece of which had been a mock medieval tournament in which young British officers, including it seemed Mary's two brothers, decked out in elaborate costumes had contended as knights of old for the favour of select Queens of Beauty, each of whom was attended by damsels-in-waiting dressed as Turkish concubines. This had been watched in largely stunned silence by the audience of stolid local Quakers.

A grand regatta on the Delaware river had followed and a magnificent banquet at which black slaves, likewise dressed in oriental costumes, had served a meal of twelve hundred dishes. The event had ended with a dramatic fireworks display, whose 'pièce de résistance' was a figure of Fame and the words in letters of fire, 'Thy laurels shall never fade!' The affair was so weird that Charles had scarcely known what to say as he listened to Mary's account, remembering all the while that his friend Francis Johnson was desperately struggling to survive with General

Washington's forces in the nearby hills.

Thomas wheeled his mount to a halt and met his gaze. "This foolishness can have only one end of course. You heard the nonsense that William Cathcart wrote to Mary. Does that strike you as prosecuting a dedicated war?" He snorted in disgust and rode on quickly.

Charles cantered after him. "So you are sympathetic to my people in this war?" he asked bluntly.

Thomas rode in silence for so long that Charles began to fear he had gone too far in his new confidence. "Let us say," Thomas eventually said heavily, "that I find myself much in sympathy with our American cousins. I am certainly quite prepared to see them govern themselves, well or badly, as they see fit. Lord Chatham, William Pitt as was--- a man I respect above all, though he is perhaps rather more of a Tory than most of my friends, has expressed the stupidity of this war infinitely better than I can ever say. He has repeatedly called for reconciliation."

Charles rode quietly on, smiling secretly to himself. He could ask for no more from his new friend. His mind was also taken up by the contents of his own mail, for the courier from Lord Stormont had to Charles's surprise carried not one but two letters for him.

The first was an awkwardly worded, formal and badly spelled account from Juliana Ritchie of her meeting with Benjamin Franklin, the essence of which was her astonishment at Franklin's apparent lack of concern at their disclosures about Bancroft and about the treachery that so surrounded the great man in Paris.

> "You will scarcely believe me, Charlie. But when I told him about those secret messages to Stormont and Silas Deane's corrupt activities, Franklin simply beamed at me. ' Madam,' he said in that affable way of his, 'what am I to do? Were you to offer me irrefutable proof that my personal valet was a British spy, why I think I might keep him on! Provided of course he was a good valet!' I was outraged, as you will imagine"

In spite of himself Charles smiled. He could well imagine Juliana's outrage at that.

> "But as I made my way back to Paris I began to wonder how much Mr F already knew about the affair. Perhaps there are plots within plots. Could he be feeding Stormont with false information? Oh, it is all so confusing! I swear I do not know what to think."

This letter was signed simply, 'Your friend, Juliana Ritchie'.

The second was shorter. There was no formal introduction and clearly it had been dashed off in great haste. The spelling was even more eccentric.

"Oh Charlie, what have you done? I hear that you are to fight that old fool de Lapouyade. And over that stupid girl! Oh how I blame myself yet again and pray that you emerge unscathed, though I fear that he is an experienced duellist. (I dare say he has ample excuse with that creature under his protection).

May God protect you, Charlie. Your dearest friend. Juliana."

Charles folded the letters away thoughtfully. Was she truly his dearest friend? He scarcely knew now what his feelings were.

Spa proved to be a delightful little town huddled against the cool sides of a heavily wooded valley, set about with attractive houses and old country inns, some of traditional design but many, especially in the centre of the town, in the most modern and stylish fashion of the day, elegant with the finest neo-classical columns, pilasters and domes. More importantly the town was dotted with the small artificially created fountains and bathing places that had made Spa famous and attracted the nobility and other wealthy invalids from around the Europe for hundreds of years.

It was only in the past few decades however that Spa had become fashionable with the English. But in recent years it had become very fashionable indeed. As Mary loyally explained to Charles. "It is quite as thronged with aristocrats now as Brighton or Bath," she advised him. The gentle days wore on quietly, with Mary patiently submitting to a variety of treatments under her husband's watchful eye, either by immersion or even worse by consumption of the warm foul-smelling waters. Making wry faces, Mary would drink the disgusting waters, urged on by Thomas who, she noted wistfully, was never tempted to drink the awful liquid himself.

For Charles the summer passed as a delightful idyll, luxuriating in Mary's almost continuous company day after day. Each morning Mary would go with a female servant to bathe in one of the medieval fountains while Thomas worked on his correspondence, sending instructions to his factor in Perthshire concerning all manner of estate business. One day he would be planning the building of cottages for his workers, giving precise details of the lay-out of roads and paths; the next he was making arrangements for the purchase of new stock for the herds or proposing the latest agricultural process to promote the growth of crops.

While the Grahams were so engaged Charles would take the opportunity to stroll about this small country town and to observe the

English at their leisure. And very peculiar some of them were, he thought. Especially the unknown gentleman whom he regularly saw riding slowly through the town's main street, seated backwards on his horse, shaded from the morning sun beneath an umbrella fixed to his saddle and deeply engrossed in his book, totally oblivious to the stares of the locals and apparently equally careless of the direction taken by his docile mount.

When he mentioned this strange spectacle to Thomas Graham his friend simply nodded. "Ah yes. I have noticed him. I do not recall his name and we do not seem ever to have met socially. Though I fancy I remember him vaguely from Christ Church. He played cricket and was a touch odd even then."

Later in the day it became quite accepted that the three of them would ride out together, perhaps to picnic in the formal gardens around la Source de la Géronstère or in one of the nearby sheltered valleys. Then as Mary grew stronger they would venture further and visit one or other of the romantic old castles that were scattered about the area.

Whether because of her new regime of the waters or perhaps simply as a result of rest after a difficult journey, the fresh clean mountain air and the warm sunshine and good plain food, Mary's pale features glowed again. Her eyes sparkled with new life and her delicate frame seemed a shade stronger. It was the happiest of times and Charles noted how relaxed his friend Thomas had become. Truly it seemed that the long and exhausting expedition had been justified.

However, the delights of Spa were not limited to such healthy activities. Charles discovered that the town had also developed a reputation for its social life and La Redoubte, the established casino in the centre of the town, had for many years provided entertainment and refreshment for visitors interested in gambling. The English of course, not content to share their sporting activities with lesser breeds, had commissioned their own pleasure dome on a hill behind the main fountain and christened it Waux-Hall. Visiting gentry eagerly seized on it as a substitute for the famous gardens of the same name in London.

Like the famous London attraction in which many of the English visitors were used to spend long nights and much of their wealth, the casino above Spa offered a series of stylish gaming rooms and was laid out with similarly elegant formal gardens. There the visitors and their ladies could stroll before supper and later, if they could tear themselves away from the fascinations of the hazard or pharaoh tables, they might snatch a breath of night air to clear befuddled heads between games. It was also whispered that they might, with almost as much discretion as in London, arrange a rendezvous with the lady or gentleman of their choice.

Although Thomas Graham was not a gambler--- that much at least he shared with his countryman Thomas Coutts--- the beautiful Mrs Graham was such a social catch that the Grahams were habitually invited to Waux-hall as guests at the many decorous suppers and receptions that filled long summer evenings. As their special friend, Charles too was invited and increasingly accepted as a member of the fashionable set in Spa.

Intrigued by the spectacle of the gaming tables, Charles usually opted to stay on to observe the players after Mary had returned to the inn. At first Thomas made a point of returning, slightly uncomfortably, to join him at the casino after Mary was settled in their accommodation.

"I know that there are great men behind this project," Thomas said one evening as the two men strolled through the gambling rooms sipping glasses of sillery. "Good men---, I mean. The President was the Duke of Cumberland himself, a patron of my own father-in-law. But I must confess, Charles, that I find the thing sad and little pathetic." Then quite obliquely he added. "This sillery wine? Are you enjoying it?"

Charles nodded. "I am afraid that I know next to nothing about wine." The truth was that he knew nothing at all about wine, it not having been a subject that had appeared in Sir William Johnson's library.

"There is no dishonour in that," said Thomas seriously. All too aware of his young protégé's rashness in Paris, Thomas had come to feel a special responsibility for advising Charles in the ways of the world. "The Marquis of Sillery was the first fellow to introduce champagne to England, you know. That was in the last century. This sillery wine comes from the same area and is a great deal cheaper."

Lady Christian's Calvinism had left an indelible mark on her son, thought Charles, nodding impassively but secretly pleased with the notion that it was his welfare that prompted Thomas's remarks. He was also flattered beyond all that Mary, whose hand he detected behind his friend's remarks, cared at least a little for his fate. They paused at the pharaoh table and stood for a moment watching the frantic efforts of the crowd to lay their wagers and the relentless pace of the professional banker as he turned over the pairs of cards that fixed the fate of the gamblers.

"To see great estates and inheritances brought to ruin!" went on Thomas. "And the bizarre things these fellows get up to in order to change their luck! Turning their coats inside out! Changing their hats! It is frankly madness!" Thomas shook his head in puzzlement. "And why do they take such risks in pursuit of money that they do not actually need? I tell you, it is a mystery to me."

"Certainly," said Charles thoughtfully as they strolled on, "it is a great myth to think there is a thing called luck." He gave dry laugh. "And even more foolish to think your behaviour can change it!"

Thomas stared at him. "You do not mean to say that these games are based on skill? Surely it is all luck, for good or ill."

"Oh, there are games where skill does certainly play a part and there are others where it plays virtually no part." They passed into the almost silent card room, a haven of peace compared to the tables outside. Groups of hushed players studied their hands intently, the only sound being the rustle of the cards or the occasional clink of coins as money changed hands in settlement.

Charles continued. "Whist, or piquet if you prefer a two-handed game, or quinze all involve skill to some degree."

"But not luck? Surely----- ."

"Probability, Thomas! That is all that men mean by luck. And probability has nothing to do with individual behaviour. It is a remorseless invariable set of laws that cannot be evaded for long."

Thomas frowned at him, obviously perplexed, as Charles gestured towards the tables. "There are some immutable laws at work there for example. The chance of holding any one particular card of a suit is thirteen in fifty-two, or one in four. And the chance of holding any two cards is one in four multiplied by one in four, in other words one in sixteen. The chances against holding seven trumps at whist are a hundred and sixty to one and equally it is twenty-six to one against holding six trumps!" He smiled. "So you see, bad luck consists simply in betting constantly against the probabilities."

"But take dice," Thomas said eagerly. "You must confess that is all a matter of luck! I have seen men undone in a flash at the hazard table; failing to throw a five or a seven or some other number to which they had pinned their fate."

"Hazard is certainly a dangerous game. But even there the probabilities reign, if you can only recognise them. And after all, are not the odds clearly announced at each throw by the groom-porter?"

Thomas shook his head in bewilderment. "Well, it beats me," he said. "You speak as though it were possible to win at will."

"By no means, Thomas," the young man said. "It is however possible to estimate the risk at which you stand in any situation. That can be an advantage for the player if only he keeps his head."

They had almost completed their circuit of the casino and were approaching the pharaoh table again. He nodded towards the crowded table. "Half of these people are drunk," he shrugged. "But they are enjoying the excitement of the game and seem to care nothing for the fact that they are throwing their money away in pursuit of that particular pleasure."

Although at heart not much more of a gambler than his steady, sensible friend, Charles did at least understand the attraction of the tables. Not of course that he approved of the drunken reckless gambling nor the wildness with which some of these gentlemen, and ladies too, seemed determined to throw away their money. For Charles could sense an impulse to self-destruction that seemed to drive some of them on, beyond all reason it seemed.

He recalled the words of Blaise Pascal, 'The heart has its reasons that reason knows not of'. Pascal was no mean mathematician himself, Charles thought, a master of probability from the previous century. But such wild gambling Charles did not attempt to justify. Though he did recall his grim father's oft repeated counsel about allowing people to go to hell their own way!

Yet in spite of his reasoned analysis there was something that attracted him powerfully to the tables. For a few weeks he was content to be a mere observer, assuring himself that his interest was intellectual only; that what he felt was a mere curiosity about the theoretical balance of risk and reward. But as he watched he realised with a growing excitement how his elegant theories might be made to work in practice; how the probabilities might be manipulated if one were but sufficiently disciplined. Gradually a belief grew in him that he found more and more difficult to ignore. Slowly the temptation to put his knowledge to the test became irresistible.

Almost in spite of himself he found that he gravitated more frequently to the casino, every night drawn by his conviction that the cool calculation of the turn of a card, the rapid assessment of odds and the mental challenge of staying ahead of a fast moving banker was a world in which he would be in his element.

Mr Coutts had transferred enough of his funds from London to ensure that cash was not a problem. But even without these resources, he knew that his alliance with the highly respected Grahams would establish him in credit for all but the most extravagant of ventures. Although by no means rich compared to the men Thomas so despised for their foolishness, Charles knew that he had an ample income for his modest needs.

But fate seemed to have thrust him into such a milieu as he had never anticipated and his standards had been quietly transformed, only half noticed by himself, from his early days in the Mohawk Valley. As a consequence Charles was aware, increasingly and uncomfortably aware, that he still had to make his way in this new demanding world.

One evening, alone in the casino after Thomas had decided to remain with Mary at the inn, Charles began to gamble.

SIXTEEN

The evening began in a familiar enough manner, Charles strolling past the crowds of frantic pharaoh and hazard players, their piles of guineas scattered over the tables as they chattered and drank while their money vanished. Entering the more sedate card rooms he noticed that most of the tables were already occupied by serious games of four-handed whist or intensely concentrating pairs of piquet players.

Standing about observing the games were a few small knots of men sipping from glasses of wine and occasionally exchanging comments in subdued voices. Charles started to edge past one such small group and at that moment a tall impressive looking man standing with his back to him turned around, apparently sensing his presence.

It was Pierre Augustin Caron de Beaumarchais, as elegant as ever. For an instant the two stared at each other without recognition. Charles had barely time to record the splendid coat of blue and silver with its usual impressive order pinned to the front before Beaumarchais's good-looking face broke into a delighted smile. "My dear young friend," he cried and Charles stood frozen in horror as Beaumarchais seized him by the hand. "What a pleasant surprise!" he said and throwing an arm around his shoulders he took Charles in an affectionate embrace.

Charles felt himself cringe at the man's touch and Beaumarchais, sensing the reaction, said merrily. "Ah, but I must remember that you Anglo-Saxons do not like to be embraced in public! And especially here in your own English club. Forgive me my friend." He beamed at Charles, who stood appalled and speechless, feeling his insides turn to ice.

This was an encounter he could never have expected, least of all here so far from Paris and its memories. But he forced himself to look the man in the face, even to produce a faint smile. Though how he did so, haunted as he was by the sudden image of Juliana and Beaumarchais together, was a mystery.

Desperately he tried to shut the scene out of his mind. But unbidden he saw Juliana writhing under the embrace of this man. In pleasure real or simulated? What did it matter? His mind spun and for an instant the whole room seeming to darken about him. He actually felt faint. He could hear his blood pounding in his ears. Somehow he managed to pull his wits together. "M. de Beaumarchais," he stammered. "I am quite taken aback. What brings you here?"

Beaumarchais, still beaming fondly at him, indicated one of the men sitting at the nearby whist table. "I am a guest here, of course. My friend and colleague of the theatre, Mr Richard Sheridan, suggested I join him in Spa to take the waters. Do you know each other?" A long sallow-faced young man with deep-set eyes and wearing his own hair cut short, glanced sullenly at them from his cards and gestured vaguely in their direction before returning his attention to the game.

Charles shook his head, his thoughts still in turmoil. It was clear that Beaumarchais had no idea he had been Juliana's lover. Or else the man was a much better actor than anyone supposed. No, Charles decided, Beaumarchais had no idea that they were rivals---- that they had been rivals, Charles corrected himself quickly. Juliana Ritchie was now in the past. As to that fact, if any doubt had lingered this ghastly encounter had settled the matter.

But how was he to survive this unacknowledged ignominy, faced with this smiling unknowing enemy? He suddenly remembered Lapouyade in his pistol sights, all the time wishing it had been Beaumarchais. Would he have fired wide had it really been Beaumarchais? No, he thought savagely, he would have dropped him there in the Champ-de-Mars. And to hell with Thomas Graham and Stormont and all the other consequences.

"Come, let us take a glass of wine together. There is much happening now concerning your country and mine." Beaumarchais led the way to a side table some way from the card players and signalled to a waiter. When they were seated he leaned forward confidentially. "You did not take up my suggestion that you might help our cause in Spain."

Charles shook his head. "It seemed to me that I had no special credentials for that kind of thing," he said coldly.

Oblivious to Charles's coolness Beaumarchais went blithely on.

"In any case the matter is much further advanced now and it is increasingly clear that my country will soon enter the war against England." He beamed at Charles. "There will then be no need for further subterfuge in providing aid to your people. All that is required now is an American victory of some kind to sway the doubters who surround the King. Of course they are all too willing to strike. But fearful of the consequences."

Charles smiled faintly. "Perhaps the King is not enthusiastic about encouraging the people to overthrow a monarch, even in America."

Beaumarchais waved the comment aside. "There is no shortage of French money available, I can assure you. Never has been. The sums that have passed through my hands!" He paused. "Had I been less devoted to the cause, less honest even, I could easily have diverted large sums to my own benefit. Others have done so, I know."

Charles recalled Fullerton's comment about Beaumarchais. 'Money always plays a part, of course---- usually other people's money'. How much of a buffoon was he? Juliana had thought him harmless--- with a wince Charles once more forced all the memories of her from his mind.

"Now my friend Richard Sheridan over there, he is a man who understands money," Beaumarchais went on glibly. "We are discussing various business ventures together. You may know that he has but recently written a great success for the London stage. 'The Rivals' it is called. Do you perhaps know it?"

'The Rivals', Charles thought despairingly. He shook his head, his composure almost recovered now. "No. I know little or nothing of the theatre, whether in London or in Paris," he said shortly, staring at Beaumarchais in wonder as the man chattered on, clearly unaware of his companion's cold reserve.

"Ah yes! 'The Rivals'. It is a brilliant success, though it is said to have been unfavourably received on its first night owing to the poor playing of the part of Sir Lucius O'Trigger." Beaumarchais shook his head despondently.

"Those damned actors," he said mournfully. "Why do they think they know more about the part than the author himself? But the defects were all remedied and since then it has been hugely successful for Sheridan." He leaned forward confidentially. "Do you know, he made so much money on it that he has been able to negotiate with Garrick for the purchase of the Drury Lane Theatre. The bargain was completed only last summer. Is that not a splendid achievement?"

"Garrick?" said Charles vaguely, looking about anxiously for a means of escape.

"Oh, my dear sir!" Beaumarchais said patronisingly. "I see that you do not interest yourself in the theatre. Well, it is not to everyone's taste. But David Garrick is probably the most distinguished actor and theatrical impresario in Europe." He smiled with a modest inclination of the head. "Well, in England at least! The Drury Lane Theatre was bought from him for £35,000 by Sheridan and his friends. So now Sheridan is famously rich and richly famous, ha ha! Quite taken up by all fashionable society. At least the Whig part--- he is a great friend of Mr Charles James Fox and a sympathiser of the American cause. A useful man to know in London."

Charles glanced to where Sheridan sat focussed on his cards, surrounded by piles of golden guineas. "A great gambler too, I see."

Beaumarchais nodded. "Do you play at all?" he asked artlessly.

Charles shook his head. A vague idea was forming in his mind. "No," he said in perfect truth. "I know some of the games in theory; the rules and so on. But I must admit that I have never played in earnest and certainly never for money."

Beaumarchais beamed at him. "So you have no moral objection to cards or dice?"

Charles shook his head again. "Not in the least. But I seem never to have found the opportunity to play."

Beaumarchais led him to one of the small tables. "Perhaps you will let me introduce you to the gaming table? I am a great lover of the game piquet," he said. "Do you know of it? It is relatively simple," he said thoughtfully. "Perhaps we might begin with a few hands of piquet."

"I think I know the general outline of the game." Charles smiled pleasantly at his rival. Piquet he knew was in fact a fiendishly complicated game and potentially costly for a beginner. It was eminently clear to him that Beaumarchais intended to fleece him. "It is played with only thirty-two cards, is it not?" he asked innocently. A revenge of sorts seemed almost in his grasp.

"Indeed," said Beaumarchais absently, as he picked up a pack and began to discard all the cards of value seven and below. "Shall we wager a guinea a point?" Before Charles had time to reply, "and let us cut for deal?" he went on casually. "Low card deals. A partie of six hands to begin with?" Charles cut low card and dealt.

Beaumarchais discarded the maximum of five cards in preparation for the declaration stage of the game. "Point of four," he said, instantly and unwittingly revealing the structure of his hand to Charles.

Charles had taken the three remaining cards from the talon and now held a long run of Clubs, though not a great deal else. "No good," he said quietly.

"Sequence of three."

"No good," said Charles.

"Three aces," Beaumarchais announced in a faintly exasperated voice which Charles noted with satisfaction.

"That is good," he replied. Beaumarchais scored three points for his aces, his first points of the hand.

Charles then declared his point of five Clubs and a sequence of four and they proceeded to the play with Beaumarchais leading. The tricks were more or less equally split between the two players and at the end of the first deal Charles found himself ahead by five points, an untypical outcome given his disadvantage as dealer in drawing only three cards. He won the next hand by twenty points and lost his second deal by a narrow margin in a low scoring hand. The fourth hand went well and once again he was some twenty points to the good.

By now he thought that he had the measure of Beaumarchais and his approach to play, which seemed to favour a high-risk strategy of discards. In the fifth hand Charles as dealer drew a crucial nine of Clubs, completing a very strong run of that suite and in addition drew an ace of Spades as cover for a king that he already held. From the remainder of his other cards he could see that Beaumarchais was strong in Hearts and Diamonds and might have four queens. Beaumarchais began the declaration with a point of six. "Not good," Charles said.

Beaumarchais stared at him. "Are you sure?"

Charles smiled. "Oh, quite sure."

Beaumarchais snapped out, "Fourteen for queens, then."

Just as Charles had thought. "Good," he said imperturbably.

Charles declared his point of seven Clubs and because he had a straight run of seven to jack in that suite he followed it with, "Quint to jack for fifteen points, making twenty-two."

"Damn me," scowled Beaumarchais. "I never saw such a run of cards. One for leading," he added sourly, playing the ace of Hearts. "And one for winning the trick." He took the next three tricks with the ace of

Diamonds followed by the queen and a seven. Thereafter Charles won every trick with his strong line up of kings and aces, scoring a bonus of ten points for eight tricks. He ended up with forty-one points to Beaumarchais's eighteen.

The partie was now at a vital stage. Charles was already over the crucial one hundred points mark, which can mean the difference between a substantial loss or gain. Now as non-dealer he also had the advantage of drawing five cards from the talon. His opponent had just eighty points and while Charles knew that it is rarely correct for the non-dealer to play defensively, if in the present circumstances he could keep Beaumarchais below the hundred point mark he would win convincingly.

He found himself with a good hand of five Spades including a king and queen, plus two other aces. After cautiously discarding he went on to win by forty points to just eleven.

Quickly calculating the scores, Charles smiled across at Beaumarchais. "One hundred and sixty, plus your ninety-one and with another hundred points bonus, as I understand it." As he spoke it flashed into his mind that in just a few minutes he had accumulated the equivalent of almost two years income from the safe investments of Mr Coutts!

Beaumarchais did his best to smile graciously. He called for glasses of champagne and they resumed the play. The next partie went much the way of the first, except that Beaumarchais made the critical hundred points mark so that Charles won only the difference between their scores plus the bonus. "One hundred and fifty points," he announced blandly, relishing the look of frustration on his opponent's face.

As the night wore on Beaumarchais tried everything he knew to recoup, gulping down glass after glass of the Waux-hall's best champagne as his debts mounted. When he finally called a halt he owed Charles a little over twelve hundred guineas. Shaking his head and reaching for pen and paper he grunted, "You will accept my note for this?"

Charles hesitated, uncharitably enjoying the moment. "It would be more convenient to have cash." He paused. "I have certain payments that must imminently be made here in Spa. Then I am off to England with my friends the Grahams. If what you say about war is true it may be some time before I can call on you in Paris for settlement." He forced a smile.

Beaumarchais flushed. "But as an American, sir, you will be free to travel to Paris regardless--- ," Charles decided to turn the knife. He gestured towards Sheridan. "Your English friend has had a good night at his cards," he interrupted. "Cannot he cover some or all of your debts?"

Beaumarchais lurched to his feet and leaned over Sheridan,

whispering in his ear. The Englishman looked across at Charles and laughed. "Why my dear Beaumarchais, you should never pay your creditors! It only encourages them!" Charles heard him say loudly.

Charles simply smiled politely at the pale untidy figure of the playwright, sitting surrounded by his newly won rouleaus of guinea coins. "Tell you what, Beaumarchais," Sheridan said. "Give me your note for this." He pushed half-a-dozen fifty guinea rouleaus across the table. "And let us hope that before too long I can collect from you in Paris!"

Charles accepted the three hundred guineas and Beaumarchais's promissory note for the balance. Then stuffing the money into a leather pouch offered by one of the staff he excused himself with a stiff bow which his shaken opponent barely acknowledged. He walked slowly through the great hall. Why did he feel so horribly tainted? By his skill and judgement he had just added significantly to his sum of capital and at the expense of a man he had good reason to dislike. That was assuming of course that Beaumarchais honoured his note, he thought bitterly.

Yet somehow Charles could feel no sense of triumph. His emotions, he realised, were dominated only by a sense of disgust. Was it disgust at Beaumarchais? The still painful disgust at Juliana? Or was it most of all disgust at himself? Was this what Thomas had meant by the evils of gambling? Suddenly he wanted nothing so much as to rid himself of Beaumarchais' gold.

He headed towards the crowd around the hectic pharaoh table and stood for a moment watching the players frenetically tossing away their money. In spite of himself Charles could not prevent some cold corner of his brain reminding him of the dangers of the game. Pharaoh was an essentially simple but very fast moving game. As quickly as the players placed their bets the professional banker spun out two cards; one to his right hand and the other to his left. All bets on the right hand card were lost. All bets on the left hand card won and on these the banker paid odds of two to one to the winners, collecting all the losing bets for himself. Wagers on any other cards neither won nor lost and might be left on the table for the next deal or removed, just as the punter chose. The game appeared deceptively favourable to the player, since at almost every deal someone round the table won and the excitement grew apace, especially as some of the wins were dramatically large.

However Charles knew that by the rules the last card of the pack was always a void and inevitably landed on the left-hand winning pile. In the nature of the game therefore there were more chances of losing than of winning. In the early play with almost a complete pack of cards the dealer had only a slight edge. Charles rapidly calculated that it represented a probable advantage to the dealer of about four percent. But as the cards were progressively dealt out the odds moved remorselessly against the players, until by the final stages the dealer's edge was closer to twenty percent.

Charles began to play at the start of a deal and tossed all of Beaumarchais money on a card chosen at random. There was no point in trying to anticipate specific cards at that stage. The buzz of conversation around the table stopped as he said quietly, "Three hundred guineas." He stood watching almost impersonally as ten pairs of cards were dealt out without his choice either winning or losing.

By now half the cards were out and in spite of his mood of revulsion, in some remote corner of his brain he could not escape a rational response. He indicated that he was barring his bet to cancel the wager. The deal proceeded and he had the faint satisfaction of seeing his choice, a six, lose in the very next deal.

After a brief pause to clear the board and accept new wagers the next deal began. Charles chose six again and saw the six of Hearts drop down on the winning pile almost at once. The banker silently added six hundred guineas to his stake. Charles indicated that he was leaving the entire nine hundred to ride on the same card. Two more inconclusive deals followed. Then the six of Clubs dropped on the winning pile and a shrill cry of excitement went up round the table.

Charles now had almost three thousand guineas to his credit on the table. He shook his head in amazement at this turn of events. Then he laughed and indicated that he wanted the bet to run for a third time.

His card did not appear for another five deals and the tension amongst the watchers mounted. Then reason at last prevailed. Calculating that the odds had moved unacceptably against him Charles was on the point of picking up his money. But at that moment the dealer turned over the six of Spades and it dropped onto the winning pile again!

As the dealer arranged for his winnings to be paid to his credit Charles stood impassively considering these events. Almost in spite of himself, in a matter of minutes he had won more heavily at this game of chance than in an entire evening of skill against Beaumarchais.

'The heart has its reasons that reason knows not of, indeed', he thought grimly. When he had cared nothing for the outcome it seemed as if he could command the cards. Or at least anticipate them with enough certainty that the element of risk was much reduced. He smiled to himself. Was he deluding himself, like the men Thomas Graham so despised?

He accepted a draft in his favour from the casino cashier and made his way back to the inn. With what Beaumarchais owed him, he thought as he blew out the candle in his bedroom, he could add some nine thousand guineas to the capital sum that Coutts held for him in London. In a single night he had more than doubled his fund of capital!

Charles lay back and smiled into the soft darkness. The old Scots banker would be proud of him, he thought sleepily. But then again, would he? And what would Thomas Graham say?

SEVENTEEN

Charles returned to Paris at the end of that summer in a tumult of emotions. Parting company with the Grahams had struck deeply at him, more deeply than he could ever have imagined. For the first time in his life he was thrown into a mood of black depression, the kind of mood that he had frequently observed in his Highland father but had never before experienced himself.

Of course watching Mary Graham depart had been central to his gloom. But he was also aware for the first time that Thomas Graham's strong handshake and steady gaze had come to mean almost as much to him as Mary's tearful farewell. Though little was said openly he realised all at once that he had become more than a friend to the Grahams; he had become part of their family. For Charles this was a novel and special feeling, given his own peculiar background.

But part they must, at least for a time as Mary said sweetly to him. Thomas had decided that Mary should try the autumn waters at Brighton which had become quite fashionable since Dr Russell had written his book on the benefits of sea-water bathing for invalids. Then they would travel north to Scotland where Thomas had pressing business on the family estates; business that should be settled before the winter there became too hard for Mary's delicate health.

Charles rode darkly back to Paris conscious that important issues were at hand. As the city that had launched him into his new life drew nearer he found himself beset by a growing sense of excitement and trepidation that was difficult to analyse. Yet in spite of his immediate concerns he had the strongest presentment that great events were moving; events that would impact decisively not just on his own future but on the whole of Europe.

At the meanest level, he must settle his own petty financial business with Beaumarchais, though the idea of enduring more of that obnoxious bonhomie disgusted him. None the less, Charles was determined to collect the money that was due to him. Not, he marvelled to himself, entering the bustling streets of Paris from the north, that nine hundred guineas was as hugely significant as it would have seemed only a few months earlier. For Charles had enjoyed a remarkable few weeks following his dramatic winnings at the pharaoh table.

Irresistibly he had found himself drawn back to the Waux-hall, though in deference to the unspoken disapproval of Thomas Graham he made a point of not gambling every night. He did however play two or three times each week and though never again did he wager so extravagantly, restricting himself to relatively modest games of piquet and whist, he steadily enhanced his reputation as a master of cards and one eagerly sought out by other serious players as a valued partner.

Whether in partnership or alone he continued to win steadily night by night and though never on the scale of that first evening it was rare for him to leave with less than seventy, eighty or even a hundred guineas added to his growing account. Most gratifyingly for him, the winnings were the product of skill and cool analysis rather than the indifference that he had uncharacteristically displayed that first night.

In spite of his new affluence however Charles was determined to extract the money owed him by Beaumarchais, who had become a kind of Nemesis to him. 'No,' Charles savagely cast aside that idea, 'not that---- he would not grace the man with such a notion.' Beaumarchais was no more than a squalid opportunist, a mountebank with whom Charles must settle and then eliminate from his life as speedily as possible. There was certainly no need to feel excitement or trepidation on that account.

On taking his leave of the Grahams he had promised Mary that he would again lodge with Lord Stormont. By now Thomas would have written to prepare the way for him. Was it his reception at the Embassy that concerned him? Charles smiled at the thought. It was a measure of how far he had travelled since that first day when he had arrived nervous and uncertain at Stormont's grand house. He also knew rather more about Davis Murray, Lord Stormont, as a man. And what he had learned from Thomas in the course of their evening conversations in Spa made the Stormont seem an altogether more human figure.

"David has risen far in very difficult circumstances," Thomas had said thoughtfully, "and will probably rise still higher. He and his uncle, the Earl of Mansfield, seem to be ascending together through the hierarchy of the British state--- remarkable when one realises that the Murray family was badly tainted by Jacobite sympathies. David's own father was gaoled for his activities in 1715 and another close family member was actually Secretary of State to Prince Charles Edward Stuart himself."

Thomas shook his head in wonder. "Of course, that kind of history is not so unusual in our great Scottish families. But there has been such an open mood of anti-Scottish sentiment in London since 1745 that David's success has not been easy---- no accident of birth, in other words. Far from it, indeed. But David Murray has always had his eyes firmly set on the heights, always determined to restore the family reputation. That was clear even when he was at Christ Church, my old college. Though of course," Thomas added disarmingly, "David was a deal cleverer than myself. He actually left with a degree and a very good degree at that! He is quite the scholar and has written books--- devilish deep books on European law and the like."

Stormont would by now know all about his stupid disagreement with Lapouyade, thought Charles. More important however was what the ambassador might have to say about Charles's dangerous contacts with Ben Franklin. Lord Stormont or his agents would undoubtedly have monitored those activities closely. So far as the duel was concerned, one of Stormont's own personal staff and indeed his own brother-in-law had been actively involved. So what could he say about that?

Probably nothing, Charles decided. Stormont would simply ignore the episode. Probably too there would be no more than a diplomatic warning on the Franklin front. For if Beaumarchais was anything like correct about the state of relations with the French, the Ambassador would have more on his mind than the social solecisms of a young American in Paris.

However, regardless of Stormont's reaction Charles simply must see Franklin again. If only to collect his promised letters of introduction, he thought selfishly. While he looked eagerly forward to that, Charles was aware too that such a meeting was no longer the hugely exciting prospect that once it had been. But see Franklin again face-to-face he must, when he would impress upon him all that he knew about Edward Bancroft. How would Franklin react, he wondered? Well, whatever the consequences Charles was determined to expose the treachery that surrounded his mission in France.

Could Juliana have failed to impress the great man with the seriousness of the situation? That was unlikely, knowing Juliana, he thought with a wry smile. Ah, Juliana! Yes, he thought uneasily. That was the true source of the excitement he felt pounding in his chest--- and the trepidation too, if he were honest. How would she receive him after what had happened? And how was he to behave when they met again?

In the event his reception at Lord Stormont's residence could not have been better. The servants sprang forward to help him dismount; the groom to lead away his tired and travel-stained horse and all the staff greeted him with warmth. Then as he walked a little stiffly into the great colonnaded reception hall there was William Fullerton waiting to welcome him.

"It is good to see you back, sir," the grey-clad secretary said, taking his hand firmly and fixing him with his usual keen gaze. But this time the gaze was accompanied by a friendly smile. "We received Mr Graham's letter and your rooms are prepared. I dare say you want a soak in a warm tub after your journey. I'm afraid his Lordship and Lady Stormont are away at present. But they will soon return, I imagine, as there is much for Lord Stormont to do here." Charles detected the slightest flicker of meaning that crossed Fullerton's eyes.

"However they send their regards and regret that they were required to travel at very short notice to London. His Lordship is on official business, while Lady Stormont is taking the opportunity to visit the Duchess of Atholl." Charles remembered that Louisa's older sister had married the Duke of Atholl in a joint ceremony with Mary and Thomas and he knew how close all the sisters were to each other. Any excuse to visit London, and Charles could guess the reason for Stormont's sudden departure, would have been an irresistible attraction for Louisa.

He had barely time to settle into his rooms when there was a knock at the heavy mahogany doors and John Sewell entered, a broad smile on his usually taciturn features. "Welcome back sir," Sewell said. "It's a pleasure to see you again. I hope you haven't had any more cause to practice with the sword!" Charles seized him by the hand, aware that unaccountably he truly felt that he had come home. While still with half his mind reflecting on that odd feeling, he saw that Sewell was actually beaming at him. "But by God, sir, I don't think I have ever seen marksmanship like it." Sewell burst out. "If there are many like you in the colonies it is little wonder our lads are having such a rough time over there."

Charles smiled. "Oh, there are many marksman in the backwoods as good or better than myself. Especially with the long rifle." He paused and laughed awkwardly. "Though they are not so good with cold steel. That takes a different sort of man. Or perhaps you have to be bred to it." He paused. "Tell me, what news is there from America?"

Sewell looked uneasily at him. "There is nothing official yet. But rumour has it that General Burgoyne has met with a serious reverse at a place called Saratoga. Do you know where that is, sir?"

Charles nodded. "I do indeed. It is not many miles from where I was raised." He remembered the letter from Francis Johnson. Would he have been involved in such an action? A pang of regret struck him briefly that he had not been there to support him. Then he shook his head. Where did his sympathies truly rest, he wondered? Immediately he put the question out of his mind. It was too confusing an issue to handle, at least for the moment.

But John Sewell was usually well informed and there was every reason to think that he would be in this case. It sounded as if the support Burgoyne had expected to receive from General Howe in Pennsylvania had not materialised. In which case a defeat at Saratoga might prove to be a costly affair politically and exactly the impetus the French court needed to enter this unfortunate war. Just as Beaumarchais had anticipated, he thought bleakly. "Tell me John, what do you know about a man called Beaumarchais?"

Sewell laughed out loud. "Why sir, he is a rogue!" Then he looked slightly abashed. "Well sir, I do hope he is not a friend of yours. I think I recall you--- had some social contact with him here in Paris," he ended lamely.

Charles knew perfectly well that Sewell, a trusted agent of Fullerton and the Ambassador, would know chapter and verse of his dealings with Beaumarchais. "He is no friend of mine, I can assure you of that. It is only that I had some dealings, literally dealings, with Beaumarchais at the card tables in Spa during the summer. As a result of which he owes me a sum of money. What do you know about his current finances? Am I likely to be able to squeeze my money out of the man?"

Sewell pursed his lips and looked thoughtful. "Well sir, he is a slippery one, that I know. But recently a large amount of money has passed through his hands, I understand." Sewell glanced thoughtfully at Charles. "I dare say you are aware, sir, of his dealings with the French government and their supply of arms to your countrymen. If I know Beaumarchais, some of that money will have stuck to his fingers. So this may be a very good time to collect from him."

He brightened up. "You could always fight another duel, sir! If you killed him, and I am certain you could, think what a great service to mankind that would be!" Later, luxuriating in a hot bath Charles briefly imagined having Beaumarchais at the end of a pistol before regretfully dismissing the notion as impractical.

Then almost reluctantly he found his thoughts turning to a question that he had always managed to avoid. Just where lay his true sentiments in the matter of this war? He had moved a long way in his sympathies, he realised. But how far? Had he slowly and imperceptibly, unnoticed at least by himself, become less of a patriot?

At the very least he knew that he was more in sympathy, a great deal more if he were honest, with men like Thomas Graham than he could ever have imagined; those men who did not at heart support this pointless internecine war. Perhaps there was a middle way for him too, he thought wearily. If such a thing was possible.

Later comfortably seated before a blazing fire in his room, he wrote two letters. The first was to Benjamin Franklin, a simple and straightforward request for an interview, though he knew the discussion was likely to be far from simple.

The second letter was infinitely more difficult to compose. Charles must have begun and then destroyed half a dozen drafts before he finally produced a brief note to Juliana, asking if he might see her again. He could only hope that he had somehow found the right balance between warm friendship and cool formality--- and that Juliana wanted to see him at all.

EIGHTEEN

Two days passed without response and Charles found his apprehensions mounting afresh. What if both Juliana and Franklin ignored his letters? Franklin must be every bit as pressed as Lord Stormont, if political events in Paris were moving as rapidly as Charles imagined. Knowing Juliana, was it not quite likely that she was involved elsewhere by now? After all, woman as attractive as Juliana would not have to seek male company. She might well feel that Charles was no more than an unwelcome reminder of an unfortunate incident, an incident best forgotten.

Then came some relief for Charles. Lord Stormont and Louisa arrived home in a great flurry of excitement from their trip to London and to his very real pleasure both seemed to welcome him like a returned brother. In particular he could detect no hint of reproach in the ambassador's demeanour when early one morning, he was summoned by Fullerton to Stormont's office. Nothing was said on the awkward issues that Charles had feared. On the contrary, the conversation was all of Mary and Thomas and the enjoyments of their time together in Spa.

Lord Stormont gripped him warmly by the hand. "Louisa will join us shortly, for she is eager to hear your news of Mary at first hand," he said with a friendly smile. "Though the ladies write to each other almost every day, Mary's letters I fear say all too little of her health--- which is a worry in itself, of course." He looked down thoughtfully at his empty desk for a moment. Then he met Charles's gaze frankly. "As you know, that is a matter of concern for us all." Then he relaxed slightly. "And I expect you may be interested to hear her latest news from taking the waters in Brighton. I think you are as attached to her as any of us."

As they waited for Lady Stormont to appear, Charles decided to take advantage of this new intimacy between them. "Tell me, Lord Stormont, do you know anything of a man called Butler? John Butler? I think he is a Bishop of somewhere in England."

Stormont shot an interested glance at him. "You are well informed my boy," he said mildly. "Butler was only consecrated Bishop of Oxford in May of this year. How did you come to hear of him?"

Charles smiled and gestured vaguely. "Oh, someone spoke of him one evening in the Waux-hall at Spa."

Stormont nodded pensively. "Well, he is quite the coming man," he said. "Has become very much in favour with the Court. He was asked to preach the fast day sermon in the House of Commons last year and made a very good impression." He went on dryly. "Though it was not always so. At one time he was a confirmed Whig of the old school and not too enamoured with the established church."

Stormont tapped his desk idly. "But now Butler seems to have changed his views and he has some powerful patrons, so it would not surprise me if he went even further in the church." Stormont smiled faintly. "He has also married well, which will do him no harm. His second wife has good social connections and he seems to have no difficulty acquiring wealth and property. No oath of poverty there." He shot a quick look at Charles. "No lover of the American rebellion either."

"I dare say he is not alone in changing his political colours," Charles remarked, thinking of his own father's change of heart. For the moment he was oblivious to the effect of his words on his companion. "I suppose many families have shaken off strong Jacobite associations and yet risen in the British establishment." Instantly he regretted his words, recalling too late what Thomas Graham had told him of the Murray family history. For several long seconds he felt a chilly frisson descend on their conversation.

Finally Stormont spoke again. "Yes," he said smoothly. "Our poor country has endured many difficult years and it has not been easy for some families to prosper or even to survive." He sighed, tapped his desktop again thoughtfully and stared at Charles appraisingly in silence. Then obviously concluding that malice was not intended, he went on. "As I say, Louisa is eager to hear your news of her sister."

With that the door flew open and Louisa burst in, closely followed by Fullerton, making a vain attempt to announce her. "Yes, yes, Fullerton," she said impatiently, waving him away, her plump face flushed with excitement and her dark eyes shining. She seized Charles as he rose awkwardly from his seat and embraced him warmly while Lord Stormont sat back watching her indulgently.

"Now Charles, you must tell me how you found Mary. How is she truly? We were not able to see her in London though I knew she was in Brighton. So aggravating! It was all such a rush. All this political business and this or that crisis! 'No time to lose' at every turn. How very vexatious it was!"

"Your sister seemed considerably better in her spirits as the summer wore on," Charles said carefully. "The journey was wearing for us all and your sister was quite tired at first. But the clean fresh air and perhaps the bathing and taking the waters helped her general health. As the summer, which was a delightful one, wore on we rode out frequently to take picnics and to examine of the sights and the countryside. She enjoyed it all, I am sure."

Louisa beamed at him. "Oh I am sure she did. She more than once said in her letters what a blessing you were and how you were always on hand to assist her." Charles flushed with surprise. He had not realised that others, least of all Mary, had noticed his attachment. Then Louisa frowned darkly. "But I am very concerned, for Mary has suffered a setback it seems, an attack of pneumonia which Thomas says has set her coughing and weakened her somewhat. Still, he is hopeful that sea bathing and a course of drinking the waters in Brighton will set her right again."

Charles looked quickly across at Lord Stormont and thought for a second that he detected a brief flicker of scepticism before the ambassador's features resumed their normal calm reserve. "Is there nothing that traditional medicine can do to help, sir? I wonder whether sea bathing in October is quite the thing for someone, well, as fragile as Mary?"

Stormont shrugged and raised his hands in a gesture of helplessness. "It is all the rage now, my dear boy. Brighton is becoming as fashionable as Spa."

Louisa interrupted him. "In any even Mary has found a new friend. Her letters are full of it and the friendship seems to have raised her spirits hugely. So that is to the good, at least."

"Really," said Charles coolly.

"Yes! And a very famous friend at that. While walking with Thomas on the sea front one afternoon she met the great Duchess of Devonshire, Georgiana Cavendish. Now the two ladies are inseparable. They spend every day together and by all accounts write to each other every other day."

Lord Stormont raised his eyebrows. "Well, well!" he said gently. "I almost wonder at such a friendship. Our Mary would seem to have little in common with the little Duchess," he smiled across at Charles, "who is, shall we say, colourful? Though undoubtedly charming." He shot a glance at Charles. "You may have heard about the so-called Cavendish set. The 'ton' as they like to call themselves, a self-selected group who even have invented their own language or at least a way of speaking, I should say. And very affected and mannered they are too." He looked vaguely disapproving. "Some of the members of the 'ton' are, well, quite raffish, not to say dissipated, with drink and gambling and indeed much more it is said."

Louisa burst in, "Yes David! But were you not an admirer of the Duchess when first we met? Was it not you who gave her the first of those huge ostrich feathers that she wears in her extravagant head dresses. That has become almost an emblem of the 'ton'! Actually banned by the Queen in Court circles. So it is all your fault, my dear husband!"

Stormont's face darkened. "I hardly think so," he said shortly. "Georgiana is not short of bad influences and certainly I do not count myself amongst them." As Louisa giggled and leaned over him to kiss his forehead, he continued speaking directly to Charles. "One of that set is Richard Sheridan, the playwright and an opportunist if ever I saw one. They say his latest play "School for Scandal" is based on the escapades of the Cavendish set and that Georgiana is actually the model for one of the more foolish characters."

"Well," exclaimed Louisa, her pretty face flushed. "Is it a wonder that Georgiana is a little wild? By all accounts she receives precious little guidance from the Duke who seems to ignore her for the most part. After all, she became the châtelaine of Chatsworth when she was little more than a child. He seems to care only for his gambling and his drinking and---- and--- oh I, I don't know what else!".

Stormont pondered for a moment. "The Duke had a strange and lonely upbringing," he said thoughtfully, "and perhaps as a result he is unnaturally reserved and withdrawn. So he and Georgiana are certainly ill matched in that regard." He hesitated and smiled at Louisa fondly. "Let us hope that Mary will become a sort of elder sister to the Duchess. For I can think of no-one better equipped to set her a good example."

"Amen to that," said Louisa. "But then all the Cathcarts are paragons of virtue, are they not, David?" Stormont ignored the remark. But as Louisa giggled her way from the room Charles detected a small smile play for an instant about his usually stern mouth.

"I met a Richard Sheridan in Spa," Charles said absently. "A dramatist, I understand. I cannot say I took to him. But did you say that Cavendish is the family name of the Duchess? Is she by chance related to Henry Cavendish, the natural philosopher? The man who has done such notable work in the latest field of electricity?"

Stormont looked interested. "Not by chance; not in the least by chance," he said with a smile. "But by marriage. Georgiana is a Spencer by birth and a Cavendish only by marriage. Your man, Henry Cavendish, is in fact her husband's second cousin. But I believe the little Duchess rather likes and even cultivates him, though he and the Duke have nothing much in common. The two men do not, I think, get on well." Stormont gave a dry laugh. "Henry Cavendish is immensely wealthy in his own right, so unlike Sheridan and his sort he has no need of the Duke's patronage."

The ambassador shook his head in perplexity. "Though I must say that to judge by his meagre life-style, you would not take Henry Cavendish for the affluent man he is. He is strange fellow--- almost a recluse. In that respect perhaps there is a similarity with the Duke, you know. But Henry dresses most carelessly and goes nowhere socially, if you do not count meetings of the Royal Society, of which he is a Fellow." Charles made a mental effort not to contradict the ambassador at that point.

"Henry Cavendish claims not to like women and avoids them like the plague whenever he can. Though Georgiana seems to be the exception to that general rule." Stormont paused. "As to his electrical work, I cannot comment. Though I did hear that he recently spent some weeks on top of Schiehallion." Seeing Charles's blank look, Stormont added as an aside, "the mountain," he said. "In Scotland, you know." Still seeing no response he went on quickly. "Anyway," he said, "that is really of no matter. But I understand he was doing something up there with instruments of some kind. Is that the sort of thing you mean?"

Before Charles could think of a sensible reply Stormont continued. "In spite of his great wealth---- his very great wealth," he said with some emphasis. "Henry Cavendish seems to care not a jot about money. He spends almost nothing and refuses even to discuss its investment with his banker! Not remotely interested!"

Charles gave an inner smile. Henry Cavendish was certainly not a man of whom Thomas Coutts would approve, at least in financial matters. Charles slowly became aware that Lord Stormont was gazing at him with renewed interest. "You know, Charles," the ambassador said approvingly, "you seem to have a knack of making the acquaintance of some interesting fellows. You have clearly not wasted your time since coming to Europe."

Charles decided that the source of his information about

Cavendish was something best kept to himself at that stage, Benjamin Franklin not being a name to drop into this conversation, especially since Stormont was at last warming to him. "Oh, people chatter in a place like Spa," he muttered vaguely, which seemed to satisfy his host. But it was a salutary warning and Charles realised that he need be circumspect about his dealings with Franklin if he wanted to maintain this new found intimacy with Stormont. And equally cautious about Juliana Ritchie. If ever he heard from her again, he thought ruefully.

Two more days passed before a brief but friendly letter arrived summoning him to Passy. Charles scrutinised it carefully, searching for clues as to how he might be received. One cryptic phrase of Franklin's raised questions in his mind; 'I hope you can join me at Passy tomorrow, when you will meet another old friend'.

Charles rode thoughtfully out of Paris, noting absently that the green chestnuts of spring had now taken on a glorious golden colour, rich and lovely even against the grey and overcast northern sky. Yes, he reflected, these trees were beautiful. Yet, without the vivid reds of the New England maples and the pale yellows of the aspens, how essentially pedestrian they were compared with the blazing forests of his childhood. Slightly to his surprise, he felt a sudden pang as he realised just how much he missed the brilliant colours that would now be drenching the hills around the Mohawk Valley.

Here in France it would take only one sharp frost or a heavy rain, both depressingly possible, for the leaves to be all stripped away and the land plunged into brown and gloomy winter. He sighed, feeling unaccountably depressed in spite of the importance of his mission as he rode on through the outlying villages.

NINETEEN

As he rode his thoughts turned to Franklin's obscure remark. Another old friend? Whom could he possibly mean? Was it intended as a warning that some kind of confrontation awaited him at Passy with Silas Deane perhaps? For Juliana would certainly have done her best to make clear the nature of Deane's activities. Ah, Juliana! Surely he did not mean that Charles would meet Juliana at Passy? He found his heart thumping unnaturally in his chest as he turned into the long driveway leading up to the grand house.

Charles was expected and was shown directly into the great reception hall where Franklin, dressed in his usual plain brown home-spun coat, rose to greet him, bowing graciously. Charles was instantly struck by the faintly absurd notion that Franklin somehow contrived to look exactly like his popular image; the long greying hair falling straight about his face, the thinning dome and of course the famous spectacles perched on the end of his rounded nose. He even propped himself up with his cane, just as he was usually portrayed and indeed exactly as Charles had last seen him.

It is all carefully contrived, Charles decided. Yes, contrived was the correct word. Every detail designed to project the image that Franklin had chosen: the simple man of the people, a little out of his depth in sophisticated Paris, but honest and sincere and essentially trustworthy.

"My dear Mr MacPherson, what a delight to meet you again. How go your studies? Do not let me forget that I have promised you those letters of introduction. I expect you want to get on with your travels, eh, do you not? Come along with me." He showed Charles into a smaller study equipped with a splendid walnut bureau scattered about with papers. "Now where are they?" he muttered. "I know that Bancroft prepared them for you." He glanced at Charles, his eyes glinting through the strangely ground spectacle lenses that he had invented to allow himself both to read clearly and yet to see longer distances. "Of course you know Edward Bancroft, do you not? But take a seat while I find the correct papers."

Charles took a deep breath. This was clearly his cue to tell his story. Quickly he outlined his fears and suspicions about Bancroft, describing from the beginning the events of that night in the Gardens of the Tuileries; the strange letter with its secret writing that went directly to Lord Stormont; Bancroft's known association with Paul Wentworth, William Eden and the British spy network. To his growing irritation Franklin seemed to be only half aware of his words, fussing with papers on his desk, occasionally muttering. "Ah dear me! Yes, yes. No, do please go on, Mr MacPherson, I am listening, I am listening. Ah yes, there they are!"

Franklin turned to him holding a sheet of paper in each hand. He waved them triumphantly and then handed one to Charles. "Pray, read that my boy. I decided against writing several letters, each one saying essentially the same thing. So I hope this will suffice. And here," he said holding up a list of ten or more names and addresses, "are some of the men on whom I think you should call. Do give them my regards."

Bemused by Franklin's lack of interest Charles helplessly glanced down at the letter, quickly scanning down the lines of writing. 'This letter introduces---- a good friend of mine and a loyal American patriot---- keenly interested in the study of electricity and magnetism---- would be grateful if you will give him what assistance you can'.

He stammered out his thanks. "I am most extraordinarily grateful to you, Mr Franklin. I cannot thank you enough" He sank back into the elegant velvet chair, momentarily speechless. Then he recovered his wits. "But Mr Franklin, what of this other matter?" he said. "Is it not of grave concern that those close to you are probably treacherous and certainly corrupt?"

Franklin stood looking down at him in silence, a fatherly smile creasing his face as Charles went on to recount the events that had befallen him in London. He told him about Sayre and Silas Deane's secret financial ventures, as well as Bancroft's apparent involvement in them. "Ah!" Franklin said simply. "London! How I miss it." He beamed at Charles. "A great city is it not? Tell me, who else did you meet there?"

Charles could no longer restrain his irritation. "Mr Franklin, I--- I am deeply unhappy at the situation I have outlined to you. But you, if I may be so bold, seem remarkably sanguine about the whole thing."

Franklin thought for a moment. He beamed. "Yes," he said carefully. "Sanguine! That is a good word." He paused and studied the young man amiably for a moment. "You see, Mr MacPherson, it is said that the world is a comedy for those who think and a tragedy for those who feel!"

"Oh come sir," Charles said in desperation. "I know you love to make these clever remarks, these deep jokes. But truly, treachery is a serious matter, is it not? Surely not a comedy!"

"Sadly I must admit that remark is not original to myself. I was merely quoting my good friend Horace Walpole, whom I hope you may meet someday." Franklin gave a broad smile. "But you were going to tell me whom you met in London, were you not."

Too astonished to dispute further Charles distractedly told him about the gathering at Charles Dilly's home. "Excellent, excellent!" Franklin beamed. "So John Wilkes was there eh? Did you by any chance also come across a wonderful woman called Catherine Macaulay?" Charles stared at him in wonder. Nothing he could tell Franklin seemed to come as a surprise.

Then Franklin suddenly looked serious. "Now Mr MacPherson, I must thank you for your confidences. They are truly appreciated, they really are. But I assure you that you need not worry yourself unduly about these matters."

He patted Charles on the shoulder and handed him the list of names he had been holding. Charles glanced down at the document, scarcely able to record them in his confusion. But they were all there, he could see. There was Volta, Henry Cavendish, Joseph Priestley, Galvani; the greatest names in the field of electrical studies. This was a compliment of staggering proportions for a young man such as himself. He stared at Franklin in astonishment. "I cannot thank you enough---," he started to say, gesturing to the list.

Franklin waved his words aside. "Oh, let us say no more." He paused. "But it may relieve your mind to know that Mr Deane is no longer a member of the American delegation here." He smiled winningly. "He is even now on his way back to America where I imagine Congress will have some interesting questions to ask him about his finances. As for Edward Bancroft--- ," he sucked in his breath, inclined his head and wrinkled his nose confidentially, "I suggest you leave that matter to me."

Before Charles fully realised it the audience was at an end and he found himself walking, stunned and silent, his head in a whirl, into the reception hall, clutching his letters of introduction. So preoccupied had he been with the discussion and Franklin's curious response that he had failed to notice how the autumn sky had steadily darkened. Now the great hall was unnaturally gloomy and as he made his way across the dimly lit flagstones a powerful rumble of thunder suddenly rattled the tall windows. Overhead the first serious rain of the season lashed against a glass cupola in the roof.

Charles hesitated and peered about the dim hallway. Shadows seemed to have gathered rapidly, filling every corner and alcove. Then in the dimness he became aware that by one of the ornate columns a tall figure stood motionless, totally still in the deep shadows. It was a man, and strangely familiar. The man stepped forward into the half light, a smile lighting up his dark features. "Hello Charlie," he said. "I am so very pleased to see you here."

Charles gasped. It was Francis Johnson! But Francis Johnson dressed in the latest French fashion, complete with white jabot! Charles stared in amazement for a second before he seized his friend by the hand, before the two young men threw their arms about each other laughing delightedly as they exchanged greetings.

After a moment Francis drew Charles into a small side chamber. It was clear that he knew his way about the house. "In here," he said firmly. "We must speak and this is a secure place." He shook his head. "A house like this has few secrets, I can tell you."

Charles followed him, still stammering words of pleasure and surprise. "But Francis," he said eventually, "how do you come to be here?" Before his friend could reply he burst out again, "How fit you look!" he said, eyeing Francis's lean figure "Stronger, if anything." Charles paused and stared at his friend again. "Though older too. I fancy you have gone through some hard times, Francis. Yet how perfectly you seem to fit in here in Paris! What brings you so far from the war?"

Francis shrugged silently. A fire blazed already in the elegant fireplace and the two young men stood together before it, Charles still beaming at his impassive friend. A solemn look came over his companion's dark features. "There is not much that I can tell you, Charlie. Let us say I am simply a courier. But a bearer of good news, indeed excellent news. There has been a magnificent victory for us at Saratoga where General Burgoyne and his entire army, or what was left of it, surrendered to General Gates."

Francis smiled. "Gates took over recently from Philip Schuyler as commander in the north, a popular move as the ordinary folk never took to the old patrician. But now some seven thousand British and Hessians are being marched off as prisoners to Boston! It is a crushing blow and of course one that will surely stiffen the resolve of our French friends." He paused. "I can tell you that they are providing us with a very large sum of money for the purchase of weapons."

"Tell me more about Saratoga," Charles begged him. "Were you there?"

"Yes, I was attached to General Benedict Arnold's force the New Hampshire Regiment, who have rather been in the thick of things as it happens." He smiled contentedly at Charles. "How I wished you had been there, Charlie! I have been used mainly on scouting duties. But I did take part in some of the set battles. We fought the British and their Hurons all the way from Ticonderoga, for it was essential to prevent them reaching Albany, where they might have linked up with Clinton and split the state from top to bottom." Charles saw his friend's eyes glint with pride. "What a man Arnold is! He fought in the front line like a man possessed, all through the final battles."

Then his expression darkened slightly. "Though if Gates had supported him sooner, the victory would have been even more complete. We lost a lot of men unnecessarily it seemed to me. But Gates does not like Arnold for some reason. Chiefly I think because General Arnold has persisted in giving staff jobs to friends of Schuyler." He glanced at Charles apologetically. "It seems impossible to escape from politics, I fear, even treachery at times." He shook his head sadly. "So much goes on away from the battle field and in politics nothing is quite so clear cut as honest conflict."

Charles nodded with more comprehension than even Francis could possibly know. "But what of you, Francis." he said. "How long do you stay here in France?"

"Not long, I fear Charlie." Francis lowered his voice. "I am on my way to London, secretly of course." He smiled. "My Spanish is passable now and I travel as a merchant in wines and oil from that country. I've had something to do with assisting the shipment of arms to our forces using a Spanish company. With the new French cash that is on its way, there will be much to do."

'Damnation!' Charles thought briefly. Then, "I suppose you know Beaumarchais?"

Francis frowned. "Yes, though he is an odd one. I dare say he is loyal enough. But I suspect money sticks to his fingers. Still we have to deal with all kinds in this war." He glanced at his friend and shrugged. "Now, Charles, listen to me. There are people in England whom I need to contact, sympathisers who can help us. You probably know that it is impossible to trust the mails." He stopped abruptly and stared at Charles. "But tell me, what have you been doing all this time?"

Rapidly Charles sketched out what he had discovered about Bancroft and Silas Deane. Francis showed no surprise. "That fits my understanding, Charlie. But I'm glad to see you have not been wasting your time here. You know that Deane is in disgrace and is being replaced? Moreover his replacement is a man of impeccable credentials, John Adams from Boston."

Charles frowned. "Not the John Adams who defended the British troops charged with murder after the Boston Massacre?"

"The same," said Francis. "But have no doubts about him. For he is a man of unshakeable integrity and a loyal patriot if ever I saw one."

He stared at Charles, his dark face impassive. "But Charlie, what of you? When are you coming home? The situation has changed greatly and your encounter with Pemberton will be long forgotten, swamped in a positive sea of blood sadly. People now neither remember nor care about that episode, though the old divisions between patriot and so-called loyalists still rage in places. Is it not time for you to come back and help the struggle? There is no need to stay away now. Especially once the French throw in their lot with us."

Charles struggled to find suitable words to explain his true feelings his friend. "Yes," he replied slowly. "I shall undoubtedly return to the Mohawk Valley one day." He look Francis frankly in the face. "But I must stay for a time. I have things of a personal nature to settle and I fear I cannot return home just yet." He hesitated. "But if I can help you here, then I am at your disposal."

Francis stared without emotion at his friend for a long moment. Finally he nodded his dark head. "I know you well enough, Charlie, to be sure where your heart lies. You will join us when you can, I know." He paused and added thoughtfully, "However perhaps you can assist us here in Europe, Charlie. Especially in England."

He pondered over his next words. "I have some confidential business there. The British fleet is a major problem because of its ability to blockade our ports. If we could destroy even some of their dockyard capacity it would have an immense impact on their ability to wage this war. That could save many thousands of lives on both sides."

"We had plans to that end. But sadly one of our best agents, John Aitken by name, is hanging in chains on a gibbet at Block House Point outside Portsmouth Dockyard. What's left of him, that is to say. Coated in tar to preserve his body as an awful warning to others."

Francis gave a half smile. "John the Painter was his popular name, for that was his trade in the dockyard." He glanced at Charles. "It may interest you to know that he was sent to England by Silas Deane and secretly briefed for the assignment by your friend Edward Bancroft in London."

"Bancroft!" exclaimed Charles. "My God!"

Francis pursed his mouth. "Yes. In view of what you tell me about Bancroft it is little wonder that Aitken was betrayed. I had guessed as much, frankly. How much bearing did his meeting with Bancroft have on his unfortunate end? We may never know, Charlie." Francis inclined his head silently for a moment. "In any event John the Painter failed in his task and has paid the price. Perhaps I can find more reliable agents in England."

Charles stood staring silently into the blazing fire, his thoughts raging. But Francis went on remorselessly. "I also have business of a personal nature that I am still determined to settle. You see, I have not forgotten our old adversary Snape." At the sound of that name Charles stared sharply at him. "You recall what I told you in my letter?" Francis went on. "I am certain the good Reverend Snape was behind Pemberton learning the truth about you and his wife. I need not remind you what resulted from that," Francis added dryly.

"But more importantly I have my private grievance. For I have not forgotten how he betrayed my people at Fort Stanwix. Make no mistake, I will find him sooner or later, Charlie. And when I do he shall be rewarded for his treachery."

"You say that Charlotte Pemberton is his mistress now?"

Francis nodded. "I suspect she always was, Charlie." As his friend shook his head in disbelief, Francis went on urgently. "In any event, try to find him, Charlie. I guess you can move freely in English society these days, thanks to your new friends in high places. Certainly more freely than myself." Charles shot a questioning look at his friend but Francis betrayed no sign of disapproval. "But Charlie, never forget that Snape is an enemy and an enemy with powerful friends. He is a follower of the man Butler, who is influential in England. So find Snape for me, Charlie." He fixed Charles with his dark eyes. "Do that for me, if you do nothing else to help the cause."

The rain had ceased by the time the two friends finally parted, though thunder still rumbled uneasily in the distance and Charles rode back to Paris more morosely even than he had come. Through a dripping world of sodden trees and dark brown fallen leaves he rode, while overhead heavy clouds trailed long low tendrils of grey across a bleak sky.

Unable to rid his mind of the parting words of his friend he found himself again imagining the blaze of colour that would now be filling the Mohawk Valley.

For in parting Francis had gripped him by the hand and stared fiercely into his eyes. "Come home, Charlie! There is so much to be done."

TWENTY

Next morning Charles made his way across Paris in bright and sunny weather, his mind in a whirl of expectation. For a letter from Juliana had been waiting for him on his return from Passy! The merest note but at least it was a reply to his own tentative approach. The note was equally if not more guarded in tone, with hardly a single spelling error.

'Dear Charles,

I am so pleased that you have returned to Paris. Come tomorrow morning , if you can, around eleven o'clock?'

Your good friend, Juliana'

There was not a great deal to be deduced from that, he thought, recalling how painfully they had parted. He did note with a cold frisson of uncertainty that Juliana had reverted to being merely a 'good' friend. No longer was she a 'dearest'. Just what was he to take from that? What did that say about how he might be received? On the other hand, the lack of spelling errors suggested that she had drafted several versions before settling on this final one, which spoke of some concern on her part.

But what might that signify? After all Juliana could by now be living openly as Beaumarchais' mistress. 'God forbid!' he thought to himself desperately. That he would not be able to tolerate.

On the other hand was it not likely that some other gentleman had emerged to capture her favours? And if so could he blame her? After all, Juliana had made no secret of her need for independence. Far from it indeed. She had made that clear from the very outset. So she owed him nothing, of that he was well aware. But see her he must, regardless of the consequences. If only, he thought, to let her know of his strange conversation with Ben Franklin. Though in his heart he knew that this was a mere excuse and that his true motive was simply a desire to see her once again.

Charles was shown with gratifying speed into Juliana's private sitting room, a pretty little room lit by the low sun and opening, he recalled with a pang, immediately off her bedroom. Juliana rose to greet him, reaching out her hand with a pale smile. No impulsive embrace this time, he noted. "Welcome back, Charlie. I am so very glad to see you again."

She was wearing a simple morning dress of white and pale green, tied by a white ribbon demurely at her throat. Very different, he reflected from the gown of dramatic green she had worn that first night at the house in the Rue du Temple. But this was a different Juliana and though the glorious red hair still tumbled unrestrained onto her shoulders she looked strained and tense.

Charles took her hand and bending forward kissed it formally. Straightening up he found himself looking directly into green troubled eyes. For an instant he trembled on the verge of taking her into his arms. But some inner voice told him that this would be wrong and certainly premature. "I cannot tell you how much I have looked forward to seeing you again, Juliana." he said self-consciously.

Her pale face was suddenly flushed. "Oh Charlie," she exclaimed. Then she stopped short and quickly turned away from him towards a small mahogany breakfast table set out for morning chocolate with a jug and two cups of the finest white china; two cups only, he registered unconsciously. Juliana composed herself on a small sofa. "Come," she said in a voice that he could tell was only half controlled, "and sit here beside me. Tell me about your summer. No more dangerous adventures, I hope," she said with a thin smile. "I was so---." She stopped and stared at him in silence.

Then she shook her head wordlessly at him. Charles noticed only how her auburn hair shimmered in the sunlight. "Charlie, I was so damned worried," she went on quietly. She paused again and then burst out. "Yes, I was worried about you! And so damnably angry too! How could you have been so stupid, Charlie? To fight over that silly girl! And don't sit there grinning at me, Charlie MacPherson. That awfully Frenchman might have killed you!"

The day seemed to lighten miraculously and Charles threw himself down beside her, taking her hands in his. "There was little chance of that, Juliana. But would you have mourned me so very much?"

Juliana shook him off in irritation. "Oh, what an ass you are, Charlie," she murmured and leaned forward to pour two cups of chocolate with an elaborate concentration as Charles watched her with growing pleasure. They sat together sipping the rich sweet drink while Charles briefly outlined the events of the summer, omitting only his encounter in Spa with Beaumarchais, whose name he simply could not bring himself to utter.

Juliana listened in silence, her eyes firmly fixed on his. Each time he mentioned Mary Graham he noticed a curious expression flit cross her face. Then, as he enthused about how the waters at Spa had benefited Mary so miraculously well, Juliana finally sighed. "Ah yes, Mrs Graham! So beautiful, so intelligent and so kind. It seems almost too much," she muttered in a tone that Charles found hard to identify. He glanced at her in puzzlement and was about to ask her meaning. But as he had already begun an account of his meeting with Franklin and as Juliana seemed eager to hear about the great man's reactions, he allowed the moment to pass.

"It truly is a mystery to me, Charlie," Juliana said when he had finished, "why Franklin is so unconcerned about Edward Bancroft. The man is obviously a villain. I wonder if Franklin has not become senile while he has been here in France. After all he is not a young man any more. Has he lost his senses altogether?" She shook her head in despair, a frown creasing her features. "At least," she went on, "Silas Deane is on his way back to America to face Congress and John Adams is without doubt an honest man. That is a step forward, at least. Let us hope Deane receives a just reward for his duplicity."

Then she turned and looked at Charles strangely, her green eyes darkening. "Charlie," she said determinedly, seizing both of his hands in hers. "I have something to tell you; something important." He gazed at her, a sudden cold chill gripping him. Juliana spoke rapidly, "Charlie, I have decided to go home to Philadelphia. Oh, I know it is still in British hands. But I'm sure it will not be so for long. The French will soon come into the war and then everything will change."

Charles stared in consternation as Juliana tightened her grip on his hands, her eyes fixed on his. "Charlie, will you not come back home with me?" she blurted out. "There is so much you can do there for our cause; things we could do together! And---- and," She released him and rising quickly to her feet moved across to the sunlit window. Standing with her back to him, staring out at the little garden she went on more slowly, choosing her words carefully. "Charlie, I would like us to be together. For together I believe that we could build something special." She turned to face him with the winter sun lighting her hair gloriously.

Her voice trembled as she quickly went on. "Need I say that I have never before asked any man such a thing? I think you know me well enough to believe that when I say so." She raised one hand to cover her mouth for an instant. Then, "Oh Charlie," she said almost in a whisper. "I know these things are fragile as glass and I suppose you will think me incredibly bold--- and probably stupid too." She gave a nervous little laugh. "But I want you with me, Charlie. I can't tell you how much---." Her voice broke and she stood there in silence, holding out her hands to him. Charles moved towards her, every rational thought wiped out in the moment.

Almost an hour later they in silence side by side in Juliana's bed. Their love-making had been as passionate as ever. But this time it had been different and both of them had recognised the difference. There had been an edge of desperation about it and Charles knew that the tender artlessness of their earlier love had gone. In place of a glorious sense of satisfaction he felt only a strange, empty, inexplicable regret.

Finally Juliana spoke. "It will not do," she said sadly. "You do not intend to come home with me, do you?" Her voice made it clear that it was a question that required no response.

Charles sat up in bed staring straight ahead, not daring even to look at her, and spoke the only words he could find. "Juliana, I am sorry," he said quietly. "But I have things still to do here in Europe. There are people here to whom I have come to feel a loyalty." As he heard his words he knew how hurtful and senseless they would sound to her. "How I wish it was different," he said urgently.

Juliana rose swiftly and wrapped herself in a robe, avoiding his gaze. "Yes, I wish it had been different too, Charlie." She gave a bitter smile. "What a fool you must think me." Then, cutting short his protestations she walked calmly out of the bedroom. "You will excuse me," he heard her say as she vanished from his sight. "I dare say you will find your own way out."

Charles groaned and sat for an age in silence holding his head in his hands. First he had disappointed his dear friend Francis and now he had undoubtedly lost Juliana for ever. How had he contrived to reject two of the people he most valued in the world!

How had this come about, he asked himself desperately? But in his heart he knew the answer. He had made a choice and come what may he was committed now to a life in Europe, at least for a time. A life such as he could never have imagined a mere twelve months before, so very different was it from the old one he had left behind in the Mohawk valley.

Left behind for ever? Well, he thought distractedly, at least for the present. One day he would return to America, of that he was certain. For he was still a patriot at heart. Was he not?

TWENTY ONE

In spite of his agonising however, his first step on leaving Paris late in the year of 1777 had been to return to London, where he enjoyed a cheerful reunion with Thomas and Mary Graham. They had asked him to join them for the winter season at the Cathcart family home in Grosvenor Place and soon after his arrival he confided in them that he hoped to travel more widely in Europe.

"What a splendid idea," Mary said with a gentle smile and an approving nod of her elegant head. "A tour of Italy is essential for a young man to complete his education, do you not agree, Thomas?"

"Certainly." Thomas smiled approvingly at Charles. "Or so I was assured by my guardians, Lord Kinnoull and my uncle Lord Hopetoun, who arranged the whole thing for me. Though I cannot honestly say, Mary dear, that I learned a great deal from all the old buildings, the fine statues and paintings and so on that I was made to stare at!"

"Oh come, Thomas," Mary smiled gently. "Did you not learn to understand all those difficult foreign languages? French and Italian too? And I seem to recall that you were much taken by some of those ancient ruins. Especially the Tomb of Virgil at Naples, I remember."

Then as an after thought she added "Oh Charles, when you visit Naples, which you must of course, as it is an essential for a young man of style these days, you will stay with my uncle, Sir William Hamilton. He is a delightful man--- he was my mother's favourite brother--- and has a wonderful collection of classical works of art."

Thomas grunted. "Has almost ruined himself buying all these old things. I imagine that's why he has to live abroad, where it is cheap. But true enough, he is a very nice fellow."

"You will enjoy Naples, I am certain." said Mary firmly. "Sir William is our Ambassador there and of course knows everyone. I shall write to say you are coming." She clasped her small pale hands and beamed at him. "Come, let us design a special Grand Tour for you! Oh Charles, you shall miss nothing! What fun! It will be almost as good as going ourselves." Charles did not have the heart at that stage to explain to Mary that the arts held no particular attraction for him; that his interests lay in quite another direction. For Charles had his own objectives and his own list of great men to meet and all the latest news of modern electrical research to acquire.

Still, the chance to bask in Mary's undivided attention was too much for him to resist and for a succession of afternoons he took delight in being closeted with her in a snug private sitting-room as she made eager lists of the places he was obliged to see, galleries he should visit and the works of antiquity he must admire. "Naples, Florence and Rome," Mary said delightedly. "How I wish we were going with you."

Charles studied her cautiously as she bent over her writing-desk concentrating on her list making. Mary looked paler than ever, he thought. Still lovely of course. But thinner and more frail than he recalled from the warm days in Spa. She was coughing more frequently too, sometimes in spasms that could last a minute or more and shook her slight body painfully and were as painful for the onlookers to see.

In those moments he would see Thomas look at her with something like anguish written on his bluff open face. But then she would recover her strength for a time, sometimes for several days on end. Cheerfully she would tell Charles her family news.

"William and Charles are still in the army." A cloud passed over her gentle features. "How I wish this dreadful war would be over. But William has been promoted again and by all accounts he has a brilliant career ahead of him."

Thomas intervened with a smile. "He's been made a Captain in the 17th Dragoons. His brother Charles seems to be enjoying himself as well, though I doubt the army will be where he makes his life's work. He's a clever young devil and I expect he'll end up as an Ambassador somewhere important, just like his father."

"But he had a shocking narrow escape on his way home recently." Mary said with concern in her voice. "His ship was captured by pirates!"

"Well, not exactly pirates," said Thomas. "It was a French

privateer, my dear. And by all accounts they treated him well enough when they learned that he was a gentlemen. In fact he was released to continue his journey quite quickly. Though of course once the French have officially entered the war, as seems inevitable now, there might not be such a happy conclusion. A French prison would not be a pleasant spot to pass the war." Charles recalled the grim bulk of the old Temple in Paris and nodded his agreement.

"Ahem!" Thomas coughed, quickly changing the subject and becoming much more utilitarian. "Now, how do you propose to travel, Charles? You'll wait until spring before setting off, of course. Horseback, which I know you prefer, is all very well in good weather for a fit young fellow like yourself and better at any time than a coach in mountains or over rough ground, of which there is plenty. But in winter,--- you do realise a journey like this will take twelve months or more? So you will not escape at least one winter and at that time of year the weather can be foul, particularly over the mountains. The best plan is to hire a chaise or a berlin as you go. Or a coach if you plan to have a great deal of baggage."

"He will need servants, will he not Thomas?"

"Yes. At least one." Thomas noticed Charles staring at him in horror. "Now I know you like to go your own way, Charles. But you should have a companion of some sort, certainly." He paused thoughtfully. "You can have one of my men, if you like. I dare say there is some young fellow on the estate who would go with you like a flash on such an adventure."

He went on. "Anyway, you will find that the local form of transport, whatever it is and however extraordinary it may look, will generally be best suited in any particular area. But be sure to take local advice. I found that people were usually helpful and trustworthy, though others had different experiences. But there you are," Thomas said with a wave of his strong hand, "you must take people as you find them."

"Incidentally," he added, "the roads in France and Italy are uniformly atrocious. Or were in my day---- they may have improved now, which I doubt. I'll give you the names of some friends who would be happy to offer you hospitality as you travel. And I dare say your financial man will fix you up with letters of credit and so on. It's still old man Coutts, is it not?"

Suddenly struck by the thought, Thomas drew Charles aside. "I say, Charles my boy." he said in an undertone. "I take it there is no difficulty about money or that sort of thing? If you are short--- ."

"No, no, thank you Thomas." Charles said with a smile. "It is a kind thought and one that I appreciate greatly. But I seem to be pretty well fixed in that regard at present."

"Yes." Thomas said half in wonder. "You had an amazingly good summer in the casino at Spa, they tell me. It seems you are quite a phenomenon with the cards." He shook his head in puzzlement. "Never could see the point myself."

Soon after his arrival in London Charles had sent Thomas Coutts a draft for nine hundred guineas, Beaumarchais finally having paid his debt and in the greatest of good nature. So much so that Charles decided uncharitably that the latest French subsidy must have passed recently through his hands and that part of it had as usual stuck to his fingers. Still, Charles had accepted the money as a small kind of triumph and stiffly taken his leave, thankful to be finished with the man and all his works. He wrote now to Coutts, outlining his plans for a European tour and arranging to call at the bank in the Strand to discuss financial arrangements.

In addition, the opportunity to put Franklin's letter of introduction to the test in London was irresistible and having received no reply to an initial communication and recalling Henry Cavendish's reputation as a recluse, he boldly determined to call on the famous man of science at his home.

Approaching the Great Marlborough Street address he observed standing outside the house an exceptionally grand looking coach, with in attendance a swarm of idle livery-clad servants. Charles frowned. This hardly fitted the image of Henry Cavendish as a byword for parsimony. Drawing still nearer he was intrigued to see that the doors of the coach were indeed emblazoned with the Cavendish coat of arms. Charles sent in his name with a brief reminder of his connection with Benjamin Franklin. Then he waited by the entrance, conscious of the curious stares of the lounging servants.

It was only a brief wait however before he was ushered by an elderly manservant into a small reception hall and left alone to look about curiously. The house was a solid old structure. But by no means luxurious, though as he reminded himself ruefully, his standards had somewhat changed since his exposure to the aristocracy of Europe! The reception room in which he stood was quite empty but for a dusty chair in the corner, on which lay a three-cornered cocked hat that looked as if it might date from the previous century. Charles, himself now the very figure of a fashionable young man, frowned. This was certainly an odd sort of house, he mused.

Abruptly a door opened and an extraordinary figure lurched awkwardly into the room. It was a very tall man with grey hair worn roughly clubbed down his back and wearing a coat of faded crumpled velvet of a colour that Charles guessed had once been violet. It had the high collar and frilled cuffs of an earlier era and Charles knew at once that he was observing the owner of the old hat.

The man's large rectangular face was plain with heavy features but pleasant enough at first sight, Charles decided. The newcomer's eyes, large, dark and intelligent, darted about nervously, sweeping over Charles several times as if reluctant to confront him directly.

When he spoke it was in a thin, squeaky voice, curious in such a big man. Hesitantly, he said, "Ah Mr Franklin--- no, no of course. You are not Mr Franklin! No, I know Mr Franklin. Met him several times at the Royal Society. A much older man altogether." A nervous smile twitched at the thin mouth. "No, you are Mr MacPherson, are you not? But a friend of Franklin's? Is that not so?"

Charles admitted that he was indeed Mr MacPherson and a friend of Mr Benjamin Franklin. It was remarkable how easily that statement seemed to come to him now. He presented his formal letter of introduction, which Cavendish read at a glance. "Splendid, splendid," he said vaguely. "So you are interested in things electrical. Well, we must talk about that sometime soon. Yes, I dare say we shall." He stared at Charles almost furtively from under his eyebrows. "But it happens that I have another visitor at the moment."

Charles started to apologise for the intrusion. But Cavendish brushed his words aside. "Not at all, not at all. It is only my young cousin. We are taking some tea in the sitting-room." He smiled awkwardly. "She has quite taken me up socially." He sighed and looked perplexed. Shaking his head he said, "Don't understand it at all. Most confusing." He straightened his stooping shoulders. "Still, there it is. Come and take some tea with us." He frowned. "This seems to be my day to be sociable! Ha, ha!" He gave a thin creaking laugh and led the way into a much more spacious room, well-lit with large elegant windows looking out onto the street.

By the wide fire-place was a small circular mahogany tea table at which sat an elegantly dressed young woman. Charles studied her curiously and noticed that she returned his stare boldly. 'Odd,' he thought briefly, 'this is not what I had been led to expect of the reclusive Henry Cavendish'.

The young woman was tall, as tall as Mary, with a mass of light auburn hair tumbling down over her shoulders and large luminous hazel-coloured eyes set in a round attractive face. She wore a gown of pale gold, with a froth of lace about her bosom and throat. Altogether the effect was striking. She was not of course as beautiful as Mary Graham. Nor as spectacularly handsome as Juliana and perhaps tending a shade too much to plumpness. But there was a good-natured openness about her manner and the ready smile playing on her red lips made him warm to her instantly.

Henry Cavendish, his thin voice almost breaking with embarrassment, stuttered out "Now my dear, this is---- is," he glanced for reassurance at the letter he still clutched in one large workmanlike hand. "Yes, this is Mr Charles George MacPherson. Mr MacPherson, may I present my cousin, Georgiana Cavendish." He paused. "Georgiana, the Duchess of Devonshire. There now," he said to Georgiana with an awkward bow. "I did that quite well, did I not." He gave another creaking laugh. "Don't get a lot of practice at all this social business," he muttered half to himself.

"Mr MacPherson is a friend of Mr Benjamin Franklin," he went on, "of whom I expect you have heard. He is a member of the Royal Society and has done some very interesting work on lightning conductors and, and,--- that kind of thing." He halted, clearly at a loss. "Mr Franklin, that is to say. Not Mr MacPherson. Though I dare say he has also done some interesting work." His voice faded away again as Charles recovered his wits in time to stoop to kiss Georgiana's white hand and murmur something about 'your grace'.

He looked up to see her regarding him with even more interest. Her voice was light and charming. "So you are a friend of Mr Franklin," she said. "Mr Fox tells me that we have treated him and our American friends abominably. Do you come from America then?"

"Yes, America. But via Paris most recently."

"And are you to be in London for some time?"

"For the winter at least. I am at present a guest at Lord Cathcart's home. More correctly I suppose, I am a guest of Thomas and Mary Graham, who are residing at her family home for the time being."

"Oh, you know dear Mary!" the Duchess cried in delight. "Oh how I love her! You know we met in Brighton and I was much taken with her. Such a sweet dear woman." Charles had formed a good opinion of the Duchess almost immediately. But now he warmed to her completely and the more so at her next words.

"Why, you must be the Charles of whom Mary speaks so highly!"

Charles flushed with pleasure. Now he would have cheerfully died for Georgiana. "I admire her more than anything, Your Grace," he said.

"Oh call me Georgiana," she said. "Everyone does. Do they not, Henry? And by the bye I am not your cousin. Not exactly. I fancy I must be your second cousin by marriage to be precise." She beamed at Henry

Cavendish, who twisted in embarrassment like a schoolboy. Turning back to Charles she fixed him with her brilliant eyes. "Cousin Henry does not care for my husband," she said blandly. "But that is no matter. There is no need for him to meet the Duke." She gave a charming laugh. "Indeed I rarely see him myself! In polite society it is regarded as bad form for a husband and wife to be seen too much together." Charles inclined his head wordlessly towards her, incapable for the moment of replying.

"Now Henry," the Duchess went on, "I expect you and Mr MacPherson want to talk about your electrical fish and so on. Did you know that Henry has constructed a cunning model of one of those strange creatures? And he has designed conductors to protect us from lightning flashes. He is so clever!"

Cavendish hung his head in embarrassment, his voice becoming thinner and squeakier. "Oh no, really," he muttered.

Torpedo Fish, thought Charles. "Do you perhaps know a man called Edward Bancroft, sir? I understood that he has done work on these electrical fish."

Cavendish looked uneasily at him and then at Georgiana, as though blaming her for his predicament. "Ah, Edward Bancroft, the physician. Yes, he did some early work on the phenomenon." He paused and gazed desperately about the room. "Strange fellow, Bancroft. Bit of an eccentric."

With difficulty Charles repressed a smile. To be called an eccentric by someone who was renowned throughout England as an eccentric seemed to damn Bancroft totally. To change the conversation Charles pressed desperately on, "I understand, sir, that you recently spent time on a mountain in Scotland making some special measurements."

"What?" said Cavendish. "Oh no, no. That was Maskelyne, the Astronomer Royal, you know." He flushed. "I don't get about a great deal. Simply gave him some advice on instruments and that sort of thing. Measured the mass of the earth. Very interesting. In fairness, it is Charles Hutton who is doing most of the calculations. Though I'm still not convinced the figure is correct. Needs a lot of work." He stared moodily at the fireplace and shook his head. "Yes, needs a lot of work."

Georgiana rose. "Now cousin, I must leave you and Mr MacPherson." Turning to Charles she fixed him with her large luminous eyes. "You shall visit us at Devonshire House," she said firmly. "We are here for the winter, thanks be to God. I cannot abide the country and all those dreary sheep and things."

Charles stared at her speechlessly. "No, I dare say not," was all he could think of as a reply.

Luckily she had sailed on regardless. "Tell me Mr MacPherson, do you ever play at cards?"

"Not seriously," he replied, wincing as he was instantly conscious of how untrue was the statement.

"Oh good!" the Duchess said gaily. "We never do anything seriously at Devonshire House! Come along to supper one evening. Wednesdays and Saturdays are best, for then the political gentlemen are free to join us and there is a great deal of merriment, as you can imagine. We have some music and supper and then play cards. So until Wednesday then?" She exited in a flurry of perfume and lace, leaving the stage curiously dull and empty.

Charles and Cavendish stared at each other in silence for a moment. "Strange girl," muttered Cavendish. "But charming. Don't know why she consented to marry my cousin. Still, there you are," he ended inconclusively.

Then he stared at Charles. "So you are interested in the electrical studies? I expect you have read the paper I produced for the Royal Society last year on the electrical model of the Torpedo Fish. No? Oh well it wasn't very good. I expect I have a copy somewhere. I'll send it to you. Used pewter plates to simulate the sort of discharge the fish seems to create naturally. Joseph Priestley came here to try it out." He gave another of his creaking laughs. "You should have seen him jump! Made him admit that God is not the only one who can make electricity!" He looked thoughtful. "Not a great deal of spark though, in spite of linking four dozen Leyden jars. Must give a bit more thought to that. More research needed."

"You are working on lightning conductors too?"

Cavendish scowled. "Oh, a lot of nonsense," he said. "This dispute between Franklin and Wilson has become a political issue. Points or knobs on the conductor! You know I chaired the Society's committee on the protection of our arsenal at Purfleet? Though there is no doubt that solids do attract differently according to their shape, as I expect you've noticed." He gazed at Charles apologetically. "But look here, you do realise that most of my work these days is on gases and atmospheres. Who else do you plan to see?"

Charles retrieved his precious letter. "Well sir, I hope to travel to Italy."

"Ah, then you must see Galvani and Volta. They have been in touch with me to discuss their work. Most interesting. I'll write to them and let them know you are coming." he sighed. "I tend to do my work here, in my laboratory. Would you like to see my electrical torpedo fish? It's very boring really."

Later in the day Charles called on Thomas Coutts in the Strand, where he was received with the zeal his new financial status justified. This time there was no long wait in which to consider the crowded street below. Instead he was ushered straight into a private drawing room where Coutts welcomed him like a returning son.

"My dear Mr MacPherson! I am delighted to see you back in civilisation," he said in his Scots accent, his long dark face splitting briefly into a broad smile. "Though I see from your letter that you are off on your travels again soon. Dear me! But let me see. How does your account stand now?" His gaze flicked rapidly over a ledger that lay on the table before him.

Charles had developed an eye for such matters since his original impressionable visit and noted that Thomas Coutts was dressed simply but fashionably in sober clothes of an expensive cut and with a spotless neck cloth of best linen. He was also well aware that Coutts already knew to the last penny how much money lay in his account.

"In round figures, Mr MacPherson, you now have fifteen thousand pounds on deposit. A good sum and one which at the rate for government funds is producing--- " He paused and regarded Charles with an enquiring glance and a small smile. "At a safe three and a half percent?"

Charles said automatically "Five hundred and twenty five pounds per annum."

"Correct," Coutts said, beaming at Charles like a proud Scottish dominie. "Well done! I see you have lost none of your quickness in the calculations. It is not great wealth of course. But an income that will allow you to travel in some comfort, I believe. Now tell me what are your plans and I shall arrange for Mr Muirhead to provide you with letters of credit against convenient banks."

"I take it you will be visiting Turin, perhaps Milan? And certainly Florence and Rome of course." He summoned his confidential clerk, a lean morose lowland Scot who appeared if anything more Calvinistic than Coutts himself. Muirhead listened with evident disapproval of such frivolous expenditure, shaking his head and occasionally tutting audibly, before vanishing to deal with the correspondence.

Coutts turned back to Charles with a smile. "Mr Muirhead does not entirely approve of expenditure of this kind. He has a low opinion of foreigners in general and Italy in particular, it being irredeemably Papist. But he is very efficient and you may be assured that funds will not be a problem for you. Now, tell me, how are you to spend the winter?" he asked. "For I dare say you will not want to leave much before February or March. Will you learn some of the Italian language? It may save you from being taken advantage of in that country. I understand they are not very trustworthy. No great moral standards when it comes to financial matters." He paused. "Or indeed in other," he gave a slight cough, "other more personal matters," Coutts said, looking embarrassed.

In the awkward pause that followed Charles intervened to fill in the gap in conversation. "I believe I shall be quite busy in London. My friend Thomas Graham has plans for me. And I have been invited to supper at Devonshire House," he remarked casually. "The Duchess--- ,"

"My dear young man! You have been invited to supper by the Duchess of Devonshire? The great Georgiana?" There was a mixture of pleasure, astonishment and perhaps a tinge of envy in his voice. "My word! You have truly arrived in society." Coutts stood up and shook Charles by the hand. "Pray give my regards to the Duchess. But in a judicious way, of course." He looked knowingly at Charles.

When Charles recounted this exchange to Thomas Graham his friend laughed amiably. "You must have impressed the little Duchess! My word, old Coutts would sell his soul for such an invitation. He has three daughters, you know. Pleasant enough young ladies to be sure," he hesitated for a moment, "though in the normal way not quite the thing to be presented at court. Though that is something Coutts wants desperately. Such a thing would, as it were, set the seal on his own place in society. As a money man Coutts is of course distinguished, indeed highly distinguished. It is well known that he gives generously to deserving charities."

Thomas laughed again. "And to some not so deserving cases! But he is not what you would call top drawer socially, for all his bounteousness to the aristocracy, most of whom owe him large amounts of money and are never pressed for repayment. So that to date he has quite failed to have his daughters presented. Though I dare say he will succeed eventually," Thomas added. "The girls are quite presentable, so to speak, and in time someone in society will owe him enough."

"Is that truly how it works?"

Thomas silently inclined his head. "You know of course that the Devonshire House set are notorious for their loose style of life and excessive gambling debts." He pursed his mouth and stared at Charles. "You know my views on that." He frowned. "But gambling is the least of it there, Charles, and the women are as bad as any, I'm sorry to say. So I hope you will be careful, Charles. There are some hellfire rakes associated with the Duchess. For charming as she is, the young lady seems unaware of the impression she creates."

He looked unhappily at Charles. "Many of that set are frivolous and quite louche. Fellows like Derby and Cholmondeley, who should know better, are regularly pilloried in the broadsheets and don't seem to care a jot for their reputations." Thomas paused. "I understand that Georgiana has recently taken up Charles James Fox, the politician, who stayed at Chatsworth earlier this year. Fox has many fine qualities, Charles, and is a brilliant debater in the House. He is of course a good Whig who resigned on principle over the American War, so I dare say you will sympathise with him there."

"But gambling is almost a disease with him. He plays at Almack's most nights and will no doubt be a stalwart at the new Brooks's Club when it opens next year in St James's. He's been known to play for days and nights on end. He will win and then lose ten, fifteen or twenty thousand pounds at a sitting, so that his debts are crushing, even for the son of Lord Holland, who has untold wealth of course. But unlike you, Fox despises games of skill, preferring the excitement of sheer chance."

"Oh no!" Charles was genuinely shocked at such a perverse preference.

Completely misunderstanding his look of disapproval, Thomas was encouraged to continue. "And then there are the hangers-on. Those who attach themselves to the Chatsworth 'ton', as they like to call themselves. Fellows like the two Craufurd brothers. Fish and Fowl they call them; the one cold and the other corpulent and both pretty ugly in more ways than one. And James Hare, though he's not such a bad fellow, if constantly on the edge of bankruptcy. Then of course there is Richard Sheridan, the playwright and an inveterate drinker and womaniser. But a clever devil, witty and quick and in consequence welcomed in that set. And some of the women--- ," Thomas Graham shook his head in silent condemnation. "Many of them are from the best aristocratic families too."

"Yes," said Charles slowly. "I met Sheridan in the casino at Spa. I did not take to him, I must say."

"I am glad to hear it," said Thomas shortly. He paused. "Tell me, how did you get along with Henry Cavendish? He received you, at least, which is remarkable enough."

"Indeed he did," Charles said, grateful for the change of subject. "He showed me a most remarkable device he has constructed to simulate the electrical effect of the Torpedo Fish. It replicates the astonishing characteristics of the South American electrical eel, which can kill a man or even a horse."

Enthusiastically he described the apparatus he had seen. "Cavendish has cut pieces of leather to the shape of the fish and placed inside thin plates of pewter, to simulate the electrical glands of the fish, you know? These are connected to a battery of Leyden jars. Oh, forty or fifty of them, which generate a charge one can feel quite strongly when the whole thing is submerged in salt water." He stopped short, seeing the uncomprehending frown on Thomas's face and suddenly aware that he was in danger of sounding like Edward Bancroft. "But no matter," he ended lamely. "It---- it was very interesting."

Thomas nodded vaguely. "I dare say." There was an awkward moment of silence. "Now Charles, there is something I want to say to you and I hope you won't mind me mentioning it." Charles instantly felt himself bristle. What was to come? Some warning about gambling. Or the dangers of associating with the Devonshire House set?

Thomas went on obliviously. "It seems to me that perhaps some time at Angelo's fencing school might be a good way to make use of the winter. Let us say two or three mornings a week? What do you say to that? It might be as well to polish up your technique with sword and sabre." Thomas coughed awkwardly. "I think you will agree it does need some improvement."

Charles, bowed his head in graceful acknowledgment.

"Italy is reasonably civilised, on the whole," Thomas went on reassuringly. "But one never can tell what emergencies may arise on the road; brigands and so on. And after all, a gentleman in your circumstances is expected to be a reasonable practitioner with the smallsword at least. By the way, I gather from David Murray that your friend John Sewell might be available to travel with you, for at least part of the journey, if that would be congenial to you." Charles smiled. Sewell would be a pleasant enough companion on the journey, he thought.

"For reasons that you will understand, Lord Stormont expects his residency in Paris to be cut short quite soon. So Sewell will be at a loose end thereafter." Thomas frowned at Charles contemplatively. "He would be a useful fellow to have beside you in a mêlée, should such a thing unfortunately arise on the road. He has been a soldier and has travelled widely on the continent, though his social contacts will of course be very different from your own. Still, he speaks tolerable French and some Italian too, I am told. Which reminds me, we must do something about getting you the rudiments of that tongue before you leave."

Thomas shrugged. "Of course the sort of people you will meet socially are happy to converse in French and the ordinary folk do tend to speak their own horrible local dialects---- the country is fragmented into a positive mosaic of petty states and duchies. It's all very inconvenient. But a grasp of the Italian language might be useful and I should judge that you will pick it up quickly enough."

TWENTY TWO

Under the watchful eye of Thomas and Mary Graham Charles spent an enjoyable winter in London. The weeks seemed to speed past, between his fencing lessons and his intensive language sessions, until in the spring of 1778 Thomas declared himself well pleased with his young protégé. By then too Charles was eager to set off on his travels, the more so since he knew that Thomas had business on his Perthshire estates and that he and Mary would soon be leaving London.

Charles's regular visits to the Angelo establishment in Carlisle House had made him fitter and more agile than ever and after one last extended sweaty session Angelo had finally pronounced Charles the finished article. Leaning on his sabre point to catch his breath the young Harry Angelo, dark haired and slim, made an extravagant gesture towards Charles.

"Mr MacPherson," he declaimed. "In my opinion you now have as much of these skills as any respectable young gentleman should ever require. Your smallsword is now quite excellent and in that you need fear comparison with no-one. Particularly, if I may say so, when combined with the dagger. Which weapon," he added dryly, "I rather fancy you still prefer if the truth was told. But it is of course no weapon for a gentleman."

Charles bowed his head in acknowledgement.

"But I have to say, sir, that your sabre is as good as anything I have seen outside the military." Angelo also bowed graciously to Charles. "To tell the truth, I pity anyone unfortunate enough to cross you on your travels." Charles, winded and soaked with perspiration, knew this was praise indeed. Presenting his sword correctly he returned the bow, remembering the elder Angelo's much repeated admonition that his school was as much one of manners as of arms.

Fortunately for Charles not all his time was spent under Thomas's fatherly eye and he found that his social life also blossomed. Devonshire House was the key to this and though it saw Charles only intermittently he soon discovered that his acceptance there ensured him an entrée to any of the fashionable houses in London.

Had it not been for social convention, Charles might easily have strolled across to Devonshire House from the Cathcart home, both being set in the new 'polite' west end of London. Instead, on his very first visit he travelled the short distance by chaise. At first sight the house was a disappointment, presenting such a cheerless facade to the world that he imagined momentarily that his driver had delivered him mistakenly to some anonymous block of warehouses.

But boring as was the exterior aspect, when once he had passed inside the forbidding brick curtain wall and mounted the sweeping staircase from the courtyard, it was with difficulty that Charles prevented himself from gaping in sheer wonder. This was grandeur and affluence of a measure he had never before encountered, never even imagined could exist. Nothing he had experienced in Paris had prepared him for this.

The first floor reception hall soared a full two storeys above him and was lavishly furnished, the walls adorned with paintings by artists whose names even Charles recognised. On each side of this hall lay two equally massive drawing rooms and at the rear of the house was a third drawing room of the same heroic dimensions. In addition there was a spacious dining room and a maze of smaller ante-rooms into which guests could wander for the kind of private tête-à-têtes that the Cavendish 'ton' relished. On special occasions it was said the house had comfortably contained a thousand guests.

The tall first floor windows gave out on splendid uninterrupted views across Green Park to the south. Within sight was Georgiana's childhood family home, Spencer House and further away beyond St James's Park lay Buckingham House, which it was rumoured King George himself planned to purchase. Gazing in a kind of controlled awe Charles found that in spite of his new-found sophistication there was still within him enough of the country boy to wonder at wealth on this scale--- and to guess at how it had been acquired.

But all the strangeness vanished as the Duchess greeted him with a generous warmth. "Come, Mr MacPherson. You must meet my very special friends. Lady Melbourne, may I present Mr MacPherson, who has recently come to us from America," she said gaily.

A tall woman of commanding presence, dark haired with deep-set intelligent eyes, coolly appraising, silently inclined her head. "Mr MacPherson is a particular friend of the beautiful Mary Graham, whom I met this summer in Brighton. As you know, I think the world of her." Charles flushed with pleasure. If anything more was need to endear Georgiana to him these words were enough.

"And Charles, here are two more of my special friends, Lady Derby and Lady Jersey." Two more elegant women acknowledged him graciously, with rather more sincerity he thought than Lady Melbourne. One of them, something above average height, was strikingly handsome and of statuesque build with rich auburn hair piled high and wide-set blue eyes of a particular loveliness; the other, smaller, with hair elaborately coiffured in formal ringlets, had no great beauty it seemed to Charles. But Lady Jersey carried her head with a grace that somehow made her seem more beautiful and undoubtedly she radiated a tangible charm. A glass of champagne was thrust into his hand and soon his head was spinning in a blur of new names and faces: Mrs Damen, Mrs Bouverie and Mrs Crewe.

Charles became the centre of a group of superbly attired ladies, each it seemed more beautiful than the other. Moreover, unused as he was to the ways of women of this class, Charles could not fail to detect a predatory gleam in the eyes of some of Georgiana's female friends, particularly as the evening wore on and the wine was consumed, glass after glass after glass. More than one of the ladies he noticed had looked appraisingly at his tall athletic figure.

Though flattered by this, frankly he soon found the attention a shade embarrassing. For nothing in his experience of women, with Juliana or Charlotte Pemberton or indeed any other woman, had prepared him for this kind of open invitation. Natural appreciation was one thing, he thought, without false modesty. But this was something else. And from women significantly older than himself, whom he did not know and indeed had scarcely met.

They all wanted to hear about his savage upbringing in the wilds of America and his adventures with the dangerous native tribes. Was it true that they took even women's scalps, they asked with delighted shudders? The notion appeared to excite some of the boldest ladies as they crowded eagerly about their latest novelty, fans aflutter, eyes blue or dark, wide and gleaming. Charles decided it would be prudent to keep to himself any account of his real life and adventures in the woods with Francis and his Mohawk friends. My God, he thought, how distant seemed that day with Pemberton!

But hearing of his relatively civilised early life in the home of Sir

William Johnson and his hours of lonely study in the library the ladies soon lost interest in him, turning to more familiar prey with shrieks of delight as a group of men appeared together in the grand drawing room. "Oh, the gentlemen have arrived from the House," Georgiana cried out. "Forgive me, Charles, for I must greet them." With that she was swept away in a mass of admirers.

These were almost the last words that Charles managed to exchange with his hostess that night. But at least he was now free to circulate, to introduce himself and to speak informally to some of the male guests, who had been eying him quizzically for some time.

As more and more wine was drunk he noted that the atmosphere grew ever wilder. Excitement seemed to mount and Charles found himself observing the behaviour of the famous Cavendish set even more critically. Drunkenness and bawdiness had never attracted him, particularly in people who should know better, he thought to himself. Although he did not think of himself a prude, far from it, as the alcohol continued to be consumed in impressive quantities he was actually shocked by the libidinous behaviour on display in these elegant drawing rooms.

Georgiana's behaviour he found especially difficult to understand. In early part of the evening she had been quite as natural and friendly as at their first meeting in the home of Henry Cavendish. There was an unforced charm and directness about her that Charles found almost as attractive as Mary Graham's more gentle appeal. It was little surprise to him that the two women should have become such friends. But as the evening unwound he could not fail to notice that the Duchess drank too much, becoming more voluble and extravagant in her manner. In an effort to impress? But to impress whom, he wondered? Were these people really so important? He shook his head in silent puzzlement.

As the supper tables were cleared away he made his way into the rear drawing room. There he saw that the room had been set up as a gambling casino, complete with a table for faro, as the English chose to call it, and another for his old friend hazard. Georgiana and her friends all clutching glasses of champagne or punch were already wildly staking fifty guinea rouleaus on the most outrageous wagers, quite oblivious to their losses.

Behind the faro table stood a tall soberly dressed man with the hard-bitten face and the smile of doubtful sincerity that marked him clearly as a professional gambler. Charles noticed that Georgiana took a central role at the tables and that she gambling more and more outrageously.

"She tries too hard to please these people," Charles thought unhappily. "Unhappy woman! I wonder what the problem is?" He frowned as he watched her toss money away. Then recalling the consequences of his last attempt to advise a lady in similar circumstances, he moved quietly away towards the great front windows of the house and stood staring out into the darkness of Green Park, making his plans for a polite escape.

As he stood in silence he became aware that nearby were two men speaking together in low voices. They were some of the most recent arrivals, having entered with the sudden influx of parliamentarians. One was a neat composed figure of medium height and trim build who glanced around, aware that company was within earshot. This man bowed to Charles with a pleasant smile. "Good evening sir. I do not believe we have met." It was an open friendly intelligent face, Charles decided. "May I introduce myself. I am Robert Greville. And this is Mr Edmund Burke."

"Oh! The famous Mr Burke." Charles spoke spontaneously. He had heard of Burke's speeches in Parliament condemning the war with the colonies and looked at the man with approval.

Burke, tall and burly, with a square ruddy complexioned face and an air about him that was almost rural, bowed graciously. "Famous is perhaps putting it too high," he said with a distant smile but in a pleasant enough tone. He spoke with a slight accent that Charles recognised as educated Irish.

Charles returned the bow. "My name is Charles George MacPherson and I am a visitor to your country from New York. Of course Mr Burke's views on my own unhappy country are well known."

Greville gazed at him in interest. "Ah, so you are from New York!" He smiled again. "Since I meet you in this hotbed of Whiggery I take it that your sympathies are for the American patriots? As you know, Mr Burke and many others have spoken out against this foolish war."

"Indeed so," said Charles. "I consider myself a good patriot. And, yes, I have read Mr Burke's speeches on the war." He bowed to the big Irishman again. "And I honour him for his views."

"Well, ah," Burke looked pleased, if slightly embarrassed. "That is gratifying, most gratifying sir." He shifted awkwardly from one foot to the other and stared uneasily round the room. "I suppose they are at their foolish gaming again," he muttered with a frown. "Ungracious as it is to say so in the home of our lovely hostess."

He glanced at Charles from under lowered eyebrows. "To tell you the truth sir," he said frankly, "I should not be here at all, were it not for my Lord and master." He looked about him again disdainfully. "This is not quite my thing and certainly no great advertisement for society in my view. But the Marquess of Rockingham understandably feels obliged to appear from time to time at informal gatherings of our party. As ever he requires me to be at hand."

As he spoke a tall man of aristocratic bearing appeared in the entrance to the hall and hovered there, looking about uncertainly. "Ah, you will have to excuse me, Mr MacPherson," Burke said. "I suspect my political master has done his duty and is ready to depart. I must also take my leave of our hostess." He shot a shrewdly penetrating glance at Charles, "I expect we shall meet again." He vanished in the direction of Rockingham, leaving Charles and Robert Greville standing alone together.

"I am thinking along somewhat similar lines," said Greville. "And if I do not mistake it, you too were on the verge of flight." They drifted back into the drawing room and stood for a moment watching the throng around the gambling tables, waiting to catch the eye of the Duchess. The table was littered with piles of coins and even gold rings and brooches, in lack of ready money, had been thrown down to make a wager. In the background, sprawled on a large couch a tall man, a glass of punch in one hand, was engaged in whispering secret words into the ear of a lady who was making a feeble pretence of fighting off his advances. Charles recognised the auburn hair of Lady Derby.

Greville stared appraisingly at the frenzied activity around them. He grunted disapprovingly. "I see Dorset is enjoying another good innings." He turned to Charles. "Say what you will of their behaviour, and I care for it as little as Burke, these are some of the most beautiful women in London. And the most fashionable people, if you can believe that. But you must not judge our society by this gathering alone." He gave a droll smile. "Though there are as many again who would kill to be invited here."

Seeking to deflect the conversation Charles enquired. "Who is that very lovely woman with the dark hair? Over there, standing talking to the tall man by the punch bowl. She seems rather more composed than the others. More tasteful, if I may say so."

"Ah," Greville said with a laugh. "That's the famous Mrs Crewe. 'True blue and Mrs Crewe' as they say in these parts! She is a Greville, I believe, by blood," he said, looking modestly down at his feet. "But prettier than most of us, I must say."

"So she is related to you?"

"Yes, a kind of cousin-german. Her father, Fulke Greville, was a first cousin of my grand-father." He laughed. "Obviously the good looks didn't go with the title!"

"Ah," said Charles, far from clear what a cousin-german meant. "You have a title then?"

"Oh lord no! Not me," Greville said hastily. "My eldest brother George is the Earl of Warwick. I'm a mere third son. But no matter," he added with a dismissive wave of the hand. "What of you? Do you come recently from New York? What can you tell us of events there?"

"I have been in France for the past year or more, so I fear I am a little out of touch." Charles paused, aware again of the incongruity of what he was about to say and the inexplicable events from which it arose. "I was the guest there of the British Ambassador, Lord Stormont."

Greville face changed instantly. "So you met Louisa!" he burst out. "Do tell me! How is she? I have not seen her since---." His enthusiasm faltered. "Since she became Lady Stormont," he ended lamely. Charles noted that for a moment he seemed quite downcast. "You see, I have known Louisa since she was a mere girl. Not that she is much more than that now," he added sadly.

"She is a bundle of energy and exuberance," Charles said.

Robert Greville gazed at his fondly. "Yes, ain't she though," he said wistfully. He sighed and shook his head. "Ah well." He stood silent for what seemed like several minutes, staring blankly at the frenzied crowd around the faro table. Then he recovered himself. "And where do you stay in London? It occurs to me that if you are about to leave, we can perhaps share a chaise?"

Charles explained where he was staying with Thomas and Mary Graham. "Of course! Louisa's sister, the beautiful Mrs Graham---." He smiled at Charles. "You know, I still rather prefer her younger sister! But I dare say you have gathered that," he added with a wry laugh. "But what a splendid fellow Thomas is. And how devoted to Mary."

He glanced at Charles. "Thomas is a countryman at heart, you know and no great lover of London or Paris for that matter. He would much prefer to be on his estates or riding to hounds somewhere, rather than this kind of thing." He waved his hand dismissively. "As a matter of fact I know he has his heart set on buying an estate in Leicestershire, where he can hunt to his heart's content." He laughed. "But Lady Christian, his mother don't you know, has other ideas! Doesn't entirely approve of spending money on mere pleasure!" He nodded towards the crowded gaming table. "Not quite the same here, eh?"

Rattling through the silent London night he sat quietly beside Charles in a shared chaise until they arrived outside the house in Grosvenor Place. Greville turned to Charles and stared so strangely at him that Charles became quite uneasy. Then he blurted out. "Tell me, do you think she is happy? I mean, as happy as one could expect?" His voice tailed away lamely.

Charles gazed at him. "Mary? Oh yes, I suppose so. Although---."

"No, no!" He said. "Not Mary Graham. Louisa! Do you think Louisa is truly happy?" Then Greville turned away and stared out of the dark carriage window. He shook his head. "Forgive me, my dear fellow. That is very unfair of me. Shouldn't ask such a thing. Damn me, certainly not. Very bad form."

Charles silently considered his response. "I take it you are fond of her then?"

"Oh Lord yes," Robert Greville said simply, staring at him in amazement. "I guess everyone in London knows how I feel!" He laughed wryly. "Everyone in England, come to that! Always have done. Since I saw her when she was still a girl at school. We are cousins, you know," he added inconsequentially. "Our mothers are both Hamiltons and sisters, you see."

Charles hesitated. He hardly knew this man and yet there was a bond of sorts already forming between them. "You must have been--- . I mean, it must have been very difficult--- ."

"When she married Stormont?" Greville said harshly. "Fit to hang myself for a goodly time." He took Charles by the hand and gazed at him for a moment. "You are a splendid fellow and you must forgive me for being such a bore. Still, I'm sure we shall see more of each other in London. If you care to, that is. For there are one or two people you should meet. You'd find my friend Charles Fox interesting. You might like him---- most people do---- and he certainly shares your views on America. Now good night, my dear fellow."

As Charles stepped down from the chaise Greville called out to him. "And if you should speak to her, please do give her my very best----." He stopped abruptly in mid sentence. "Oh damnation," he muttered. Then, "Drive on, will you," he called to the driver and the chaise trundled away in the direction of Buckingham House.

After that sudden unexpected moment of intimacy Charles found his friendship with Robert Greville developed rapidly. The two men enjoyed each others company and Greville, after his abrupt and candid admission concerning Louisa, seemed somehow to accept Charles as a confidant and a sort of kindred spirit.

Moreover, as their friendship blossomed, Charles discovered that

Greville in spite of his diffident manner was very much an inner member of the London elite and through him Charles was to meet many of the personalities of the day. Greville's natural home was with the traditional Whigs of the landed gentry. But he seemed somehow to have cultivated friends right across the spectrum of politics and one of the first of those whom Charles encountered was Charles James Fox.

Fox was a curious figure at first sight: of no great height, untidy in dress and usually so unshaven that with his swarthy colouring he presented a distinctly unprepossessing appearance. Yet within moments of meeting him Charles found himself, like most of the world, caught up by Fox's almost magical conversation and flowing wit. It was impossible not to like Charles James Fox, "unless you were King George" as Greville remarked dryly when Charles commented on this to his new friend.

"Charles Fox is marked by brilliance, beyond a doubt." Greville added. "And he will make our party great. Or possibly destroy it." He looked thoughtful for a moment. "For there is a young man of equal talent who may yet prove to be Fox's political nemesis. William Pitt is just coming down from Cambridge where he has proved himself to be quite brilliant. Moreover Pitt has all the steadiness and resolution of the Grenvilles on his mother's side to complement his cleverness. He is the son of Lord Chatham, of course. So as you might imagine young Pitt has been bred to a political life almost since infancy." Greville grimaced. "He will be a formidable adversary if he keeps his health, which is a little shaky by all reports."

Fox, after a precocious spell of power at the Admiralty Board at the age of only twenty-one, had for a time been the special protégé of the Prime Minister, Lord North. But then, impulsively, Fox had broken with the administration, after which his oratory and cleverness made him a natural leader of the opposition, attracting a substantial following in the House. Charles also learned that unusually for a parliamentarian Fox had a broad popularity in the country. He had courted radicals like John Wilkes and encouraged the development of the new local 'corresponding societies'. Though according to Robert Greville not everyone was happy with the extreme ideas these societies were spreading amongst working people.

Still, Fox's intellect, his sheer brilliance and mastery of a brief even after a night or more of non-stop gambling and drinking, as well as his scathing criticism of the administration's policies towards the American colonies had made him a great favourite in some Whig quarters. His friendship with Edmund Burke had recently led him to attach himself and his followers to the powerful Rockingham party, so that he again had hopes of high office before long. Small, plump, untidy and unshaven as he was, Fox somehow generated a powerful charm that worked as well on men as on women. He was quite simply a charismatic figure, Charles decided.

"Now then," Fox had said to him one evening at Devonshire House. "When Brooks opens his new Club you must join us there some evening. For some supper and perhaps a game or two of cards. I take it you do play cards? And dice perhaps?" he added anxiously. "For if not," he added with a smile, "you are preparing a very dull old age for yourself." Charles laughed and Fox gave him a secret rueful grimace. "Not original I'm afraid, old fellow. M.Tallyrand said it firstly. Now there is a clever fellow! Especially wise for a man of the cloth, don't you think!"

"Well, sir," Charles remarked, with a bow. "If M. Tallyrand did not say it, I expect he will sooner or later!"

Charles was secretly very pleased with his riposte, which was so well received by the company that he was instantly credited with the reputation of a wit, something Charles had never set himself up to be. But the exchange cemented his approval by Fox and when repeated around London it undoubtedly ensured his acceptance by the rest of Greville's friends. Privately Charles was left to wonder at the ease with which reputations were gained in the society of which he had so mysteriously become a part. The Mohawk valley seemed further away than ever.

On his occasional visits to Devonshire House, although still careful to avoid the gaming tables, Charles found himself drawn into a handful of casual dalliances with one or two of Georgiana's friends--- it seemed to be quite the expected thing. He was, he suspected, passed from one curious lady to another, each eager to experience this new young savage from the American woods. At first he was content to be cultivated in this way, though the affairs were fleeting and never in the least as intimate and certainly not as intense as the emotions he had experienced with Juliana Ritchie.

For as time went by he found that Juliana seemed to loom more and more in his thoughts rather than less, usually at the most inopportune moments. More than once he found her image interceding in the loveless couplings that followed from these affairs. Not, he thought sadly, that the ladies in question seemed to notice his distraction.

He also found time to visit Henry Cavendish again, who on the strength of his friendship with Georgiana now seemed to regard Charles as a trusted associate. "You would do me a great service Mr MacPherson, on your travels, if you will deliver this note of mine." He thrust a sealed document into his hand. Charles glancing at it saw it was addressed to M. Charles Augustin de Coulomb. "He is doing some very valuable work on a torsion balance at present." Henry Cavendish said vaguely. "I have asked him to send details to me. Especially his calculations. Which I think are most interesting. Yes, most interesting."

Charles noted that there was no address on the document. "Ah, can you tell me where I am likely to find M. Coulomb? I know him by name and reputation of course. But--- ?"

"What? Eh, what do you say? Oh, an address! Well, I dare say any French official in Paris will tell you where to find him. He is quite well known. Does work for the government." He peered at Charles in a puzzled way. "The French government, that is to say. He has developed a most interesting mathematical solution to the problems of fortification construction, I understand. Very interesting indeed," he said musingly. "Quite radical."

With a war looming, Charles thought bleakly, he imagined exactly how he would be received if he made enquiries about Coulomb in Paris! It was just possible, he supposed, that he could convince them he was an American ally. But an ally who was in the habit of residing with the British Ambassador?

Cavendish was gazing blankly into space. "I seem to recall," he said musingly, "that Coulomb has been out in the West Indies. Building fortifications there, if I recall. Against our navy, I dare say. Ha ha ha!" Oh God, thought Charles. "But ah no!" said Cavendish, suddenly beaming. "My dear young man! Of course! He is now at Cherbourg, supervising the construction of fortifications there!"

Against the British navy, thought Charles gloomily, as he tucked the document carefully into an inside pocket. Possibly a letter from someone as distinguished as Henry Cavendish would speak well for his virtue in the event of a contretemps with the French authorities. Though he did not exactly know what a torsion balance was, he realised with a frown.

Still, he did not doubt that Henry Cavendish was above such petty issues as espionage. Indeed he doubted whether Cavendish had any notion that his country was soon to be at war with Coulomb's. No, the letter would be innocence itself, of that he was certain. Or so Charles hopefully thought.

TWENTY THREE

The journey to Paris was now tolerably familiar and Charles was received back into the Stormont household like an old family member. Next day over coffee the ambassador solemnly brought him up to date with political events. "The French have signed a secret treaty of mutual support with your friends in America," he said, looking concerned. "It is therefore only a matter of time before we have to consider ourselves at war with them, I fear. Then of course I shall be forced to leave Paris and take up whatever duties my country sees fit to offer me."

Charles nodded. "I understand, Lord Stormont. I suppose you know my plans? I had hoped to travel across France and into Italy, across the mountains to Turin. Thomas Graham will have explained that to you. Do you see any problem with that plan. Will this new situation allow such a trip? "

"If you plan to set out in the next few weeks there should be no difficulty for you within France. But travel in Italy is rarely a straightforward matter, as I expect Thomas has told you. For the place is little more than is a proliferation of petty states, which in itself creates complication. The Kingdom of Sardinia, you may be astonished to learn, actually has territory that lies astride the Alps in Savoy and Piedmont, through which you will inevitably pass. Then further to the east there is the Duchy of Milan, which is in reality controlled by the Austrian empire."

"It sounds fiendishly complicated."

Stormont paused. "Well, you see the city of Milan commands one of the key routs from the Tyrol and hence is vital to the interests of the

Hapsburgs in Austria. Then even further to the east there is Mantua, another key Austrian fortress. To the south there is Parma and Tuscany, to name only two more places closely tied to Austria, while around Rome the Papal States complicate the matter further, diplomatically speaking. Add to that the decaying old republics of Venice and Genoa, both fallen on hard times and ripe for revolution! Then again the entire southern half the peninsula in the shape of the Kingdom of Naples is a ramshackle affair, cobbled together by dynastic bonds."

He paused and laughed. "So not an easy land in which to travel! But rewarding, for all that. Now I understand from Thomas," he said quietly, "that you might care to have the company of John Sewell on your journey, for at least part of the way? I should warn you that it may be a week or two before I can allow him to leave, as I have urgent duties for him here. As you can imagine, there is much to be done in Paris at present."

Charles was aware that he had never been clear on the precise nature of Sewell's duties, apart from collecting messages in the dead of night. But, "I would indeed welcome a companion like Sewell," he said with a smile. "I have learned to value him greatly and a delay of a week or two will be no problem as it transpires. For I have a mission of my own to perform before I leave for Italy--- a rather curious mission on behalf of Mr Henry Cavendish which it will involve me in a journey to Cherbourg. I am bidden to deliver a letter from him to a Monsieur Coulomb."

Stormont glanced at him sharply. "Augustin de Coulomb?" He paused and then shook his head in astonishment. Or as near to that sentiment as David Murray was ever known to display. "Well, well." he said slowly. "Charles MacPherson, you do move in the most--- ." He stood up and placed his arm round Charles's shoulders. "You never cease to surprise me, my boy. Truly you do!"

He paused for a moment. "Well, let me speak to Sewell about your plans." Suddenly he beamed at Charles. "I am quite certain he will be delighted to join you on your grand tour." He paused. "Perhaps if I can arrange his duties accordingly he may even be free to travel with you to Cherbourg."

In fact it proved that John Sewell was indeed free to travel to Cherbourg with Charles. "You will be glad to learn that I have rearranged his duties to the satisfaction of all concerned," Stormont announced the very next day. "You will understand that, ahem, matters are somewhat confused and uncertain at present. But it does look as if you will have a chance to get to know Sewell better. Perhaps decide if he is indeed the man with whom you want to spend so many months travelling around Italy, for inevitably you will be thrown much together on such a journey.

Perhaps as well to put it to the test, do you not think?"

In fact the two of them had no difficulty on the journey from Paris. Sewell's part in the infamous and now faintly ridiculous duel seemed to create a certain camaraderie and Charles found him a good companion from the outset. He also found him a man of surprising and hidden talents. He had been aware of course that Sewell was an experienced man-at-arms. As a veteran soldier this was not surprising, particularly since Charles was well aware that his new companion had frequently acted in confidential and trusted roles for Stormont.

But one evening in a quiet wayside inn near Caen, sitting before the fire, Sewell diffidently produced a bundle of sketches. "What do you say to this?" he said almost shyly and held out a very good likeness of Charles seated on his mount and staring off into the remote distance, a likeness rough but undoubtedly accurate.

Charles gave an exclamation of delight. "Why, John! It's very good indeed. I had no idea----." He turned over a few pages and saw a series of commendable little sketches, mostly of the rolling landscape through which they had travelled during the last four or five days, though here and there were images of village streets, churches and old stone walled towns. "My word! You are a veritable artist, John! I never imagined that you were talented in this way."

"Ah! Well!" Sewell flushed and looked embarrassed. "It's a way I have to pass the time. Done it all my days during my travels. A pastime, nothing more." He packed the rest of bundle hastily away in one of his saddle bags. "But I thought you might like to have that little sketch as a keepsake," he muttered.

In the bustling town of Cherbourg it proved much easier to find Coulomb than Charles had feared. Indeed, the two travellers had scarcely crested a range of low hills at the southern base of the peninsula and began their descent towards the ancient seaport before a patrol of suspicious French cavalry had ridden urgently up and ordered them to halt. After an awkward few minutes of questioning, Charles, having urged Sewell to remain silent and adopt the role of servant, had explained his mission.

No, he was not an 'anglais', but in fact an American ally. Moreover he was a friend of the illustrious Mr Benjamin Franklin, travelling to meet Charles Augustin de Coulomb on matters of a scientific nature. After much muttering amongst themselves the patrol uneasily accepted this account and the young officer in charge saluted Charles gravely. "With such a recommendation, monsieur, you are of course welcome. We honour the name of Benjamin Franklin in France. And of course M. de Coulomb is well known to us. Please follow me." With a sharp word of command the patrol wheeled about and escorted the travellers down the slope to a charming old inn on the waterfront where it appeared Coulomb had based himself.

From the heights above the town they soon found themselves looking down on a great natural harbour jutting out into a grey and storm-tossed Channel and it quickly became apparent that the whole area was buzzing with activity. Workers swarmed around a series of massive fortified gun emplacements around the wide bay and further out in the approaches enormous barges seemed to be engaged in some great construction enterprise.

"They are working like beavers," Sewell whispered as they rode. "Sinking huge caissons out there in the deep water. Making a new sea wall, if I am not mistaken. Quite a project, for the water there must be sixty feet deep." Charles grunted, his mind more on his imminent meeting with Coulomb than on Sewell's observations. For how would he be received?

After a certain initial stiffness, Coulomb could not have been more charming. A tall man with large intelligent eyes, a strong chin and nose and darkly arching eyebrows, his reserve melted completely on reading the letter from Henry Cavendish. "My dear Mr MacPherson!" he said instantly. "I can easily have a model of my new torsion balance built and sent to our mutual friend. There are several excellent model makers in Paris from whom I can commission--- ." He stopped suddenly. "Ah!" he said, glancing thoughtfully at Charles. "Though current events may create some difficulty, of course."

He pursed his lips for a moment, then smiled affably. "Still, let us think about how best to meet Mr Cavendish's request." He paused again. "If all else fails I shall write to him with a detailed description of the device. I dare say there are competent craftsmen in London. But now let us dine! The food here is very good and I can recommend the pork cooked in calvados. And let us talk! You can tell me what our friend is working on at present and also what your own plans are." Charles swallowed hard, thinking desperately back to some of the ramblings he could recollect from his encounters with Henry Cavendish. "You are acquainted with your own great countryman, Mr Franklin? A very great man and a good friend of France, as you know."

The next week passed off easily enough, with Charles spending his days travelling with Coulomb as he inspected the many construction sites around the sweeping harbour. "This kind of engineering is not truly to my taste," Coulomb confessed to Charles as they gazed out across the waves towards the caissons of the developing sea wall. "But I seem to have gained a reputation for designing fortifications. Not that it is difficult in truth, as it is usually a simple matter of geometry. But it is a case of 'when the king commands'." He shrugged. "I suppose it is inevitable that sooner or later we shall have to fight the English again and when we do it is vital that we have a secure naval base on La Manche, what in their insufferable arrogance they call the English Channel."

One incident only disturbed the even tenor of the visit and that was on the very eve of their departure. Charles returned from a final stroll around the harbour area to find Coulomb in the company of a French officer. "Ah, Mr MacPherson," Coulomb said uneasily. His normal relaxed manner seemed to have deserted him. "This is Captain Duchampe of the military garrison. It appears there is a matter of security that he wishes to discuss with you."

Duchampe bowed. "The security of the area is my principal responsibility, monsieur. Certain peculiarities of behaviour have been reported to me that I must ask you to explain."

Charles frowned. "I can think of nothing that might interest you, Captain. But if I can be of assistance, please continue. What is the behaviour that concerns you? For the most part I have spent my time most enjoyably in the company of M. Coulomb here."

Duchampe smiled. "That is not the issue, monsieur. My concern is with the behaviour of the man who is I think your servant." Charles felt his heart sink as Duchampe went on. "He has been observed on several occasions making sketches of the harbour area and the surrounding hills. As you will understand this is a matter of seriousness for us in such a sensitive location."

Charles gave an uneasy laugh. "Oh Sewell! Why yes, he is a great sketcher! He spent most of our journey from Paris drawing old buildings, churches and town halls. Even perfectly ordinary broken down stone walls." He shrugged. "He is no great artist, of course. Quite an amateur in fact." He paused, conscious that Duchampe was staring at him with a sceptical gaze. "Though he does draw a very good likeness on occasions. Come, let me show you one of his works."

Charles led them into his room and opened one of his travelling bags. Pulling out the sketch that Sewell had done for him near Caen he handed it to Duchampe. "Not a great masterpiece of course. But a good likeness, don't you think?"

Coulomb visibly relaxed a little. "Do you not think, Captain, that this explanation is adequate? It seems an innocent enough activity."

Captain Duchampe wavered. "With respect monsieur, I should like to see the man myself and examine his--- other work." He shot a glance at Coulomb. "I need not tell you how valuable information of our defences would be to an enemy." He turned to Charles. "This man Sewell, he is

English, is he not? How does he come to be in your service? You, a patriotic American, as I understand."

Charles thought quickly. "Oh, he was in the service of some friends of mine in London. Friends of America too, for there are many in London who do not care for the war." He laughed. "They have planned a trip for me around the classical sights of Italy and being a touch paternalistic they feel that I need a companion and servant on the way. My visit to Cherbourg is almost incidental. I am sure M. de Coulomb has explained the reason for that."

Duchampe nodded. "I see," he said shortly. But Charles knew he was almost won over. Then he straightened up. "However, I must speak to this man directly and also examine any drawings he has in his possession."

Charles bowed. "Of course. I understand that you must satisfy yourself completely in this matter." My God, he thought, I hope Sewell has done nothing stupid. "I think he is about the place somewhere," he added carelessly. "Perhaps we can have him summoned?"

"No," said Duchampe after a moment's thought. "Let us go to his quarters. I would prefer to see him under those circumstances."

Sewell proved the soul of cooperation, playing the part of the modest dabbler in sketches as he pulled a pile of drawings from his half-packed baggage. "These I did on the journey from Paris," he started to explain.

But Duchampe waved them away. "Only the drawings you have done here in Cherbourg interest me."

Sewell spread a few out on a rough table. "These are general views, from the hills to the east."

Duchampe stared at them. "Go on, please."

"Then this is a sketch I made of M. Coulomb and Mr MacPherson together, lunching by the harbour. I thought you might like to keep it, sir. It seemed not a poor likeness. Not bad for me, I mean," Sewell added ingenuously.

Coulomb gasped. "Why, it is charming! I shall be delighted to have it. Thank you, Sewell. It will remind me of a very amiable visit. I hope, Duchampe, that your fears are allayed?"

Duchampe silently leafed through the rest of the sketches. "I regret monsieur that there are several drawings here which, in the wrong hands---. Please understand that I do not doubt your intentions, monsieur. But in the wrong hands these could be damaging," he added stiffly. "I fear I must confiscate these."

Glancing over his shoulder Charles saw that Sewell had made a series of landscape drawings, some of which revealed the position of the gun emplacements. Others showed the extent of the new sea wall. They looked innocent enough and might well have passed as genuine landscapes by an enthusiastic amateur.

"Ah," he said smoothly. "Yes, I can quite see that these will not do. I am sure that Sewell here included the scenes unwittingly. But I can quite understand that from your point of view---. No, sir, you have your duty to perform."

Turning to Sewell, he said sharply. "I am afraid the officer will have to take these sketches from you. They are simply too sensitive to be permitted. You could not be aware of that, of course. But there it is, I fear."

It was only when they were well on their way back to Paris, having taken an affectionate farewell from Augustin de Coulomb with promises of future meetings and good wishes to Franklin and Cavendish, that Charles raised the issue of the sketches. "Do you regret the loss of those drawings," he asked him as they rode silently side by side along a country track.

"Oh it's a damned nuisance," Sewell growled. "But I think I know the disposition of the guns well enough to re-create them for the Ambassador."

Charles halted his horse and grabbed Sewell's bridle, hauling him round. "Damn me!" he shouted. "So you are a spy! One of Stormont's spies! You could have put us both in gaol at the very least! What were you thinking about?"

Sewell gazed at him coolly. "Why do you suppose Lord Stormont allowed me to come on this little trip?" he asked with a short laugh. "A golden opportunity to see the new works at Cherbourg! Make no doubt, sir, it will not be long before our ships are blockading that harbour, when what I have learned may save English lives. Just where do your loyalties stand, Mr MacPherson? Just where do your loyalties stand?"

TWENTY FOUR

Much of the next two years was spent travelling leisurely through Italy following Mary Graham's carefully planned itinerary. Moreover, despite his reservations, for the most part Charles did so in the company of John Sewell.

The long ride back to Paris from Cherbourg had been made in a strained silence while Charles pondered on Sewell's frank question. For it hit the mark acutely. Just where did his loyalties stand? That it was an issue which he must one day confront, he was perfectly clear. For he knew that increasingly his loyalties were indeed divided. Francis Johnson, with his usual perception, had divined full well the conflict in his mind and Charles winced as he recalled that awkward last meeting at Franklin's house.

Where was his friend now, he thought guiltily. Covering himself with honour on some New England battlefield? Or possibly freezing to death at Valley Forge, for Charles had heard that Washington's army had been forced into winter quarters on starvation rations. Or was Francis still moving quietly about Europe, plotting England's downfall and at the same time hunting the odious Snape? But was Francis Johnson so very different from John Sewell? And if not, how then could he blame Sewell for his actions at Cherbourg?

Then again, what of Juliana Ritchie? It seemed so very long since their last painful parting. Would he ever see her again? Of course Juliana was another true patriot. Charles bit his lip and groaned. Francis and Juliana! The two people who should be closest to him and both loyal patriots. He admired and envied them for their single-mindedness, for their total lack of doubt on the issue. Yet it seemed he could no longer share their sentiments in the same way.

The journey through Italy went wonderfully smoothly. He had only to flourish Benjamin Franklin's letter of introduction and doors miraculously opened that otherwise threatened to be closed, while in those places where Franklin's writ did not run that of Thomas Graham or Robert Fulke Greville or Lord Stormont almost invariably did. As a consequence the two travellers were seldom short of hospitality. For there were only the two of them, Charles having refused the offer of an English manservant from Lord Stormont on the secretly held grounds that another man might be more trouble than he was worth.

Though Stormont had been surprisingly insistent for a time. "You will find the sort of fellows you can hire along the way will cheat you, my dear Charles. Steal your possessions if they can. For they think young travellers like you are fair game." But finally he had relented. "Very well, Charles, as you wish, though Thomas did think that you should---. Still, there you are, eh! You must do as you think right. But do listen to Sewell. He has experience of the area and speaks the language well enough for practical purposes." He shook Charles warmly by the hand. "Goodbye my boy, and good luck. Do not forget these," he added, handing over a bundle of letters of introduction to various English and Italian dignitaries.

"Fullerton has as usual thought of everything that might be helpful. And be sure to give my regards to Sir Horace Mann in Florence. He is our consul there and has lived in the city for longer than I can recall." He hesitated for a moment. "Mann is rather an odd fellow. Thomas may have mentioned him to you? Well-meaning and endlessly welcoming to English travellers. Especially to young men, if you take my meaning." He frowned apologetically. "Still he will be very useful if you need anything at all in Florence."

Charles smiled his thanks. With the introductions Thomas and Mary had provided, in particular to her uncle Sir William Hamilton in Naples, these new credentials added to his prized letter from Benjamin Franklin meant that he was unlikely to lack for social contacts along the way.

The journey began uneventfully, travelling southeast across France, delayed only by poor roads turned into muddy tracks by frequent heavy rains and early spring days that fell quickly into darkness. They broke their journey thankfully at Dijon, which Charles found interesting and with surprisingly good food for a small provincial town.

The thought instantly caused him an inner smile. How his standards had changed! Paris and London or even Spa were now the comparisons! Yes, it was a far cry from the Mohawk Valley.

In general, even where civilised introductions were not possible, they usually contrived to travel as comfortably as possible given the diabolical roads and the unsanitary conditions in the hostelries they were sometimes forced to endure. Here Sewell's experience indeed proved invaluable and perhaps as a result of the chastening effect of events in Cherbourg, he proved to be a good companion, competent, undemanding and eternally resourceful. It seemed to Charles that the two men had at last struck a working relationship.

From Dijon they continued southeast through Savoy and into Piedmont, towards mountains which daily grew ever more conspicuous on the horizon. Soon, each evening they could be seen clearly, tipped by the rosy sunsets, for the north facing slopes were still snow clad. "Going to be a cold crossing, even this late in the spring," Sewell grunted, screwing up his eyes as he stared at the looming bulk of the Alps. "But there is no alternative. The Mont Cenis is the only way across from here. Straight up the mountain and through the high pass. Still, with luck it will be fully spring on the other side."

For several days more they climbed steadily into the foothills of the Alps, the air growing colder by the hour until finally, in a high desolate clearing, they came to an isolated village. There Charles with some relief paid off their uncomfortable coach while John Sewell went off in search of porters to take them up and over the mountain.

Charles stood about, stamping his feet and gazing curiously at the miserable cluster of huts that seemed to constitute this village. He was well wrapped up in a grey flannel prudence against the chill air, but even with the warmth of the blanket round his shoulders he was still almost numbed by the cold, his breath turning to steam before his eyes. With astonishment he realised that he could neither taste nor smell in this icy atmosphere.

But when he looked upwards, despite the deadly cold he stood enraptured. For there above him rose all the magnificence of the western Alps and Mont Cenis, with its ancient pass used by travellers since the time of the Emperor Charlemagne— probably even earlier. Range after range of superb mountains fell away in folds on each side, reaching to the clear blue remote horizon. Away to the north the Massif de la Vanoise and to the south the Frejus. Charles had seen nothing like this before, certainly not in New York where the hills, round and green and tree-clad, rose to a mere 2,000 feet or so.

When Sewell returned he was accompanied by a party of roughly dressed men with whom he had apparently struck some kind of bargain. Though in what language the arrangement had been agreed Charles could not imagine. For the men seemed not to understand either French or Italian, instead grunting in a crude and impenetrable local dialect.

Shivering, he stared at them in horror. They were big ugly lumpish creatures, swollen eyed, heavily goitred and buck-toothed, their arms unnaturally long swinging apelike by their knees. "The product of generations of inbreeding," Sewell confided to him in a whisper. "in some benighted mountain village."

But the men were strong and they knew their business. Swiftly they loaded Charles and Sewell onto an 'alp machine', a kind of crude sedan chair made from two stout tree trunks between which were twisted thick ropes on which the travellers sat, with a few wooden boards serving as a back and another hung before them to support their feet. A second of these contraptions went before them carrying their baggage and the whole elaborate caravan set off up the mountain pass, half carried on the shoulders of four of the men and half sliding over frozen hard packed snow, which in places was still six feet deep on each side of the path.

At one point Charles caught a glimpse of some small deer-like creatures who stared nervously at the party before bolting suddenly into the snow. "Chamois," Sewell said to Charles. "Their skin is wondrously soft. But they don't eat too well. Not unless you are desperate."

At the top of the pass the porters paused to recover and Charles stared around at the stunning mountain spectacle. Now he could see that it stretched away, crystal clear and cold, in all directions. They had actually reached a shallow depression, a high plain which contained a tiny village and a church and the Hôpital des Pèlerins where, Sewell explained, poor pilgrims were entitled to receive shelter and food in extremis, in return for attending mass.

A priest who spoke French seemed pleased to see them and invited them to join him in an evening meal, taken in his comfortable kitchen before a warm log fire. Charles ate the simple meal ravenously, the keen mountain air having given his appetite an edge. One would have thought he had carried the alp machine himself, as Sewell commented jovially.

"I cannot remember, sir," Charles said, "when I last enjoyed a meal so well. Pray, what was in that delicious pie." A particular kind of white partridge, he was told, that lived only in the Alps. The pie and the rough red wine, with fresh bread and a cold capon sent Charles to bed in a simple bunk to sleep a dreamless sleep--- the best he had enjoyed in many a night. Almost since the Mohawk Valley, he thought drowsily as he drifted off.

Next morning they hired horses and started down the smooth green southern slopes of the mountain, Charles having left a small contribution with the grateful priest. As Sewell had predicted, suddenly all was warmth and sunlight. Most certainly it was spring here and Charles felt his spirits soar still higher as they made their way towards the city of Turin.

As they drew near to the city Charles turned to the itinerary that Mary Graham had so painstakingly prepared for him. There were great sights that he must see, churches and palaces and the like that she would expect to have described for her by letter. A sudden pang of guilt struck him as he realised that for several weeks he had not written the regular letter she would be anticipating.

In the warm spring sunlight Turin looked splendid, with wide modern streets driven through the old medieval town in a way that made Charles think longingly of doing the same for cluttered old Paris. The people they met were polite and serious in manner and for the most part speaking French, at least in polite society.

"We should stay at the Bonne Femme," Sewell said. "That is where all the young English gentlemen stay. But let me warn you, sir. You must make a strict bargain with them regarding food and lodgings, else they will cheat you blind. Don't be mislead by their nice manners, sir. And be especially careful of the valets they offer you. Let anything out of your sight and it will vanish for certain. They are foreigners you see and don't have the same standards."

Robert Greville had mentioned the inn to Charles and the Bonne Femme proved to be everything he expected: a magnificent old auberge built around a central courtyard where their horses could be safely stabled, the stout outer doors securely bolted after dark. Charles was welcomed like a prince and given the best room in the house at a rate that Sewell, with a sharp intake of breath, said was extortionate. To Charles however Turin was everything that he had hoped for, modern, clean and efficient and he immediately set about exploring its attractions, following Mary's instructions religiously, if was the appropriate word.

On the first day they rode out of town a little way to inspect a great Basilica, recently constructed on the very top of a curiously conical shaped hill. Charles stood beneath its magnificent portico and surveyed the surrounding landscape. Away to the north loomed the white-tipped Alps and the chilly Mont Cenis Pass, a stupendous backdrop to the city, while to the east and south lay mile after mile of green cultivated farmland that spoke of ancient civilisations. It was through these fields, Charles reflected that their future route lay.

After almost a week in Turin, during which Sewell vanishing by day to entertain himself in his own way, Charles had dutifully ticked off the churches on Mary Graham's list. "The Church of San Lorenzo," she had said exultantly. "The Royal Chapel! That you must certainly see!"

San Lorenzo was indeed a revelation, though the exterior was modest enough by Italian standards. But the interior took his breath away, such was the blaze of light from enormously arching lunettes, all set in a vast dome of incredible engineering skill and illuminating a splendid diversity of ornamentation. Over the great altar Charles noted there was a smaller dome, tiny by comparison, but with lunettes that cleverly echoed the huge ones soaring overhead. He shook his head in wonder. This was civilisation such as he had never seen, not even in Paris or London. He grimaced at the memory of Sir William Johnson's mansion, which not so long ago he had imagined to be the height of sophistication.

"And the Opera! Do not forget the Opera! In Turin!" Mary had cried, as she added it to the list. And with Thomas grunting reluctant approval she had written it down in a firm hand. "It is the very finest thing," she said definitely. "And not to be missed on any account. The Italians have created something truly magical. Mark my words, opera will sweep Europe and become an essential part of any civilised person's experience."

So Charles went one night to the Teatro Regio. "There are two theatres in Turin, But the Regio is infinitely more fashionable than the Teatro delle Feste. So the Regio is definitely where you go to see--- and to be seen." So he was advised by other travellers at the Bonne Femme.

Once in the theatre he found himself seated in one of the vertiginous banks of boxes that rose straight above the crowded stalls, looking down on the noisiest rowdiest crowd scenes he might have imagined. On stage were a small group of singers, battling vainly to be heard over the clamour, as the audience shouted, laughed or called for food from the strident vendors or made arrangements to meet in the casino.

Was this the new art form, he thought as his eye roved around the boxes. A few of the audience leaned forward as if indeed straining to hear the music. But more often the boxes were taken by small parties of elaborately dressed men and ladies, drinking and eating and apparently more interested in each other than in the performance, flirting openly and in some cases shamelessly doing rather more than that in the darker recesses of the box. After half-an-hour or so Charles had more or less decided to leave when the curtain at the rear of his box was pulled back and a tall handsome woman, magnificently attired, glided into the box and took a seat beside him. Charles rose to his feet and introduced himself, hoping that he had not accidentally strayed into a private box.

"Not at all," the lady replied in excellent French. Then clearly pleased with his manners and appearance she introduced herself. "Contessa Emilia da Bonito," she said gravely, eyeing him so carefully that Charles was quite glad he had worn his most fashionable Parisian clothes.

Though much older, how much older Charles never knew, there was something about the Contessa that reminded him of Juliana Ritchie. Her hair was a similar dark red, though less lustrous, and her eyes were green like Juliana's. But not the sharp clear green that even now sent a pang of loss and regret through Charles. The Contessa's eyes, beautiful enough he decided, were rather a tawny hazel in colour, with here and there flecks of yellow that gave her a curiously feline appearance.

Her features had been very fine, although now an indisputable heaviness lay around her chin and neck. Still, the overall effect was striking, especially in the shadows of the box, and almost in spite of himself Charles found himself first staring and then smiling and finally chatting quite freely, oblivious to the public performance beneath them and the more private ones taking place around them. When the opera finally ended---- Charles never did discover its name, except that it seemed to have some classical Greek connection--- the Contessa smilingly took her farewell. "I have enjoyed meeting you, sir. It is always a pleasure to meet a young man of culture."

She stared at him directly. "If you are in Turin for a time, please to call on me at the via Principessa. If it will amuse you, come and take breakfast with me there tomorrow. Around eleven in the morning?" Then she swept out without a backward glance, leaving Charles blinking in astonishment. Was this an assignation? Or simply a polite gesture from a respectable lady of society, doing her duty by a young foreign traveller in her city.

Next morning Charles presented himself at the house in via Principessa, where he was solemnly received by an elderly uniformed impassive manservant and shown into a small but elegantly furnished boudoir. The Contessa lay stretched out on a small chaise-longue, with a small side table already set out with fine white china pots and cups. Uncannily, she wore a morning dress of the same dramatic green that Juliana had worn that first night at the Rue du Temple.

"Mr MacPherson," she murmured and with her white hand waved him towards a seat beside her. "I am so very pleased you have come."

They drank the warm chocolate and exchanged pleasantries for half-an-hour or more, by which time Charles decided that he had reached the limits of a polite visit and that his imaginations of the previous evening had obviously been misplaced. Thinking of a suitable exit line he casually remarked, "And M. le Compte, is he at home?"

Her tawny eyes fixed him boldly. "No," she said shortly. "My husband is not at home." She gave an abrupt laugh. "He seldom is at home! He is in Rome on business. Or so he says." She smiled sadly at Charles. "And will be for most of the summer." The Contessa lowered her eyes and took one last mouthful of chocolate. Then she stared at him again. Her eyes were suddenly darker and heavy lidded. "So you see I am quite alone. You need not fear that we shall be interrupted." Her tawny eyes never left his face as she lay back on the cushions.

The invitation was obvious; too obvious to resist. Charles moved across to sit beside her on the chaise and slowly and gently kissed her, feeling her warmth melt into him. After a few minutes Emilia da Bonito freed herself and stood up, taking him by the hand. "Come," she said and led him through into her bedroom.

An hour later Charles lay looking down into her face, her red hair in a tangle on the silk pillow and her cheeks flushed with pleasure. She had, he noticed, lost herself or at least lost herself to him in the last stages of their lovemaking, rather in the way that Charlotte Pemberton had done. In fact, he decided, there was more of Charlotte about her than there was of Juliana. Now that he saw her completely there was none of Juliana's smooth youthfulness.

Indeed her flesh was old; older than Charlotte's, her breasts softer and even pendulous, so that Charles found himself giving her pleasure with a faint sense of self-disgust. The Contessa had clung to him as he left. "You will come to see me again? Tomorrow at the same time, caro mio?"

Charles made his way back to the auberge with all the mixed sentiments of a young man who has found an older woman. "At least for the time being," he thought almost angrily. "For nothing more can come of this."

That afternoon he and Sewell, who had returned as mysteriously as he had vanished, rode out to see another of Mary Graham's wonders. It was the hunting lodge of the King of Piedmont, the Palazzina di Caccia, set in the midst of flat farmland. But this was a hunting lodge on such a scale, of such baroque magnificence, that no one from northern Europe let alone the Americas could fail to be struck silent by its extravagance. It was in reality more a palace than a hunting lodge, with a gigantic dome crowned by a true-to-life but immense figure of a stag that must have been visible for miles around. It was a stunning statement of wealth and power, of arrogance even, that took away his breath.

But the interior was even more luxurious and he wandered astonished through a confection of marble staircases and terraces, vast rooms with beautifully painted panels of hunting scenes from antiquity, huge carved fireplaces, ornate columns and capitals and overhead a myriad of elaborate chandeliers. Yes, it was a hunting lodge. But a king's hunting lodge and grander than many a royal house in the north. Charles returned to the Bonne Femme silently aware of what Thomas and Mary had intended him to learn on this tour.

Next morning he returned to the via Principessa where Emilia greeted him with delight and once again they spent part of the day in bed. By now however Charles was beginning to feel uneasy. He knew that very soon, indeed in the next day or so, he and Sewell would have to move on to Milan. How would the Contessa react?

When, gently, he hinted at his plans Emilia shrieked hysterically. "No, no, no! No, you must stay with me! Stay with me longer, dearest Charles! Caro mio! Stay until the summer at least. I cannot bear to lose you!" She threw herself on the bed sobbing, her whole body heaving dramatically. Charles stood in dismay, shocked by what he had done.

By the time he returned to the auberge a note from her was already waiting, tearfully imploring him not to leave her. He groaned, allowing the paper to fall to the floor from his hand. Sewell had been watching him with a grin on his face. "Woman trouble?" he asked calmly.

Charles groaned again and clutched his head. "I had no idea," he muttered. "How could I have done it."

"Oh, it's easy enough," Sewell said brightly. "Especially here in Italy where the women are so easy. And now she doesn't want you to leave, I suppose?"

Charles stared at him. "Easy?"

Sewell nodded. "I suppose I should have warned you about the women, sir. The married ones at least," he added casually. "The young single ones are kept fairly close--- in nunneries or at least under lock and key until they are ready to be married off." He laughed. "After that they are pretty free to do as they see fit--- once they've produced an heir for their husbands."

Charles frowned at him and Sewell smiled. "After all, sir, is it so very different in England? For some, I mean." Charles silently recalled Georgiana's lady friends of the Devonshire House set.

"But this is one of the most libertine countries in Europe," Sewell went on. Then he sighed. "Still, I should have warned you, sir. But, well to say the truth, I never thought of it. Never thought it necessary. Thought you would know. For tell you the truth, a lot of these ladies--- ." He paused as he stressed the last word heavily. "From a lot of these ladies,--- ." Again he hesitated. "Well sir, to put it blunt, you can get yourself a dose of the pox from them as easy as from a doxy in Wapping docks."

Charles sat quietly for a time. Then he said firmly, "John Sewell, let's get out of here. First thing tomorrow morning. Let's get on our way to Milan--- very early tomorrow."

TWENTY FIVE

Charles settled their account that evening and long before daylight a servant from the auberge brought them their hot chocolate. A vigorous douche under a cold pump in the darkened courtyard and then Charles mounted up and followed Sewell out onto the highway to the east. Clinging half awake to his bridle Charles muttered sourly. "It's a pity I had not tried the cold douche before this. It might have kept me out of trouble." He bit his lip. "But Sewell, I do feel badly about this. What will she think of me when she finds I have fled in this way?"

Sewell reigned in his horse for a moment and stared at Charles. "Where did you meet this lady?"

"At the opera the other night."

Spurring his mount away Sewell called back to him over his shoulder. "Then don't you worry, young sir. I expect she'll be at the theatre this very night, looking for some other young tourist! It must be a prime hunting ground for her."

'Heartless and unfeeling,' Charles thought to himself, shaking his head as he rode quickly after his companion.

It was six days later as they were nearing the outskirts of Milan that Charles became aware of the burning itch. That night he examined himself and was aghast to see how red and inflamed he was. "No! It cannot be! This is too much."

But when awkwardly he informed Sewell about his predicament

his companion only nodded. "Can't say I'm entirely surprised, sir. The lady is obviously very generous." He sniggered. "She's certainly given you a little going away present! But what do you expect?" Charles stared at him in dismay. "Oh, don't worry about it sir. We'll find an apothecary and get you a treatment; a sulphur or a mercury. They usually work a treat." He paused. "But it will cramp your style for a few weeks, I'm afraid."

Charles rode on in silence for a mile or more. "The Contessa Emilia da Bonito!" he muttered grimly. "Never again in this accursed country!"

It was as well that Stormont and the efficient William Fullerton had provided them with official passports and bills of health. For these proved essential as their route, by roads tortuously twisting, seemed to change direction with no apparent logic. This, combined with the confusion of petty ducal states, meant that more than once they found themselves by nightfall re-entering a state they had with great ceremony left only that morning!

At each border crossing their documents were solemnly studied by self-important officials wearing what Sewell contemptuously described as 'fancy dress--- right Bartholomew's Fair outfits.' But had it not been for Sewell the delay and frustration of these arcane controls would have driven Charles to despair, especially given his state of mind regarding his health. Fortunately the guards who scrutinized them with such suspicion proved susceptible to financial inducements and so Sewell was able to ease their path across northern Italy with the expenditure of relatively small sums of money. They reached Milan before dark on the third day, just as the great city gate crashed shut behind them, securing the populous for the night.

According to Mary Graham there was in Milan only one essential sight, though she did whisper secretly to him that the city was renowned for wonderful textiles, silks, satins and velvets. If he should find space in his baggage--- but only if--- well, blue was a colour that she thought suited her especially well. The tailors of Milan were apparently famed for the skill and speed with which they could produce a suit of clothes for a young man of fashion and during his short stay Charles took the opportunity to add an Italian touch to his predominantly French wardrobe. He also purchased a length of the finest pale blue silk for Mary, his mind reaching far ahead to the pleasure his gift would give her.

The morning after their arrival he found the Dominican Monastery of Santa Maria della Grazie and strolled into the cool dark interior of the small dining hall, all set about with rough wooden tables at which the resident monks ate their meals.

An end wall was covered by a vivid mural showing Christ and his disciples seated at a long table. Charles studied his notes. It was the Last Supper, painted by someone called Leonardo da Vinci and it was an acknowledged masterpiece. Or so Mary Graham claimed and in his present penitent mind Charles did not feel inclined to doubt her word.

He stared at the image. It seemed to his eye curiously divided right and left and he almost wondered if the artist had deliberately constructed it in two sections. Moving closer he studied the figures carefully. Now he could see quite clearly where sections of the original paint had flaked off. Also one of the figures seemed curiously feminine in appearance to be a disciple, sitting with his head on the shoulder of his neighbour, long auburn hair falling gracefully in beautiful folds about an oval face. "Hmm," Charles mused. "Well, what do I know about art?"

After Milan they travelled southwards the short distance to Pavia where Charles eagerly hoped to use his letter of introduction from Ben Franklin to gain an audience with Alessandro Volta. Sewell, once he had delivered his charge into safe hands, apparently had business of some kind in nearby Cremona and the two of men agreed to part and to rendezvous there in a few days time.

Pavia was small but delightfully situated: a very ancient university town set pleasantly in a wide loop of a tributary of the River Po and surrounded by vineyards, rice fields and fertile meadows. After a night in a comfortable family inn just off the Piazza della Vittoria, Sewell looked about him sourly. "No," he said. "There's not much to interest me here. We'll meet again in Cremona, a two day ride to the northeast of here. It's easy terrain so you should have no difficulty. I'll look for you by the main gates each evening--- let us say in ten days hence? Will that give you time to complete your discussions with Mr Volta?"

Suddenly alone Charles found himself relaxing into independence. First he spent a day or two simply strolling idly through the narrow streets of the old town, watching the rapid flow of the Ticino past the walls and under the old Ponte Coperto, simply absorbing the quiet even tenor of life: merchants opening their stalls and shops in the pale spring morning and closing them up in the mellow glow of evening.

He quickly identified the University--- it was by far the most prominent building on the main street, apart from the splendid Duomo. But he felt curiously reluctant to attempt his introduction to Volta. Sitting one morning over his chocolate in the piazza, he examined his reluctance to proceed. Did he fear a rebuff? There was certainly no reason why a man of Volta's reputation should waste his valuable time on Charles. Or was he worried about being exposed as the fraud he still secretly felt himself to be? For he was an ignoramus so far as the true subtleties of electricity were concerned, in spite of Franklin's endorsement. And Volta he had heard had a very short way with stupidity.

Still, did he not know Cavendish and Coulomb? And if not on equal terms, far from it indeed, he had nevertheless seemed to understand something of their work. Besides he had come so far--- and with an introduction from Benjamin Franklin himself. For what more realistically could he ask? With a smile of resignation he called for ink and paper and began to compose a short note to Senor Alessandro Volta.

In the event Volta could not have been more charming. Tall, elegant and intelligent, he welcomed Charles to the University. "I expect quite soon to be appointed Professor here," he had said casually. "A great compliment in such an ancient seat of learning." He showed Charles around his laboratories and entertained him to dinner in his rooms--- local food, including eggs poached in a light broth, a risotto with sausage and a delicious freshwater fish grilled and washed down by a fine wine from the Valtellina. It was the best meal Charles had eaten since that simple supper at the top of the Cenis Pass.

Nor had Charles any need to fear exposure as an amateur. In fact he freely admitted the fact in his first meeting with Volta and his comment was waved away. "My dear fellow, are we not all amateurs in the true sense of the word within this field! Some of us simply have more resources." He gestured around the large sun-lit room where half-a-dozen assistants bent over an array of tanks of liquid, piles of metal discs and lengths of wire connections. "But we are all at the very beginning of this journey."

Charles moved closer to the work area. "Some of this looks quite similar to the model of the Torpedo Fish I saw at Mr Cavendish's home," he ventured hesitantly.

"Ah," cried Volta. "And do the electrical piles function well? I sent Cavendish a description of my devices but had not heard from him." He paused briefly "Mr Cavendish is not a good correspondent, I find." he said with a smile. "And sadly for us all, he seems rarely to publish his findings." He shrugged. "That is a luxury a poor university academic cannot afford."

Charles nodded. He had seen enough of Henry Cavendish to know that he was far from a normal savant, if there was such a thing. He stared at Volta's elaborate structure of metallic plates. "Can you----- ? I mean, is there any way to measure the electrical output from your equipment?"

Volta beamed at him. "That of course is precisely the point!" He looked so delighted that Charles instinctively returned his smile. Volta had achieved some major breakthrough it seemed. He went on, "But the honest answer is not yet! There is no way to measure accurately, to calibrate the output. But it is progress to ask the correct question, is it not?" He beamed at Charles again. "Of course we can feel the difference as more and more cells are added---, I have decided to call them cells, incidentally. But how can you describe feelings? No, we need an instrument of some kind to measure the effect consistently. Come! Look here."

With that he took Charles over to a large glass dome to which an evacuation pump had been fitted. "This is a gold-leaf electroscope and it does indicate generally the level of charge on a plate." He shook his head. "But it is too crude, too approximate a device. What I need is an instrument that will react to some other effect of the electrical charge. A side effect, as it were, that is easier to measure at low values."

"Magnetism," Charles murmured half under his breath.

Volta seized him by the hand. "My dear fellow, you have a flair for this kind of thing! Must you go on with this tour of yours? For indeed magnetism! That was my most recent thought! Stay on here as my assistant---- we can work on the problem together."

It was a considerable temptation. For Charles liked Pavia and he liked Volta and the prospect of being associated with the very latest work in the field did excite him. But Sewell awaited him in Cremona and besides he had Mary's agenda to complete. She would never be well enough to enjoy the wonders of Italy in person, he knew that now. And so she needed him to do this for her, to report it all for her as well as he could. There was little enough that he could do for her, given the facts of their relationship and the all too solid existence of Thomas Graham.

He shook his head and sighed as he lay in the early stages of sleep at the inn. No, it was impossible to stay longer. He must continue with the tour, if only for Mary.

TWENTY SIX

Yet in the event he remained with Volta for almost two weeks, making himself generally useful in the laboratory and gradually developing an understanding of where Volta hoped his experiments would lead.

At one point Charles mentioned that he was to see Galvani in Bologna. "Ah, Galvani!" Volta said coolly. "Of course you know that we disagreed on the fundamentals of the question. He is a very nice man. But I doubt if you will learn much in Bologna." He smiled sadly. "He and his frogs! Do you know," he said dismissively, "that he actually thought the electrical spasms came from the dead tissue! Preposterous! But what can you expect from someone who is scarcely more than a biologist. Though, to be fair," Volta added, "he did eventually realise that atmospheric electricity from lightning discharges was providing the motive power."

But he recovered his usual good manners quickly. "Still, Galvani is a good-natured fellow and you will enjoy meeting him, I am sure. Please give him my compliments." He beamed at Charles. "As you know, errors are almost as important in research as the truth. Provided of course you can tell one from the other!"

Charles finally took a belated leave of Volta with real regret and with a promise from the future professor that he would be sent a model of his first successful measuring instrument. Then he left, riding slowly out of Pavia and into the flat valley of the Po, staring in curiosity at the black water buffalos standing shoulder-deep in the swampy marshes on each side of the road.

Why exactly was he going to Cremona? Charles frowned and

referred to Mary's notes. Ah yes! There was a world renowned violin maker there by the name of Amati and Charles was sure to call at his workshop; perhaps even to purchase one of his famous instruments, which would be much cheaper in Cremona than in London or Paris.

No, decided Charles firmly after he had looked about the pretty little town. 'I do not believe I will buy a violin.' In fact there seemed to be a positive orchestra of local fellows all making violins in Cremona and in truth he was at a loss to distinguish Mr Amati's instruments from the others. According to Mary the next important thing he must do in Cremona was to mount the Torrazzo, an immense tower in the centre of the town, from the top of which he would sample a panorama which promised to be uniquely spectacular.

"Exactly five hundred and two steps," Charles groaned as he counted his way up and gasping found himself on a precariously narrow platform at the very top of the tower. The ancient clock showed almost noon and the early summer sun beat oppressively on him as he stared down into the town. Like so many others in Italy it was entirely set within strongly fortified walls and the broad river sweeping past was still swollen by the winter snow melt from the nearby mountains. Yes, there was the Duomo and directly facing it across the piazza the splendid town hall. Church and State in opposition, Charles thought briefly. But no ducal Palazzo he noted. For he had learned from Thomas that Cremona was one of the many small city states of northern Italy that still guarded their independence jealously.

Gingerly negotiating around the vertiginous platform, to his astonishment he came upon John Sewell. He was leaning back at the top of the tower, sketch book in hand and intent on his drawing. It was a complete surprise for both men; they had not expected to meet until their planned evening rendezvous time. But suddenly there he was. "Five hundred and two!" Charles panted out aloud. "Damn me, Thomas was right after all! This must be the tallest tower in Italy. Why, John Sewell! What brings you up here?"

Sewell had slammed his sketch book firmly shut at the sound of approaching footsteps. Now he peered around cautiously. Then, seeing there was no one else on the tower, he relaxed and gave Charles a forced grin. "These defensive walls in Cremona are continuously being changed," he said. "Clever devils these Italian engineers when it comes to fields of fire and covering approaches." He glanced awkwardly at Charles. "Lord Stormont will enjoy my drawings, if no one else does."

Charles stared at him aghast. "What do you mean? Not again! More espionage, Sewell? Will they not arrest you if they learn what you are about?"

"Oh," Sewell smiled and shrugged his shoulders. "As for that, why there are foreign agents all over the place. The authorities know perfectly well that half the young gentlemen who pass this way take information away with them." He laughed. "Which is one reason why they keep changing the fortifications of course."

Charles stared and shook his head. "You make it sound like a kind of game."

"That's exactly right, sir. It's a great game, though." Sewell smiled again, grimly this time. "Until the killing starts that is. Until some poor sods have to storm this place from across the river. Or through that horrible mess of swampland there. Then it becomes a different sort of game."

"But if they keep changing the defences, what is the point?"

Sewell shrugged again. "The point is, sir, to keep up to date. You never can tell when it's going to be needed."

Charles stared at Sewell in silence. Painfully and reluctantly he realised that he was travelling across a foreign land with one of Lord Stormont's secret agents, much as he had tried to forget the fact. "But look here Sewell, you are a common spy! First that business at Cherbourg. And now this! You're one of Stormont's spies, are you not?"

Sewell laughed. "A spy, sir? No, not me! I--- I only run errands for the Ambassador, sir. You know, deliver things here, pick up things there! But a spy? What an idea, sir!" He seemed to find the notion almost entertaining.

"That's all very well." Charles was determined now. "But, damn it all Sewell, I saw you myself in Paris picking up letters from Edward Bancroft in the Tuileries!"

"Oh did you, sir." Sewell responded blandly, though Charles detected the slightest hesitation. "Well now, that's what I mean. That's exactly what I mean. Just fetching and carrying, that's all I do." He smiled at Charles. But behind the good humoured gaze was just the hint of a warning. "Not a spy, sir," he repeated. "Oh no, sir. Just fetching and carrying."

"But I know that Bancroft is a spy," Charles blurted out. "He is Benjamin Franklin's secretary and you were carrying papers from him to the British."

"Oh really, sir?" Sewell's mask was firmly back in place. "Well, he is an odd one, that Bancroft fellow from what I've heard. But a spy? Well sir, I wouldn't know about that." Slowly Sewell rose to his feet.

On the small platform Charles was aware of the low parapet that skirted the top of the tower, uncomfortably aware that it was scarcely knee-high. From the corner of his eye he glimpsed below them the strangely miniaturized piazza. It seemed suddenly very far away--- all five hundred and two steps down and the platform curiously cramped. For an instant Sewell swayed a shade closer to him. Charles put his hand casually on the hilt of his dirk, as if to adjust it in his belt.

His companion's eyes narrowed slightly and an awkward silence hung for a moment between them in the shimmering heat. Then Sewell laughed. "Well, well, sir," he said. "I'm sorry you feel that way about things. Still, I think we'd better get you back to the inn. I took rooms near the piazza, just as you said, sir. And very pleasant they are too," he added mildly.

Charles followed him silently down the tower. But their relationship had irrevocably changed and early the following morning when they set out for Parma, the next of Mary Graham's recommendations, they were in a sombre mood. They rode the thirty miles to Parma in near silence. But behind the silence lay a tacit understanding that soon their paths must part.

Much to Charles's relief Sewell appeared to show no interest in Parma and so he was free to spend a few days wandering aimlessly on his own through the narrow streets, examining the array of food shops displaying all manner of exotic pastas and dried meats. He also spent a good part of his time trying to avoid being run down by the hordes of small town carriages that raced dangerously through the streets, swaying and rattling over the stone-flagged roads, each drawn by two fast moving horses with a complete disregard for pedestrians.

He soon found the Teatro Faranese and wrote for Mary a painstaking account of what she had said was 'the first theatre in Europe with a modern proscenium arch'. It had been built by a Grand Duke for his private entertainment but he had used it so rarely it seemed that now the citizens regarded it as one of Parma's civic treasures.

On three sides a swathe of seating rose up in high steep banks and this had the effect, accidental or intended, of creating an arena with quite remarkable acoustics. Charles noticed how even a low conversation held on the stage were clearly audible at the rear of the theatre. He pondered briefly on how sound could be transmitted with such purity over such a distance. Had Cavendish, he wondered briefly, ever addressed himself to the issue of sound? Or perhaps Franklin? He must ask them about that one day.

Then he went into the Duomo and stared dutifully at what Mary assured him was a masterpiece painted on panels in the interior of the dome by some fellow in the 16th century called Correggio. To Charles they appeared to be an uneven mass of dull shapes, almost impossible to see against the bright sunlight that streamed through the cupola. He sighed but dutifully included the experience in his weekly letter to Mary.

'And much pleasure may it give her,' he thought grimly as he sealed the letter that evening. 'But how I hope that her health is improved. And also that there may be letters from her somewhere along the way.' In his lonely bed he wondered, not for the first time, why he was undertaking this journey. After all, would she not one day come and see these wonders for herself.? But in his heart something told him that such a thing was impossible.

Mantua was another day or two towards the east and there Charles noted that Sewell openly spent most of his time sketching the massive defensive walls. It was clear even to his eye that these walls would secure the city on three sides from direct assault, plunging as they did straight into the swirling waters of the River Po on one side and into two deep lakes on the others, giving Mantua a remarkable natural protection.

All pretence of innocence had been abandoned by Sewell. "This place could be crucial in the event of the French moving into northern Italy," Sewell grunted as he closed his sketch book one evening. "It's part of the famous quadrilateral of Austrian fortresses along with Verona, Legnago and Peschiera. They guard the way from Austria into Italy." He pushed a rough sketch map towards Charles. "We have good relations with the Austrians at present, you see, for they hate the French as much as we do."

"What do the Austrians have to do with it?" Charles asked absently, staring at the map.

Sewell nodded in the direction of the mountain passes north of the city. "Why, there they sit, sir. Right behind those mountains. And if Froggie comes into this part of Italy the Austrian army will be pouring through those passes before you can say 'kiss my hand'. Mantua would be critical then, as I say." His eyes met Charles's for an instant, frankly. "I think sir," he added quietly, "it is probably time for us to be going our separate ways."

Charles nodded silently. That seemed to be the only solution. He was far from comfortable with Sewell as a companion now and increasingly anxious to return to the role of innocent tourist. In any case it was time for him to turn south--- to Bologna, where depending on his reception from Galvani he hoped to spend some weeks exploring that ancient university city. As he had guessed, Bologna held no great interest for Sewell.

"Where will you go next," he asked.

John Sewell smiled. "Oh north, sir. Definitely north! Towards Venice and a ship home, hopefully. Or perhaps on to Vienna and home overland that way. It will be high summer soon and too hot for me in the south," he added with a wry smile. "And unless I'm much mistaken, events are moving rapidly. I dare say there will be instructions from Lord Stormont when I reach Venice. Some odd jobs, as you might say, on the way home to England."

Home to England, Charles thought, half enviously.

TWENTY SEVEN

Bologna in high summer and the sun beat mercilessly down. Charles, exploring the wide streets and piazzas, dutifully followed Mary Graham's instructions but wherever possible stayed within the blessed shade of the long covered arcades. These had been cleverly constructed to offer protection from the heat of summer and the snow and rain that plagued Bologna during its equally extreme winter. But for now, under their civilised protection, Charles was able to walk in relative comfort from one side of the city to the other.

"The Due Torre are an essential sight," Mary had written. "They lean at an extraordinary angle one to the other and seem liable to collapse at any moment. Though I am assured that they have survived in that condition since the 15th century and are unlikely to do so." Charles frowned at the ancient battlements soaring high above him as he stood, buffeted by the busy throngs of merchants and traders and their rumbling carts. These people at least were oblivious to any impending disaster, he thought uneasily. Nevertheless he plunged into the cool interior of a wine shop in the Via San Stefano for a glass of the local red wine to settle his nerves. Then he set out to find the Basilica of San Petronio, which was next on Mary's list.

The church proved simple to find, its façade dominating even the huge expanse of the Piazza Maggiore. Charles paused for a moment to stare at its solidity with some satisfaction. Sadly the fine exterior decoration of its walls had been abandoned only half completed in the 14th century, when some Duke ran out of money. But in spite of this the Basilica stood foursquare and substantial, almost filling one side of the great square. 'But at least,' Charles thought, 'there is no likelihood of it falling down any time soon.'

"On each side of the main portal there is a group of wonderfully realistic carved panels by Jacopo della Quercia," Mary informed him, "depicting scenes from the Old Testament. They are acknowledged masterpieces of the Renaissance." It seemed to Charles that his eye for this kind of thing must be developing, for he did find beauty in these carvings.

But he was glad nevertheless to pass into the cool vast echoing Basilica; the sun was almost at its dazzling zenith and the heat in the piazza was intense. To his surprise he found the interior of the massive, almost brutal, structure was astonishingly lovely; airy and suffused with light, the high soaring gothic arches and the pale pink tones of its brick pilasters illuminated by glorious stained glass. 'It is like a true vision of heaven,' Charles thought as he gazed around in wonder. 'Perhaps there is something in this art business after all.'

Then he frowned as he noticed an extraordinary single beam of bright sunlight that plunged downwards from high in the roof, casting a spot of light onto the ancient floor. Peering up Charles could just make out a distant aperture, set far above him in the giant dome, from which the beam obviously came. He walked towards the spot of light and saw that set into the marble floor nearby was a long strip of brass running far into the interior of the Basilica.

Charles studied the brass strip with some puzzlement. Mary had made no mention of this. Yet the arrangement looked old: very old and very intriguing. Then he saw that the stone floor beside the strip was marked off in a series of irregular measures with next to each various letters and numerals. The letters he quickly worked out were abbreviations for Latin words; probably the months of the year, he decided. Then he noticed that little by little the spot of light was drawing ever closer to the brass line. The truth dawned on him. 'It will cut it at any moment,' he thought. 'The whole concept is an elaborate sundial, effective at midday!'

Then he heard a voice echoing in the empty Basilica. "Subito!"

Glancing up he saw an untidy figure standing half hidden by one of the great pillars; a man, elderly and shabbily dressed, but respectable looking and mild in appearance. He was juggling awkwardly with a bundle of loose manuscripts, a long measuring rod and an old-fashioned writing stylus. For the moment he seemed oblivious of Charles, peering short-sightedly at the brass strip in the floor. Then he looked up and addressed Charles in a rapid stream of local Romagnian dialect. Clearly he was asking something. But what?

"Mi scusi senore. Ma non parlo bene Italiano--- ."

The man ignored him and darted forward, peering at the strip again. "Ah, gli Inglese!" he muttered. Then, in a weird mixture of Italian and struggling English, "My eyes are not so good. Mi ochi? Can you read for me the number on the---. There, just where the sun falls!" He thrust the measuring rod into his hands. "Give me the accurate diameter of the spot."

Charles quickly read off the numerals and carefully measured the sun spot on the floor. "Twenty-six centimetres," he said. "Ventisei," he added, falling into this strange bilingual conversation. He watched with barely concealed amusement as the peculiar figure added this information to a long column of numbers on his paper.

Then the man relaxed and beamed at Charles. "Mille grazie, senore," he said and extended a hand. "Mi chiamo Alberto Massimo." Haltingly he went on in English. "Every day at noon, summer and winter, I come here and record the variations." He held up his bundle of papers with a charming smile. "The seasonal variations of course are part of the planetary system--- the days of the month and the hours. But also the size of the sun as it changes. The apparent speed of the sun as it crosses the horizon in summer and winter?" He gazed at Charles hopefully.

Charles thought he grasped what was going on. This entire structure was a giant sun dial, just as he had imagined: but an extremely sophisticated one. That hole--- squinting up into the light he saw that it was positioned eccentrically high up on one side of the back wall of the basilica--- that hole generated a spot of light that would cut the brass strip at midday on the correct day of the appropriate month. He shook his head in wonder. It was as if the entire Basilica, the whole great structure of San Petronio, had been designed as a measuring device. But what genius could have calculated the exact relationship between the distant hole and the long brass strip, which he now realised functioned as a meridian? And to calibrate it so accurately!

He studied the irregular floor markings. Of course! In winter when the sun was low in the sky, the shaft of light would throw a spot of a very different shape. The apparent size of the sun would seem to change, as well as its speed of travel! This whole concept was complicated in ways he was only beginning to grasp. He whistled in amazement. Glancing up he saw that Massimo was beaming at him, aware that Charles had begun to understand. "Capisce? Bene, bene!"

Charles nodded slowly. "Si capisco. Penso!" he added with a wry smile. "You mentioned variations? Exactly what variations are you trying to measure?"

Massimo shrugged and gave him a delighted glance. "Ah, that is something I do not yet understand! But there are curiously regular variations as measured by my chronometer," he went on eagerly. "I have been recording them for the past twenty-five years and there seems to be a pattern of some kind." His face fell and he shook his head sadly. "But I do not understand them--- not yet."

Charles blinked. He thought he must have misunderstood the little man. "I'm sorry. You mean that you have been coming here every day at noon for twenty-five years!"

Massimo nodded glumly. "Yes," he said with a shrug. "Summer and winter. In illness or in health. Some days it is not so easy."

Charles did not know whether to laugh or cry. "So, no shortage of readings," he murmured weakly.

Massimo beamed at him. "No shortage of readings. For in addition I have studied the work of Eustachio Manfredi, who had access to eighty years of observations. He published his studies in 1736 so, as you say, no shortage of information. But still it is difficult to understand."

"You say the variations occur in a regular pattern. What could explain that?"

Massimo sighed. "What indeed?" He shook his head sadly and shrugged his shoulders, dropping the measuring rod with a clatter on the floor of the silent Basilica.

By now Charles was intrigued. Was the old man a crank? Or a serious researcher? Astronomy and the movement of the planets was not a subject Charles had encountered before. It had simply not figured in Sir William Johnson's library, from where Charles had derived his patchy education.

On an impulse Charles determined to study the old man's figures in detail. He took Massimo by the hand. "I must go for the moment. I must arrange an appointment at the University." The old man looked impressed. "But I should like to discuss this question with you again. Perhaps we can study your numbers together, if you are agreeable. Can we meet some time?"

Massimo bowed graciously. "You will have no difficulty in finding me, my friend." His brown wizened face split in a broad and friendly smile. "At least once each day!" Charles returned the smile and took his leave of the curious gentleman.

Making his way across a small piazza to the University to present his letter of introduction to Galvani, he mused on the encounter. The man's tale had begun to weigh on his mind. Yes, he decided. If I have time I shall seek out the old fellow again and find out more about this phenomenon he thinks he has discovered.

"Professor Giovanni Galvani is away from Bologna for the rest of the summer, enjoying the cooler airs of the lakes," an obviously envious university official told him haughtily. "He will not return here until September." Charles nodded abstractedly. Galvani's absence would not be a problem, for Charles had always intended to spend the summer in Bologna rather than venture further south into even more intense heat. Galvani's absence gave him the excuse he needed. He left his letter of introduction and made his back into the town.

Next day just before noon he returned to the Basilica. The faithful Massimo was there and seemed delighted to have Charles's help with the readings of the day. Every day for a week Charles presented himself just before twelve o'clock and soon he and Massimo had become firm friends.

Charles found a comfortable inn only a short walk from Massimo's rooms and during the long summer evenings became accustomed to sitting with his new friend, drinking the local wines and studying the thousands of observations that Massimo had accumulated so systematically over the past quarter of a century.

Alberto Massimo, he discovered was a retired school-teacher and greatly respected by his pupils, some of whom still helped him in his work. "The meridian on the floor of San Petronio is actually the work of Domenico Cassini," he informed Charles. "It was he who replaced an earlier and shorter line that had been there since 1575 and it was he who calculated the exact position of the 'eye' for the much longer meridian that you see today." Charles inwardly wondered at the complexity of the calculations involved in even that simple statement.

Massimo went on. "His avowed purpose for creating such a huge meridian line--- it is the largest in the world you know--- was to determine accurately the length of the tropical year." Seeing the look of puzzlement on Charles's face he stopped. "That is the time between subsequent spring equinoxes. This was necessary in order that the new Gregorian calendar should be made as accurate as possible."

He paused again. "The equinox is when the sun is directly above the earth's equator. When the earth has equal amounts of its surface exposed to sunlight as it revolves around the sun." He looked sharply at Charles. "It is well established that it is the earth which revolves and not the sun. Since Kepler and of course Galileo."

"I see," said Charles vaguely.

"But that was not Cassini's real motive."

"Ah," said Charles noncommittally. This was going to become even more complicated, he could tell.

"No," Massimo went on happily. "Cassini's real motive was, by measuring the size of the sun's image and comparing its rate of change with its apparent speed across the sky, to prove that in summer when it is further away from the earth, it truly does move more slowly."

"Hold on!" said Charles. "In summer you say the sun is further away than it is in winter? That hardly seems logical!"

Massimo pursed his mouth and stared at Charles, wondering what kind of ignoramus he had encountered. "The position of the sun at summer solstice, or winter solstice come to that when it is nearest to the earth, is not what causes the seasons, you know."

Charles waited silently. He was beginning to think that after all he had encountered a true eccentric. "No," said Massimo. "The reason for the seasons is that the earth is tilted on its vertical axis as it spins around the sun."

Suddenly Charles visualised the system Massimo was describing. "So that the northern part of the earth," he said slowly, "has summer while the southern part is in winter?"

"And vice versa," Massimo said with relish. "What is more, Eustachio Manifredi, whose observations I have been studying, proved that the angle of the earth's tilt changes regularly over time. This has the effect of changing the time of the seasons. There is, as it is called, a precession as the earth seems to be straightening slowly in its orbit."

"But---," said Charles.

"Yes," Massimo added quickly. "If that is indeed the case we will eventually have no seasons."

"In fact, if it continued," Charles said with a laugh, "the earth would in theory tip right over! But that is clearly ridiculous! Since it would surely have already happened at some time in its history and there is no evidence of such a catastrophe!"

"Precisely! That is why these other variations that I seem to have detected are of interest. At least to me!"

"Tell me about these!" Charles cried and Massimo beamed

delightedly at him. It was what proved to be the start of a long intensive summer of study, as slowly and systematically they arranged and analysed the information.

Gradually Charles began to see what was implied by the readings his friend had collected. Then, with his curious instinct for numbers, he began to see a new pattern emerging: a pattern that his friend Massimo had missed completely. One evening towards the end of August Charles flung down his pen. "There it is, Alberto," he said quietly. "It is quite clear what the trend is! If what you tell me about astronomy is correct, which I do not doubt, there seems to be only one possible explanation for these numbers. The change of tilt is in fact a periodic change and not a continuous one. In other words the angle of the earth's axis to its orbit around the sun varies, too and fro, back and forth on a regular basis. So our seasons are safe after all!"

Then he sat bolt upright. "In fact," he went on slowly. "It could well be explained by a circular movement, a second rotation, causing the tilt of the axis to change in two planes. It is slowly gyrating, rather as a spinning cone wobbles! Alberto, you must document this for posterity, my dear friend!"

By the end of September when the university resumed Charles had become almost fluent in Italian, thanks to many evenings spent with Alberto and his band of loyal pupils. "Or at least I have become fluent in the local Bolognaise dialect which is what is mostly spoken hereabouts," he wrote to Mary. He wrote to her every week now without fail, hoping that the accounts of his experiences were giving her vicarious pleasure. Hoping too, fervently though unexpressed, that she and Thomas were both well and happy.

Giovanni Galvani, he explained to Mary, proved to be a small, rather stout and endlessly cheerful man, without the least pretension about him. He welcomed Charles enthusiastically, Franklin's letter working its accustomed magic again. "I was quite mistaken at first," he admitted to him frankly. "Observing the muscles of the frog spasm I assumed that the energy came from within the creature--- a kind of vital life force." He shrugged and laughed. "I now realise that I was simply conducting electricity from the air into the body."

"Well," said Charles shamelessly, "I suppose one learns almost as much from a failure as one does from success."

"How very true, young man!" Galvani cried, regarding him with new respect. "How very perceptive of you. Now, what would you like to do while you are in Bologna? I am sure we can find something useful for you here in my laboratories."

Later that night Charles rather guiltily wondered at the ease with which he had gained this credibility in the field of electricity. The great men of the subject seemed to accept him at face value and he was beginning to half believe his own reputation! 'Still,' he thought, 'I must do something to justify these good opinions or I shall think myself a total fraud.' He decided therefore to spend his winter working as one of the professor's assistants and Galvani, having quickly identified his aptitude for numbers, made full use of him on all his quantitative work.

So it proved a memorable winter. Nor was it all work. For he had come to enjoy the confidence of Galvani and under his tutelage had also learned to enjoy the food for which the area was renowned. Wild boar shot on hunting trips into the hills around Monte Donato--- once again Charles had established his reputation as a deadly shot by dropping one dangerous wicked-eyed pig as it charged out of the undergrowth straight at the petrified Galvani--- were butchered there in the snow and roasted deliciously over open wood fires. Later, some were turned into wonderful sausages or hung up to dry to produce the local version of preserved ham. This, eaten cold with cheese and freshly baked bread, made a meal for Charles on many a freezing winter day.

What he did not enjoy about Bologna however was the persistent bone-chilling cold that drifted into the city from the flat grey misty plains of the River Po. Dampness hung menacingly about the streets, penetrating it seemed to the very marrow of the bones. "It is much, much colder here," Charles wrote to Mary, "than on the peak of Mont Cenis. For though we were there surrounded by snow and ice, the air was beautifully clear, crisp and dry. In the present season it is difficult to believe that Bologna is the same town in which we laboured in such overpowering summer heat. Still, I can now fully appreciate the dual function of these miles of covered arcades, particularly on the all too frequent days when the fog is temporarily dispelled and the icy rain descends!"

'But this place would have killed poor Mary', he thought as he silently sealed the letter.

TWENTY EIGHT

By the end of March, though it was still far from spring in the Po valley, Charles had decided to resume his travels and headed southward towards Florence. Recalling Thomas Graham's advice and as a concession to the fickle weather he hired a carriage, bade Massimo and Galvani fond farewells--- he had become genuinely attached to both of his genial savants---- and set off across rutted mountain roads through the Apennines.

On parting, Alberto took him by the hand and with tears in his eyes thanked Charles for his assistance. "Never forget the meridian of San Petronio, my son." he said intently. "Think of it as a measure of your own life etched there on the floor of the Basilica, illuminated by the eye of the meridian. For it is God's light that brings comprehension, however clever the mathematician."

Embarrassed, for he had no religious feeling himself, Charles mumbled his good-byes. But he had plenty time to ponder on Massimo's words as the fifty miles to Florence, long and wearying, passed painfully and slowly. Roads were narrow and dangerous and on each side steep valleys rose shrouded in mists and low cloud, dankness dripping from the dark green forests that crowded down onto the road. At night he was offered a succession of lice-ridden hostelries where the food was uniformly execrable. "This is certainly no place for a tourist," he muttered to himself on many a night, frequently opting for a cold restless slumber wrapped in his greatcoat inside the coach.

But short of starvation there was no way to escape the dire cooking. At one inn he was offered a revolting mess which, so far as he could understand the local dialect grunted out by a filthy peasant with a cleft palate, consisted of crow's gizzards with mustard. Charles toyed with it in dismay, hoping that he might have mistranslated the dish and fearing that he had not.

But eventually the misery ceased and crossing over into Tuscany all became miraculously sunlight and astonishingly warm. Suddenly it seemed to be spring or even early summer and he gazed in wonder as the carriage crested the last barrier of hills at the village of Fiesole. There spread out beautifully before him lay the city of Florence, a mosaic of terracotta and pale umber dominated by its spectacular Duomo.

The Duomo, Mary's notes informed him, was topped by a unique dome of so great a span that for forty years it had proved impossible to construct. Finally the incomparable Brunelleschi solved the problem for the frustrated city fathers. 'At great expense to them, I dare say!' was Charles's uncharitable thought as he approached the city. But Florence had so much at which to marvel that Charles, completely captivated, was happy to spend several weeks simply walking the streets and absorbing the sheer loveliness of the place.

Ben Franklin's writ did not seem to run this far south. But Charles did have a letter of introduction from Lord Stormont to Sir Horace Mann, the British Consul in the city. Thomas Graham also had assured Charles that Mann kept open house for British travellers. "He—humph--- has a particular fondness for young men, I understand. Which may explain why he has remained in Florence for so many decades," Thomas muttered awkwardly. "Not that this should concern you, Charles. He seems to prefer young men of a certain type."

In the event Sir Horace proved to be quite charming and the very soul of hospitality, if to Charles's eye a trifle affected in speech and manners. "My dear young sir," he had trilled, when once he had extracted from Charles his social connections with Thomas and Mary, the Cathcart family, Thomas's mother and the Hopetouns, and of course Sir William Hamilton in Naples.

Charles studied him cautiously at first. Sir Horace was a tiny figure, always fastidiously dressed with his hair still heavily powdered in the old way and extravagantly mannered. 'But also quite ugly,' he remarked to himself. 'With a large nose and heavy features. Not unlike a fussy toad!'

"Now what news do you have for me from London?" Sir Horace had enquired. When Charles explained that he had been travelling for more than a year his host obviously could not contain himself. "Ah, then you will not know about the latest scandal! Poor Lady Derby! She has left her husband, intending I dare say to set up house with her lover, Lord

Dorset." Charles nodded. He seemed to recall something of that sort going on at Devonshire House.

"But after a few weeks," Sir Horace went on delightedly, his eyes gleaming, "Dorset abandoned her! Completely stranded! He went off with someone else--- an actress of sorts, I believe. Imagine that! She had left her husband and three children! And now of course she is no longer acceptable in polite society, poor woman. Left quite high and dry, for Lord Derby refuses either to take her back or to give her a divorce. What a tragedy!" He paused. "Of course she should have known her man. Dorset is a notorious womaniser."

He gave a disgusted shudder. "But it scarcely seems fair, does it?" he appealed to Charles. "And this is a man who claims to be the patron of cricket! Do you know," he went on eagerly. "He once sacked a mistress because she ran him out when batting with him in a game!"

Charles tried to look concerned. "Is it such a heinous offence then? To run someone out at cricket?"

Mann waved his arms dismissively. "Oh, I know nothing of cricket! Or any other sport for that matter. But it does seem to betray a lack of human compassion." He paused. "Still, I dare say you do not know the principals of whom I speak."

Charles bowed his head slightly. "I believe," he said casually, "that I did see the unhappy couple together one evening at Devonshire House."

"Devonshire--- !" For a moment Sir Horace's ugly face was a picture of astonishment. Then it quickly changed to delight. "You know the Duchess socially?" he said in hushed tones and this was enough to seal Charles's acceptance. For the rest of his stay there was nothing that Sir Horace would not do or arrange for him in Florence.

Sir Horace Mann lived in an elegant villa in a secluded area of Florence, surrounded by shaded gardens, splashing fountains and terraces that caught any breeze from the stately River Arno. There he held his notorious garden parties, when he would always be surrounded by a bevy of delightful young men. As Thomas had tactfully warned, his host at first seemed to take a special interest in Charles but quickly recognised where Charles's inclinations lay and confined himself to improving his young guest's aesthetic appreciation. He thoroughly approved of Mary's recommendations and added a few snippets of information of his own, usually of a scurrilous nature.

"This is a Medici city and you simply must see the Palazzo Pitti, which is ugly on the outside but well worth exploring. It is a treasure trove of the most exquisite works of art. And you must see the bed-chamber of the last Medici Duke!" He fluttered his eyes grotesquely at Charles. "Where he entertained his 'rispanti'" Charles looked at him enquiringly. This was not a word he had come across in his travels.

Mann gushed on. "His naughty boys---- if you know what I mean!" He pretended to look shocked. "His painted catamites!"

"I see," Charles said grimly. Thomas and Stormont's warnings had not been misplaced.

"And of course you must see the Uffizi. Titan's Venus is at one end of the hall and something of the same sort by Zoffany at the other." He sniffed. "They may be to your taste, I dare say." He glanced at Charles coyly, with a tilt of his head.

"But for me the finest thing in Florence is the figure of David, Michelangelo's masterpiece! It stands in the loggia of the Piazza della Signoria." He smiled winningly at Charles. "It never fails to excite the most extreme sensations in me. Sometimes I am so overcome that I simply take to my bed until my feelings are controlled."

Charles first came upon the figure of David after dark, when it was illuminated by flaming flickering fire-brands and in these dramatic circumstances the sheer brooding power and beauty of the young David moved him to agree with Mann. It was the most impressive of any sight he had yet encountered. 'Including,' he reflected, 'even the Alps! For this is the work of a human hand! Remarkable indeed!' Next day, still awestruck by what he had seen, he made his way to the Church of the Santa Croce, an ancient gothic structure where he had learned that Michelangelo was buried.

But this was to prove a disappointment. "It is a poor tomb for such a giant of a man," Charles wrote to Mary. For even to his eye the carving and the design was of an inferior nature. 'What a pity he couldn't have carved his own tomb,' he thought inconsequentially. 'He'd certainly have made a better job of it.' But there was much to tell Mary in his letters, which Sir Horace insisted on sending back to England with his own speedy private service, including a covering note to Mary telling her how quite delightfully charming he had found her young protégé and of course sending his regards to Thomas's mother, Lady Christian.

The weeks slipped away in a pleasant succession of introductions, garden parties and dinners, marred only by one unfortunate evening when Sir Horace was so overcome by horror at the behaviour of a guest that he fled his own table in anguish and took to his bed for two whole days.

When eventually Charles saw him again he was still pale and

shaken. Enquiring after his health, Sir Horace visibly blanched. "My dear boy, I cannot endure to think of it!" he shuddered. "That dreadful fellow! He--- he sat there chewing, with his mouth open!" Mann flapped a hand weakly. "No, I mustn't think of it again. I mustn't--- no! Please do not make me!"

Soon after that regrettable incident Charles left again on his journey southwards along the lovely old road to Siena and Rome, with the good wishes of Sir Horace ringing in his ears and more warnings about corrupt passport checks and unscrupulous inn-keepers.

It was high summer again and Sir Horace insisted that Charles take a carriage to see him over the next hundred and fifty miles of the Via Casia in comfort. "Otherwise you will find the heat utterly enervating, my dear." He shuddered exquisitely. "I should simply die." He smiled at Charles adoringly. "Though you are so young and strong." But he gave him the gift of a blanket, of leather so fine that it might have been made of cotton. "Wrap yourself completely in it, dear boy, if you should have to sleep in one of those awful inns," Sir Horace said with a shudder. "You will find the lice cannot penetrate the leather."

It was a kindly thought and Charles departed with something like affection for his generous host. "A strange man. But perhaps there is more to him than is immediately obvious."

He reached San Gimignano on the first day, a strange town with hundreds of tall towers set on a hill with charming views across the surrounding countryside. Gazing out at a manicured landscape that stretched on all sides as far as he could see, he was struck by the essential civilisation of the place. 'Yes, that is the word; civilised,' he thought. 'These fields must have been farmed for a thousand years. How very different from the hills of the Mohawk valley!'

How, he wondered, was his friend Francis? Was he still pursuing old Snape? Or was he by now caught up fully in the patriotic struggle? Once again Charles was struck by a pang of guilt. He had somehow imagined, listening to Fox and Edmund Burke, that General Burgoyne's disaster at Saratoga would bring the war to a speedy end. But Sir Horace had given no sign of any official dismay. He shrugged as he watched the rich scenery drift past the carriage window. America and the war seemed curiously unreal.

His next stop was Siena, another glorious city of umber yellow and red where Sir Horace had insisted he must see the Duomo. "It is quite stunning, with a perfect façade of pink and white marble." Mary had said that he must not miss the wonderful pulpit, carved by Pisano in the 13th century and Sir Horace had agreed. "A work of true genius."

Writing to Mary, Charles was happy to admit that he was indeed impressed with Siena. He noted that either his Italian was improving or the Siennese were speaking a purer version of the language than he had encountered elsewhere. The women of Siena were welcoming too, though he omitted mentioning this in his letter. Since his unfortunate experience with the Contessa in Turin, Charles had been circumspect about entanglements of that sort.

But here in Siena he felt sufficiently confident, taking appropriate precautions, to enjoy the company of one or two of the local young ladies. During his daylight strolls he also had time to notice the curiously shaped piazza where they had since time immemorial, or at least the previous century, ran the annual palio horse race. This was a momentous event he was told, but one which sadly he had just missed.

Then he was off again towards Rome, with a stop at Orvieto, yet another fairy tale city on a hill, with an outrageously beautiful cathedral glowing in the evening sun. Another set of old masters to record and then at last long final leg of the Via Casia to Rome.

From London he had covered a thousand bone-rattling miles of rough road and sometimes no road at all, thought Charles bleakly as he gratefully abandoned his carriage at the vast Piazza del Popolo and stared at three noble radial roads that led straight and wide, though narrowing gradually as they receded, into different quarters of Rome.

Rome, the eternal city, he thought! Expectations were high, for Mary Graham had complied a daunting list of sights that exceeded in quantity any other city along the way. Even from his boyhood reading in Sir William Johnson's library he was filled with recollections of Roman ideals: honour, loyalty and faith. Here it all lay before him at last.

The immediate reality was rather different, Charles noted in dismay as he forced his way through a mob of dirty, noisy, gesticulating porters fighting to gain his patronage. These were the fellows who made a living of sorts from the thousands of tourists and pilgrims who by law were required to leave their carriage at the entrance to the city and to make their way into the centre on foot carrying their baggage.

Charles selected the least scrofulous looking individual who, with little more than a glance at him, trotted off towards the Piazza di Spagna, an area in which Robert Greville had assured him "the English live in a kind of ghetto". Indeed, as Charles discovered, so English had the area become that it was known as 'little Westminster'. With no difficulty Charles found comfortable rooms half way up a splendid stone staircase that even the locals called in English 'the Spanish Steps'.

But his first opinion of Rome were not good. The buildings looked scruffy and uncared for, unspeakable objects lay in the streets and there was sewage and filth everywhere. The over-riding impression indeed was of dust, dirt and wandering goats and over all hung an unpleasant miasma of urine and garlic. Was this really the place he had come so far to see? Rome he discovered had fallen a long way from its illustrious height.

It was of course still a major city by any standard--- it took him a full two hours to walk from one side to the other. And it was undoubtedly thronged with people. But there seemed to be no commercial life, apart from catering to the needs of tourists like himself. Was there no normal population such as you would expect to find in a city of this size? All he saw as he wandered its streets following Mary's itinerary were equal numbers of beggars, prostitutes, priests and nuns. The rest of the population it seemed were aristocrats of various nationalities, degraded and debauched, many exiled Catholics and Stuart supporters from England.

He found his way to the Forum, his mind still half filled with noble images of stirring speeches by Pompey, Marc Anthony and Julius Caesar. What he found was a medium sized field of grass, with a herd of cows peacefully grazing amid the ruins of stone temples and triumphal arches. Above him ranged the pleasantly shaded Palatine Hill and from there he walked to the Circus Maximus, where he found yet another ruin.

As he stared at the vast empty expanse he could conjured up in his mind frantic chariot races, drivers whipping the horses and everything else that impeded them and a hundred thousand wildly cheering or cat-calling spectators. But Charles shook his head. The greatness had all passed away, he thought sadly. What could he tell Mary? Still, he squared his shoulders. There was work to be done and he set off to see the other spectacles on her list.

In fairness, he reflected, one hot evening relaxing in a small taverna on the Piazza Navona, some of the city had lived up to expectations. Right before his eyes was the most elaborate, if tasteless, fountain he had ever seen. Waters poured from four carved sources which seemed to represent the great rivers of the world, though he had to admit to Mary in his regular letter that he had no idea which they were.

Nor did any of the locals seem to know or care, though one did tell him that on special holidays in the past the entire piazza had been flooded and mock sea battles of antiquity recreated. This Charles rather doubted, though his informant, a strangely well-spoken beggar insisted it was true.

He found the Pantheon and marvelled at the sheer immensity of its walls and gigantic dome. Constructed in the lifetime of Christ, he thought with genuine awe. Of course, it struck him! This was the model for the Pantheon Theatre in London, in which Benjamin Wilson had recently conducted his spectacular demonstration on the rival merits of points or spheres on lightning conductors. He thought again of Ben Franklin and wondered how events in Paris had moved.

He went on to stare at the immense ruin that was the Colosseum and wondered at the stories of teams of hired gladiators fighting to the death in the dust of the arena; of 5,000 wild animals killed in a single day to entertain the Roman crowd. Now it was a mere empty shell echoing to the noise of pigeons wings, the only other sound the cries of welcome from the hundreds of prostitutes who found their living in the shadows of the darkened galleries. Charles fought down an impulse and hurried away in search of something more spiritual.

He found it across the River Tiber at Bernini's astonishing St Peter's and as he entered the gigantic church he could not contain a gasp of astonishment. This, he thought, was architecture on a scale that rivalled the ancient Roman structures on the other side of the river. Immense soaring pillars and enormous curved domes towered above him, with everywhere elaborately decorated ceilings and a seemingly endless array of spectacular memorials and tombs carved in marble and bronze.

He drew nearer and nearer still to the Grand Altar. The distances were very deceptive, that he realised. Then suddenly the true scale of the four massive columns of elaborately wrought bronze of the baldacchino over the Altar became apparent to him. Bernini yet again he thought, glancing at Mary's notes. Yes, this was architecture designed to reduce man to his proper insignificance. Even Pope Alexander's splendid tomb, carved in rouge marble and crowned with studied moroseness by a human skeleton waving a large sandglass sent the same silent message.

At High Mass Charles saw the throngs of young girls, dressed in white like Vestals, with about their heads crowns of thorns, preparing to take their vows as nuns. Across at the Colosseum were their sisters, equally committed to a very different life, he mused silently.

Finally he found himself standing silently before the Michelangelo's Pieta. In spite of himself he was moved almost to tears at the sheer beauty of the white marble figure of the dead Christ, lying naked across the knees of his grieving surprisingly young mother. A sudden pang of regret struck Charles. He had never known his own mother, only his rough and remote dead father. Would she have cared for him so pitifully? He wiped away a suspicion of moisture from one eye. He never thought of his mother. What was the point?

The summer of 1779 was drawing to a gentle close when one evening he took a carriage out to a village in the surrounding Compagna countryside. "Tivoli!" Mary had said. "You must see the wonderful things there--- and you must tell me all about them, for I fear I shall never see them for myself." She had smiled lovingly at him as she said those words. Was lovingly putting it too highly, Charles wondered? His feelings for Mary had not diminished in any way since that first astonishing 'coup de foudre' when he had seen her at Stormont's home in Paris--- so long ago it seemed now, though scarcely a year or two had passed.

Mary did care for him, of that he was certain. But more and more, if reluctantly, he had come to realise the nature of that love--- if he could even apply that word to the sentiment she felt for him. It was a feeling like the Pieta, he realised in a flash of insight. That was what he meant to Mary. A surrogate son--- no more than that, he thought sadly. But no less either, he decided with a sort of satisfaction growing within him. And in his own way, Thomas too regarded him with fondness. Of that Charles had become increasingly aware. Suddenly he longed to see them both and to return to England.

But first he enjoyed for a few hours the innocent delights of the Villa D'Este gardens at Tivoli. The Medici family in a typically high-handed gesture had redirected a major tributary of the Tiber, thus depriving the local peasant communities of its water. They had then used it to embellish their already lovely estate, creating a true pleasure garden as it tumbled down the hillside in an endless cascade of fountains, sudden jets that would surprise and delight their guests, graceful streams full of flowers and carved figures from antiquity.

There were also extraordinary entertainments, created by the cool tinkling waters of the streams pouring down through the gardens and bringing to life artificially constructed grottos. There were devices engineered to produce lifelike sounds of bird songs and even the hooting of a predatory mechanical owl which seemed to scare the other birds away for a time! After dark the gardens were illuminated by flaming torches without number and altogether Tivoli was a place of absolute delight. Charles thought that he had never seen anything so wonderful: Vauxhall by comparison seemed tawdry.

Late that year he rode on from Rome in a changed mood towards Naples, where he would meet Mary's favourite uncle. That thought gave him an obscure sense of pleasure. For then he would go home at last, by sea.

TWENTY NINE

"You will travel more speedily and more safely in one of His Majesty's vessels," Sir William Hamilton had announced to him. "Moreover you would oblige me greatly, Charles, if you will supervise on the voyage a package of my personal possessions which I am consigning to London."

It was early in 1780 and Charles stood propped comfortably against a heavy stanchion on the weather side of the quarterdeck as HMS Niobe under the command of Captain Corbin plunged towards Gibraltar. Beyond that lay the open Atlantic Ocean and then America, Charles thought fleetingly. When was he to see his country again?

Moments earlier a young lieutenant called Merryweather, who had befriended Charles in spite of being turned out of his cabin to make room for him, had quietly uttered the magic words, "Captain on the quarterdeck". At that the entire watch of officers and midshipmen had moved across to leave the holy starboard side free for the captain. Charles, by now quite accustomed to these mysterious rituals at sea, had automatically followed suit.

Captain Corbin bounded up on deck, swept the horizon with an experienced eye, glanced with a nod of satisfaction at the trim of the great pyramid of white that towered above them and stared at the sky for a few minutes in silence. "We are making excellent progress," he announced to no one in particular. Then looking about he spotted Charles and boomed out, "Ah, Mr MacPherson. I was thinking about our conversation at dinner yesterday."

Now that he had been officially recognised, Charles cautiously made his way across the sloping deck to grasp the lee shrouds. "Did you ever see the St Elmo's Fire?" asked Corbin cheerfully. "The masts and rigging, even the bowsprit, all aglow with a strange blue-white light? It's as if----, well, it's as if a flash of lightning had been slowed right down and poured itself over the vessel's extremities. It happens from time to time in the Tropics. Where the atmospherics are right, I presume."

Charles admitted that though he had never seen this phenomenon, that he had never even been to the Tropics, he had read accounts of this effect. "It is thought to be a strange form of static electricity, Captain. So your poetic metaphor is perhaps well chosen."

Corbin grunted. "Poetic metaphor, eh." His round brown, rather simian face screwed up in doubt. He was unusual in the service, or so Merryweather had told him during a long warm sleepless night spent on deck. For Corbin had started his naval career in the lower deck as a foremast jack. Looking at his long powerful almost apelike arms, Charles could well imagine a young Corbin leaping about on the upper yard-arms and grappling with the heavy iron-hard topsails in the wildest of weather.

By an unlikely succession of circumstances Corbin had been made up, first to midshipman as a result of almost the entire quarterdeck being wiped out by fever in the West Indies and then to acting lieutenant to fill a gap left when the sloop on which he served had the misfortune to encounter a Spanish heavy frigate. Without influence in the Admiralty, Corbin did however have powerful admirers at fleet level and after a number of years of steady service he had finally been made Post Captain and given the frigate Niobe.

"Now he has command of a frigate, sir," Merryweather whispered to Charles in the quiet of the night. "Why, there is no limit to how high he may go! It would not surprise me if in time he became an Admiral of the Blue."

Charles had nodded sagely at this. "I suppose that is highly prized?"

The young lieutenant gasped. "Oh Lord yes, sir! Why,--- ! Well, I don't quite know how to explain it." He had stared at Charles in silence, wondering how an intelligent fellow could be so ill-informed about such important things. "For then he would hoist his flag, sir: blue at the mizzen! As a Rear-Admiral, do you see!"

Charles nodded sagely.

"First as a Rear-Admiral of the Blue." Merryweather went on. "Then, in due time, of the White and finally of the Red!

"I see," Charles said .

"Perhaps even become a Vice Admiral," Merryweather went on.

"Of the Blue?" Charles asked, eager to show comprehension.

"Then the White and eventually the Red!" Merryweather beamed at his companion, happy in the thought.

"And on what qualities would these promotions depend?" Charles enquired.

"Qualities, sir? Why service, of course--- years of service."

'So it's dead men's shoes,' Charles thought, hardly daring to express his reservations. 'Perhaps hardly as admirable a process as Merryweather seems to think.'

Be that as it may, the indisputable fact was that the crew adored Corbin and the Niobe, a complex organisation of men, ropes, canvas, metal and spars ran with a calm efficiency that Charles could recognise and admire. The miles between Naples and London in consequence slid past happily and speedily.

Sir William's 'package of personal possessions' turned out to be several substantial wooden crates which had been swiftly stowed away somewhere below the water line. "It's not likely that we will run into a French vessel. At this stage they are not really prepared for war at sea. We might run into an American privateer out in the Atlantic where they are starting to be a nuisance to our shipping, though no privateer in his right mind is going to tackle a 32-gun British frigate. But should we have such an encounter there will be no chance of a stray cannon ball messing up the boxes down there."

Charles was well aware that this arrangement with HMS Niobe was far from regular. Indeed his very presence on board a man-of-war was entirely due to Sir William's patronage. He also knew perfectly well what was in the crates. Sir Horace Mann, who seemed to know everything about almost anyone of consequence, had explained it to him.

"Hamilton is a charming and delightful man. You will like him." He had smiled winningly at Charles. "And I just know that he will like you." He had leaned forward and patted Charles affectionately on the thigh. "But he has no money to speak of and is entirely dependent on his ambassadorial salary, poor fellow." He grimaced. "He made the cardinal error of marrying," he waved one pale hand disparagingly in the air, "a woman of no great looks or influence and tragically without money."

"Ah," said Charles diplomatically. "A love-match, I suppose."

"Well!" said Sir Horace acidly. "One would like to think so, certainly. Though what her attraction could be I am at a loss to know." He sat back in contemplation of Hamilton's folly. "But the point is that he spends most of his time collecting works of art and antiquity from around Naples--- he has little else to do except to charm the ghastly Queen of Naples." He shuddered delicately again. "But no," he muttered. "I must not think of her! She is simply too ugly for words." He shook his head to free himself of the awful image.

"So Sir William," he went on, "acquires the best Greco-Roman artefacts he can find, sculptures and ancient marble pediments and so on. He does have excellent taste, mind. Then he sells them to wealthy collectors in England, when he can bear to part with them that is. Or when he is desperate for money. Which he regularly is." He paused. "Recently he has been dealing mostly with the new British Museum in London. So he is paid for them by the government therefore, which in a way seems only right, if you follow me. But you will love Naples," he had added irrelevantly. "It is not Florence, of course. But still--- ."

Charles had indeed loved Naples, if for no other reason than the letters that finally reached him there. The first was from Thomas Graham.

'My dear Charles,

I trust that your journey to Naples has gone well and that you are benefiting from the wonders of the classical world, which Mary assures me you must. Here this momentous year of 1778 has come and almost gone, with so many issues of great moment that I wonder how we can emerge from it in a stable condition. There is no doubt that change is in the air all about us.

As you know, France had now entered the war against us and Spain waits in the wings: not of course with any real sympathy for the cause of your young country, but rather like jackals, hoping to pick up scraps. It is all so very sad and unnecessary. One tragedy sums it up. The great Lord Chatham, who railed so continuously against this foolish war, died making one last speech in the House of Lords.

As you know, his views were broadly those of the Rockingham Whigs: Fox and Burke and your friend Robert Greville. But now the French are playing a hand the game has changed, with the religious issue introduced again. We need more soldiers than ever and to that end parliament introduced a Catholic Relief Act to revoke an earlier Act that, in theory at least, required recruits to renounce the Pope. The change however has been so unpopular that I fear it could become a burning issue with the mobs. Popular feelings are hugely inflamed against the government of Lord

North and I wonder seriously how long the present political settlement can survive.

Of course we need reform, of that there is no doubt. Our system of parliamentary representation is hopelessly out of date and economic mismanagement is rife. Our naval power is a mere shadow of what it was and French fleets cruise the Channel unimpeded. Their waste is regularly washed up on our beaches and the people are outraged, rightly so. As I say, change is in the air. I only pray that when it comes it will not go too far, as I have always feared will happen in France one day.

In spite of all this, mainly because the King will abdicate rather than appoint Fox, Lord North seems more secure than ever. Also the war in America goes well for us again (though I realise you will take a different view of this) and the setback at Saratoga is now forgotten. General Burgoyne is back in London on parole and everywhere treated as a hero. Meanwhile Clinton and Cornwallis seem to be conducting a successful campaign in Virginia in an effort to bring this sorry affair to an end before the French can intervene too forcefully.

Mary's health continues to give us concern. But she maintains her usual good spirits, which are greatly raised by your regular letters. She sends you her sincere and affectionate regards and will, I think, write to you under separate cover with her own news.

Please give our regards to Sir William Hamilton with whom you must by now be residing.

       I am as ever,

       Your friend, Thomas Graham

    (By the bye, Charles, you should visit the Tomb of Virgil near Naples. I found it quite memorable.)

    Even without his cherished letters Charles would have loved Naples. To his surprise, so late in the tour it proved to be a high point on a tour of high points. It did not have the powerful emotional impact of Rome nor the raw excitement of the Alps. Or for that matter the sophistication of Turin or the drama of Mantua. Nor did it provide the intellectual challenges of Pavia and Bologna. Yet fall in love with it he did, as Mary had anticipated, and completely.

    For Naples was a gracious city set in a lovely golden curve of coastline dotted here and there with magnificent villas and fertile gardens. It was also a very ancient city: Greek in origin and built on a range of low hills around the bay. Its principal streets were wide and well-constructed of square blocks of lava firmly mortared and its public buildings were stylish and solid.

The finest street, Via Roma, ran splendidly half the length of the city with at one end the Royal Palace, while to the east, towering rather uneasily over the city was the isolated summit of Vesuvius, the volcano that had once destroyed a nearby town.

Charles had taken to Sir William Hamilton instantly--- Lady Hamilton he rarely saw, though he remained with them for more than two months. It seemed that she suffered from a succession of illnesses and when she did appear she struck him as a pleasant, if colourless, woman of no special distinction. Charles was of course predisposed to like Sir William, who was after all Mary's most dearly loved uncle. And like him he certainly did. Tall and elegant, his host was an agreeable man and an engaging conversationalist, with a personal warmth that could not fail to delight Charles, so reminiscent was it of Mary's own charm.

Sir William was also an extraordinarily well-informed art-lover, Sir Horace not having exaggerated in this regard. Since it appeared that the duties of Ambassador to the Kingdom of Naples had been for many years less than onerous, Sir William had used his time to good value and had acquired an enormous collection of paintings, sculpture and furniture to adorn his villa, the Palazzo Sessa. As Mann had indicated, whenever the balance between his income and expenditure required some adjustment, one or two of the choicest pieces would be regretfully packed up and sold to some wealthy friend in England or increasingly to the new British Museum.

Charles found himself caught up by Sir William's antiquarian enthusiasm, even developing some slight insight into the significance of this artist or that furniture-maker. Pietro Fabris was currently Sir William's favourite painter and Charles took the opportunity to watch in wonder as his compositions took shape on canvas and transformed themselves before his eyes into beautiful views of the bay or elaborate churches or palazzos. Perhaps, he thought not for the first time on this trip, there was something in this art business after all. At least he knew now what Mary had wanted him to discover when she had planned this long involved journey.

But one final experience was yet to come: an experience that for Charles would have a more poignant significant than he could possibly then have imagined. It was a still warm morning, late in the year, when he first mentioned the Tomb of Virgil. "Thomas Graham recommended it highly to me," he said.

"Well, I'm surprised!" Sir William laughed. "I mean not that Thomas is mistaken. Indeed I could not agree with him more. In fact I was going to suggest something of the sort myself. It is certainly a place of wonder and beauty, though of a dark kind, it has to be said." He smiled at Charles. "I suppose I am faintly surprised that Thomas Graham should show such sensitivity; such sensibility. For I'd never have taken him for a poet. Or even much of a scholar. Clearly there is more to Thomas than meets the eye!" Then he beamed. "There must be indeed, else why would someone like my niece be so devoted to him!"

A few months earlier Charles might have secretly resented the implications of such a comment. Now he merely nodded. "I am certain there is a great deal more to Thomas Graham than meets the eye," he said. "But if I may borrow a horse from your stables and perhaps one of your fellows to act as a guide, I should like to pay my own respects to Virgil."

But Sir William would not hear of it. Instead they went by coach, the two of them, out on the road heading north from Naples along the sparkling coast to Pozzuoli. Barely a mile or two outside Naples Sir William drew the carriage into a dusty narrow track. "It is better to walk from here," he said and strode off towards what looked to be the mouth of a dark cave. The track quickly vanished into the darkness and gazing about him Charles saw that he was in fact in a deep man-made tunnel built into natural walls of towering rock.

"This is the entrance to the Grotto, which is actually a tunnel half-a-mile in length that runs right through to Pozzuoli. The Emperor Nerva had it built for his convenience in travelling. If you look to your left, Charles, there on the side of the cliff you will see the Tomb of Virgil, who was of course perhaps the greatest of the Roman poets."

Charles studied the structure which clung precariously high up on the side of the Grotto. It was of classic simplicity, constructed of the local stone carefully shaped and fitted, rusticated at its lower levels but rising in tiers of increasing sophistication to a plain sloping pediment.

"Vigil had his body brought here from Brundusium in BC19. The poet Statius, who was born in Naples, describes composing his own poetry while seated here in the shade of Virgil's tomb." Sir William paused to catch his breath as he led the way up the slope. "That, of course," he panted, "was scarcely one hundred years later. So there is little reason to doubt the authenticity of the report."

Soon they were standing on a broad ledge beside the Tomb which rose reassuringly above them. "Apparently it was originally shaded by a gigantic bay tree of great age," Sir William said, placing one hand respectfully on the rough stone walls. "But the tree is said to have died at the moment of the death of Dante Alegheri. A pretty thought, don't you agree? But there is another tale that the entire grotto was created by the fierce power of Virgil's intense gaze! So one never knows!"

Charles walked slowly through a low doorway, stooping into the plain interior of a square vaulted chamber, poorly lit on three sides by small windows. He looked around the empty space. There was nothing to see. And yet the place was curiously redolent of something; perhaps a sense of some enormous loss?

"From early in the 16th century there are descriptions of the actual funeral urn which contained the ashes of the poet. It stood here in the centre on nine small marble pillars. Some say that Robert of Anjou removed it in 1326 to a place of safety. Another account is that the Cardinal of Mantua took it--- Vigil was born in Mantua of course." Sir William glanced at Charles. "Mantua me genuit--- and so on," he muttered softly, as if they were in church.

Charles nodded. "I have no Latin. But Thomas was absolutely right. This place is very special. What became of the urn and Virgil's ashes?"

"Lost, I am afraid. It is said that the Church disapproved of his pagan values and may have caused their disappearance. Even so, this place has not lost its power to attract."

Charles nodded. There was a mysterious atmosphere about the Tomb of Virgil which would stay with him for ever and the two men walked back to the carriage in a curiously sombre mood to return to the Palazzo Sessa. Perhaps, thought Charles, his low mood was bound up in the sense that his long journey was nearing its end. Perhaps that was creating this strange sense of melancholy in him.

At the Palazzo some papers had arrived, mostly official documents for the Ambassador but among them more letters for Charles that immediately lifted his spirits. One was clearly his long awaited letter from Mary Graham. His hand trembled over this. But he put it aside as a treat reserved for a private moment. Instead he opened the other, which proved to be an amiable letter from Robert Greville dated June 1779.

'My dear Charles,

I was delighted to learn that you will soon be staying awhile with Sir William Hamilton. He may not have mentioned, and I saw no reason to do so until very recently, that I am one of Sir William's several nephews, though it is fair to say that he has always had more in common with my brother Charles than with myself. He and Charles share the same passion for things artistic, an interest which I do not claim for myself.

Events in London run a familiar course. The King still loathes Charles Fox, who misses no opportunity to tweak his royal tail, especially over the conduct of the American War. But increasingly also about constitutional reform. As for the war, it seems to have taken a turn for the better from our perspective. But I cannot see anything but disaster from this unnecessary conflict, particularly since the French have become involved. Fortunately they are in a poor state of readiness, for all their long months of scheming against us.

Still on the political front, a young man is emerging who may well become a major player. I think I mentioned him to you once before. William Pitt, the son of the late Lord Chatham is a formidable intellect and even at his tender age is a powerful debater. Having left Cambridge he is now reading law at Lincoln's Inn. But I am certain he will soon be in parliament, where Fox will undoubtedly welcome him as an ally. Pitt's views on America are very close to those of Fox, Burke and Dundas and in some respects it is a natural alliance.

But sooner or later I anticipate that young Pitt will prove to be a painful thorn in the side of Fox and the Whigs. There are many constitutional issues, I fancy, on which they will differ. It may seem strange to be writing thus about such a young and unproven man. But I sense that William Pitt is no ordinary young man.

Now I must reveal how I come to know of your visit to my uncle! For at last I have overcome my reticence and written to Louisa, who sent me a very friendly reply. She informed me that her sister had arranged for you to call on Sir William, who is of course also an uncle to the Cathcart family. From this you will see that Louisa and I are cousins. I do not know if that fact had any bearing on Lord Cathcart's choice of a husband for Louisa. Probably not, as there is no history of madness on either side, though you may wonder at that!

However, my dear Charles, I ramble! Do hurry back to London, where your friends miss you and speak of you frequently. Charles Fox in particular has asked me more than once about the whereabouts of my "witty young American" as he likes to name you. He frequents the new Brooks's Club, which is up and running and where fortunes are won and lost at the tables most nights, often by the same people!

Please give my kindest regards to my aunt and my best hopes for her improved health .

    I remain your good friend, Robert Greville.

    Charles smiled. Suddenly London seemed all the more like home.

He retreated to his room and opened the letter from Mary Graham.

'My dearest Charles,

His heart pounded strangely at those words. He read on;

'My dearest Charles,

I do so enjoy your regular accounts of your tour and the vivid and realistic descriptions of those wonderful places. How I long in particular to have seen the fresco of the Last Supper in Milan. But your words bring it to life again each time I read your letters, which I confess I do almost daily.'

Charles felt his head swim at the exquisite notion of Mary reading and re-reading his letters.

'By now you will be with my favourite uncle and I hope you will give him my very warmest regards. It is so long since I have seen him. He seems to prefer living in the warmer climate of Italy, something that increasingly Thomas and I find ourselves considering also. Though it is not something I would chose to do except for reasons of health.

Not that I have much to complain of in that regard. We spent a very pleasant summer on the family estates in Perthshire, frequently riding out together into the lovely hills in excellent weather. It was curiously reminiscent of that charming time we spent with you in Spa. Oh Charles, that does seem so long ago and though I know your absence is in part of my own engineering I do look forward to your return.'

Charles felt himself flush with pride. This was more than he had ever dared to hope.

'On our rides together up a valley known locally as Glenalmond, a beautiful place that I hope you will see one day, Thomas discovered an old cottage. It is really more of a small country house with extensive if dilapidated gardens. It is called Lynedoch House and Thomas plans to buy it, have it refurbished and for us to live there, rather than to continue to share Balgowan House with Lady Christian, kind though she is. Now we spend much time mulling over décor and furnishings, (at least I do!).

My brother Charles is now studying law and seems destined to be a diplomat, while his brother William goes from strength to strength in his military career. He is soon to marry a lady from New York, so I fear his future lies in North America. I shall regret that as I do miss him. My sister

Louisa and Lord Stormont both send you their regards.'

Ah yes, Stormont, Charles thought sourly, the clever John Sewell's lord and master.

'Yet another person who asks to be remembered to you fondly and who looks forward to your return is the Duchess of Devonshire. She always speaks warmly of you when we meet. I see her frequently and we exchange letters almost every day now. She has become a very dear friend, though I fear not a very happy one. I trust however that you are!

Your dear friend, Mary Graham.'

THIRTY

London seemed strangely changed. It was not more crowded nor any noisier nor dirtier than Charles remembered. Yet it struck him that somehow there was an underlying sense of menace on the streets, a threat that he had never before noticed. In the past he had wandered freely throughout the city, however insalubrious the area. Now he sensed a sullenness and a suppressed anger that had been absent or at least unobserved by him in the past.

At one level he picked up the threads of his old life much as he had left off. There was of course the disappointment that Thomas and Mary Graham were not there. They had indeed been away in Scotland for almost the past two years, Thomas much occupied with estate matters in Perthshire. This was frustrating, for Charles longed to see Mary again and to recount directly to her the experiences of his journey, which he knew she also longed to hear. In addition it was clear from her letters to sister Louisa that the Scottish climate was doing her health very little good.

But at least Robert Greville was in London, to say nothing of Fox and Georgiana and the entire Devonshire set, less one or two social casualties such as the unfortunate Lady Derby. Charles was also delighted to renew his friendship with Harry Angelo, his one-time fencing instructor. Angelo was happy to see him back in England, safe and sound and a credit to his training, though he was faintly disappointed it seemed, that Charles had not had an opportunity to display his prowess with cold steel somewhere along the way.

In some respects then London in the spring of 1780 was agreeably familiar and Charles enjoyed the comfortable sensation of having returned home. He was received warmly back into society; so much so that his life fell quickly into an easily round of parties and dinners, not least at Devonshire House where Georgiana now treated him as a confirmed part of the 'ton'. Lord Stormont too was in London, having returned from Paris as soon as war with France was confirmed and Charles was particularly welcomed at his home, though little was said on either side about John Sewell.

Thanks to Charles Fox, Charles was introduced to the new Brooks's Club, where if anything the play ran even higher than before. A regular guest, Charles however made a point of never gambling, despite Fox's frequent encouragements. Not that the play was too rich for him now, though he was aware that one careless evening of hazard could still ruin him in spite of his relatively secure financial footing. Rather it was the wildness of the gambling, the wholly irrational nature of the wagers that offended him.

For the scenes in the gaming rooms struck Charles as simply bizarre. Under the glare of the great candelabras the players sat with a sort of visor to protect their eyes, while the more affected of the young members adopted wide-brimmed straw hats, ludicrously decorated with gaily coloured ribbons and even fresh flowers. On occasions they would turn their coats inside out, whether to protect the garment from dripping candle-wax and splashes of wine or out of some weird superstition Charles was never able to decide.

But it was the dice table to which Charles was most frequently drawn now. This was where Charles Fox was usually to be found, surrounded by his companions and hangers-on, the table piled high with fifty guinea rouleaus. At hazard the play was particularly high. It was by no means unusual for the wealthier and more reckless of the members, among which Charles Fox was prominent, to lose ten, twenty or even forty thousand pounds in an evening and to be apparently unmoved by either experience. According to Greville, who rarely gambled himself, it was considered 'not quite the thing' to show emotion, whether in triumph or catastrophe.

This hazard is a game well named Charles thought, as he watched family fortunes made and unmade in an hour. Sometimes entire estates change hands at a few rolls of the dice. Was he alone in thinking of the terrible effect this casual entertainment could have upon the lives of hardworking labourers and tenant farmers, oblivious of such frivolous activities a hundred miles or more away?

Charles wondered too at the wildness of the play. For in spite of its risks hazard was a game of more or less fixed mathematical odds, called out clearly at each throw by the presiding groom-porter, a paid official who sat on a high chair overlooking the table. From there he watched impassively as events unfolded, giving the players all the information needed to minimise their risk and maximise their gain. For people like Charles Fox however, and he was by no means exceptional, it seemed merely an excuse to throw away or occasionally to gain money; little more than a source of gratuitous excitement, though little of this excitement was actually displayed by the players. Charles shook his head in puzzlement. Perhaps Thomas Graham was correct in his opinion of gambling.

Thus was Charles reintroduced to polite London society. But it was out on the streets that he sensed the new undercurrent. Out there in the real world, he thought grimly. Recently he had taken to doing what he had done during his early days in Paris--- it seemed so long ago now--- wandering through the streets of the most unfashionable districts after dark, dressed casually and inconspicuously and with his dirk hidden inside his jacket.

"It is nothing like a mood of revolution," Greville said to him. "God forbid that it should ever come to that in this country. But there is considerable unease and dissatisfaction with the way the government is handling the war." He hesitated and glanced at Charles apologetically. "As you know, there was a wide-spread sentiment at all levels that the war against our kith-and-kin in America was misguided. So our half-hearted efforts at the war were tolerated rather than condemned." Charles nodded and Robert Greville continued. "But now the French have taken a hand the public mood is quite different. The people want the matter pursued much more effectively."

He paused. "And there is a new factor at work. There are elements, extreme Protestant groups, who are openly agitating against any measure to relax the laws against Catholic participation in public life. Their adopted leader is a wild fellow, a Scotchman called Lord George Gordon. He is a member of Parliament, which of course gives him a ready platform." He smiled wryly. "The Gordon family have long had a strain of instability. His mother was once observed riding on the back of a cavorting pig down the High Street in Edinburgh. High spirits only, I dare say!" Robert said, rather charitably.

"Be that as it may, Lord George has been seized on as a kind of messiah by certain extreme sections. So much so that they say there are three parties in Parliament now: the Ministry, the Opposition and Lord George Gordon! There is even talk of a march on Parliament to force the members to recant, as it were, on the Catholic Relief Act. A measure passed with the very best of motives by the House, I can assure you."

Curious to sense the mood of the city Charles made his way one evening along the Strand and into the more dangerous east-end. Nearing the Exchange he noted Jonathon's Coffee House and wondered fleetingly what had become of Stephen Sayre. In gaol again or even dead? Or perhaps gone home to Philadelphia like Juliana Ritchie, to whom his thoughts frequently turned in the night.

Wandering more or less aimlessly Charles found himself in the Poultry and on a sudden impulse presented himself at the front door of Charles and Edward Dilly. The very same doorkeeper took his name and asked him to wait, giving no sign of recognition. After a short time he was ushered upstairs into the large comfortable drawing room that he well remembered.

But it was a very different scene that greeted him now. There was no glittering array of talent as on his previous visit. Alone by the fire, lit in spite of the warmth of the spring evening, was Charles Dilly, a smaller, less flamboyant figure than his elder brother. Indeed Charles had hardly been aware of him on that earlier occasion, so dominant a figure had Edward been.

Charles Dilly rose to greet him courteously. "Why Mr MacPherson! What a pleasant surprise to see you. You are the friend of Mr Franklin. I remember you well. My dear brother commented on how impressed he was with your scientific interests."

Inwardly marvelling at the ease with which his reputation had been established and secretly longing to justify it with his new familiarity of Volta and Galvani, to say nothing of the great meridian of San Petronio, Charles bowed. "How is your brother?" he asked politely.

Charles Dilly's welcoming face clouded over. "Ah! You have not heard? Edward died early last year. He is buried in Southill churchyard. His health declined rapidly with the dreaded consumption." He himself gave an almost involuntary cough. "It has become a positive scourge and always it seems to take the brightest and the best." Charles felt a cold spasm of dread as he thought of Mary Graham. It surely could not be? He must arrange to see her and Thomas soon.

"My sincere condolences, sir. No, I did not know of your loss. I have been out of the country for the best part of two years, travelling in Italy."

Dilly waved him to a chair by the fire and poured him a glass of hot punch. "My brother and I were close, you know. Very close and I miss him greatly. Neither of us has other family. Never married, you see. So now I devote myself only to the publishing business."

He sighed. "Edward was a good-natured and well-disposed man and an excellent man of business. But I have to admit that his politics were tainted by some extreme views. Radical views that were too much for me, in truth. Though I am of course just as pro-American."

Charles nodded silently. Then he took the opportunity. "I suppose you have not come across an old friend of mine in London," he asked. "A good friend from my childhood in the Mohawk Valley by the name of Francis Johnson? He may come to London from time to time, on business as it were."

Dilly frowned. "I know the name. And I believe I have heard it mentioned not so long ago. But as for his whereabouts, no sir, I have no knowledge of that."

"Or a churchman named Snape? He too was in New York when I lived there."

Dilly's face darkened further. "Yes, I have heard something of him," he said shortly. "He is in the service of Butler, the Bishop of Oxford and when last heard he was living in Butler's house in Leicester Fields." He looked at Charles in a puzzled fashion. "But Mr MacPherson, the Bishop is no friend of America, I can assure you."

"So I understand," Charles said hastily. "And Snape is no friend of mine." Then, largely to change the subject, he enquired about the strange mood on the streets that he felt he had detected.

Dilly looked thoughtful. "Do you now? But yes, you are correct. And I do not like it," he said slowly. "I am not a man for violence, least of all directed against a legitimate constitutional government. More especially when innocent members of the community are the most likely to suffer, the rich for the most part being able to flee or to defend themselves if they stay." He fell silent for a moment. "I know that for some all is fair in love and war. But I pray the American cause is not sullied by association with the scurrilous mood that seems to be abroad on the streets."

Charles frowned. "Is that likely?"

Dilly waved his hand vaguely. "Oh there is talk, you know." His mood seemed to change and he rose sharply from his seat by the fire. "Well, it has been a pleasure to see you again, Mr MacPherson. I hope you will look in again. Sometime." Charles took his leave and went out into the night, feeling that he had unwittingly trodden on dangerous ground.

Over the next few weeks this conviction grew as his nocturnal visits to the lower taverns and coffee houses convinced him that Robert Greville was right. There was a growing mood of discontent among the poorer members of the community and specifically directed at anyone suspected of Catholic sympathies.

Though some of the targets of this anger seemed absurdly badly chosen. Even the Earl of Mansfield, Lord Stormont's uncle and the Lord Chief Justice of England, was being cursed at openly as 'a damned Catholic and a Jacobite', bent on overthrowing the government!

And everywhere he heard tales of the wonderful orator Lord George Gordon and the great gathering which he would soon address.

THIRTY ONE

Then one night at Brooks's, for reasons he never could explain even to himself, Charles departed from his golden rule on gambling. It was a decision taken impulsively and one that was to change entirely the future pattern of his life.

Ironically, that very day he had called on Thomas Coutts and listened with inner amusement as the dour banker expressed in almost paternal tones his satisfaction with the state of Charles's finances. "I have known extraordinary sums spent on such a journey as yours." Coutts looked benignly at Charles. "Some young men have been outrageously extravagant in travelling about Italy. Ruinously so in some cases. I do not speak of money spent in acquiring great works of art and so on. For those may be justifiably considered as in the nature of an investment, which in time hopefully will appreciate in value."

He gave Charles a steely smile of approval. "But you Mr MacPherson, if I may say so, have been an example of modesty in your expenditure. Why, even Mr Muirhead was moved to comment favourably! And he is not an easy man to impress in matters of financial restraint, regarding as he does every account as if it were his own personal fortune!" He gave a creaking laugh at the thought. Charles gave a polite smile, privately convinced that the austere Mr Muirhead only reflected his employer's own dearest sentiments.

"You will see that in your absence your capital has actually grown over the period. That is largely thanks to some judicious transactions in and out of government funds at what proved to be highly profitable times." Coutts smiled at Charles contentedly. "So that your account now stands at a sum in excess of £25,000." Charles blinked. This was a sum he had never envisaged having at his disposal.

"So you are now a young man of substance." Coutts gave him another frosty smile of approval. "Yes. I think we can say that. All you require now to set you up for life is a wife! One of similar financial ballast, of course. I take it you have no suitable young lady in mind as yet?"

"Ah, no, no!" Charles hastily disclaimed. "No! Far from it. No ideas of that sort." He ran rapidly in his mind's eye the list of young women he had encountered in London. Then he shook his head decisively. "No! Definitely not," he said firmly.

"Humph! Well, that is a pity of course," Coutts said in disappointed tones. "For such a union could quite set you up as a magnate almost. Then with careful management----." He paused thoughtfully. "Still, there is time yet, I dare say. Yes, there's certainly time yet." He paused again and then seemed to brighten up. "Nonetheless your finances are in prime order, I am happy to say." He actually beamed at Charles. "And together we shall keep them in that condition, eh, Mr MacPherson?"

Thomas Coutts would have been distressed to think that it was probably this very conversation that caused Charles finally giving way to Fox's frequent boisterous invitations to join in the play at Brooks's that evening. Certainly the realisation of his new wealth played a part. 'Even so,' he thought cautiously, 'I shall venture £1,000 and not a penny more.'

He stood by the large circular hazard table watching the dice pass from player to player as, one by one, they threw out and lost their stakes. 'Yes, that is a sum that I can apparently afford to lose, though it is not by any means insignificant and once would have seemed a great fortune to me. But when that has gone,' he thought firmly, 'I shall simply cease to play.'

In the course of the evening he had noticed one young man in particular; fair haired and good-looking but clearly more than half drunk and gambling wildly with, it seemed to Charles, a ridiculous disregard for the groom-porter's odds. He commented quietly on the young man to Robert Greville, who had joined Fox at the hazard table. Greville almost never gambled, whether from principle or poverty Charles could not tell.

"That is Stavordale," Robert Greville said evenly. "His father owns half of Leicestershire. He plays high. Often loses or wins many thousands in a night. But he drinks too much to enjoy his winnings and I sometimes wonder at his motives."

Charles nodded and took the dice as his turn to cast arose. Hazard he knew was essentially a simple game in which the caster was required to select a number between five and nine, announce this as his choice of 'main' and then, placing on the table his wager to be matched by one or all of the players, attempt to throw his 'main'. There were then three possible outcomes.

Either the caster won immediately by throwing the 'main' or a specific other number associated with it, thus taking all the money on the table. Or he lost immediately by throwing one of several fatal losing numbers, most notably twos or threes.

In the event that neither of these outcomes came to pass the game then moved to the next phase, with the actual number thrown becoming his new 'chance'. He then continued to cast the dice until either he won by throwing his 'chance' a second time or lost by throwing his original 'main'.

Charles could of course calculate the odds of the various wagers as accurately as any groom-porter and had observed that frequently players selected the number seven as their 'main'. Presumably this was because the number seven offered the maximum number of chances, six in all, out of the thirty-six different ways two dice might fall. In addition there were a further two combinations which would 'nick' the wager by throwing the number eleven. More likely though, he thought with an inner grimace, seven was often selected from some mystical sense of destiny associated with the number.

The problem with that particular strategy lay in the almost equally large probability of throwing an outright losing number: two or three or twelve, or of throwing a 'chance' that offered a lower probability of success in later throws. With the odds now firmly against the caster the rest of the players would plunge in with substantial wagers which the caster was required to cover.

Charles took the dice and pushed half of his money into the centre of the table. It was a comparatively modest wager by the standards of some of the players and he noted that Stavordale promptly covered the full amount with a laughing aside to one of his companions. "Five," Charles called.

The dice bounced around the deeply bevelled table and finally settled to reveal a four and a three. "Seven to five," the groom-porter called out in a voice quite devoid of emotion, indicating that Charles now stood to lose with a five and win with a seven. "Odds of three to two in favour," he added in the same detached voice.

Charles now had to make a decision. To risk his entire stake or to continue with his original wager. He glanced around the table. Several of the players were already tapping their rouleaus in anticipation. By the standards of Brooks's the money involved would still be trivial, he decided, reaching down to push the rest of his fund into the centre. The odds were after all in his favour. In fact they were unlikely to be much better. Immediately his wager was covered he cast the dice again.

For several throws the result was inconclusive, with neither the 'main' nor the 'chance' appearing. 'In theory,' he thought, with a silent laugh, 'I might go on throwing all night.' But in fact he knew that with only thirty-six possible combinations, seven in any of its six variations or a losing five in one of its four possible arrangements would not be long in appearing.

Just as he calculated, on only his third throw the dice spun out and came to a halt. "Five and two. Seven wins," the groom-porter called. His stake, now more than doubled, he decided to wager in full. He threw for his next 'main' and again selected five. As he cast the dice he noticed that Stavordale had covered his entire bet. Charles 'nicked' it with an improbable eleven, to Stavordale's obvious irritation.

After only three more winning casts Charles glanced again at the table. There was more cash lying there than the entire fortune that had so delighted Thomas Coutts that morning. 'I must however bear in mind that only one thousand of that money is truly mine,' he reminded himself. 'The rest is, as it were, found money. But still--- .' He felt a frisson of excitement. By now the regular gamblers had been joined by some casual spectators, drawn by the news that the clever young American fellow was actually playing and for high stakes.

Fox, who had, Charles estimated, at least ten thousand of his own money on the table, gave a guffaw and slapped him on the shoulder. "My word! I think I've lost enough for one night! At this rate dear sir, you will be able to buy up half of New York, what with the poor depreciated Continental dollar. But you must crack on! When fortune is with you it is ill-mannered to reject it."

Robert Greville drew close to him, sipping a glass of port. "You have done well Charles. Why not stop and let someone else win." He smiled. "Or more likely, lose."

"No sir!" Stavordale's voice was loud and blurred. "I say carry on! There's a lot of my money there and I insist on a chance to recover it."

Charles glanced at him coldly. But before he could reply Fox had intervened. "Insist?" he bellowed. "What do you mean insist, Stavordale? Do you not know that the caster has the right to play or not to play? It is not for you to say, sir!"

Stavordale stared sullenly at the table, swaying slightly. Greville took him by the elbow and started to say something to him quietly but Stavordale shook him off. "I want another cast," he muttered and pushed his remaining guineas into the centre of the table. Charles took up the dice and called his 'main' as five yet again. The wager was now at even money and he knew that he could live with the disappointment of a loss.

But as he listened to the dice rattle in their box a strange silence seemed to descend on him. It was as if Stavordale and Greville and Fox, indeed the entire room, had dissolved into oblivion and he knew with total clarity how the dice would fall. They clattered across the table, bounced off the deep edge and came to rest. "Damn me," said Stavordale, reeling back.

"Poor form, that," Greville whispered to Charles. "He can well afford to lose. He has estates of his own, inherited from his mother's family, quite apart from his father's wealth."

"I take it the game is all done," Charles announced politely, looking around the table and trying to avoid addressing Stavordale directly.

"No, by God!" Stavordale said. "Here, give me paper and ink," he shouted to one of the nearby club servants. "One more throw, I insist." Then he had the grace to add, "I beg you, that is to say. I've no more ready cash but I'll wager my estate at Ragley against the table. It's worth at least what we have there." He began to scrawl out a note of assignment. "Fox! You can witness this for me."

Charles turned to Greville in alarm. "Robert! I do not want to take away a family estate! Besides," he said wryly, "what in the world would I do with it? I know nothing about farming and that sort of thing."

Greville turned his back on the table and looked him steadily in the face. "It's difficult, Charles. To refuse him now, in his present mood and before all these people, might be taken amiss."

"Amiss? What do you mean--- amiss?"

"Well," Greville said awkwardly. "Between gentlemen it might be taken as an insult." He shrugged. "He might even call you out. He is a hot blood. And while a fight is no uncommon thing and I dare say you could handle him, think of how your other friends might receive the news. The Grahams, for example. And Louisa would probably blame me!" he added with a rueful smile.

'Oh God, Mary and Thomas!' Charles thought bleakly. 'Another duel! What would they make of him?' He turned to Stavordale and bowed shortly to him. "Very well, sir. As you please."

He picked up the dice, called "Seven." and quickly threw them onto the table, But even as they were spinning to a halt he heard Stavordale shout out loudly, "Dice!" The dice settled, showing a winning seven. But the throw had been voided by Stavordale's use of his privilege to ask for new dice.

'A desperate ploy in the hope of changing what he regards as his luck,' Charles thought disdainfully. Inevitably there was a delay while the groom-porter produced a new set of dice. Charles was calm. But he could feel the tension mounting around the table. Stavordale stood staring silently at the heap of golden guineas that filled the centre of the round table, topped now by a single white piece of paper that held the futures of a hundred or more individual estate workers.

'This is not at all proper,' thought Charles. 'People's lives should not be wagered in this way. But the die is about to be cast.' Charles Fox watched with his usual jovial interest--- such a wager was nothing new to him. Meanwhile Robert Greville stood nearby trying to appear relaxed. Charles picked up the new dice and showed them. "All well?" he asked calmly. Stavordale licked his lips and nodded abruptly.

Once more Charles calmly called "Seven". As the dice left the cup he knew with a strange certainty that he had won. The two small cubes of ivory flew across the table, rebounded from the deeply bevelled edge and came to rest. "Six and one," droned the groom-porter impassively and a buzz of excitement burst out around the table. "Seven wins."

THIRTY TWO

May was a heady month for Charles, for in addition to his spectacular win at Brooks's he had the supreme pleasure of being reunited with Thomas and Mary Graham, however briefly. Mary's health was still a problem and so their journey south from Scotland was to take them onwards and back to the waters at Brighton.

Nevertheless the meeting was happy and affecting. Thomas grasped his hand and shook it energetically. "My dear boy," he said. "My dear boy. How glad I am to see you." For Thomas, this was a rare outburst of emotion and moved Charles greatly. It was, he recognised, the greeting of an older brother; or even that a father.

For the first time however Charles became aware of just how physically slight Mary had become, though her spirits seemed as high as ever. She poured out a torrent of questions about his experiences in Italy. "You did not tell me much about the opera in Turin! Perhaps you did not enjoy the experience?"

"No, I can't say that I did in truth," Charles said guiltily, recalling the Contessa and the painful consequences of his meeting with her.

"But you actually saw Leonardo's Last Supper," Mary sighed. "How wonderful! And how you made it come to life for me, Charles! And my uncle William? And poor Lady Hamilton? She does not enjoy the best of health, I fear. The eccentric Sir Horace Mann in Florence! What excitement! And how amusing your letters were!"

The three of them spent the best part of a delightfully idle week together; dining, riding in the park or simply talking endlessly of their recent experiences and their plans for the remainder of the summer. One afternoon when even Mary's questions were finally exhausted and she had retired to rest, Thomas took the opportunity to speak to Charles privately.

"I hear that you have made a great coup at Brooks's," he said diffidently. "An estate in Leicestershire, so it is said." He looked at Charles enquiringly. "Or is that an exaggeration? The story grows with every telling."

Charles stared frankly at his friend, aware of his views on gambling. "No, I have to say that the win was substantial. Though of course," he added hastily, "I have no intentions of keeping the estate. What would I do with such a thing? I have put the matter in the hands of Thomas Coutts and I understand that Ragley is likely to be bought back by Lord Stavordale's father."

Thomas nodded. "That might be the soundest thing," he said. "Let it stay in the family." He gave Charles an almost guilty smile. "Though I confess that I have long thought of owning an estate in that part of England! It's excellent hunting country you know. And from what I've heard Ragley has a lovely run of country. Generates a nice steady income too, in spite of being still largely unimproved. There's a great deal that could be done with it. Mind you," he went on, "my factor in Scotland could learn a lot from farming methods in that part of the world." He glanced ruefully at Charles. "I'd make you an offer for it myself. But Lady Christian is reluctant to spend money on that sort of thing. Actually regards fox hunting as a frivolous activity!"

Charles barely concealed his amusement. This was the man who disapproved of gambling as an entertainment! "To tell you the truth, Thomas, this estate business has made me think seriously about my future. Money is no longer a problem for me, so it would seem. But I find myself increasingly torn between returning to America, which in a sense is my duty, or staying on here to enjoy the company of my friends. An estate in England would only have complicated the situation."

Thomas nodded seriously. "I quite understand. Which brings me to a question I intended to ask. Mary and I are going on to Brighton to try out one of Dr Russell's bathing machines. The waters there do wonders for the health. And to say the truth, Mary did not benefit from the weather in Perthshire this spring." Charles nodded solemnly. This was the nearest Thomas had ever come to acknowledging the problem. "So Mary and I plan to travel south in search of a better, softer climate. We go to Gibraltar and then home slowly by land through Portugal and Spain. Perhaps the sea air will help her."

Recalling his own experiences in the Atlantic, Charles wondered at the wisdom of that. But Thomas had continued, "You must be aware how much Mary enjoys your company. I see her spirits rise whenever she speaks of you. The point is," he stumbled on awkwardly. "Well, we wondered if you would care to journey with us? You might enjoy it and Mary, well both of us really, would enjoy you companionship."

Charles barely had to think. He seized Thomas by the hand. "My dear friend, I can think of nothing better!" He laughed shamefacedly. "If nothing else it means that I can defer my painful decision about America for a few months more. For I don't mind telling you that I am greatly torn. What a splendid idea! When do we leave?"

"Later next month," Thomas said. "It all depends on available vessels. I think an Indiaman would provide Mary with the comfort she needs and they are going out in convoys now for security. There are still a few French frigates about and the odd American privateer, though the danger is much diminished since Rodney destroyed the Spanish fleet off Cape St Vincent. But the East India trade is taking sensible precautions. Their vessels are large and reasonably well armed and there are often naval ships along for good measure. And by the way, if this Ragley business is not settled, you might like to help me with some of my estate papers, just to see the sort of things that arise. My factor usually sends anything important on to me wherever I am bound."

"But are we not soon to be at war with the Spanish? Will we be able to travel through their country safely?"

"I'll take letters of safe passage from some influential people I happen know." Thomas looked slightly uncomfortable. "I still keep up my social contacts in France and Spain, you know. They are really quite civilised about that sort of thing, once they know what you are about. A few English visitors still mix socially with the French at Spa, you know. War can't be allowed to interfere with pleasure!"

Charles smiled. "Well, It's a wonderful idea. I cannot think of anything I should rather do." He paused. "To tell you the truth Thomas, I'm rather glad that you and Mary are going to be down at Brighton. I don't like the feeling on the streets here, with this anti-Catholic protest march being planned."

"Oh, that!" said Thomas dismissively. "You needn't worry about that! Not here, Charles. The average fellow in England is not going to start a riot, far less a revolution! No, no! They are far too sensible."

"I do hope that you are right, Thomas," Charles said doubtfully.

A day or two later he was taking coffee one morning in Robert Greville's rooms when Robert tossed him a copy of the London Evening Post. Charles glanced at the large advertisement that covered the front page with a banner headline. It declared boldly:-

"PROTESTANT ASSOCIATION, Whereas no hall in London can contain forty thousand men---."

Charles looked across at Robert. "Forty thousand men! Will they truly attract that many?"

"There's little doubt of it," his friend said, looking a shade more worried than Charles had expected. "And a motley crew they are, gathering already from all over the country. Including thousands from as far away as Scotland."

Charles read on; "---it is resolved that this Association do meet on Friday next June 2 in St George's Fields at 10 o'clock in the morning to consider of the most prudent and respectful manner of attending their Petition, which will be presented the same day to the House of Commons."

The rest of the announcement outlined in almost military terms exactly how the crowd was to be ordered. There were to be organised in four divisions; London, Westminster, Southwark and Scotland, arranged in formation, with Scotland on the left and London on the right wing. "By God Robert," said Charles. "It sounds like an army they are preparing!"

"Indeed," Greville nodded. "They even stipulate a uniform dress, with blue cockades in their hats 'to distinguish them from the Papists' as they say. For those who make a financial contribution to the Association there are special cockades with gold and silver decoration and specially woven labels such as 'No Popery'. So they certainly do not lack for funds, wherever it comes from."

"St George's Fields is across the river, is it not? Is there room for so many people there?"

Greville nodded. "Just about, if they are well organized. Getting across the bridges will be a crush. But they seem to have that planned too."

"I see that they are requesting, as the organizers put it, that the magistrates of London, Westminster and Southwick attend the meeting to ensure good order?"

Greville grunted. "Well might they! But what is going to happen outside Parliament when that mob converges on New Palace Yard and blocks all the streets? I only hope the Members will be protected. Though I cannot see the Civil Magistrates and their handful of constables being able to control a crowd of that size if it should turn violent."

"What about the army," Charles asked. "Would troops not be better equipped to deal with something like this? Have they been alerted?"

Greville shook his head. "It is very difficult. There are many in the House who would resist that kind of solution. In fact there are no powers to do so constitutionally. In theory only the Lord Mayor can invite troops of regulars or even militia to assist. So strictly speaking the government can do nothing in that direction until and unless asked."

"But that seems ridiculous," Charles burst out. "If public order is threatened!"

"You must realize, Charles, that we place a high value on our freedoms in England and one of them is freedom to protest peacefully."

"That did not seem to count for much in Boston or New York," said Charles sourly.

Greville smiled. "But bear in mind, Charles, that many of these marchers will be openly pro-American and in favour of ending the War. Now that is a sentiment with which you and I can both identify," Greville smiled. "You see how feelings can be so mixed. Just let us hope it does not come to violence."

By nine o'clock on Friday 2nd June the pavement was already scorching beneath his feet as Charles made his way across the massive stone bridge at Westminster. He paused for shade in one of the recesses of the bridge and stood for a time observing the crowds of men as they scurried past him.

There was a steady flow, all heading for St George's Fields; some walking alone, some in twos and threes and some in larger groups of ten or more carrying large blue flags. All were similarly decked out in the trademark blue ribbons and cockades of the Protestant Association, moving forward eagerly but in an orderly and indeed almost a solemn fashion. Soberly dressed, they looked for the most part the best kind of respectable working man. Studying the marchers as they passed Charles decided that Greville's fears of violence protest were misplaced: though there was a curiously fanatical air of self-righteousness about some of them and a kind of religious fervour seemed to glint in their eyes. He frowned and made his way across the river.

By ten o'clock the Fields were already thronged by thousands of protestors and thousands more were pouring in over the bridge or streaming in from Southwark to the east. Hearing the sound of a bagpipe playing Charles found himself drawn almost against his will to the farthest edge of the Fields where it appeared that the Scotch Division was already drawn up in military order, headed by a highlander complete with kilt and claymore.

By eleven o'clock when Lord George Gordon drove up in his coach there must have been at least fifty thousand gathered for the march, all arranged in more or less orderly divisions. Charles was too far away to hear much of what Gordon had to say when he addressed the multitude. Indeed by that time the crowd was so excited, crushing forward and cheering wildly at any excuse, that it is doubtful if many of those present did hear his words. But at least he had a good view of the famous orator; tall, pale-faced, with long lank hair and darkly clad in sombre clothes.

Charles learned from those about him in the crowd that Gordon would soon go directly to the House of Commons where he was to receive the petition against the Catholic Relief Act from the marchers. This petition, Charles was assured on every hand, had at least one hundred thousand signatures and its various component parts were being sewn together as they spoke, making such a roll of parchment as would need several men to carry it, working in relays, on the journey to the Commons.

Charles had fully intended to retrace his route across Westminster Bridge directly to Parliament. But such was the mass of people that he found himself instead forced to follow the enormous press of marchers across Southwark to London Bridge and hence into the city further to the east. It was a clever strategy, he realised, designed to create maximum impact and visibility throughout the city and a mark of just how much planning had gone into this protest.

The vast column, shoulder to shoulder and ten or twenty deep, crossed London Bridge and marched silently and peacefully up Fish Street Hill and Grace Church Road and turned left down Cornhill and Cheapsides. Then down Fleet Street they tramped and past the Temple Bar into The Strand and Charing Cross. At various points the column was swelled as they were joined by other supporters, many on horseback or in coaches. Always the march was conducted in a more or less decorous silence, with mostly only a steady murmur of conversation rising from the ranks. Now and then however a loud cheer would break out spontaneously as they passed a church.

But in the narrow mean streets between the river and Bishopsgate the column had been silently joined by some very different figures, ill-dressed sinister looking men, some of whom carried not flags but clubs and heavy wooden batons. The leaders of the march of course, being far ahead, had no idea that they had attracted this new type of follower and continued their peaceful progress down Whitehall and Parliament Street. The only diversion was when a side party broke off to cheer John Wilkes's house in Great George Street.

Suddenly, as they reached New Palace Yard outside Parliament they stumbled to a halt, face to face with the rest of the march which had taken the direct rout over Westminster Bridge. At that instant both groups erupted in a deafening burst of cheering and shouting. Charles pushed his way to a convenient vantage point and gazed about in astonishment.

Every approach to Parliament was completely blocked by a mob of thousands crammed shoulder to shoulder, waving blue flags and chanting their slogans of 'No Popery' and 'The Protestant religion for ever' in ever wilder enthusiasm. But the march had obviously changed in character, for among the crowd Charles could see scores of common ruffians and street boys, pick-pockets and prostitutes, all determined to extract what they could from the mob and certainly devoid of any religious fervour. Here and there he also spotted the hard-faced men whom he had noticed earlier, hanging about on the fringes and apparently operating to some as yet unclear plan of their own.

Soon after two o'clock, he noticed that some of these men had taken up positions on the surrounding roof tops and were signalling to their companions below, as if to warn them of the approach of their targets. Somehow, no-one ever knew how it came about, the order was spread throughout the mob that any unpopular Members of Parliament should be stopped, forced to wear the blue cockade and to join in the cry of 'No Popery'.

Penned in by the mass of bodies Charles watched helpless to intervene as distinguished Lords and Commoners alike, irrespective of their known religious or political inclinations or indeed their support or otherwise for the offensive Act, were abused and physically attacked.

The frail aged Lord Bathurst, a former Lord Chancellor, was dragged from his coach and splattered with mud. This seemed to excite the mob further and to his horror Charles saw that when Lord Stormont's coach arrived it was instantly set upon by a dozen or more of the roughest members of the crowd. It was out of the question for Charles to help, so dense was the crush and he could only look on in anger and disgust as the carriage was toppled over and then systematically wrecked. Wheels were wrenched off, panels beaten in and the glass shattered. Burning with frustration he watched as his old host was kicked and pelted with ordure all the way to the shelter of the Lords.

The Duke of Northumberland for some weird reason was taken to be a Jesuit. Or so the cry went up. He was then dragged from his coach and beaten and kicked like Stormont. Even Lord Mansfield, the Lord Chief Justice himself, had every window of his coach smashed and his wig pulled off, only just reaching safety, shaken and trembling. There seemed no sense to the attacks. Staunchly Protestant churchmen like the Bishop of Lincoln and indeed the Archbishop of York had their ecclesiastical gowns ripped from them and were plastered with mud and filth. Charles saw the Archbishop seized by the throat until blood poured from his mouth and the old man forced to croak out the watchword of the mob, 'No Popery', to a mixture of cheers and boos.

For some reason the Members of the Commons seemed to attract less venom, though Sir George Savile, who had moved the Catholic Relief Act in the House, had his carriage completely wrecked. From the distance Charles noticed that his honourable acquaintance Edmund Burke was also bitterly abused, but in his case only verbally.

Burke at first had shown some sympathy for Gordon, particularly on the American issue, and had actually spoken on his behalf. But soon he had realised what an unstable and disruptive figure Lord George was becoming and then he had spoken against Gordon in the House in his usual devastating fashion. Clearly he not been forgiven for that. There were organising minds behind this protest, Charles realised, who were surprisingly well informed politically.

Then excited word spread through the crowd that Lord George Gordon was in the process of presenting the petition to the House. The huge roll of parchment had apparently been carried into the Chamber and dumped on the floor before the doubtful members. By now according to Gordon the number of signatories had grown to one hundred and twenty thousand, a startling rate of increase on its journey across the river, thought Charles wryly.

The news seemed to inflame the crowd further and soon a rabble of ten thousand or more of the wildest and most determined were hammering on the doors of the House itself demanding access. Finally they did force their way in, filling the lobby with a drunken howling mass, the noise of which almost drowned out the voices of Members in the Chamber.

This chaos continued for several hours, with the Members nervous or angry according to their temperament. But all besieged and virtually at the mercy of the mob outside. At last the vote was taken and Gordon's motion to consider the petition immediately was defeated by 192 votes to 6. When this news spread through the crowd their mood once again flared into ugly violence.

But at last some effort at law and order was achieved and Charles was relieved to see a small detachment of Foot Guards with some mounted cavalry enter the Palace Yard, led by a civil magistrate. The soldiers quietly took up a position at the east side of the Yard waiting, it seemed to Charles, rather nervously for orders.

The mob however were not in the least cowed by the arrival of the troops. Indeed they became if anything more aggressive, jeering and taunting them, pelting them with stones and advancing right up to them, knocking off their hats or poking them with sticks, all of which the soldiers took with remarkably good humour and restraint. It was almost, Charles felt, as if there was some bond of fellowship between the soldiers and the crowd.

Then Justice Addington addressed the crowd, asking them politely to disperse. This sparked off even more violence and another barrage of stones and missiles. Finally Addington asked the senior Guards officer present, a Captain Topham, to give the order to charge. But the foot soldiers had no effect and the crowd was so thickly packed that even the cavalry, unwilling to use their sabres, could make no progress. Finally they withdrew a short distance, regrouped and charged straight into the mob, scattering them to all sides, riding right through them to emerge on the other side of the Yard.

Wheeling around they saw the absurd spectacle of the crowd piled up in heaps, mostly unhurt but looking for all the world like a pack of cards strewn across the street. Then as a result of some odd alchemy, the mood of the crowd suddenly changed as the foolishness of the scene struck home. Many of the on-lookers could not refrain from bursting into laughter and Addington, taking advantage of this new mood, rose in his stirrups and in a good-natured way offered to dismiss the troops if the crowd would promise to disperse quietly.

Some of the more sensible of the marchers immediately shouted their agreement. The soldiers were marched off and the crowd melted away, abuzz with excitement and conversation but mercifully peacefully. Someone even called for three cheers for 'Good old Addington' and a large portion of the crowd actually obliged him with a good-natured hearty cheer! Charles too made his way home, still puzzling at the curious nature of the country in which he found himself.

But the day was not yet over. Nor yet the night.

That evening Charles and Harry Angelo had been at supper with friends in Long Acre where they had been regaled by accounts of events in the House that day; of how Gordon had been threatened with running through by some of the military Members who had come armed into the

Chamber, if he failed to call off his rabble outside. At one stage, they were told, Members had been prepared to fight their way out sword in hand at the end of the session. "It has been an extraordinary day," their host said to them at about nine o'clock as Harry and Charles were about to leave. "I hope you will be safe on the streets after such a day."

Angelo laughed and tapped the short and heavy hanger that Charles carried at his side. "You need have no fear! I have seen Mr MacPherson use that particular weapon! And if there is anyone of the mob left standing when he is finished, why I believe my own sword might have something to say!"

"I can think of no two young gentlemen better equipped to deal with trouble in the normal way," their host said slowly. "But against a great mob? Do, I pray you be careful."

"Have no fear," Charles said with a bow. "I imagine the crowd is so well satisfied with its day that it is probably quite besotted with drink by now."

However no sooner had they stepped out on to the public thoroughfare then they discovered that the city was not yet peaceful. In the darkness there was the sound of running feet and the shouting of many voices and hurrying down to Great Queen Street in the direction of the noise they saw a large column of marchers, still with the blue flags and cockades of the morning and moving in a surprisingly orderly fashion. But these men were hard-faced and somehow sinister as they tramping purposefully in the direction of Lincoln's Inn Fields. These were not the passionate protestant protesters of the morning.

"This is something different," Charles said, glancing at Harry Angelo, who simply nodded and instinctively loosened his sword in its scabbard. Then Charles saw with a chill that some of the men were carrying burning torches, fashioned in the form of fiery crosses, while others bore pickaxes, crowbars and heavy hammers.

"It is serious mischief," Angelo called to Charles. "I hear they are headed for the Chapel of the Sardinian Ambassador in Duke Street, just off the square. And this is more than a protest, I fear. Come! I want to see what is going on."

As they ran, to their astonishment the two friends saw many bonfires burning in the streets, often with a tar soaked cross fiery in its midst. "These are the homes of Catholics," Harry panted out as they passed. "Some of them are friends of mine. I pray they will be safe tonight and that this is only a warning."

Entering Lincoln Inn's Fields they drew up short in amazement. For the way ahead was barred by a solid mass of people and the night illuminated by a sea of flaring torches. The original hundred or so grim marchers had now been joined by hundreds more, including the usual gangs of street urchins and girl prostitutes out for excitement or illicit gain. Others were merely drunken rabble, would-be spectators for the promised entertainment. But as Charles stared around the square he noticed that there were also a few other men in evidence, well-dressed men who stayed in the background. 'More spectators,' he wondered. 'But a different class of people. Who are these men?'

Then over the heads of the crowd Charles saw one of the leaders of the march, a big man with dark hair and a moustache, walk directly up to the chapel of St Anselm and St Cecilia on the west side of the square and calmly thrust his crowbar into one of the stained glass windows, sending a shower of shattered fragments everywhere. The act was greeted by a loud cheer and as one the mob threw themselves forward against the chapel. Within minutes sledge hammers and crowbars had broken down the locked doors and the excited crowd poured in, ripping out pews and even the altar and smashing them into pieces.

Soon every piece of furniture, indeed everything flammable including fine works of art, gowns and hassocks and the remains of the altar was dragged out into the square and piled up in a great heap. Then with a howl of approval from the laughing cheering throng several of the flaming torches were tossed onto the pile. Within minutes in the dry summer night a blazing bonfire was lighting the square with a strange flickering orange glow.

In that strange light Charles caught a glimpse of a vaguely familiar figure lurking in the shadows across the square. Then a burst of flame from the fire illuminated the figure and Charles instantly recognised the pale features, the fair hair and the wispy beard and moustache. "Harry," he said quietly to his companion, "Wait here a moment. There's someone I want to speak with."

Angelo nodded. "Mind your step, Charles. There are some odd ones about tonight."

Charles made his way silently round the edge of the crowd until he was standing just behind his quarry. "Good evening," he said in a low voice. "How is Silas Deane these days?"

Stephan Sayre jumped away from him and spun round in the same motion. He appeared still to be wearing the same old fashioned black court-dress that Charles remembered from Jonathon's Coffee House. Sayre's hand went automatically to the hilt of his sword and he stared at Charles with the same angry eyes. "What the devil---?" Then he blinked against the glare and narrowed his eyes. "Damned if it isn't the famous Mr MacPherson!" His thin mouth twisted in a sardonic smile. "What are you up to here?"

"My question for you exactly," Charles said. "I would not have taken you for a man of strong religious convictions."

Sayre relaxed slightly. "So," he said, his eyes constantly moving as he stared around the square. "How are things in the Mohawk valley? Or have you not been there recently." Charles felt himself bridle at the implied criticism, particularly since the jibe was well aimed.

At that moment a tall figure materialised out of the half-darkness. It was the big man who had smashed the windows of the chapel. He knuckled his grimy hand to his forehead. "What next, captain?" He spoke in a coarse London accent.

Sayre studied a small piece of paper. "Bishop Challoner used to say mass here," he said shortly. "He lives nearby in Gloucester Street." He looked over to where the mob had now pushed the remains of the bonfire against the doors of the chapel. "So burn him out next, if you're still in the mood for action."

By now the chapel was well ablaze. Too late, at last Charles saw some evidence of law and order as about one hundred Foot Guards from Somerset House Barracks arrived and formed a cordon around the burning building, catching the rioters as they fled. But by now it was only the drunken rabble who were being arrested, the original attackers having moved quietly away out of trouble.

"Captain?" said Charles dryly. "That is in the Continental Army, I suppose."

Sayre grunted. "It's just his way of speaking. The man's a fool, but useful. And no, I do not have strong religious principles, as you may know from our last little chat." He stared at Charles with another twisted smile.. "Not that you didn't do well by me that night, I recall."

Charles saw that Sayre's shoes were still badly worn and his dress decidedly shabby. 'Whatever he's getting out of this, it does not seem to be money,' he thought. As if in answer Sayre went on sharply. "If you think I'm doing all this for religion you are duller than I took you for. This Catholic Relief Act is designed to provide more troops to fight against us in America. That is reason enough for me to oppose it."

'So Sayre is helping to organise this violence,' Charles thought. 'But who else is involved? The like of that fellow there--- ,' he glanced across to where the big man with the dark hair was whispering instructions to a group of his toughs, '--- that kind of man doesn't act without some financial reward.' He was struck by a sudden idea. "Do you know if my old friend Francis Johnson is in London?" he said abruptly. "He and I grew up together. He's a dedicated patriot. So you may know him. If he is here, tell him I would like to speak to him."

Sayre stared hard at him. "Francis Johnson is it, eh?" He paused and wiped his pale hand across his watery eyes. Then he appeared to make a decision. "Well, it could be that he is in London. Folk get about these days. Tell you what, young Mr MacPherson. If I do run across him I shall give him your message."

Charles started to tell Sayre where he could be contacted. But the strange little man interrupted, "Oh, don't worry. He'll know where you are. If he's here, I mean!" With that Sayre darted off into the shadows, following a small group of dangerous-looking men who faded away from the square, leaving the soldiers to deal with the remaining rabble.

Charles slept very late in what was left of the night until he was aroused by Robert Greville who had come to share a belated breakfast with him. "The trouble seems to be over," Greville said as he sipped his chocolate. "Even when the prisoners were taken to Newgate the mob seemed in good humour. Let us hope so, at least."

"Over? I wonder," said Charles quietly. "For I suspect there are forces at work here more powerful than the mere whim of the mob."

Greville looked at him sharply. "It is true there are all kind of wild rumours going about. Quite sensible people have the strangest explanations for what has happened. Tales of very great people at the bottom of this. Everyone is being blamed, from opposition Tory politicians to French and American agents paying the mob with gold sovereigns." He shrugged. "It seems more likely that there is a simpler explanation."

"Perhaps," said Charles quietly.

By nine o'clock that evening trouble broke out again. This time it was in Moorfields, a rundown working-class district in the east of the city where large numbers of poor Irish immigrants had settled, attracted by low rents. Private houses were attacked and chapels burned, while individual Catholics were assaulted in the streets, spat on and even beaten. Eventually, late on Saturday night, Alderman Kennet, the Lord Mayor sent for troops and things quietened down once again.

Next day was very hot and being Sunday almost nothing stirred for a time. But when evening came and temperatures dropped Charles decided to venture out again. Somehow he was sure that Sayre or perhaps even Francis himself would try to make contact with him He headed towards Moorfields, noting that crowds had already begun to gather and move in the same direction. As he approached the area he saw that a full scale riot was already in process. "What's about?" he said to one excited onlooker.

"Why sir," the man said with his eyes gleaming. "It's the damned Romans! We are burning them out! They intend to take over the country otherwise and burn us all at the stake for being Protestants!"

Charles watched in horror as house after innocent house was broken into. Doors and window shutters, even floor boards, were smashed up and along with every stick of furniture dragged out into the street to create bonfire after bonfire. Any food and drink was looted and the mob proceeded to set up impromptu picnics around the fires, singing and chanting and becoming steadily more drunk.

There was no attempt to restore order and when at last a handful of soldiers did arrive they merely stood about watching events and waiting for orders from the civil authorities, orders that never came. This orgy of looting; the burning of everything Irish or Catholic was to last for two full days and nights and eventually it was to spread far beyond Moorfields.

Charles moved cautiously through the chaos, his hand on the hilt of his hanger, scanning the fringes of the mob for a face he knew. Then he felt himself poked hard from behind. Wheeling around he saw Stephan Sayre standing before him in the flickering light of a fire. "Could have dirked you like a dog, young MacPherson! What kind of a fighter do you call yourself, eh!"

"The kind that does not stab a man in the back in a crowd," Charles said coolly. "As you very well know." Sayre stood wordlessly swaying to and fro, half sneered and half giggled. He was very drunk, Charles decided. "Let us have no more foolery, Sayre. Have you spoken to my friend?"

"That I have," the little man said solemnly, suddenly serious. "He wants to meet you. Be at the old inn behind the Foundlings Hospital in the north of the city at nine pm on Monday."

"Does this inn have a name?"

"Of course," said Sayre dismissively. "Else how would anyone find there way there? It's 'The Boot'. You must be the only one in London as doesn't know the name."

"'The Boot'?" Charles repeated.

"That's right, Master MacPherson. 'The Boot'. A nice quiet spot and quite secure." With that Sayre lurched away into the darkness.

THIRTY THREE

By Monday it was clear that the chaos was spreading. Fires were blazing in parts of town with no Catholic associations and it seemed that all manner of dissidents and criminals and even respectable members of the working class were joining in the orgy of burning and looting.

"The riots have no longer the slightest pretence of a religious protest. General law and order has almost collapsed," Robert Greville admitted to Charles gloomily that evening. "It seems that you were right. There is a good deal more to this affair than meets the eye. Why, as I passed Leicester Fields the homes of men without any history of support for the Act were being attacked and set alight. The square is a positive sea of flaming torches!"

"Why were all the bells tolling this morning? More trouble? When in the world will the government act?" Charles said in exasperation.

Greville laughed. "Those bells, believe it or not, were to celebrate the King's birthday." He slumped in a wing chair and sipped a glass of port. "Come Charles, I told you how it is here," he explained patiently. "This matter lies with the Lord Mayor of London. The government can do nothing at this stage for the constitution requires Alderman Kennet and the civil magistrates to declare the situation out of control and to ask for troops. But for the most part Kennet seems content to let the mob's anger burn itself out, quite literally."

He shook his head in bewilderment. "Though I cannot say I see much sign of that happening. You have heard that Sir George Savile's house, he who moved the bill in parliament, has been looted? All the poor fellow's furniture was piled up in the square and set on fire. Edmund Burke's house in Charles Street was targeted too. But he had been warned that the mob was coming and was able to save his books and papers. He and his wife have taken shelter with General Burgoyne, who has all manner of waifs and strays under his protection. The city is awash with rumour and speculation, some blaming members of the opposition for spreading the trouble and others say it is financed by French gold.". He paused. "Or even, saving your presence, a plot by Benjamin Franklin and the Americans."

"Well, sooner or later someone will have to take a firm grip, constitution or not," Charles said grimly. "Remember, I saw New York once the loyalist mobs had finished with it. It looks to be happening again, right here in London."

It was not yet dark when Charles left his rooms to keep the rendezvous with Francis but already he could see the red glow of fires in the sky all across the city. 'The whole damned place is going up in flames,' he thought. 'I hope Francis has a good reason for all this.'

His route took him north out of the city on the Gray's Inn Road. At first he encountered a few individuals and even small groups of two or three people hurrying eagerly towards the city. 'Can't wait to join in the fun,' he thought disgustedly. But soon he found the road deserted, with on both sides a seemingly empty expanse of fields intersected here and there by a few rough lanes.

Occasionally a darkened cottage or a small farm building would loom out of the night. When he paused and looked back there was still the ominous red glow in the sky. 'This inn must be hidden away somewhere in that maze of lanes on the left. But how to find it? An isolated area like this, so close to the city must have been a den of rogues in earlier years,' he mused. 'And probably still is.' Charles walked on, loosening his dirk in its scabbard as he did so. After several false trails Charles eventually struck upon the correct lane and found himself unexpectedly outside a ramshackle building that appeared abruptly out of the darkness. He stared about carefully.

Directly opposite the inn a roughly painted sign bearing the name of the place swayed from the limb of a miserable looking tree. 'Not unlike a gibbet,' he thought briefly. But to his surprise there were lights in several of the windows and as he drew nearer he heard sounds of laughter and conversation from inside the rambling old building. Clearly not everyone had the same difficulty in finding the place.

He started to mount the few stone steps that led up to the front door. But from nowhere a tall figure appeared in the doorway, barring his way completely. "Well, captain? What can we do for you?" It was the big man with the dark hair whom Charles had seen smashing his way into the chapel of the Sardinian Ambassador. He still carried a crowbar, which he wedged firmly across the entrance.

Charles, resisting an impulse to draw his dirk, forced a smile. "Not captain, I am afraid. But a friend nonetheless. Seeking another friend, by arrangement to meet here," he added as pleasantly as he could manage.

The man scrutinised him. "Aye," he said with a frown, slowly. "I know you. You were with the captain at Lincoln's Inn Fields the other night. I think you are expected in there." He jerked his thumb in the direction of the inn. "What would your name be?"

"MacPherson," Charles said shortly.

The man stood aside. "That's the name I was told," he said. "In you go, captain! I dare say you'll find your friend." He scowled. "But don't take too much interest in the others in there. They don't take kindly at the Boot to folk as shows too much interest in the company."

Charles shook his head silently and passed on into the inn. There was a large room to the right set up with a rough wooden table from which a scruffy unshaven old man was serving ale. A fire blazed in the old-fashioned hearth, partially illuminating the darkness. He stood gazing about as his eyes accustomed themselves to the gloom.

The room was surprisingly crowded, for the most part by the type of roughly dressed, dangerous-looking individuals he had seen at the various scenes of turmoil in the city. Bizarrely, somewhere in the dark interior of the building Charles heard a fiddler playing what sounded like a Scottish reel. He shook his head again and moved towards the fireplace.

Two men, better dressed than the rest, stood deep in conversation beside the fire. One, a dark, surly looking individual, was every inch the gentleman, with boots shining, his cravat spotless and a coat of the finest cloth. The other, tall and slim and dark haired, stood with his back turned to Charles. But he was instantly recognisable.

Charles approached quite closely to him and said quietly in the Iroquois dialect, "Good evening, my brother."

Francis spun round, a smile instantly on his face. "Charlie!" He threw his arms around his friend and embraced him. Then he stood back and looked at Charles in the flickering light of the fire and the few wax draped candles that spluttered on the stone fire surround. "My God! You look well. Thriving on this European life!"

Charles nodded and studied his friend. Francis looked thin and tired. But before he could reply, the well-dressed gentleman intervened. "Who might this be, Mr Johnson?" he said arrogantly. "I cannot say I approve of all and sundry being party to our conversation."

Francis waved away his complaint. "Oh, by no means all and sundry. Have no fear, Maskall. Charlie and I go back a long way to childhood days. He is as reliable as---." He stopped and gave a short laugh. "I was about to say, as reliable as the Bank of England. But that may not be such a recommendation, eh?

"My name is Charles George MacPherson." Charles said stiffly. He already disliked this man. "And you sir?"

The man scowled and shot a suspicious glance at Francis. "Another damned Scotsman," he said contemptuously. "Like our gallant leader, Lord George Gordon. I suppose that was Gaelic you were speaking," he added with a sneer.

"You suppose quite wrongly," Francis said cheerfully. "Charlie, allow me to introduce you to Mr Henry John Maskall, who is helping us with our endeavours here in London. But Charlie, please excuse me for a moment while we complete our business."

With that he drew Maskall away to one side. A few final low words were exchanged, the man nodding his agreement. Charles saw Francis hand him a sheet of paper and a small leather bag that clinked heavy with coins. The man nodded again to Francis. Then they shook hands briefly and Maskall left the room without a backward glance.

Francis returned to Charles. "I'm sorry about that fellow. But needs must."

"He's a surly devil."

"Well, he has contacts in London where we need them." He embraced Charles again. "But come and sit down. Have a glass of brandy and tell me what you have been doing. Italy, was it not?"

Charles looked at him in surprise. "How---?"

Francis laughed. "Oh, I keep track of my friends!" His mood darkened suddenly. "I have few enough that can be trusted." Then he smiled at Charles again. "But with you it was easy!" Charles frowned in puzzlement. "Ben Franklin," Francis said simply. "You surely didn't expect him to lose track of his young electrical protégé!"

"It had not occurred to me that I was of such interest."

Francis waved across to the makeshift bar and two glasses of brandy appeared as if by magic. "Franklin knows pretty much everything that's going on in Europe. Everything he wants to know, that is."

Charles was struck by a sudden thought. "Edward Bancroft?" he asked. "Does Franklin know about him? For I am as certain as I can be that Bancroft is a British spy."

"Oh, there is little doubt of that now," Francis said calmly. "For that reason he is a useful conduit for information Franklin wants to pass to the British."

"You mean false intelligence, of course?"

Francis smiled. "Some of it is false, certainly. But consider, Charles. This war will not last forever and when it does end we will almost certainly want to negotiate a settlement separate from the French. They have their own plans and you can be sure that their interests will not coincide with ours." He shot a glance at Charles. Then he shrugged his shoulders. "This war has become a murky business, Charlie. At least for me," he added sadly. "So very different from the fresh certainties we shared back in the Mohawk Valley." He grimaced. "I wish sometimes that I could return and play a role in honourable battle again."

"Francis," said Charles. "Are you responsible for the bedlam that is happening here? The fires and the looting?"

"Oh, not all of it. This kind of thing only requires a push in the right direction. Then local rascals take over and after that almost anything can happen."

"And men like Maskall and Sayre are your agents?"

Francis detected his tone. He looked keenly into Charles's face. "Do not confuse them," he said quietly. "Sayre is a patriot. I can't truly say what Maskall is--- in it simply for the devilment, I suppose. For reasons of his own that I do not enquire about he seems to hate his own society. He does not need the money, that is clear." He paused. "Do I take it, Charlie, that you disapprove of what I am doing?"

"You talked of honourable battle. This is scarcely honourable, Francis"

Francis laughed bitterly. "Honourable? Well, it's a fine word. But when you have seen what I have seen; men starving and freezing to death at Valley Forge for months on end, honour is a strange word."

His thin handsome face darkened. "Nor have I forgotten what

happened at Fort Stanwix, where Snape set the loyalists against my people and killed my own sisters. If I am honest, Charlie, that is my other reason for remaining in England as long as I have."

He stared at Charles impassively, his eyes hard and cold. "Snape is here in London. For a time he was under the protection of his master, the Bishop of Oxford. Now he has moved up in the world and is a member of the household of the Archbishop of York himself! Snape and his housekeeper, so-called--- by which I mean Charlotte Pemberton. You may recall her." Francis permitted himself a faint smile.

"Old Snape and Charlotte in London! What a curious turn of events, to bring all four of us together again in this way," Charles slowly said. "You truly mean to hunt Snape down? To kill him?"

Francis nodded silently.

"Well, I cannot say I approve of the shambles you are creating in the meantime," said Charles frankly. "So many innocent people are suffering."

"As innocent as my sisters?" Francis asked.

"Francis! Let us not quarrel. But I pray that this turmoil will end soon."

"Charles, my friend, it has scarcely begun!"

THIRTY FOUR

Francis had not exaggerated. On Tuesday the Members of Parliament were again attacked as they arrived at the House. Then the Justice who called out troops to allow them access to the House of Commons had his own house attacked and burned, his possessions thrown into the street and set alight. The same thing happened to the home of Sir John Fielding, the famous 'blind beak', who was Chief Magistrate in the city.

But that was as nothing to what came when night fell. First a mob of more than a thousand attacked and burned Newgate Prison, the largest in London. Harry Angelo told him it was like a well organised military operation. "First they posted sentinels at vantage points to warn of approaching troops," he said. "Then they set fire to the Keeper's house and forced him to release all the prisoners, many of whom were convicted murderers awaiting execution. The prisoners could be seen hobbling away into the darkness, still chained and manacled, presumably to find the nearest blacksmith!"

Next the crowd broke into a nearby public house and looted the cellars of gin and wine and brandy. Soon they were utterly intoxicated. "Drinking gin from their hats!" Harry Angelo reported. "Actually drinking from their hats. Charles, you must come and see this. It is unbelievable!"

By the time the two of them arrived at Newgate the main prison building was furiously ablaze and towering flames were sweeping the night sky. "It is a scene from hell," Charles said, half to himself. Above them drink-crazed figures danced on the burning battlements and the collapsing walls, some actually urinating on the fire! Gazing around in horror Charles noted the now familiar sight of a small group of well-dressed men standing in the shadows. One of them was Henry Maskall, calmly studying a piece of paper.

Suddenly a fresh cry arose from the mob. Where it came from no-one knew for certain. But somehow the message spread, "Roast alive Lord Mansfield and the Archbishop of York!" Within minutes a contingent of toughs had marched off in the direction of Bloomsbury Square.

"Come Charles! We must see this."

Charles shook his head. "No, Harry. I've seen enough to know what is afoot. I shall hear all about it later, I fear."

It was Robert Greville who woke him late on Wednesday morning after a restless night. "Charles, it is total anarchy out there!" he burst out. "Even when the troops are called out by the magistrates, as they were last night in Bloomsbury, they do nothing!"

"Did you not explain to me that it is because of the constitution," Charles said sarcastically.

"No, no!" he said angrily. "This is different! Someone has spread the pernicious idea that because the military is sworn to uphold the Protestant religion the troops cannot legally fire on anti-Catholic rioters. It's scandalous!"

'Clever!' thought Charles as he struggled into fresh clothes. 'That sounds just like Ben Franklin! Or perhaps Francis.'

Greville went on furiously. "The mob actually destroyed Lord Mansfield's library of law books! Burned them in the street! With all his furniture broken up and thrown onto the flames. Disgraceful beyond words," he said indignantly.

"Finally a magistrate was found with enough courage to read the Riot Act and to order the troops to open fire. Five or six of the mob were shot dead. After that the streets were cleared, as you might imagine, with just the few dead and the dead-drunk lying about in the gutters. Then the soldiers marched off to their barracks and all was quiet. But within an hour the looters returned with boxes of wood shavings soaked in turpentine and proceeded to burn down Mansfield's house! When a fire engine arrived they refused to allow it to approach."

"And Charles," he went on urgently. "More rioters burned down Brideswell Prison and New Prison in Clerkenwell last night. All the prisoners released, including murderers! God knows what they will do! I mean, what do convicted murderers have to lose?" he laughed bitterly.

"What about the Archbishop?"

Greville looked at him with interest. "How did you know about that? The Archbishop was forced to flee in a neighbour's coach with several members of his household, mostly women. He left some of his male servants to guard the house."

'Well,' thought Charles. 'It's a pound to a penny that Snape will not be among the gallant defenders!'

"The Archbishop had to be disguised in a borrowed coat and hat. But even so he was spotted by the crowd and chased." Greville shook his head in wonder. "They say there were so many fires that it was light enough to play cards in the street, which some of the rabble did! Sitting at impromptu picnics, drinking looted spirits and eating stolen food.

"The Fleet Prison was broken into and more prisoners released. But then it became even more serious, Charles! For the mob has broken into the Artillery Ground and stolen muskets. So now they are armed and roaming the streets, while prostitutes, pick-pockets and other low-life flock after them, collecting money from law-abiding folk with threats. Yet even now that reprobate John Wilkes is speaking against the use of military force!"

"Have some chocolate," Charles said calmly.

"Charles, the King has proclaimed martial law."

"Well, thank God for that at least."

"Yes. Sadly, it has come to that in England! The army and the county militias are gathering in Hyde Park. All the most likely targets are being guarded heavily; The Bank of England, the Royal Mint, the Arsenal at Greenwich, the Tower drawbridges are up and the moat flooded. Every shop in London is closed and locked up! Many people are leaving the city. Even Georgiana is leaving Devonshire House! And as you know she is not a lady to panic. Oh, and Lambeth Palace was attacked last night. But it is now well protected by troops."

"Thanks to God that Mary and Thomas Graham are not here," Charles said half to himself. Then he glanced at Greville "I should have thought Georgiana was safe enough behind those great walls, though if they can break into the Fleet--- ? By the bye, Robert, who lives in Lambeth

Palace?" he enquired.

"Really Charles, I sometimes despair of you! It is of course the official residence of the Archbishop of Canterbury across the river. Not far from St George's Fields as a matter of fact." He departed shaking his head in wonder.

By nightfall open war had been declared on the streets of London, with troops everywhere. But the rioters, emboldened by the stolen muskets, seemed in a mood to tackle anyone. In spite of the stories he heard of virtual anarchy Charles decided to go out into the streets.

"I must find Francis. I must make him stop this," he said to himself as he headed eastwards, towards the latest reported riots. "Surely my old friend can be made to see that this is not the way to conduct warfare."

But as he walked he saw that the worst of the tragedy was only now unfolding. A large Catholic-owned distillery was attacked and smashed. Then, while the mob drank themselves into a stupor on the escaping alcohol, the building was set alight.. Dozens of men and women, even babies in arms, were burned to death as they lay too drunk to escape from the flames. Unrectified spirit, pumped up from the vats using a handy fire engine that had been commandeered by the crowd, was scooped up and gulped down as it poured into the gutters. Scores of the rabble who drank from this deadly stream collapsed and lay where they fell, poisoned, burned, even drowned according to chance. "It is a scene of hell," Charles repeated grimly as he scoured the streets searching for Francis. "Pure hell."

He walked, scanning the crowds carefully for a sight of his friend. There were fires on every street corner it seemed and though the sun was going down it was still as bright as day from the flames. Gradually it dawned on him that he was seeing familiar faces in the crowd. The same men were always present, usually in small groups of two or three: men whom he had seen in the vicinity of every incident since Friday's demonstration began--- and how innocent that now seemed by comparison!

These men were usually well-dressed by comparison with the rest of the crowd. They stood in the shadows, rarely taking an active part in events, except now and then to exchange a few quiet words with the leaders of the mob or occasionally to make a signal or to pass a message.

Finally the sun went down and a new cry arose from the crowd, "The Bank! The Bank!" As if by magic the entire horde, hundreds strong, moved as one up Cheapsides in the direction of the Bank of England. But the Bank was now well guarded by ranks of regular troops augmented by militia from as far away as Northumberland. Some of the militia men had marched day and night to arrive at the capital and now stood exhausted but resolute, awaiting the mob.

The troops were drawn up across the Poultry, Cornhill and Threadneedle Street, effectively sealing the Bank off from every direction of attack. Shops and taverns were closed and shuttered and heavy naval hawsers had been tied across the roads to prevent any mass attack. "My God!" Charles gasped. "They have actually placed cannon in the courtyard of the Bank! There will be a massacre if this assault continues!"

Finding a vantage point on the corner of Old Jewry he studied the scene. Hundreds of rioters were milling around and exchanging excited calls of "No Popery" and "Burn the Pope". Then without any obvious signal they charged in a screaming mass towards the front of the Bank. But the hawser did its work and as they encountered it the crowd was checked and broken up into smaller detachments. Still they attempted to scramble over the barrier and ran on ferociously towards the defenders, some waving old rusty swords and crowbars and some firing off their stolen muskets wildly. Some still wore their blue cockades or waved their blue flags.

But it seemed to Charles that the mob had changed in nature. Now it was composed not of hard-faced agitators or religious fanatics, but of the absolute dregs of society; the kind of white-faced pathetic ruins, the derelicts that Sayre had shown him that night so long ago. It was as if they had risen from the miserable slums and doss-houses of the east-end to throw themselves in rage against the Bank, a symbol of the society that had failed them. "Oh, Francis! What have you done."

A huge man riding a clumsy dray horse headed the charge, waving broken fetters from his wrists as he yelled on the crowd. 'One of the prisoners from Newgate or the Fleet,' thought Charles. 'And mad as a hatter.'

Suddenly a crackle of shots rang out and instantly twenty or thirty of the crowd dropped. The rest stopped, milling around angrily. By some miracle the giant on the horse had escaped untouched and he rode up and down in the midst of the mob, screaming at them and trying to rally them for another charge. But the crowd sullenly retreated out of range, dragging the dead and wounded with them.

In the shadows of Dove Court just off the Old Jewry, Charles noticed the customary group of better dressed men directing the operation. He moved cautiously towards them. Yes, Maskall was there as usual, quietly organising the mob for yet another attack. The crazy escaped prisoner was still prancing about on his horse in front of the Bank, apparently immune from the soldiers' muskets.

Then Charles spotted Francis at the extreme rear of the crowd, edging away in the direction of Fleet Street. Crouched low, Charles crossed the open area between them and as he closed in on him, "Brother," he cried out in Iroquois, knowing that in this bedlam of noise it was the only sound likely to make Francis pause. But at that very moment a deafening cheer came from the rioters as they threw themselves once more in a solid mass against the Bank. The rattle of musket fire was almost continuous. 'This is insanity,' Charles thought as he pushed his way through the onlookers.

Francis had stopped and was gazing at him blankly. "For God's sake, Francis! Can't you stop this? Do you not see what you are doing?" He seized his friend by the shoulder and stared into his face. With a sudden shock he realised that he was no longer looking at Francis Johnson, for in the eyes of his friend he saw only a blood lust. Charles knew that for the moment at least Francis was more of a Mohawk on the warpath than the American gentlemen he knew.

Behind him wave after wave of attacks were being thrown against the Bank. Each time more and more of the attackers were shot down and fell in the streets or wounded dragged themselves away into the shadows. "Let me go, Charlie," Francis said mechanically, shaking himself loose. "Listen, my brother," he went on, his eyes gleaming. "I have found Snape! Just where I expected him to be. I had him watched and now know where he is headed. He has been sheltering with someone in the Adelphi. But now he is on the move again, and on foot. Now I shall kill him."

Before Charles could respond a stunning blow struck him on the back of his head. He reeled sideways and collapsed, hazily aware that the big dark haired man was standing over him. Vaguely he heard Francis's voice. "Enough! He is a friend. Let him be."

He was down only a matter of seconds. But by the time he had scrambled to his feet Francis had vanished into the darkness. He stared about at the scene, still dazed. In front of the Bank the dead and wounded were lying in heaps and the troops were calmly reloading their muskets. But by now the mob had lost their enthusiasm and many were already starting to drift away. As they passed, Charles could hear the muttered oaths. "Did you see Wilkes? He was helping to defend the Bank! John Wilkes firing on the people! The damned traitor!"

'The Adelphi,' Charles thought. Then shaking his head clear he set off at a trot, threading his way through the throng towards that fashionable stretch of houses by the river. But he could not restrain a grim smile as he ran. Wilkes had changed sides after all and with a vengeance! Of course he would! When it came to an attack on money and privilege or any real threat to this society, there was little doubt how hypocrites like

Wilkes would respond. Stephan Sayre had been right about that at least!'

Charles knew his way well through the streets of London and in five minutes he had Francis in sight again. He followed his friend unthinkingly, not at all clear what he intended, only determined somehow to prevent further killing. As he ran, intent only on keeping Francis in view, he became aware of a strangely unreal atmosphere that had settled on the streets.

Though it was late at night, it seemed that no one had yet retired to bed, fearful as they were that they would have to repel an attack on their homes. Yet every window was brightly illuminated on the orders of the rioters and almost every door carried the same scrawled sign 'This is a Protestant House.'

Here and there buildings belched out flames and smoke and at many street corners fires still blazed, marking an establishment that had failed to follow instructions. As he approached the more respectable part of the city near the Strand however, he registered the fact that most of the main thoroughfares were now closed off by strong chains, with armed groups of inhabitants standing guard as unofficial vigilantes.

Then suddenly he saw Francis, standing motionless in a doorway. Charles was close enough to see him loosen a knife at his waist. Unconsciously Charles made the same gesture. Francis was clearly waiting for someone. In that instant, from across the street, a tall spare figure in black clothing and a wide brimmed clerical hat emerged from the side door of one of the large houses and in the half darkness moved quickly away in the direction of Blackfriars Bridge. Francis followed in pursuit, still oblivious it seemed of Charles's presence.

Swiftly Charles went after them. Snape scurrying, head down in an effort to remain inconspicuous; Francis moving smoothly and easily, gaining on his quarry with each stride: the three of them reached Blackfriars Bridge almost together.

There Snape hesitated, shocked by the spectacle that faced him. For years the local people had bitterly resented the toll-houses on the bridge which obliged them to pay one halfpenny for each crossing of the river. Now the mob had turned their rage against these old wooden structures and were busy demolishing them.

As Charles drew near, the first of these burst into flames and the drunken crowd roared in delight as they smashed open the cash-box and scattered the contents into the road. By the light of the flames some scrabbled about on the road for coins, while those who failed to grasp a handful set off screaming in rage towards the booth on the Surrey side of the river.

Snape stumbled in their wake. He had lost his clerical hat now and his long black cloak billowed out behind him. Silhouetted weirdly against the red and yellow of the crackling flames he reminded Charles fleetingly of an image of a fleeing demon he had once seen in Sir William Johnson's library.

Suddenly Charles realised that at the far end of Blackfriars Bridge ranks of red-coated soldiers were drawn up to block the road. A thought struck him. 'Of course! Lambeth Palace! Snape is heading there to seek the protection of the Archbishop. But for himself only, of course, the coward!'

Francis closed rapidly on Snape, seemingly oblivious of the militia on the bridge. Charles sprinted towards him. Francis called out something to Snape. But the noise of the mob made it impossible for Charles to hear what he had said. It was enough however to make Snape stop in his tracks and turn.

Charles was close enough now to see him clearly in the glare from the fire, his eyes dead and flat. It was a strange sensation to catch sight of this man again, after all that had passed. Was this pale terrified creature truly the architect of the events that had so shaped his life? For a brief second Snape hesitated.

"No!" Charles cried out in anguish. It was too late. Francis had drawn his knife and seizing Snape by the hair had forced him twisting down to his knees. Then with a single sweep of the blade Francis cut his throat.

He was still standing over Snape's lifeless body when the first volley of musket fire from the troops rang out. In the narrow confined space of the bridge it wreaked havoc amongst the milling mob: scores were shot down where they stood and others fell or jumped over the parapet into the filthy waters of the river below. Miraculously, Francis seemed to have escaped the first volley and stood staring down at Snape's body, casually cleaning the blood from his blade, ignoring both the advancing redcoats and the hysterical crowds streaming around him.

The troops stopped, presented and fired a second volley. Francis was caught fully exposed and struck by half-a-dozen balls he was hurled violently backwards against the parapet of the bridge. There he half turned, as if aware of Charles for the first time. He opened his mouth to speak and then slumped sideways, toppling into the black waters of the River Thames.

THIRTY FIVE

Only a few weeks later Charles stood beside Thomas Graham on the lee side of the Falmouth packet as it raced north from Lisbon, the sky ahead filled with ominous low grey cloud and both men well shrouded against a chilling rain borne on a brisk south-easterly wind.

Charles had seized the opportunity to join his friends on their travels, for the hellish scenes on Blackfriars Bridge and the ghastly aftermath of that night of horror in London had burned in his mind and an escape of some sort had been essential. Of course it had also been his unspoken delight to be with Mary again.

The journey out to Gibraltar in a spacious Indiaman had been comfortable enough and Mary had seemed happy and well. Their subsequent travels by land across Portugal had been enjoyable and full of Interest and in particular he had relished Mary's delight in hearing from his own lips the account of his famous tour of Italy. Though it was soon clear that she knew the contents of his letters almost by heart, at times correcting him gently if his tale deviated from his original journals.

She had embraced him fondly, her eyes gleaming, when they met in London. "Oh Charles," she said. "I am so happy to see you safely home. Though I cannot tell you how much your letters have meant to me. It was so very kind of you to follow my rather self-indulgent itinerary so thoroughly!" She had taken his hand and smiled, gazing at him in a way that he had never seen before.

"But dear Charles, it is even more wonderful to have you back with us again," she added with the same gentle smile.

Charles had thrilled to her touch. It was the first time she had embraced him so freely and so naturally and he knew in that instant that their relationship had moved onto a new plane. Just what that relationship was and exactly what it meant to Mary he was still not sure. Yet in the moment it was enough for him to relish the knowledge.

But in that same brief instant he was also shocked to realise how terrifyingly fragile she felt in his arms, how painfully thin Mary Graham had become. Though she was still as beautiful as ever to him, Charles felt a sharp pang of dread.

END OF BOOK ONE

A COMING STORM

BOOK TWO: *The Journey Home*

With a sigh Charles George MacPherson tossed the quill down on his desk and turned to stare out across the darkening Mohawk Valley. Far to the north occasional flashes of lightning still reflected on the underside of low clouds as the late summer storm drifted away over the Adirondacks. The storm was receding, its energy almost played out and only the faintest distant rumble of thunder came to his ears.

This spectacle had been a part of his life for many years now. Yet there had been a time when the death of his friend Francis Johnson in London had seemed to sever his links with these valleys for ever. Francis was the son of Sir William Johnson and a formidable Iroquois woman named Molly Brandt, sister to Joseph Brandt the legendary war chief of the Mohawks and staunch ally of the British in New York.

Charles, largely ignored by his own dour father, had grown up running wild with his friend, learning from him and his friends the arts of survival in these valleys, until he could trap and hunt and certainly shoot as well as any Mohawk. By the same token, it had been in Sir William's largely unused library that Charles had acquired whatever haphazard education he had scratched together, alone and more or less at random. Francis, ironically, had been sent to a proper school in Connecticut where he had enjoyed an altogether more rounded education. When he returned, both of the young men had been caught up in the events of the War of Independence, in ways that were totally unexpected.

Charles George MacPherson shook his head sadly at the memory of his friend's death. All that night in London he had searched along the dark riverside wharves and across the foul waters of the Thames, desperately seeking some sign of Francis. There had been no shortage of bodies that night in June 1780, for the lunacy of the Gordon Riots had left corpses scattered throughout the city. Most lay around the Bank of England where the mob had launched their final futile attack and there the streets were littered with their pathetic remains. But the river too had its share of bodies, for the soldiers, anxious to conceal the magnitude of the disaster, had tossed the dead from bridges and embankments. Hundreds of corpses drifted downstream, spinning slowly in a fetid mass of blood and filth.

Of Francis there had been no sign. After watching his friend shot down by the militia guarding the bridge, Charles had rushed to Blackfriars Steps and peered frantically across the dark river. But the gloom, illuminated only fitfully by flickering light from the burning toll houses on Blackfriars Bridge, was such that he could see almost nothing in the black waters.

But there could be no doubt that Francis was dead. He had seen his friend crouched over the body of their nemesis, the Reverend Snape, and watched in horror as he was struck by that final volley of musket fire. He had seen Francis turn towards him and try to speak before toppling from the parapet of the bridge into the shadows below.

Charles had stood balanced precariously on the worn and slippery steps, gazing about, his mind reeling in anguish. Nearby the filthy Fleet Ditch poured its effluent into the river and the sickening miasma rising from the turgid waters made the nightmare complete.

At first light he had hired a boatman and searched the river as far down as Greenwich. He had repeated the exercise again and again, day after day, until the scouring of successive tides made it impossible that any body could be found floating free. Yet day by day he had searched, repeating the revolting process with increasing despair. The mudflats around the mouth of the river were decorated with decaying bodies for weeks after the riots. But of Francis there had been no trace.

Charles had gone on searching long after reason told him it was futile. For somehow he could not bear to think of Francis meeting his end at such a place. 'Not in the filth of Blackfriars Steps,' he thought dismally. 'From which countless felons have been shipped to America.'

Charles had even found himself hoping that his friend might miraculously have survived that volley from the troops, that somehow his eyes might have deceived him. But it was simply foolishness to think so.

[Book Two: 'The Journey Home' will be published in 2008]